Rise From Ruin

BOOK FOUR

R. M. MULLER

*For those who fight for
everything good in this world.*

MOUNTAIN WILDS
POWER SOURCE
VILLAGE
TRADING POST
GUARDIAN OUTCAST CAMP
ETONL
PRISON
VILLAGE
HUT
CATORI'S PARENT'S VILLAGE
FOREST

3: HEALERS SHELTER
4: HARM'S HOUSE
5: ARLO'S HOUSE
6: MASON'S HOUSE
7: HANGING POLE
DESERT
NUNDEEN
GUARDIAN OUTPOST
ONDO
TRINDARI
DONTERRA
SLENBIR
PERENDI
GUARDIAN OUTPOST
FARNO
GUARDIAN OUTPOST
TABARA
TRADING POST
MAREYA
INDORI
SPRING AND WATERFALL
HANOLA'S VILLAGE
W

SALVATION IS CARRIED ON EVERY
BREATH, THROUGH EVERY HEARTBEAT OF
THOSE WHO FIGHT FOR IT.

THE TIME HAS COME ...

Rise From Ruin

CHAPTER I
CATORI

Nothing is familiar.

Nothing.

The sun has long since blistered my skin and the rope around my wrists burns. The man in the grey uniform at the end of my bonds tugs me along, again. My legs falter in the dense sand. Another walks by his side, but never speaks. My clothing is different from theirs, like I don't belong between the dunes that surround us in every direction. I don't remember this place or these people. I don't remember where I was, what I was doing, or how I became their prisoner. But deep in my gut, dread twists with every heavy step through the desert. As it should.

We head north-northwest. By the second day, the outline of a village appears on the horizon. Dark-grey and black buildings stick out from the wall that winds through the dunes. The wall at least looks familiar, but I can't figure if that is because I know what it guards, or just because I have been staring at it for two days as it follows along on my left. Sometimes vanishing behind dunes, always there, like a constant companion. My foot hits a rock as the sands thin and I stumble.

"Keep up. We would like to get there before the sun disappears altogether," the uniform tugging my wrists spits. I return his annoyed glance with one of my own and track my gaze to the path in front of us. The darkness descending on the village ahead grows with every step. The pit of my stomach sinks. Fear seeps into my bones, inch by inch, as the sun hovers for a last salute before vanishing, drowning us in the dim hues of twilight. He tugs the rope again and we pick up the pace, closing the distance between the three of us and the looming mass of greyed stone.

Mere meters from the front gate, I raise my head to scan the face of the biggest building I have ever seen. And one thing hits me instantly—no windows.

This is a prison.

"Where are you taking me?"

"This is the prison on the desert side. All traitors are taken here," rope-holding uniform says.

"Traitors?" I study his face as the uninterested facade turns to amusement. Every last one of *us*? My breath stops.

"If you are thinking of trying to get out of this, don't bother." He steps into my space, huffing a laugh. I push my shoulders back and turn my head to the side, wincing as his hot, putrid breath hits my face. "Every last one of you traitors will be hanged. It's only a matter of time."

He lifts a dirty hand to touch my face, and I flinch. It feels wrong. Very wrong. My hands twitch to reach for something at my hip, but nothing is there. I school my face to remain disinterested, while my insides fling around in a frenzy of nausea and prickling heat. He drops his hand and grunts, a smirk pulling over his face.

Traitors.

That means more than just me; there must be others. Are they inside this filthy place, waiting for their last breath too? Will I recognize them? Grey uniform stands in my space for another heartbeat before turning, taking a step forward, and banging on the door. Three knocks, followed by two pair. I force my gaze from the door and look for openings or defects in the building's facade.

Nothing.

I move my gaze along. More nothing.

The door groans as it moves to open, and more grey uniforms hurry about inside the sandy courtyard of the prison. The silent uniform pulls the door back. I'm tugged forward and inside the prison compound walls. The smell of rotting flesh hits me at once, and bile rises in my throat before I can control my reaction. I gag and lean to one side. Hitting the end of my rope, he forces me forward. A cart piled with limp bodies housing vacant eyes sits to the left of me, waiting against a grimy wall. I lose my stomach onto the sandy stone and almost buckle over. Wiping my mouth on my torn grey-green sleeve, I follow behind, breathing shallow breaths. I pick up the pace to clear the cart of dead bodies.

Moments later, we stand just inches shy of the actual prison threshold. The suffering from inside echoes out to greet us. I hesitate.

"Williams, Brandon. We were expecting you this morning," a clean-faced uniform says.

"We were a little slower than usual; this one doesn't seem to travel well in the desert," rope-holding uniform says.

"Williams, take the prisoner to a holding cell for now. We will assign her a permanent spot tomorrow," clean uniform says.

So, this mongrel's name is Williams. I will be keeping that for later. Without a word, Williams pulls on the rope, not even looking back. I follow, eyes burning into the back of his head for a second before we turn into the largest room I have ever seen. Bars line both sides, broken into square cells with more bars dividing the long row. Every sad, grimy iron-and-stone space holds bodies, more skin and bone than actual flesh.

Williams stops in front of the second cell on the right. Another uniform, clean and much younger, appears by his side, keys already clicking in the lock. With a swift motion, Williams cuts the rope around my wrists with a small blade before shoving me through the door and slamming it behind me.

"See you tomorrow, traitor," he whispers through lips pulled into a smirk once again. Apparently, that's the only face he can pull.

"Oh, I hope so, Williams," I sneer back, offering him the cruelest face I can muster. My hands move to my hips again, and once again, there is nothing there.

The smirk falls from his face. He retreats into the dank, dim light of the prison, recounting the two days' walk with me to anyone who will listen. Murmurs come from behind me.

Whispers.

I turn to the voices and find three pale faces with wide eyes and painful half smiles. Their clothes are ragged and torn. They sit together on the floor. I pad over, standing above them for a moment before sinking to the floor.

"You are—who are you?" a man with shaggy dark hair says, his hands fiddling with the hem of his trousers, his legs folded underneath him.

"Your clothing is strange," the woman beside him whispers, as if not sure if she should say it out loud.

"My name is Mina," the small girl beside her says, holding out her hand. The bravest of the three of them. I take her hand and grip it in mine. But I have no name to offer her back. I don't remember what it is. Who I am. Or why my clothing is so vastly different from theirs.

"Good to meet you, Mina," I say softly, and she smiles at me.

How is a child in prison? What kind of people imprison children and leave piles of dead at their entrance? I draw in a long breath before rising to make my way back to the cell door.

I scan the surrounding cells.

More skin-and-bone people.

Misery filling every cell.

"What are you looking for, girl?" a man in the adjacent cell calls. I track my gaze across the cells to him. He stands, looking through the bars, as I do. His head is cocked to one side, as if assessing me from head to toe.

"Probably the same thing you are," I call back.

A scuffle four cells down, then a gasp. A woman dressed the same as me stands at the bars of her cell, eyes wide. Her head shakes from side to side briefly before she stands taller.

"Catori," she calls out.

I don't recognize her, or the name. Her long, wavy brown hair is down, her freckled face pressed down in concern, both hands firmly around the bars in front of her now.

"What happened? How are you here?" she calls, her voice wavering slightly.

Every person has stilled, watching the exchange between me and her. I should know who she is; she is dressed like me. Her face, her voice.

I can't place her.

I don't know who she is.

I growl past the lump in my throat and press against the bars. "I don't know." The least I can do is be honest with her.

"Catori, how do you not know?"

"I'm sorry, I don't remember—"

I know I should. I should destroy this place and leave with her. At least we seem to be on the same side, if our clothing is any indication. I cannot possibly belong here, in this world of sand and heat and endless cruelty.

My grip on the bars releases. I turn back and wander toward the far wall.

"Catori, it's Miya. Please, you have to remember me."

I stop, frozen, with my back to her words. My chest tightens. *Miya.* I try to draw up anything in my mind connected to that name. Nothing. My hands curl to fists. I want to remember. Disappointment and annoyance thunder through my head.

"Catori, please. Just talk to me." Her voice echoes through the cells.

I slump against the wall and close my eyes. How can I not remember her? How can I not remember anything? My stomach turns to stone, and tears sting my eyes. How am I supposed to get out of here and survive if I can't even remember who I am?

Something light and soft lands on top of my hand in my lap. I open my eyes. Mina's hand rests on mine and she offers a small smile, shuffling closer. I choke out a laugh of thanks and she leans her head against my arm. A small comfort.

"You will get it back, you know. I have seen it before. A lady who lived in our village once, the Guardians banged her up so bad she couldn't remember her name. But she got it back. It just took a while."

"How long did it take?"

Mina's face drops as her gaze reaches mine. "A few months."

Dammit.

That makes things complicated. A few months before I even know which way I am supposed to run. Who is my enemy, who is my family. My breathing turns ragged, and I grind out a small moan before closing my eyes and laying my head back on the wall. I stay cuddling Mina until she drifts off to slumber.

Keys click over in the metal lock of our cell door. I push Mina over carefully, her small body limp with sleep. Her mother moves closer, taking the girl from my grasp with a thankful smile.

Williams is back.

I stand and stalk to the cell door, stopping inches from it, feet apart, shoulders set back, eyes burning into his.

"Commander wants to see all of you," he spits, thrusting the door open toward me. It barely misses my face. He grabs my arm and spins me around before wrapping rope over both my wrists behind my back. Two other officers walk past, heading toward another cell. Williams spins me back around and shoves me through the door. He pauses to close and lock it.

"Let's go," he growls, his grip still on my hands. His body is so close to mine. Heat rises up my throat. I swallow, walking faster to put even a sliver of space between us.

He tugs on the rope as we approach a large wooden door and I stop. He leans forward, knocking three times. His body grazes my side as he moves back behind me. I tilt my head slightly, closing my eyes for a moment. The next time he does that, I will wrap my hands around his throat.

Footsteps come from behind, and I open my eyes to meet the gaze of the woman called Miya. Another one of her people comes to a halt beside her, eyes widening when they land on me.

"Oh no," they gasp.

Miya shoots them a look of warning.

The door opens. The commander holds the knob, his uniform immaculate. His sandy blond hair is ruffled, and his dulled blue eyes are surrounded by grey circles. His jaw sets as he scans the three of us. All dressed in green and grey, all standing the same—shoulders set, feet apart. He nods his head, and the men behind us push us into the room.

Three chairs sit in front of his desk.

Williams waits while I sit in the first one.

"Don't even think of trying anything, girl," he says, stepping behind the chair, too close.

Miya and her comrade sit, and the commander stands in front of his desk before leaning against it, arms crossed. He studies each one of us carefully. Miya holds my gaze, her eyes searching my face, as if what she needs to know is written over it like a parchment. I try to force a smile, knowing there is nothing I can give her right now, but fail.

"I am not sure what happens on your side of the wall, but on this side, rebellion is taken very seriously," the commander says.

"We don't lock up innocent children," Miya spits. The Guardian behind her slaps the back of her head. She shakes it off and raises her glare to the commander.

"The Chancellor's orders are final. And any uprising or rebellious activity is dealt with however he sees fit. That applies to both sides of the wall, desert and forest dwellers alike. Don't forget your place, girl."

"I have not forgotten my place, nor my people." Her gaze drifts to me briefly and I hold it, gut twisting with the insinuation that I have abandoned my own. "You have no right to hold us."

"Actually, without your diplomatic relationship with the Chancellor's wife, you no longer have immunity from the Guardian Regime. We have every right to hold you. We have every right to execute you for rebellion."

The words sink like stones in my chest. Miya shifts on her seat slightly and sucks in a breath.

"There must be a way to resolve this?" I say. The words sound ridiculous the second they leave my mouth. The commander turns his gaze to mine. He looks between Miya and I, as if trying to figure out who has the lead here. I sit taller in my seat, not wanting her to take the burden.

"Unlikely," he says, and gestures with a hand. Williams steps beside me, pulling me up from the chair with a hand under my arm.

"Wait, what happens now?" I ask.

Williams drags me toward the door. I shove him off me and stalk back to where the commander stands.

"What happens now?" I grind out. Miya watches from by the door, a Guardian holding her steady.

"You all die." His words are weak, his face gaunt, like he is tired of the cruelty here but is powerless to change it.

"Why? For what purpose? Anyone who defies the Chancellor is simply killed? You are the commander, how can you let this happen?" His blue eyes drill into mine, his jaw feathering.

"No purpose, that's just the way it is." He turns away from me and sits in his chair. A rough hand lands on my bound ones. Williams ushers me toward the door. I stare at the commander, their leader. He looks as helpless as we are. I step over the threshold, still watching him. His head lands in his hands as he releases a long breath.

"Hey," Mina whispers into my ear. My eyes are closed against the darkness of a morning that is yet to begin, but I am not asleep. The cold stone bites into the side of my weak body.

"Yes, Mina," I whisper back.

"That woman four cells down was calling for you, I think. She is calling you Catori, is that your name?"

I sit up.

"I think she wants to talk to you." Mina gets up and offers me her small hand.

I take it and stand.

"Thank you," I whisper into her hair, hugging her briefly. I wander toward the side of the cell. Miya is waiting at the bars of hers.

"You have to get out of here," she whispers hoarsely.

"So do you," I return.

"No, I mean, you have to get out of here. *You* do." She points to me.

"If I go, the three of us are going."

"Okay, but if it comes down to it, you are leaving. With or without the two of us." She looks behind her for a moment. Her comrade must be asleep on the floor.

"Fine, let's hope it doesn't come down to it."

She nods and sinks to the floor, hands holding the bars on the way down.

Boots thunder through the cells and four Guardians appear at the door of my cell. Mina releases a small yelp and huddles into her mother. I turn to face them, my hands brushing against my hips automatically, chasing the ghost of whatever used to hang there.

The door opens and they all step toward me.

"What's going on?" I ask.

Williams's mouth pulls into a smirk.

Nothing good then.

He stops in front of me while his comrade binds my hands. The cold air of almost morning seeps through my clothes, and goosebumps wash over my skin. Williams's gaze falls to my chest, now peaked from the cold. He releases a low growl and looks back up at me. Lust, greed, and want fill his eyes. I swallow past the rock lodged in my throat as he steps into my space, his face almost touching mine. I turn away from him and his breath hits my cheek.

"You're coming with us," he whispers. His hand grabs my chin. I flinch, setting my jaw.

"We are going on a little trip, though the sands again." He waves a hand toward the door.

"Where are we going?"

"That, girl, is none of your business."

He releases my chin and grabs my neck, wrapping his filthy hands around my thundering veins, around my windpipe.

"You best behave, or you will have me to deal with. We clear?"

I rasp a grunt against his hand, and he smiles, viciousness curling through his eyes. He drops his hands and walks out the door. The other Guardians push me through it after him. I turn back, scanning the cells. Miya stands, gripping the bars, chest heaving. Her mouth is a thin line, her eyes tight with fear. I try to tell her I will come back for her. I try to speak with my eyes, knowing words would only get the both of us in more trouble. She seems to understand, nodding.

I turn back as the door to the prison groans open. The early morning light pierces over the dunes and through the gates of the prison hold. The smell of rotting bodies wafts around the compound. My stomach twists and I breathe through my mouth, trying not to lose the contents of it on the sand.

After two days of walking, we round the last of the huge dunes before the village of our destination. Trindari. Williams hasn't laid a finger on me the whole way. And while this was welcome at first, now it's making me nervous. Why is he not taking what he wants? He could have, many times. His men definitely wouldn't interfere. The sun fades to my left as the village lights come on, one by one.

"Final destination: Trindari," Williams says, like we have been talking as friends the entire time.

I grunt in response. A hand pushes me along, and I trip over the sand under my feet. I will never get used to walking over something not solid.

He stands beside me. "Home sweet home, forest girl."

Forest girl.

Catori, Forest Girl.

Is that who I am? That would explain the clothes. But I am nowhere near a forest. Sand and trees don't usually go together.

We walk toward a tavern, the noise from inside spilling out into the surrounding village.

"We eat, then you stay in the cells here until tomorrow's bidding. You better hope someone wants to trade for you. Otherwise, it's the hanging post, girlie."

They are going to sell me?

CHAPTER 2
MASON

I have been tracking footprints through the trees and now the sand. The hot prison wall I lean against sears through my robe and shirt. Shouting floats through the air from the markets of Etonia. The mass of people ebbs and flows through the streets as they go about their daily errands. Sweat beads across my forehead. I swipe it away, pushing off the stone wall. She's not here.

I don't know whether to be relieved or disappointed. Rumors are flying through the village about the blonde forest girl. I throw my hood over my head and stalk toward the nearest market stall. An older woman looks up from behind her counter, forcing a smile. Her weathered face studies me, and I don't dare remove the hood.

"How can I help you?" she asks.

"I'm looking for someone."

"I am afraid I only sell wares, not people." Her tone shifts, sharp and guarded.

"I know that," I snap, shifting slightly, dragging in a breath. "I'm looking for the forest girl, the blonde one the rumors are about. She isn't in the prison. Where did they take her?"

The woman's face all but drains of color and she swallows, staring at me. She puts down the item in her hand on the bench carefully and steps backward.

"Please"—I raise a hand gently—"I am not going to hurt her or you. I need to find her, please."

"Show me your face," she utters.

It is highly possible she will recognize me, but I slide my hood back and meet her gaze. I stand motionless for what feels like an age before her hand flicks upward, gesturing for me to put my hood back on.

"I have seen you before; you used to wear the uniform. What do you want with the girl?"

Her words are like a punch to the gut. What do I want with the girl? She is protecting her, protecting a girl she has never met from a place she has never heard of until today. Never been to and knows nothing about. Her kindness for others seems automatic. I step up to the bench and push back my hood so she can see my face, my eyes.

"She's my match." I swallow past the lump in my throat.

The woman holds my gaze, the worry in her face melting to sadness. My gut twists with every line on her face that drops as she leans toward me.

"They took her to Trindari, son. Officer Williams was the one she came in with and the one she left with." Her eyes are tight with worry.

"Williams? Are you sure?"

"Yes. I wouldn't lose another second if I were you," she urges and turns her back to me to rearrange a stand of small kitchen items.

Williams.

He is notorious for taking what he wants from female prisoners. I rip the canteen from my side and chug water.

I weave my way through the people and head toward the outskirts of the village. I need to find her. I have no doubt Catori can handle Williams, but the stone in my gut feels like an anvil now. I round the last building before the dunes. Pulling my hood down and wrapping my face up, I scan the horizon for Guardians. The sands are quiet.

Trindari is two days' walk.

I take off running.

I hear her voice, but I can't see her yet.

She is throwing insults and cursing at anyone who moves too close. Something in my stomach flutters, raising an ache in my chest. I push through the crowd, careful not to draw too much attention. Villagers throw sideways glances at me as I weave through them. The selling platform is to one side of the Guardian officers' building on the south of the village. A few villagers still have their hoods up, having traveled here for the bidding.

Catori will be sold to the highest bidder. I have nothing to trade for her. I will have to follow whoever buys her and steal her away in the night. If she doesn't escape on her own. I wonder if they realize who they are bargaining for. Something has been turning over in my mind the whole way here: why is Catori still their prisoner? She took out twenty Guardians by herself in the tower; how can they still be holding her?

Something doesn't add up.

I push past the last person as I reach the front of the crowd. Williams and his two officers stand on the front of the platform, canes swinging from one hip, daggers glistening under the hot sun. They must all carry weapons now. Williams moves behind her and runs a gag around her mouth. She whips her head sideways trying to bite him. I suppress a chuckle and watch her face. Seeing her almost makes my body limp with relief and need. But her demeanor is off. She is angry, but she is also afraid, not an emotion I have seen in Catori before. Her hands tremble in the rope that binds them in front of her. Her chest is rising and falling at a rapid rate. Her eyes dart between Williams and the crowd constantly. If I could remove my hood and she could see me she might calm down. But I can't risk being noticed by Williams, or Catori being sold will be the least of my worries.

I fix my gaze on her face, hoping she will find mine.

She doesn't.

Williams moves in front of her again and touches her hair, trailing a finger over her cheek. She swings her knee into his groin, and he doubles over. Sucking in deep breaths to recover, he leans on the building. His comrades bind her ankles with rope, ripping the coarse twine tighter with every pass. She releases a low moan. The rope must be cutting into her skin. Heat thunders through my veins, my hands balling to fists. The second I get my hands on them, they are all dead.

A woman moves in the crowd, her polite words parting the crowd as she passes. A man follows behind closely. Both wear hoods that cover their faces. A wisp of curly blonde hair sticks out from under her hood. Her voice is so familiar. But I can't place it with all the commotion around us. I rip my gaze from the hooded duo back to Catori.

Williams stands tall and pushes off the building. He walks to Catori, facing her, loosing vicious words. He raises a hand, hitting her hard across the cheek. She whimpers, her body swaying slightly, but she glares back at him. My fists shake in my pockets, my heart flipping against my chest.

"Get on with it," someone at the back yells.

Williams turns to face the crowd.

"The forester will be traded for three months' rations, minimum. Once she is sold, her welfare is up to the owner."

Three months' rations is an insane price for her. He is weeding out the serious punters from the spectators now. Half the crowd leaves and returns to their daily chores. The woman and her companion stay. With the people gone, I can see them better. But her face remains hidden by her hood. She sinks a small, elegant hand into her pocket. She leans and says something to her companion, who is leaning down to hear her. He nods and raises his head before folding his arms across his chest.

"I'll give you four months for her." A gruff man's voice comes from behind me.

"Four and a half," another calls.

"Do we have five?" Williams calls across the dwindled crowd.

"I'll give you five," a man says, stepping up to the platform with two comrades. He looks up at Williams, holding out a hand to shake on it. I recognize him. The man Harm and Imani call Peaches.

"Five, and you have yourself a forest girl," Williams says, shaking his hand. "After you sign the contract, she is all yours, but feel free to inspect your purchase now."

Peaches steps up onto the platform and moves into Catori's space. He trails a finger across her face, down her neck, and between her breasts. She tries to wriggle away from him, and he laughs heartily.

"Oh sweetheart, you are going to have to behave a little better than that if you want to keep that pretty head of yours."

Catori's eyes widen and she breathes hard through her nose over the gag. Her chest rises and plummets. Peaches' gaze drops to her chest as it heaves with ragged breath. She tries to move backward, and he laughs at her again.

Fire spreads through my core. If he touches her one more time,

I will slit his miserable throat and gut him for good measure. Williams steps between them, brows lowered.

"I said look, not touch, filth," he snaps, nodding to his comrades.

They file in, removing the rope from her ankles and the gag. She almost looks grateful for Williams. He can't have hurt her then. Knowing Catori, he would be dead if he had.

Catori is led into the officers' building. The metal clang of the cell door echoes through the window. At least she is safe. I walk around the side of the building and lean against the wall next to the window. She sits bent over in her cell, shoulders shaking. My arms ache to wrap around her, my fingers needing to wipe away her tears and hold her face. Instead, I stand and watch her fall apart. Something else she rarely does.

Moments later, the three men leave the building, hanging around the door as they wait for their end of the bargain. The cell door squeaks, and Williams says something to her that I can't make out. But his words are not harsh. His face is inches from hers, and his jaw feathers. She shakes her head, and he sighs, taking her by the arm and leading her out the door.

"Time to get moving, sweetheart." Peaches steps up to her and she leans away from him. His comrades chuckle. "We stay in the tavern tonight, but tomorrow we head for Donterra." He grabs her arm and drags her toward the tavern. She pulls back, fighting him, and lets loose a strain of curses. He spins back to her, hand raised. She flinches and he drops his hand, pulling out the gag that was on her before. He hands it to his men, and one ties it over her mouth, pulling it tight.

"That's better. I have no use for your mouth just yet, girlie." They tug her along through the tavern doors. I follow behind, careful not to be noticed. I step inside the tavern. The tables are full, and the air is thick with chatter and smells of food and what is most likely illegal wine. This is Trindari, after all. I don't see them. Every table is full, but Catori is not in here.

"They went upstairs," a young woman says, her face as grim as my gut feeling.

"Thanks." I move quickly to the stairs on the side of the room. Halfway up the stairs, one of the men rushes past me, running back down, blood gushing from his nose and neck. I take the stairs two at a time. I reach the top and follow the yelling. Furniture crashes about. I flatten myself against the wall outside their door.

"You little bitch!" Peaches holds his neck.

Catori grinds out a slow growl. A crack, and something thuds on the ground.

"You couldn't have done that sooner?" Peaches snaps.

"She's out now. What do you want to do with her?" the other says.

"Teach her a lesson," Peaches says.

Footsteps thud up the stairs toward me in a hurry. I slink around the corner of the hallway and peer around the wall at them. The man who ran past me before runs up the stairs, carrying ropes. Bile rises in my throat.

Moments later, Catori is carried out of the room over Peaches's shoulder, out cold. I creep past the door to their room, following them. Furniture is splintered to pieces and drips of blood cover the floor. She must have laid into them good.

I follow fifty feet behind as they wander out into the desert toward a hanging pole. Old blood stains the wooden pillar, its ropes dangling in the hot winds, all but frayed.

Peaches cuts the rope from the post and ties up new binds while his men stand on either side of Catori's crumpled body on the burning sand.

They lift her up, raising her bound wrists over her head, securing her to the pole.

Good. Once they leave, I will cut her down and get the hell out of here. All I have to do is wait. Tension twists my entire body. I am so close.

She is almost safe.

Almost free.

I make my way out of the sun and back into the shadows of the last building of the ring of homes on the outskirts. Peaches and his men mill around the edge of the village, one eye always on their property. With a ragged sigh, I slide down the wall and sink onto the sands. I wait, watching Catori hang from the pole, still out cold. Her blonde hair flicks around in the winds, her breathing steady. The shape of her with her arms over her head brings back memories of us together in her home. I close my eyes and savor the image. If anything happens to her, I won't recover. My body relaxes in the warmth of the day, head leaning to one side as I watch her. Exhaustion from days of tracking and searching and running have left my body weary. My eyes fall, and my breaths shallow out.

So close.

I am so close Catori...

Footsteps crunch in the sands around my tired body. I force my eyes open. A small hand touches my hood. I grab and hold it, raising my gaze to its owner. She pushes back her hood with her other hand, and my heart almost stops in my chest along with my breath.

Nirri.

That explains the blonde curls. Marshall stands by her side, close. His taut face scans mine. His eyes void of trust. I scramble up the wall to stand. Nirri's eyes run up and down my sandy frame.

"Mason, you found her," she whispers.

"I have been tracking her since the—" I pause, closing my eyes briefly, remembering the day we were ambushed in the forest village, when they gassed the entire village. "We were in the forest village closest to the tower, just after you and Harm and Imani left. By the time we got there, almost everyone was dead. The children were gone, and three Guardians were still there. They took her and Callian. I tracked Catori from there."

"What happened to Callian?" Nirri's voice wavers. Her mouth thins out, her eyes tighten. Marshall watches her, her pain reflected on his young face.

"I don't know, Nirri, he was taken too. He may have ended up in the prison. But I didn't hear any talk of a male forest warrior; only Catori."

"That part of your training was useful at least." Her words are shallow. Nirri's brows are lowered, eyes ringed with grey. I look to Marshall. He stands a little taller beside her, folding his arms across his chest. The desert prison. Harm and Imani went to free the children with Nirri. I haven't heard anything about them in the villages either. And I saw no children. Not one.

"Where are Harm and Imani?"

Nirri's face crumples.

Marshall finally speaks. "They were both taken by the Guardians, Miya and her team also. We were the only ones to escape, thanks to Miya and Tobias."

Hell.

The Chancellor has the upper hand. The children from both sides; Harm with his ability to change the dial; Imani, the commander's daughter; and the warriors from the forest side. Catori, their leader, is hanging from a pole, leaving me and Nirri and Marshall. One defected Guardian, the Chancellor's runaway granddaughter, and a village boy. Could things get any worse?

"Mason." Her voice fades in and out, and I slide back down the wall, hitting the sand.

My head falls into my palms, knees pressing up against the backs of my hands.

"Mason," Nirri whispers, and her hands land on my shoulders.

I push through a ragged breath and raise my gaze to meet hers. Silver lines her eyes, and her mouth curls into a wobbly smile.

"I know it is bad. But we cannot give up on them. They would never leave us. We will get them back and we will win this thing. You have to believe that." Her words turn from comforting to begging.

I huff out a disbelieving sigh.

"I might be able to distract those three men long enough for you to get Catori down," Marshall offers. His hard expression has all but melted. Nirri was on a journey to find herself when she left the forest; running around rescuing her friends wasn't part of her plan. She has done so much for us all already.

"Where do you plan to go now?" I ask.

"Harm was taken to the prison in the tower. I can't get him out by myself. Last time, I had my grandmother—we did it together."

Another person she has lost because of her grandfather.

"Where do you think they have Imani? There was no talk of her in the prison of Etonia," I say.

"I don't know; there is no sign of her. It's like she just disappeared from the desert side altogether, which is not good." Nirri's hands wring the edges of her robe.

"No, that's not good," I utter. Where would they take the commander's daughter so she couldn't be found? The tower prison with Harm wouldn't work. Having two of us together would be a mistake. And Callian, they would need to take him out too, so he would have been put somewhere we can't find him, at least not in time.

I stand and brush my robe off.

Like hell we are going to let any of this happen.

"Marshall, can you make that distraction? I'm getting our people back. Even if it's one at a time."

He nods curtly and disappears around the side of the building. Nirri steps in beside me in the shadows of the building and we wait.

Moments later, a building is alight. Flames lick the nearby homes closest to Peaches and his men. I grab Nirri's hand, and we sprint across the sand to Catori.

"You hold her, and I'll cut her down," Nirri offers.

I wrap my arms around Catori's waist. Holding her raises a lump in my throat. Shouting echoes from the buildings behind us and Catori stirs.

"Hurry, Nirri, I don't want a knee to the groin." I huff a laugh and she cuts faster, both of us knowing Catori will come up swinging.

The last thread of the rope snaps and Catori slumps in my hold.

"Someone is coming," Nirri pants.

"Get out of here, go."

"Will you two be okay?"

"We will be fine. You need to hide; don't let them find you, Nirri, they're mongrels."

"We will see each other soon." She offers a broken smile, resting a hand on Catori's shoulder as I stand holding her awkwardly, like a father with a sleeping child.

Nirri takes off running toward the village. I lean Catori backward and scoop her up, one arm under her legs, the other behind her shoulders. I run south. Every burning stride, I count my blessings that I have her back.

After I pass the next village, I slow to a walk. She is still out.

Rocky outcrops flank the passage south from here, and I walk along the dark stony ridge, looking for a cave-like structure to rest in.

Halfway, a cluster of rocks juts from the ground, falling into each other, cave-like enough. Brushing away the smaller stones and pebbles, I lay her down. I pull my robe off and fold it, sliding it under her head. Her blonde hair is like silk in my hands. I run a hand over her head and kiss her forehead, so grateful she's alive.

We will need a fire.

I push up from beside Catori and wander through the rocks, looking for anything that will burn. Returning with an armful of dry sticks and branches from the sparse desert plants, I sink to the ground and arrange them into something like a fire. Catori murmurs and rolls over. Her cheek is bruised. Now up close, I run an eye over her to assess the damage they have done. I hit flint together under a bundle of grass and leaves to start the fire. The wind changes, and the smoke dances around Catori. I wave it away from her with my hands. She coughs, rolling onto her back, her eyes half-open, blinking to focus.

I shuffle closer to her. She groans, holding a hand to her face.

"Hey," I say, wanting to meet her gaze so much it's wringing out my chest.

She startles, turning toward me with a gasp before scrambling backward, holding her free hand out in front of her. Her chest rises and falls rapidly, and she looks around her, constantly looking back at me, wary like prey in the lair of the predator.

My heart sinks.

"Catori, it's me, Mason." I reach a hand toward her.

"What do you want from me?" she rasps, pulling her knees to her chest, leaning back into the rock behind her.

The ache in my chest strangles my breath.

She doesn't remember me.

CHAPTER 3
IMANI

I stare into the face of my dead cousin. At least that's what Jonah and I thought; Luca was dead. But here he is, standing in front of me, older and more rugged but very much alive. He must be around twenty-five now. It has been almost a week since I woke up strung up that frigid pole in the center of this ex-Guardian village. Sebastian hovers to his left, warm drink in hand. He doesn't say much, but judging by the way his eyes study everything—me included—he knows more than he says and silently considers everything the two of us talk about.

"So, you are asking me to risk my men and their peaceful existence to go up against the Chancellor, who now, by the sounds of it, has the upper hand and may very likely wipe the lot of you out just for trying to change things for the better?" Luca stares at me, mug in hand.

"Yes." I turn my own mug around in my grip, savoring the warmth.

"Imani, do you realize what you are asking of me? Of us?"

"Yes, I do. And it's not for just me or my friends. Jonah, your father, is part of this too. He is part of the rebellion on the desert side."

Luca stills.

Possibly I should have mentioned Jonah earlier.

"He's still alive?" he rasps.

"Very much so. He has been living with the gypsies ever since you were taken. I was with him for five years. And he misses you every day, Luca."

He stands, leaving the chair in front of me empty, and wanders to the fireplace, resting his mug on the mantel. His head drops onto his forearm beside his drink.

Seb, still silent, drains his mug and grabs his coat from the hook by the door. He offers a brief smile before pulling the door open. The icy fingers of wind shoot inward. The air outside is almost a blizzard today, Luca's words, earlier this morning.

"Imani, I can't go home."

I stand and walk over to the fireplace. I grip the mug in both hands, still shivering from the cold despite the roaring fire in front of me.

He lifts his head and turns to face me. His eyes shine with pain and tears.

"Why not?"

"This place was not much more than a breeding ground for violence and misery when I arrived. Seb and I have been working to make it better ever since I was made chief."

"How exactly did you become their chief?"

He pulls in a breath and stands, his arms hanging by his side, and stares down at me for a while, his jaw feathering.

"A fight to the death with my predecessor."

"You killed him?"

He nods. "It's not something I am proud of, but men were

dying under his *rule*, for lack of a better word. There was very little food and no structure. No order or consequences; the men were no better than savages. Seb and I were not in the regime long enough to have been affected like that, and we saw the possibility for change."

"Seb doesn't say much."

"He has had a hard life but would give you the shirt off his back without a second thought. He is the best of us. I'm just the mouth-piece and the muscle." He gives me a sly smile, and I chuckle at that. His smile is exactly like Jonah's. I see my uncle in his face so much and in everything he does, his gestures, the way he moves. They are so similar; my heart wrenches.

"What if I could guarantee you and your filthy band of outcasts could reintegrate? They could go back home."

Luca's smile falls. He walks over to the kitchen table and sits, fingers tracing the grain of the tabletop boards. He is quiet for a long time, and I pull out a chair on the opposite side of the table and sit.

"Luca, you could go home, all of you."

"Not all of the men are fit to be back in society. Some are damaged. They do things they shouldn't. Even now. Besides, we have all we need here, Imani, why would we leave?"

I study his rugged, square face, the dark beard that frames it. The hazel eyes, Jonah's. His rough, calloused hands that show years of living off the land in this wild mountain place. He runs a hand through his scruffy dark hair.

"There is one thing that you don't have, Luca."

"Oh yeah, what's that?" He leans back and folds his arms over his chest.

"Women."

His face goes static. They have been without the other half of the population for years—for some, decades. The love, tenderness, companionship, and release they can have with a woman has been denied them for years.

Luca swallows, holding my stare.

"That is true," he rasps, as if the idea of a home with a wife and a family is something he could only dream about. Desperation flickers through his eyes for a second. That is my end of the bargain then, their help in exchange for reintegration and homes, the opportunity to become Blended if they choose. The chance at a normal life, at a family, at everything having a match brings. Despite being here a mere seven days, my cousin and his comrade have looked after me well. Luca is my family by blood, and they are fast starting to feel like real family. Even Seb and his quiet ways.

"So, do we have a deal?" I ask, not wanting to lose momentum.

"I will have to think about it, Imani," he says, rising from the chair. He walks to the door and shrugs on his coat. He turns back to look at me. I offer a smile, but he looks away, opening the door. He walks into the raging, freezing winds and clicks the door shut behind him.

I sit in front of the fire, occasionally tossing another piece of kindling or a fat log on. There is no shortage of wood in this sector, but it must be dried out with all the snow. The glistening, beautiful snow. I thought it would feel soft and fluffy, but it's just wet, chilling your hands to the bone. I think I prefer the dunes to the snow. Better still, I prefer home, the forest. My gut twists with the thought of home.

I miss Harm.

I close my eyes and steady my breaths. I have no idea where he is. Did he escape? Is he in prison, is he dead—

Tears well and slide down my cheek.

"Imani," Seb barks from behind me. I am so surprised by him using my name I scramble to my feet like a naughty child. He brushes snow off his shoulders and pushes back his fleece-lined hood.

I wipe the trails of moisture from my cheeks, and he watches every move. His Adam's apple bobs.

"There is something you need to see," he utters, extending a hand.

I grab a coat from the hooks by the door and he helps me put it on. The bulky size of the coat made for men much bigger than me is awkward, but it's better than freezing to the bone outside.

He hovers for a moment, watching me arrange my hair under the fleece hood, and his gaze falls to my mouth. I freeze on the spot. A second later he shakes his head, looking up.

"Seb," I start.

He shakes his head again.

"Sorry, it's just been a long time since I have, we have..."

I laugh, loosening some of the tension between us.

"I hope you find him, Imani," he says, color rising in his cheeks.

Harm. I try to ignore the knot twisting in my stomach.

"Me too," I say.

Seb walks out the door and I follow, shutting it behind me. The bitter wind bites and I follow closely behind Seb, using him as a wind break. Men are gathered around a horse in the center of the village. Someone is draped over the back of the horse, out cold. Half frozen to death, most likely.

Seb moves the men aside, making way for me. Even through the fleecy coat I shiver, fog curling from my mouth with every breath. Snow crunches under each step and I pull the coat around myself tighter. The men mill around the horse and unconscious man. Seb barks a single word, and they back off. Luca stands holding the straps attached to the horse's head, stroking its face, talking softly as it stands patiently with its cargo.

"We thought we should ask you first, before we made any decisions," Luca says, nodding to the body draped over the horse. My gaze shifts from Luca's face to the body over the saddle. It is dusted with snow, the limbs of the man trembling with the cold. A blanket covers his head and shoulders and I reach for it.

Seb steps up beside me and my hand freezes halfway to the blanket.

"Go ahead," he says.

"Do you think he is dangerous?"

"We have no idea. But we thought you might recognize him. He was found near the wall by the forest sector."

What? I grab the blanket and toss it back over the man's back. Shaggy blond hair hangs from his head. His bulky arms swing limp in the cold. His face is bluish, but I recognize him just fine.

Callian.

"Oh! Dammit."

I place my hands on his cheeks, kneeling to get a better look at his face. His lips are blue; his body is stiff yet trembles.

"Callian," I choke out.

I trace my hands over his face, over his neck, checking for a heartbeat. It's slow, *too slow*.

I turn to Seb. "Get him down, now!" Panic rips through my voice.

Seb nods and tugs the blanket from Callian's back. He lifts him under the arms and pulls him from the horse. His stiff body is awkward and Seb stumbles under the warrior's weight. Luca steps over, getting under one arm. Callian groans something but doesn't wake. The two men drag him into Luca's home, and I follow on their heels.

He is too pale. How long was he in the snow? *Heavens above. Please don't let him die.*

"Imani, pull the cot from under my bed and shove it next to the fire," Luca says.

The cot is long and sturdy, scraping the floor with a low whine as I drag it over to the fire seconds before they lower Callian onto it.

Seb retreats, returning with a pillow and some blankets moments later. I take them from him, lifting Callian's head gently to slip the pillow under. Seb hands me a fleece blanket and I cover every part of Callian's large frame with it. I grab the next blanket, but it stays stuck in his hold. I lift my gaze to his.

"This one is for you," Seb orders, holding my gaze.

"I don't need it; Callian does," I snap.

"You do," he says, eyes tracking to my hands. They're shaking. My whole body is shivering.

"He needs it more, Seb."

"Fine," he says, releasing the warm blanket. I lay it over the first one and tuck Callian in tight. His blond hair is all over his face, stuck from the wet snow he was lying in, no doubt.

"Can you get me a bowl of warm water and a rag?" I look up. Only Luca remains.

He nods and moves to the kitchen.

I sink to the floor beside Callian's cot and sweep his hair from his face, leaving the stuck-on bits for the warm water. His blueish skin and trembling body have relented slightly. I press my palm to his neck; his heartbeat has picked up a little. Sighing, I close my eyes and rest my head on his chest. He could have died in the snow.

Boots appear beside me, and I raise my head to see Luca holding a steaming bowl and a clean rag. I kneel and take it from him, placing it on the floor before submerging the cloth into the hot water. My hands burn and tingle with the heat of the water. I wring out the rag. Luca pulls over a chair and sits beside me while I tend to Callian. With steady strokes, I remove the muddy ice coating his hair. His face warms a little with every pass. It is so easy to love this one; he has been a big brother to me since the day we met. I run the warm rag over his forehead and down one cheek. His face is almost clean. The warmth of the rag is bringing some color back to his face, and I plunge it back into the hot water before wringing it out again. I pass the other side of his face, down his square jaw, and over his lips and nose. Warming the rag in the bowl again, I run it down one side of his neck, and then the other. He moves under his tight blankets, mumbling.

"It's okay, you're okay now," I whisper and drop the rag into the bowl, resting my hand on his cheek. It is still cold to my touch. But the bluish hue has all but disappeared now.

Callian moves under the blanket again, struggling to get his arms free.

"Let him out, he might be feeling too hot now," Luca says.

I sit on the edge of the cot at his waist. My hands tremble over the fleece of the blanket as I pull it back. From the cold or fear of what I will find, I don't know. His grey-and-green clothes are torn and filthy; his arms are covered in cuts, caked with dried blood. His chest is rising and falling at a rapid rate now.

"Callian?"

Blond hair flings side to side as he turns his head back and forth, as if shaking off a nightmare.

"Callian, it's Imani; you're safe. You can open your eyes, brother." He thrashes on the cot and Luca stands.

"He's okay, he just needs to wake up," I say.

I grip his arm with both of my hands. "Callian, wake up."

He steadies but releases a painful moan.

I grab his shoulders and shake him. "Callian, wake up, now!"

His eyes fly open, and he sits bolt upright. I tumble from the side of the cot onto the floor. His eyes scan the room quickly, panic stretched over his face, hands gripping the blankets. I stand and move next to the bunk. His eyes track up my frame, until his gaze meets mine.

"Imani," he rasps.

I sink back onto the side of the cot and wrap my arms around him. He shakes, but his body is warm now. The fire crackles beside us, warming both of us. His arms raise and wrap around me, and his head sinks into my hair at my neck. He mumbles something into my shoulder, but I am not letting go yet.

"Imani." Seb's voice comes from my side, close.

"Yes, Seb," I mumble into Callian's shoulder.

"You both need to eat."

Callian releases me and takes in the two men now standing beside us before returning his gaze to me. "Where are we?"

Holding him at arm's length to check him over again, I say, "We're in the mountains. And it's cold as hell."

His jaw feathers and he stiffens.

"Imani, they took the forest children, every last one."

I rise from the bunk.

Every last one.

Miles too.

I press a hand to my chest, and my heart flings against it.

"And there is something else." Callian's voice is thready.

I turn back, pacing every breath.

Callian's face almost breaks. "They took Catori."

Heavens above, no. I grip my head with both hands and pace the floor beside the bunk.

"Food is ready on the table, if you are up to it." Luca's words crack through the ringing in my ears.

Seb walks over to the cot, offering Callian a hand to get up, and he takes it, wobbling his way to the kitchen table with assistance.

The three men sit at the table, steaming bowls of something

that smells divine in front of them. Callian starts to shiver again. I grab a blanket from his cot, and he leans forward so I can wrap it around his shoulders.

He offers up a smile. His happy face is one I couldn't live without now. I take the seat next to him and Seb nods to the food, having already started himself.

The first mouthful is hot, and the meat and vegetables melt in my mouth. I shovel more in as Callian watches me. He picks up his spoon, sipping the hot broth before making short work of his portion. He must be starving. Seb rises and returns with the heavy iron pot the meal was cooked in. He ladles more into Callian's bowl, who grunts a "thank you" between spoonfuls.

"So, you are from the forest sector, but Imani is from the desert side," Luca states.

Callian nods and I murmur in agreement.

"How, then, did you become such close friends? I thought those two sectors were kept separate?"

I swallow the last of my meal and wash it down with a mug of water. "It's a long story."

Callian looks up from his spoon, eyes filled with brotherly love.

"Well, since we are not going anywhere, why don't you entertain us with your story, Imani? I am dying to hear how my cousin made it over that wall. I am assuming it was you who went off by herself, or at least with a traveling companion."

Callian's eyes widen.

"Luca is Jonah's son," I offer, and he turns to stare at Luca who returns the stare.

"You have met my father too?"

"Yes, Harm and I traveled with him a few times, and he was at their Blending ceremony. I stayed with him and Enid once in the desert with Harm."

Luca looks back to me. "Enid?"

"Harm's grandmother," I utter.

Luca's eyebrow raises, but something playful whips over his face. Our empty bowls sit between us on the table. With a full belly and good company, I feel safe for the first time in days. The only thing missing is Harm.

"Well, this does sound like a long story. Start from the beginning, and don't you dare leave anything out," Luca says, shifting his arms behind his head and spreading his feet. Seb settles in for the story too, closing his eyes.

I start from the day Luca left with the Guardians, from the beginning. He has missed every day of his life in the desert sector since then. Missed out on years with his father. So, I tell him every small thing, down to the minute I woke up in the snow.

And he absorbs every word.

CHAPTER 4

HARM

I have lost count of how many times I have stood in one of the Chancellor's dank prison cells. The Guardians hurry about, getting things ready for another prisoner. It must be someone important—they have hung two sets of shackles, wrist and ankle ones. The same ones I was in when Emmie and Nirri got me out last time.

Voices drift down the row between cells. A little boy calls out. Miles.

I stand and hit the bars, my hands gripping the cell door.

"Miles?"

"Harm, is that you?"

"Yeah buddy, you okay?"

"Maybe, I mean, I'm—"

I sink, dropping my head onto the bars between my hands. Miles stifles a cry.

"Hey, hey, you will be okay. Where are you? Can you get to the cell door?"

Shuffling across the hallway pulls my focus. Two small hands wrap around the bars of the cell two doors down to the left. His small face and dark hair I can just make out in the dim light.

"Hey, there you are," I say, keeping my words light.

"I want to go home, Harm," he whimpers.

He must be terrified.

"I know, buddy. We will soon, I promise."

"Why did they take us?"

"I'm not sure, but you won't have to stay long, I'm sure."

"Are you coming home with me?"

His words sink like a stone in my gut. I'm not getting out this time. I grapple for air, pulling it into my lungs, one forced breath after another. "Sure am, probably after you get to, I reckon."

"Oh good. I still need help to finish that wood thing I started."

The large wooden door of the room of cells creaks, opening as Fletcher pushes his way through. He walks through the hall, taking in the crowds of children in the cells. He is alone; his officers are not flanking him today. He stops in front of my cell, pulling keys from his pocket. He opens the door.

"The Chancellor wants to see you, Travesci. He has a proposition for you."

I stand at the side of the cell, leaning on the bars, not moving. What kind of proposition would the Chancellor really have for me? Do I get to choose which way I die, is that it? That's about as far as his generosity stretches.

"It's up to you, but he rarely does deals with convicted felons. Your choice, boy."

I push off the bars and pad toward Fletcher. His blue eyes, the same as Imani's, watch my movements.

"Fine, get it over and done with." I hold my wrists up for him to bind them. He ties off rope around them before stepping aside to let me through the cell door. We make our way through the cells.

"Sir?" Miles's voice is weak and scared as he clings to the bars, staring up at his father. Petria didn't tell him that though. But she told Fletcher. He halts, yanking on the rope.

Miles stands a little taller as he grips the bars with both hands. "I remember you. I met you in the old hut one time."

Brave talking to a Guardian, even if he doesn't realize who he is talking to—the commander of the regime.

"I remember," Fletcher says. His words are not unkind, but Miles flinches a little.

"When can I go home, please?"

Fletcher shifts on his feet beside me. I glare at him. If he says anything to upset Miles, I will pummel him with tied hands. I'm dead anyway.

Fletcher doesn't respond, studying the boy in front of him.

"Please, some of the other kids are really scared. They need to go home. Please, sir. Even if it's just the really scared ones?"

He is so much like Imani. My gut twists and an ache grows in my chest. I miss her.

Fletcher's jaw feathers. He grunts and shoves me toward the wooden door.

"You aren't even going to talk to him?" I growl.

"Stay out of this, Travesci."

I huff a half laugh and turn my head to give Miles an encouraging look. His face is deflated, and his hands shake over the bars. He tried to help the others. Even after they never really welcomed him, he still tried.

We wind up the stairs toward the Chancellor's rooms. I almost know my way around now. Imani lived here for a week. I wonder what other parts of the tower she found. The memory of the moment I thought she betrayed me hits me as we pass the door to the bridge. Sunlight pours in through the large stone doorway. Callian, Catori, and I stood there, watching Mason and Imani put themselves into more danger than ever, and we all thought they had betrayed us. Hurt is pushed down by heavy guilt for ever thinking she would double-cross us.

Dammit, I hope she is somewhere safe.

Fletcher tugs the rope along, and we ascend the last flight of stairs before the Chancellor's strategy room on the fourth floor. Fletcher stops and knocks.

We wait.

"Enter, Commander," Arthur's voice calls from inside somewhere.

We step into the room. Fletcher's grip tightens on my bound hands, his other hand now on my arm. I stiffen in his hold, and he raises his head to meet the Chancellor's waiting gaze.

He stands by his strategy table covered in maps and papers. He plucks an old piece of parchment from the top and wanders over to his chair. Emmie's chair has been removed.

He settles into it and beckons us forward with a lazy hand.

"I have a proposition for you, boy. Since you are so determined to get your hands on the dial, willing to risk everyone else's necks for the chance it seems, I am going to offer you the chance to help me. With my granddaughter gone, you will take her place."

"Why would I help you?"

He laughs, but there is nothing pleasant in it. Fletcher shifts on his feet beside me.

"Why?" Arthur's gaze leaves mine and settles on Fletcher. The commander's heartbeat accelerates, and I can feel it in his hand around my arm. He is scared of the Chancellor? Fletcher's face is stone, gaze burning into his superior's.

"You will do this for me, boy, because otherwise that pretty wife of yours—the commander's daughter—will cease to breathe. And next will be her family." He raises steepled fingers to his chin, and Fletcher's grip around my arm turns painful. "And then your friends in the forest and so on. You don't really think you can traipse around my lands without me finding out what you're up to, do you?" He stands and walks over.

"I have let your shenanigans go on long enough. Surrender yourself and the rest will be *relatively* left alone."

"How do I know you won't just kill them all anyway?"

"You don't."

"Then, no, no deal."

Fletcher stops breathing.

His wife and children are the ones I am bargaining with.

"What did you say?" The Chancellor leans closer. His clothes smell of soap, his hair is immaculately combed, and his girth is wider than any I have seen.

"If you are just going to take me your prisoner indefinitely and kill everyone I love anyway, then no deal."

He walks away, fingers knitting tighter behind his back. Fletcher looks at me, his veins raging around his tensed neck, eyes pleading with mine. I loose a low breath.

The Chancellor does a full circle of the room before coming to a stop in front of us again. "I could alter the terms."

"How?" I grunt.

"I will not have your friends and family harmed, and in return you remain here and manipulate the dial whenever I see fit, in any way I see fit."

"Imani—my wife—and her family, they have immunity from the regime, or no deal."

He stares at me, jaw flexing. His arms fold across his chest. His focus alternates between me and Fletcher for a time.

"You have yourself a deal, boy," he croons, extending a hand. I stare at it, then down to my bound hands. I twist my wrists to loosen one hand and shake his. The moment my palm meets his, I know I have just bargained my life away. Fletcher stands motionless beside me.

"That will be all, Commander."

Fletcher shakes his head, as if he has been dreaming. He clears his throat and relaxes the grip on my almost numb arm a little.

Every step back down the winding stairs feels like lead. I will never see Imani again. I will spend countless years in these dank cells. I will die in here, never having lived. I will never be free again.

Breath burns in my lungs.

The second the wooden door to the tower cells opens, Miles calls out for me.

Ringing in my ears drowns out what he is saying. Fletcher pushes me into the cell and locks the door with a clank. I slump to the floor and curl up on the stone.

"Harm!" Miles's angry, desperate call splits through the piercing noise in my ears.

Imani.

Every memory of her beautiful face, her fiery spirit, I catalogue through, clinging to each one.

"What did you do to him?" Mile screams at Fletcher.

"He did it to himself," Fletcher rasps and leaves Miles wailing against the bars.

Pain splinters through my ribs. Again and again. A boot connects with my body repeatedly. Miles is screaming at them. Two of them stand over me.

"Housewarming gift from the Chancellor for his latest permanent resident," one officer says.

"You didn't think you were a guest, did you, Travesci?" the other laughs. His boot connects with my chest. I choke for air and try to roll into a ball to protect myself.

"Just like a dung beetle, rolling around in filth," the first one jokes before sinking his boot into my side again.

"Get off him, you bastards!" Miles yells. One of the officers spins around, stalking over to Miles, who clings to the bars of his cell.

"No," I gasp. "Stop." I hold out a shaking arm toward Miles.

The officer reaches through the bars and lifts him up, smashing his chest into the iron. Miles lets out a whimper.

"Not so brave now are you, little ingrate," the officer snarls.

"Let him go." Blood seeps from my mouth with the words.

Miles's face twists with hate. "Stop hurting Harm."

The officer laughs in his face, dropping him onto the stone floor. Miles sobs by the bars. One of the older children moves over and wraps an arm around him. The officers return their attention to me. A rough hand grips my shoulder, and I struggle to my feet. They shove me backward until my back hits the grimy stone. Each wrist is strung up in irons and they make to leave.

"Just five more minutes?" one asks the other.

"Five more minutes," his comrade responds, a smirk creeping over his face. I suck in deep breaths. His fist connects with my face. Sting aches through my cheek and I spit blood onto the floor.

Another fist sinks into my gut. I gasp for air, unable to bend over with my arms strung up in chains.

"Enough!" a voice roars from outside my cell.

The two officers freeze and turn slowly to face their commander.

"The Chancellor needs his property alive and functional. Get out." Fletcher's face is taut. The two officers nod their apologies and make through the wooden door with haste. It thuds shut behind them.

Fletcher wanders into the cell. His gaze travels my body before landing on my face. Blood drips from my mouth still.

He stands staring at me for an age. "Why would you do that?"

"Do what? They hit me, not the other way around, Fletcher."

"I mean for Imani. Why would you do that for her?" Fletcher is repeating himself… He's flustered.

I sway in my chains. Is he actually asking me if I love her? Or is sacrificing yourself for the person you love most in the whole world really such a reach in his mind? For a moment I feel sorry for him. Would he have done it for Petria? If what she told me about them was true, then he would have, once.

"The same thing you would have done for Petria, before you lost touch." My words are not kind. He doesn't react; instead, he studies my face, his breaths coming fast.

"You would do that for my daughter?"

His daughter? Last time we were in this position, he swore he had no daughter. He told me she was dead. He told me he was going to kill me. Like so many others.

My mother's words play over in my head, from the day Mason punched me in the face over Marla. *Kindness, especially when they don't deserve it.*

"Without Imani"—I drag in a ragged breath, fire pulling around my ribs—"I don't have a life worth living." The truth. So, I have traded my life for hers. I no longer get to have a life. But Imani will, and I can live with that.

"Why? I mean, are you really going to do whatever he asks to keep Imani safe?"

"My life in this cell is a small price to pay to give her a chance at a real life."

Fletcher's hands shake against his sides, and he shoves them into his pockets.

"Living without her in this world would be much, much harder. That would feel like dying a thousand times over."

His jaw feathers and he fiddles with whatever is in his pocket.

"Your choice, Travesci," he rasps out and turns on his heel. He closes the cell door, not looking at me. He walks to the cell where Miles is sitting with the older child, her arm still wrapped around him.

"Miles," Fletcher orders.

The boy stands on shaky feet but makes his way to the bars.

"Yes," he starts, sucks in a breath, and stands taller. "Yes, sir."

"Do you know who I am?" he asks. A risk, in front of the crowd of children. But Petria hasn't told Miles who the commander is to him, at least I don't think she has.

"You are the commander of the Guardian Regime, officer of the fourth rank," Miles says.

Fletcher sighs, relief and disappointment clouding his gaze. He stands silent for a handful of heartbeats. "That's right. Dismissed."

Miles lets his hands slip from the bars and retreats into the cell, head hanging. Fletcher reaches the wooden door, stopping at a small table by the first cell. He pulls something from his pocket and drops it onto the table. He walks out the wooden door and shuts it firmly. Every set of eyes watches the door latch. A set of keys sits on the table, merely inches from the bars of the first cell. Close enough to be reached by any prisoner in that cell.

That seed Petria planted in the forest hut just unfurled, breaking through its husk.

CHAPTER 5
NIRRI

Marshall steps through the door of the healer's shelter, pushing his hood back from his head. I do the same, taking in the rows of bodies on rough-made bunks. Moaning and the tang of blood rush me. I grip my robe, holding my breath, reminding myself, *I am here to help*. Options for work in the desert sector are limited for women; I can only hope my talent for working with Guardians is transferable to helping people heal. Marshall's cousin Felicity has her back to us, working with a patient. She looks much better than the last time we saw her in the prison with the rest of the children. I haven't seen her since we went our separate ways, when Catori was brought in. I'm three days late, but she has promised me a position as her apprentice in return for board and food, and I intend to make good on her offer.

I have spent my entire life working toward becoming the next Chancellor. Being the granddaughter of the ruling Chancellor has sheltered me for most of my life. Never in my worst nightmares would I have ever imagined suffering like this. The healer's shelter is overrun with patients. Their pitiful cries echo through the big space. Marshall stands quietly beside me, inching closer with every gasp that leaves my mouth. I close my gaping mouth and steel myself. I am here to be useful, not to add to the misery. I stand a little taller and search for Felicity, having lost her amongst the rows of bunks. She is leaning over a woman. The woman's thin hands are wrapped around Felicity's, her face twisted into a sad smile. Felicity is saying something to her, nodding as she talks. I wait until she rises, pressing her hands into her lower back, before I walk toward her, Marshall in tow.

"Nirri, I thought you had gotten lost or worse," she says, but her words are kind, a half smile playing over her pretty, round face. She wipes her hands on her apron and nods to Marshall. "Thank you, cousin, for delivering Nirri to me."

He blushes slightly, dipping his head. "It was no burden, Flick."

I watch them interact. Their connection and love filter through the playful banter.

"Well, I'm here to learn and be useful, so put me to work, healer," I say, gesturing to Marshall that he is free to go. He strides toward the door, turning back briefly with a wide smile, his curly brown hair falling over one side of his face. I will be forever grateful to him. Without him, I wouldn't have had a clue on this side of the wall. Marshall as my guide has been much more than I could have asked for, and he has quickly become like family, like a little brother to me. I return the smile and he lopes out the door.

"You two get along well," Felicity says. Her gaze breaks from the door and back to me.

"I would have been lost without him on this side of the wall, literally."

"He is a good boy, my little cousin."

"He looks up to you. He talked about you constantly on the trip here."

Felicity laughs and gestures for me to follow as she ambles

through the aisles of bunks. "We grew up in the same village, Amondo. Have you heard of it?"

"You mean Harm's village?"

"You have heard of it. I should have guessed, since you were with them in the prison."

"So, you and Marshall both survived the poisoning?"

"I did. Marshall's family moved to another village when he was about thirteen, so they weren't there when it happened, thankfully."

I don't know what to say; nothing seems good enough. Some people die, some survive. And it's anyone's guess who gets to live on the desert side of the wall. We come to a halt by a bunk with an old, greyed man, his frame so thin I can see the shape of every bone in his body.

"Gregor has been ill for a time now, three days maybe; his stomach is his main complaint. He refuses to eat unless someone sits with him. Some days he needs to be fed. Will you sit with him and get some food into him? I need to tend to some dressings."

"Yes, thank you."

Felicity walks three bunks back, greeting a young girl whose hands are wrapped in cloth. Burns, maybe.

I sit on Gregor's bunk, and he stares at me. His grey eyes run over my face, hands moving slowly over the bunk by his sides. He looks like a caged animal, terrified of his captor. A lump rises in my throat. I breathe through the panic that is climbing up my core. I am here to help. I grip my skirt with both hands, close my eyes, and loose a long breath. A heartbeat later, Gregor does the same and I open my eyes. His are closed, so I draw a long steady breath and he copies me. A smile plays over my lips, and I release the breath. He follows.

"Gregor, my name is Nirri."

He opens his eyes and tilts his head to one side. "Nirri," he echoes.

"Are you hungry? I have some food for you." I pull the small tray of food from the old wooden table by his bed and rest it on my lap. He looks down to the tray and back up to my face. He nods slowly.

"Would you like me to feed you, or do you want to try for yourself?"

He points a long, bony finger at me slowly. I nod and pick up the spoon, loading it with the lumpy white porridge. I extend the spoon toward him, and he leans forward a little, eyes never leaving my face. I hold it out for a time before his mouth closes around the spoon and he pulls the porridge from the silverware in one movement. He chews slowly, watching me the entire time.

"Would you like another?"

He swallows and takes a steadying breath. "Yes."

I load another spoonful and extend my hand; he pulls the food from the spoon easily. Warmth rises in my chest, and my face blooms into a smile. Gregor chews slower this time; his eyes tighten as he swallows. His hands are trembling in his lap now. He has gone still.

"Are you okay?"

He shakes his head no.

Oh no, what did I do wrong? I look down to the porridge and examine the spoon in my hand. Nothing looks amiss. Gregor groans and clutches his stomach. I lean in, trying to assess what he is mumbling. He shakes his head violently.

"What is it? Do you need the healer?" His body lurches forward and he loses his breakfast down the front of my tunic, coating the bowl and spoon in my hands along with my skirt and some of his bunk. For a moment I sit still, not knowing how to react. Gregor is shaking his head again, dribble hanging from his mouth.

"I'm sorry, Nirri," he chokes out.

"It's—" I rise from the bunk and bundle up my skirts, trying to stop the mess from dripping on the floor. His twisted face makes my heart ache against my ribs. I drop the bowl and spoon onto the tray and hand Gregor a cloth to clean his face and hands. He gives me a sorrowful look.

"It's not your fault—you're sick. I will clean up and come back, promise."

"Nirri," Felicity calls from across the room. I walk cautiously over to her, still holding my skirts.

"Oh, Gregor is not up to eating today, I see." She stands, replacing the instrument she was using on the trolley beside her. I shake my head, and she walks me to the door.

"My house is next door; take a bath and recoup. You can try again tomorrow. I have other tasks you can do, ones that don't see you covered in vomit."

All I can do is nod. My heart sinks for Gregor. I make my way to her home, pushing through the front door. A small kitchen sits on my left and a sitting area with two chairs and a shelf of books to my right. I pad down the hall. Two bedrooms flank the hall next. Two closed doors end the hallway. I open the one to the left. Piles of supplies for the healer's shelter cover most of the floor. I close the door and open the last one. A wooden bath sits in the center of the room. The smell of soap lingers in the small space. I walk in and close the door. A basin sits on a small dresser, a cracked mirror hanging above it. Two neat piles sit underneath, a handful of dresses and some aprons. A towel is rolled up between them. I pull out the towel and dump my rucksack on the floor.

Gingerly, I peel the vomit-soaked clothes from my skin and lay them by the door. I pluck a soap from beside the basin and step into the bath. The water is cool, but not unpleasant. A bath that's not steaming hot isn't what I grew up with. Hot water was always supplied by the maids in the tower. My baths were always drawn with oils and heat. *"To keep the skin young,"* Grandmother used to tell me so often. I descend into the water, letting it wash the remnants of Gregor's lunch away. The soap smells of lavender, and it lathers well as I glide it over my arms and chest. I miss her, but I think she would be proud of me for taking action. Even if I haven't exactly been very helpful yet. But I miss my friends.

I miss Callian.

I sink under the cool water, letting it take me down. Bubbles float to the surface as I release my breath and close my eyes. I hope he is safe. I hope he is happy. I grip my face with my hands. I was so sure, when I left the forest, what I was going to do. Find my calling. Be something more than just the Chancellor's granddaughter. I need to find out who I am. But all I want to do is run home. Home to the forest, home to my friends—if they made it back.

I stand next to Gregor's bed, gift in hand. I have no idea if he knows how to play cards, but it is better than getting vomited all over, and I did promise I would come back. So, an hour later, I am standing by his bed again. Felicity gives me a curious smile as she passes by, large bowl in hand.

"May I sit?"

Gregor nods, maybe unsure why I returned. His gaze alternates between my face and what rests in my hands.

"Would you like to play a game?"

His eyes light up, and my heart almost burst as his old, weathered face twists with excitement. I chuckle and sit on the bed facing him, tuck my legs under myself, and arrange my skirt. He watches my every move.

"This is a game of cards. The person to reach the highest number wins!"

His face falls.

What did I say?

"You don't want to play?"

"I—" His voice is croaky with disuse, and he clears his throat. "I cannot count, lass."

"Oh." I wasn't expecting that. My gut twists. "Well, I can count for you, and show you which ones are worth the most?"

"Okay, I guess that will work." He tilts his head and narrows his gaze. "How will I know you're not cheating, young one?"

"I would never do that to you, Gregor."

He straightens up and arranges himself on the bed to play, bony legs crossed in front of him. He runs a hand through his sparse grey hair. "Alright, let's play. But if I win, you have to sit with me every day. And if you win, you get to sit with me every day."

"You have yourself a deal, my friend," I say through possibly the biggest smile that has ever stretched my face.

"Not yet, lass; not yet you're my friend. But your odds are looking good."

I laugh and deal the cards. He takes a sip of water from the mug by his bed and receives the cards I give him.

We play and he asks me questions. Why am I here? Where did I come from? Why am I not Blended? Who is my family? I answer all but the last one, not wanting him to hate me on the first day. He tells me of his wife and children. He misses them all, his wife long passed and his children having moved to another village. I ask about every part of his life that I can think of. It seems to help him greatly just to talk to someone. I remember the sessions my grandmother and Hanola used to have every year, studying the practices of healing the mind. I sat in on most of them, especially in the later years when Callian was old enough to train with the warriors. He was not around to play with anymore. I draw a sharp breath at the thought of my friend and whisper a small prayer to myself that he is safe and happy for the second time today. I often think of him, but the last few days have felt off. I push the worry aside and focus on Gregor, who is sitting right in front of me.

"How did you end up in the shelter?"

He stares at his cards for a time. "I was a blacksmith, worked all my life, then one day, after losing Mary and the kids gone, I just couldn't do it anymore. I lay in my bed one morning and thought, what's the point? Work is all I have left, and it isn't something I would have chosen for myself. It was my father's trade. One I have always hated. It wears you down after a while, lass, this life."

I study his face, only now noticing the lines that shape it. The crow's feet that flank his eyes, the scars, and the deep creases over his brow.

"How long has your wife been gone?"

"Ten long, lonely years."

I mull over what to say next that could steer the conversation to something positive and helpful, remembering the sessions Hanola used to teach her mind healers. "What do you think would make life worth it again?"

"I'm"—he clears his throat—"I'm not sure."

"You can call me Nirri, you know, all my friends do," I whisper and squeeze his hands that are still wrapped around his cards.

"When we are friends—I mean proper friends—I'll call you anything you want, lass," he whispers back, winking before he puts down a card that sees him win.

"All in good time then, hey?"

He looks down at the cards on the bunk. "All in good time."

"You win, by the way."

"Ha ha! Then you must come and sit with me every day that you are here. How long will that be, anyway?"

I stare toward the door. Marshall's clothes are just visible around the door jam. He is standing guard again. He is loyal, I'll give him that. He takes Harm's instructions very seriously, never leaving my side unless I tell him to.

"I don't know, Gregor, I…"

"What don't you know?"

I search my hands, still wrapped around three cards. "I don't know who I am."

He stares at me for a moment before rounding up the cards and pushing them into a neat pile.

"Lass, not many of us do. Most of us end up what other people want us to be, and take it from me, happiness does not lie there. Many on this side of the wall think that young girls such as yourself should be Blended and take care of a home and want no more. But I was lucky, my Mary taught me better than that. You do whatever it takes to find out what lights you up and then you make sure you get to do it. Don't let a man tell you how to live your life. Meddling buggers, most of them, anyway." A grin cracks over his face. His teeth are half grey, some missing. But it is the happiest smile I have seen in a long while.

"Thank you, Gregor." I lean in and hug him.

Slowly an arm wraps around me, and he chuckles in my hold. "You know, for two people who are not even friends yet, we sure get along pretty good."

I bid him goodbye and set off to find Marshall. He must be starving; I know I am. A hand grabs my arm before I reach the threshold. Felicity holds me on the spot. Her face is elated.

"How did you get Gregor to talk to you?"

"What do you mean?"

"He has been a recluse in his home since his wife died; he ends up in here every couple of years when he has one of his episodes, not eating and so on. He never talks to anyone. And I don't think anyone in this village has seen him laugh for years."

I loose a breath in disbelief.

"I just talked to him and kept my promise."

"Promise?"

"I promised I would come back and visit."

"Visit? That's it?"

"Kind of. I used to study the healing of minds with my grand-mother and Hanola, the forest leader, growing up. I guess I have retained some of it."

"You have managed what me and the other healers have been trying to accomplish with Gregor for over a year."

"I have?"

"Yes, ever since he returned from Trindari. Poor bugger, he went there to trade and came home with nothing but a mind full of nightmares. You can sit with him every day and help him heal. I will add other patients to your load when you feel comfortable. I am good with healing bodies, but with *minds* I have no idea where to start. You could be that for us. The desert sector is in desperate need of that kind of healing. At least think about it, for me?"

"I will. Besides, I have to sit with Gregor. That was the deal, and he won the game, so I have to hold up my end of the bargain."

Felicity laughs, shaking her head. "It is good to have you here, Nirri. I will see you at home in a few hours. Make Marshall show you around the village before dark."

I nod and step into the sunlight, feeling much lighter.

CHAPTER 6
IMANI

"You can't be serious, Luca!" I pull the too-big coat tighter around my shaking shoulders.

"I am. This is not our fight, Imani. The men in this village have already lost too much to the regime. The risk for them is too high, for something they may never receive in return."

"Luca, this"—I wave my arms around me—"is not living. Your families on the other side of the wall are what's worth fighting for."

Callian stands beside me, arms folded over his chest, coat snug around his broad shoulders. His messy blond hair is surrounded by the fleece collar he has pulled up around his neck.

"We are used to living this way, and not one of us has forgotten what the Chancellor is capable of. My decision is final."

"So, that is it, the brave men of the mountain wilds just give up like a pack of spineless cowards!" I throw my hands up and stalk out the door. I need to blow off some steam before Luca receives any more of the frustration, panic, and fear that has been clawing its way up my core since the moment my eyes opened on this side of the wall, without Harm. Every step crunches the shimmering snow underfoot and I huff out cloudy breaths, heading for the trees, a habit from living in the forest.

Surrounded by snow-ladened pines, I scream. It cracks through the spans of trees, sending birds off their perches. I sink to my knees. Snow soaks my thick pants. I don't care. I grab handfuls of snow, pelting it at the rough trunks of the trees in my line of fire. Why is he doing this? It is his father, his family, we are talking about. Jonah. I stagger back to my feet. A twig snaps behind me and I turn quickly.

Callian stands mere feet from me, arms holding his coat around his chest. His eyes are lined with worry. Blood pounds through my head, and tears sting my eyes. His arms open and I fly into them. The tips of my ears burn with the cold, and I shiver, huddling into his warmth. His arms wrap around me tight. "We will get home, Imani, I promise."

I pull in a breath and wipe the half-frozen tears from my face. "I know, but not knowing where any of them are is tearing me apart."

He releases his hold and leans back. His face breaks, silver lining his eyes. It is the first time I have seen Callian falter since Hanola died, and it breaks my heart. I push my shoulders back and loose a rough breath. "Help your little sister blow off some steam?"

"What did you have in mind? I don't think I'm up to running through the snow. But we could grab some steel and make some noise?"

"Sounds like a plan," I say, more chipper than I feel, leading the way back to the village.

I duck inside Luca's briefly and pluck a sword and two long daggers from the small table near the door before heading to the clear area near the frozen lake to the west of the village. Callian follows behind. I walk the area for a moment, finding the flattest spot, then turn and toss the sword at him. He catches it with a swift motion and rolls his head on his shoulders, taking stance, his feet shoulder-width apart, the same way they taught me. I square my stance to match his and wait for his attack.

Callian lunges, sword swinging in from my right. I block with both blades, sidestep to his right, and wait for him to spin to meet me. The cold makes us slower than usual, and even the lighter blades I have feel heavier than normal. We take it slow, warming up as we go for a while. When our movements pick up pace and Callian tosses his coat onto the snow, I circle back and do the same. I run at him, both blades descending from above my head. He blocks both with an almighty clash that echoes over the village. Moments later, a handful of men are standing around watching as Callian and I match each other's blows, again and again. This feels better; it feels right. I feel more centered than I have in days.

A few more men wander over and murmurs start up. Callian holds up a hand, and we take a breather. I pull my wrap from my waist and tie up my hair.

"Ready?" He watches me as I tuck stray waves of hair under the sides of my blue wrap.

"Yep." I take the offense, moving quick. He blocks and steps into my space, trying to knock me off-center. I sidestep him and spin to come behind him, raising both blades, one at either side of his neck. He stills and chuckles.

The men watching go silent.

"What the hell are you doing?" Seb's voice barks from behind me.

I lower my blades and turn to face him.

His hands hang by his sides, fury etched all over his face.

"Training, what does it look like?" I snap.

"Women don't fight. Hand over the blades."

The snow crunches behind me. Callian stands closer.

"What? No way. I need to train. And so does Callian."

"I said hand over the weapons, Imani," he growls, stepping up to me.

I have nowhere to sheathe my blades, so I turn and hand them to Callian. Seb's eyes burn into mine. I cross my arms over my chest and tilt my head to one side.

"Why do you say women don't fight, Seb?"

"It's not proper; that's not something that women do. It's our job; we protect you."

Callian snorts and I try to school my face to seriousness, not really achieving it. I clear my throat and tamp down a smile. "I can handle myself. We needed to train, and I needed to blow off some steam."

He stares at me before studying me without the bulky coat covering most of my frame. I pull my wrap off with one hand and shake out my hair. He swallows and turns on his heel, pushing back through the crowd of men. I raise an eyebrow and watch him weave his way through the whispering men. Men who apparently need women in their lives more than they realize.

"I think you have gotten under Seb's skin, Imani." Luca's voice comes from behind me. An earthy smell follows his words, bringing with it the creak of leather and tap of hooves. I turn to see Luca wrapped up in his coat, hair dusted with snow, hands holding onto straps leading two horses. Callian tussles my hair and wanders off with a crooked smile.

"Who are those for?" I ask.

"You and me. I think we need to talk." He hands me one set of leather straps. "The reins," he says, nodding to the straps in my hands, "you steer him with those and squeeze with your legs to get him to go faster."

"Oh, no, I have never—"

"You will do just fine. If you can take on Callian, Wilbur here will be a walk in the park." He grins and puts a foot into the iron dangling from the saddle. "Stirrup," he says pointing to where his foot is now secured. He swings himself onto the horse in one move and sits back. "Your turn."

I move beside Wilbur and raise a foot into the stirrup.

"Put the reins around his neck before you get on. Easier to hold on when he takes off that way."

My eyes widen, and I lean back from Wilbur's furry warm mass.

"I'm kidding, he won't go anywhere. Up you get."

I wrap the reins around Wilbur's neck and hop on one foot trying to pull myself up. It's awkward.

"All in one big move."

I bounce one last time and pull myself over Wilbur, swinging my leg over the saddle. The seat is cold, and I shiver.

"Coat." Luca barks at one of the men still watching me. He plucks it from the snow and shakes it before handing it to me. I pull it on and do up the four buttons, lifting the collar like Callian did to keep myself warmer.

"You look good on a horse, Imani; you should take one back with you," Luca offers. Is this our consolation for going home empty-handed? One horse?

"I don't think that would be a great idea. Might stick out too much; get me noticed and strung up."

Luca clicks his tongue and tugs the reins to the side. His horse walks toward the path through the trees. I do the same and, to my delight, Wilbur walks on, following Luca. The movement under me is strange. I grip the saddle, watching the ground move past underneath.

Luca stops and waits for me to catch up. Then he walks beside me, quiet for a long time, as if trying to put what he needs to say in the right order, find the right words. I have no idea what he could possibly need to tell me that I don't already know.

"This is nice," I offer.

He smiles at me, running a hand over his beard.

"It has been over two decades for some of the men in this village, Imani," he starts, scanning the woods around us.

"Isn't that all the more reason to get them home?"

"Yes and no."

"What do you mean?"

"Not all of the men in this camp would be able to be reintegrated into the community. Some are damaged now. The Chancellor's methods are brutal, and they break people. Some of these men would be of more harm than good in a community. It would be a risk to others to take them with us. And to leave them behind would mean they could end up in the hands of the savages."

"Savages?"

"There are two other villages on this side of the wall, one south of here and one north of the mountain range, that pre-date the ex-Guardian arrivals. They are territorial and vicious. You are lucky our men found you two before the south savages did. The only reason we have been left alone for some time is because our numbers are strong. If most of us leave for a better life, the men I leave behind will be sitting ducks—they won't last more than a few weeks. The savages torture non-natives. Eventually they kill them, to prove a point or keep us scared of them, I don't know which. In any case, they don't take prisoners."

"Could you take them out first?"

"They are similar in numbers to us, and they fight hard. In my opinion, it would be a massacre for both sides. It is better to live in peace as we do now, with our boundaries firmly in place. But if they were to find out the advantage has turned in their favor, they will not hesitate to kill the remaining men in our village out of pure spite."

"I'm sorry, Luca. I didn't know any of this."

"So, you can see, I'm in between a rock and a hard place. Of course, I want to go home. I want my men to go home. But that means a number of the men would likely die because of it. How do you make a choice like that?"

I close my eyes and the ground sways. I forgot where I was momentarily. I open them quickly and grip the saddle with one hand.

"Could you come home? Even just for a time, for Jonah?"

"I have thought about that too. But what kind of leader leaves his men for selfish purposes?"

I sigh, studying his face. So much of him is like Jonah. His features and his stoic selflessness. What I wouldn't give to bring them back together.

"As for getting Harm back, I can give you some information on the places in the barracks and tower you didn't see that may come of use. But that's all I can give you now. I'm sorry, Imani."

"Thanks." I sway with each rhythmic step Wilbur takes. Luca scans the trees again.

"What are you looking for?"

"Mountain lions. They get a little brazen when we don't travel in larger numbers."

"Fantastic." I roll my eyes and scan between the trees for movement.

"We should head back; Seb will be making supper soon." Luca turns his horse and Wilbur follows.

I drop down from the saddle the moment Wilbur pulls to a halt. He turns his soft nose into my shoulder, and I stroke his head.

"He likes you," Luca says softly.

"Well, I am the only girl he's ever met." Luca laughs, handing the reins to Clancy, who eyes me up and down. I shiver and shake off the creeping feeling, and we head home.

Warmth radiates from the hearth where Callian stands waving his hands over the dancing flames.

"We prepared a house for you to stay in tonight," Seb says from the stove, not looking up. Luca glances sideways at me before walking over to his friend.

"Thank you," I say to Seb.

He shrugs.

Callian shoots a sorry smile at me.

"What's for supper? I'm starving." I wander over to the stove and stop beside Seb. I don't want to upset either of the men who have helped us.

I know they didn't have to.

CHAPTER 7
IMANI

Seb ladles a meaty stew into a bowl and hands it to me. I offer a smile, but he doesn't look at me. I sit at the table and sip the hot stew from the spoon. The three men sit down with their bowls. Callian puts himself between Seb and me. I eat every last morsel of the stew. It's delicious. I look up from my scraped-bare bowl, the others still eating, slower than I had. Luca looks between Seb and Callian and then Seb and me. "That was delicious. Thank you, Seb."

He just nods and continues eating. Luca mumbles something to Seb I don't hear. Seb drops his spoon and walks out the door.

"I guess he's off to bed then," Luca utters.

"What did I do so wrong?" I ask. "He was fine this morning."

"Seb is complicated. And *very* traditional. Women in their place, and all that. You are the first woman he has encountered that doesn't fit into his old-fashioned upbringing. Which is an issue for him, since he—" Luca freezes and shoves a spoonful into his mouth. I stare at him and then at Callian, who is very busy cleaning out his bowl with a scrap of bread.

"He what? Since he what?" I grip the spoon in my hand like a fighting knife, ready to hear the worst.

"He likes you, Imani. But he understands you're Blended. It won't be a problem."

"Oh. Are you sure it's not just because I am the only woman on this side of the wall?" I pull a silly face, but it doesn't take. The words sink in. I am the *only* woman on this side of the wall. Not counting the savages. There are how many men in this camp? I stiffen in my chair, pushing back closer to Callian.

"I don't think it's that. Seb's not that shallow." He hesitates, placing his spoon inside his bowl. "You are safe here. They wouldn't dare touch you. I would feed them to the mountain lions myself." Luca takes our bowls and places them on the bench by the sink. "You must be exhausted. I'll walk you to your house."

Callian rises and grabs both of our coats before holding mine up for me. I push my arms through and smile up at him.

"It's fine. I know where it is," Callian says.

Luca smiles at me before bidding me goodnight.

Callian's arm flops over my shoulders. "That was a weird day."

"Tell me about it." I relax under his heavy half-hug, and we wander to the house. I rest my head on his arm, yawning. Light from the fireplace spills under the door and through the gaps around the wooden windows, not shut against the cold. I push the door open to find two beds with furs and pillows by the fire. A small bowl of fruits and large nuts sits on the table on the opposite side of the home. A wash bowl and jug of water sit by the first bed. I make my way over to clean my face.

"You want a bath?" Callian chuckles from the opposite side of the room.

"What? Are you serious?" I spin around to find him standing by a screen, towel in hand, steam billowing up past the screen in the front corner of the house.

"I thought you might want one, since you seem to be so fond of them. According to that besotted husband of yours." Callian tosses the towel at me. I grab it and rush over to find a round wooden bath, steaming with hot water. It looks so deep. So good.

"I'll leave you to it. I had mine earlier." He winks.

I toss a cake of soap at his head, and he ducks before flopping onto the bed furthest from the fire.

I pull the screen around a little more and rip the heavy clothes from my weary bones. I dip a toe into the water. It burns a little but feels so good. I sink into the water, moaning as the water covers my chest, laying my head back on the edge of the tub. "Oh, that feels amazing."

"I can still hear you." Callian chuckles.

Heat creeps up my neck, flushing my face. "Sorry."

I sigh and slip under the water, releasing bubbles to the surface every other heartbeat, and scrub the soap through my hair before resurfacing. The soap lathers well over every limb. I palm it over my neck and my chest. My breath catches as memories of Harm flood in with every move of my hand. I stifle a whimper, tears spilling over my cheeks. I grab the washcloth from the side of the bath and remove the bubbles with long strokes.

Breaths turn to sobs.

I cling to the cloth, pushing it hard against my chest. I want Harm's arms wrapped around me. I want to go home. I want him to be safe. I want his smell, his warmth, his body against mine. I choke through torrents of strangled cries I can't hold back.

"Imani?"

My eyes fly open. And I swallow back the sob caught in my throat. "Sorry, I will be done in a minute."

The bed Callian is lying on creaks. His boots hit the floor. I stand and step out of the tub, wrapping the towel around myself. Clean clothes appear over the screen. I pull them down and slip them on quickly. A hand waves at the side of the screen, gripping a brush and small mirror. I huff out a small laugh.

"Where did you find that in the land of no-woman?"

"Apparently the traders come here once a year. Who would have figured? Luca has had it for a long time. Who knows what he needed it for." Callian's voice is light, but I hear the concern that underscores his words.

"It's perfect, thank you." I take the brush and mirror, placing them on the edge of the bath. I detangle my hair with my fingers before brushing it out. It's back to the length it was when I first met Harm. I plait it to one side and walk out to the bed by the fire. Callian pats the space beside him, and I flop down.

"You okay, little sis?" His face is pulled with worry and something else.

"I will be fine. What about you?"

"Every day we are stuck on this side of the wall feels like an eternity. I am worried about them all. Catori, Harm, even Mason. But I am *terrified* for Nirri, Imani. In so many ways. I waited. Now I am wondering why I did. I may have missed my chance, and that rips me apart. Damn, I hope she's alright." He hangs his head. I suck in a deep breath and grab his face with both my hands, lifting it so his gaze reaches mine.

"Hey, you didn't miss your chance. Nirri is fine, she got out. Marshall got her and another girl out, I remember that much. As for Catori, I would feel sorry for anyone who got in her way, honestly. Mason's too." As I pull in my next breath, I realize I can't account for Harm. I have no idea what happened after we were knocked out. He could be fine. He could be in prison. He could be... My face tightens, my heart hammers in my chest, and my chin wobbles as I close my eyes, my grip on Callian's face tightening.

"No, no, no. Don't you even go there. You listen to me, Imani. He is fine. Harm is going to be fine. We are all going to be okay."

I open my eyes and tears flood my cheeks. Streaks run down Callian's face, dripping from his jaw. He is grabbing my shoulders. I slap a hand over my mouth, and he shoves me into his chest. I can't breathe. His hands rub my back. He is shaking his head as he whispers words I can't hear. My hands tingle. I choke and he pushes me off his chest, scanning my face.

I roll my eyes to the ceiling and force out a harsh breath. Wiping the tears from my cheeks, I press my palm into my chest, over my heart, trying to steady its rapid pace. My body sags with the fatigue that I have been holding at bay for the last week.

Callian stands and picks me up, depositing me on my bed before laying a fur around me and tucking me in. Such a big-brother move. I huff a laugh at him, and he tousles my hair.

"Night, Imani," he says, laying on his bunk.

"Night, Callian. Love you."

"Love you too, little sis." His words sound like a smile. I huddle into the fur, grasping onto that sliver of happiness, and wait for sleep.

Heaviness covers my mouth as I lay still tucked under the fur. Callian's snore rattles quietly beside me. There is scuffing next to my bed. Something isn't right. I try to move, but my arms are like lead. I open my eyes. Inches from my face is the dirty face of Clancy. Darting my gaze side to side, I realize his hand is over my mouth. A rag comes close to my face. Two younger men stand on the side of the bed closest to the fire; one is bent over, holding down my arms.

I am the only woman on this side of the wall.

Dammit.

I bite the hand over my mouth and kick the closest man in the crotch, flying out of bed.

"Argh! You little bitch," Clancy hisses.

Callian stirs, eyes flying wide after he sees the three men close in on me. I hold a hand up and Callian sits frozen on his bed, his face stone, but his eyes track every movement the three men make. Clancy runs at me, trying to grab my shoulders. I punch his face with every ounce of energy I can muster. He staggers backward. My hand stings where it connected with his nose, which is now bleeding down his shirt. The younger men come at me together, and Callian crosses his arms over his chest. I sidestep them, grabbing the water jug from the washbowl. I slam it over one man's head, and he drops like a sack of grains. The last man hesitates before running at me. He grabs me, and I knee him hard in the stomach then slam his head into my knee repeatedly.

A sound comes from the doorway, and I look up, hands still gripping the man's head. I shove him sideways and stalk to the door, stopping inches from Seb. Luca rushes up behind him, still buttoning up his coat. Blood trickles down my cheek and from one hand. Callian rises and comes to stand behind me.

"What the hell is wrong with you?" Seb growls, but he is looking at Callian.

Luca walks in and drags the men out of the house, one by one. Callian helps with the unconscious man and Seb stands, staring in disbelief before marching outside to Callian. I return the jug to the washbowl and stand over the small table, gripping its side with trembling hands. After a handful of heartbeats, I pluck the washcloth from the side of the bath and clean up my face and hand. The cuts sting. But the bleeding tapers off.

"Why didn't you defend her?" Seb shouts at Callian.

"She asked me not to," my brother says calmly.

"She is a woman!" Seb points at me like *I'm* the villain in this scenario.

"Being physically stronger than someone doesn't make your men more capable. Imani can look after herself."

"She is literally half your size!" Seb is walking in circles now, hands in his hair.

"And more skilled, and more capable than you will ever be. The most capable people I know are women. If you want to stand half a chance on our side of the wall, you'd better remember that." Callian storms back inside. He slams the door and pulls me into his chest, so tight I have to raise my head to catch some air.

He's shaking.

I extract myself from his grip and sit him on the bed.

"I thought they would hurt you," he chokes out.

"But you just said—"

"I know what I just said, and I meant every word. But it still rips me apart seeing my family in danger."

I sit beside him and wrap an arm around his neck, resting my head on his shoulder. "Now you know how we all feel about you," I say softly. Callian is always the one to put himself in harm's way, to protect everyone else. Miya and Callian are the bravest, most selfless people I have ever met.

"I hope Luca feeds those three to the mountain lions," Callian says.

"Bit scrawny. I pity the mountain lions."

Callian forces a laugh. "Promise me we will all make it through this?"

I open my eyes and catch his gaze. "All of us will do everything we can to win this thing and go home."

"I miss them," he utters.

"Me too." I wander back to my bed and snuggle under the furs, pulling them over my head, blocking out the last half an hour. Despite the cold and the ruckus, sleep finds me easily.

I wake to the rattling snores of Callian but turn when I realize they are too far away. I sit up, rubbing my eyes, waiting for them to focus. Callian's bed is against the door, barricading it. And he is sound asleep.

Well, that solves that problem, big brother. I chuckle at him under my breath and get off the bunk to stoke the fire. Today we start the journey home.

We walk to Luca's for breakfast. Both him and Seb are already sitting down to eat when we walk through the door.

"Morning," Callian says.

"Morning," Luca offers.

"Morning." Seb rises and walks toward the door. I move to let him through, but he stops in front of me.

"Seb."

"Can I talk to you outside for a second?"

I glance briefly at Luca and nod, following Seb outside. The morning sun illuminates his pale face and red hair. His eyes track my movements until I am standing in front of him. A chair scrapes inside. I imagine Callian is sitting down at the table.

"I'm sorry for my behavior the last couple of days." He looks past me as he speaks. "I haven't been myself."

"Really?" The word is flat.

"I—"

"Forget it, Seb, I'll be out of your way in a matter of hours." I storm back through the door and throw my coat on the rack before sitting down in my spot beside Callian. He hands me a bowl of something that looks like porridge, and we clean our bowls.

"Can you give me some information on returning to the wall closest to the tower?" I ask Luca. Seb walks in and plops onto his chair, shoveling in spoonfuls of porridge.

"South-southwest. Do not track east," Luca says.

Seb stops chewing. "You're going back to the tower? That's suicide."

"I am going to find Harm."

Seb puts his spoon down. "And if he is already dead, you're walking into a trap."

Heat rises into my core, and I grip my spoon with white knuckles. How *dare* he tell me what to do; he is too afraid to leave his own hearth.

"You don't get a say in what I do. At least I have the courage to try."

"Imani, go back to the forest village and stay safe. Going to the tower is a seriously bad idea."

"I am not afraid, Seb. I am not like you; I am not going to play it safe and give up on everything and everyone I love." I stand, knocking over the chair. Luca's and Callian's gazes swing between Seb and me.

"You're crazy, you know that?" He stands on the opposite side of the table.

"No, I am not crazy. I am going to find my husband." I stalk out the door, slamming it behind me. I march back to the house Callian and I stayed in and shove the few items I have in a rucksack that Luca dropped off yesterday. The door opens behind me, and I spin around to shout at Seb again. Luca stands in the doorway, holding my coat.

"You will have to forgive Seb. He suffered more than most in that tower. He is only trying to protect you, even though I will agree he is not handling it as well as he could."

"I am not just leaving Harm there to rot. If there is a *chance* he is alive, I will find him."

"I know, Imani. We know; we are all worried. That's all."

"If you are so worried, why don't you help me?" I am almost

shouting at him now. I know his answer. He has to take care of his own, just the way I do.

I pinch the bridge of my nose and loose a breath. "I'm sorry, I know the answer to that question. And I would do the same thing."

He stands closer. "Cousin, you are the bravest person I have *ever* met. You were when you were a little girl and even more so now. And... It's okay to be scared, you know."

"I am, Luca. I am terrified."

He swings an arm around my shoulders.

"I'm terrified I'm too late." You only get three days once the Chancellor decides. A fact Luca has probably already thought of.

"You will be okay, Imani. I truly believe that."

Callian appears in the doorway and Luca gives me a squeeze before walking out the door.

"Say hello to my father for me, will you?" Luca asks. His jaw feathers, and he walks away.

Callian grabs his rucksack and plants weapons in every spot on his body that will hold them. He tosses me a set of fighting knives and a bow and quiver. We head southwest, leaving the snowy village behind. Moments later, we are swallowed whole by the snow-coated pines that sway in the mountain drafts, tracking through dense snow.

CHAPTER 8
CATORI

Why does he have to stand so close?

The stone door thuds shut behind me, trees as far as the eye can see covering the land in front of us. Mason—apparently, I know him—stands beside me, watching for my reaction to the forest side of the wall. For three days he has been watching, taking care of me, and protecting me. I have no idea why. His light-blue eyes search my face, as if it is about to reveal something so important that he can't look away. I roll my eyes and stalk into the trees.

He sighs and follows behind. The scent of this place is familiar; it feels like my childhood. It feels the closest to home I have felt in the last week, even if I have no idea where home is.

"Maybe I should lead the way?" he says.

I stop and turn back, almost bumping into his chest. He doesn't make space between us, so I do.

"That would probably be a good idea," I say at last, watching his mouth curl into a smile over his jawline. He adjusts the rucksack over his shoulder, flexing his arm. I move to the side as he passes, but changes direction slightly to the south. His shoulder brushes mine and I freeze. My stomach flips. I force my legs forward, following the man who rescued me and claims to be taking me home.

"How far is it?" I say, catching up to his quick pace.

"A day and a half, usually, but we can take our time if you need."

"Why would I need longer?"

He stops and turns back. I stand inches from his face. He sucks in a breath, gripping the strap of his rucksack tight. "Catori, I—"

"How do you know that's even my name?" Miya, the woman in the prison called me that too. I want to believe them. But without knowing for myself, all I can do is wait until my memory returns. Heavens above, it better not take three months. I don't think I can take three months of this mollycoddling.

"Because it's your name. What else would I call you?" He lifts his chin slightly, narrowing his gaze.

A lump rises in my throat. An inkling of recognition comes but flutters out instantly. Nothing but fuzzy emptiness sits in the place where the things I know to be true should be.

"If you say so, forest boy," I say and brush past him, angrier at myself than anyone else. I push through the trees in the direction he was headed. A handful of heartbeats later, I stop. No footsteps follow. I scan the trees for him.

"Mason?"

He doesn't respond. I walk back the way I came, clearing the branches of large ferns as I go. I am almost back where I started when I find him sitting on the ground, his back against a tree. His head is in his hands, knees up with elbows propped on top. His chest rises and falls in deep cycles. What did I say?

"Don't you think we should keep moving?" I ask, standing beside him.

He doesn't move.

He doesn't look up.

He doesn't speak.

He takes deep breaths before raking his hands through his sandy blond hair and looking up at me. His eyes are tight, and pain laces the blue in them. For a second, I see a man who looks like he has lost something irreplaceable.

Instantly, everything feels heavier. What has he lost that was so precious? He clasps his hands behind his neck and hangs his head for a moment before blowing out a breath, releasing his hands, and pushing off the ground.

"We should." He walks into the trees, and I follow. The stone lodged in my throat sinks to my gut. Now I feel guilty for being so obstinate. I have no clue what he has been through, what anyone around me has.

I jog to catch up through the slew of ferns and ground shrubs. I have nothing to carry, and he has done all the daily tasks, including getting food, finding shelter. I have been acting like a spoiled child for days. That ends now.

Hours later, we arrive at a clearing. A small firepit lined with stones sits in the center. Mason dumps his rucksack on the ground. "Stay here while I get some food."

Before I can offer to go in his place, he has disappeared through the trees. I sit on the ground by the fire. The ground is damp and soft. I should get firewood. I push up and wander into the trees a little way, hunting the ground for sticks and small branches. I have an armful by the time I hear him return, muttering to himself. Then silence.

"Catori!"

I turn back and wade through the bushes and ground cover plants with a load full of wood. His hurried steps break through the undergrowth.

"Catori!" His voice is so desperate, it steals the air from my lungs.

"Here, Mason. I'm here."

He stops mere feet from me, staring as if I had been lost all over again.

I reach where he stands and meet his gaze. "I just got firewood." My words are almost a whisper.

He stands still, now staring past me into the mass of trees, hands hanging by his side.

"Don't we need it?" I ask.

He nods slightly and I drag in a breath, walking past him to the clearing. I drop the wood by the fire and sit. With the larger sticks I make a triangle shape, like the tepees I used to build as a child with... My brother. I have a little brother. Cal—Callian. I slap a hand over my mouth and loose a ragged cry.

Something came back.

I have a brother.

Mason sits on the opposite side of the fire and sorts out a variety of berries and something that looks like it's moving onto two large leaves.

"I have a brother."

Mason looks up, going still. "You remembered something?"

With a wobbly laugh, I nod. A smile blooms over his face, melting the worry from earlier.

"Callian will be pleased to hear that. You hungry?"

He knows my family? Of course he must, if he was sent to bring me home.

"Starving, but whatever is moving on that leaf, I am *not* eating."

"That's funny, forest girl. You are the one who taught me how to eat them." He chuckles and throws one of the pale wriggling things at me. I jump sideways and watch as it squirms beside me. I look back. His face is filled with so much happiness, my chest tightens. We eat in silence. I toss the revolting worms in the fire Mason eventually got started and share the water in his canteen.

With a full belly, I lie back on long strips of bark from the forest trees and gaze at the few stars I can see through the gaps in the canopy. I think about the shape of my brother's face, his huge smile, his hearty laugh, and try to piece anything else about my life together.

Nothing else comes.

I close my eyes, listening to the nightlife of the forest around me. I feel so relaxed in this place. Like I am a part of it. I roll over and watch Mason sleep. I study the angle of his jaw and the curve of his lips. He is out cold. He must be exhausted. I will always be grateful to him for saving me.

"We need to make a detour," he says. We walk along a well-worn path through the trees now. My body travels the strip through the trees as if it has done it thousands of times before.

"What for?"

"We could both use a wash." Mason winks at me.

"What?"

"It has been about a week since either of us bathed. It's time, Catori."

I study his face as he grins at me. My hands hover over my hips. Once again, I am reaching for something that isn't there.

"It's okay; you can go first. We can do it separately," he says.

"Fine. Where is this water hole?"

"It's not a water hole."

He walks on and I follow. After trudging through even thicker undergrowth, we break through the trees. The sound of gushing water drifts toward us, getting louder with every step closer. Mason pushes the frond of an overgrown fern to the side and turns back to me.

"Bath time." He smiles and tilts his head toward the sound.

I walk past him, looking up at a waterfall ten times our height. The crystal-clear water cascades over the rocky edge, landing in a pool that is lined with ferns and rocks. I gasp, and he files in beside me. "You want to go first?"

I close my gaping mouth. "No, you can."

How can I not remember such a place? Mason places his rucksack on the ground by my feet and tugs off his shirt. He removes his boots and socks and pulls his belt from its loops. Loosening the waistband of his pants, he wades into the water until it is up to his navel. Water sloshes over his hard stomach, the muscles in his arms flexing as he throws water over his chest and back. He walks into the falling water and runs his hands through his hair, closing his eyes. Water runs down his face and jaw. My breaths come fast, hands gripping my hips. How can I not remember him?

I pull myself from my spot rooted in the ferns and slump to the ground against a tree. Three months is a long time to not remember who you are. Who everyone around you is to you. What they mean to you. Who is Mason to me? Who am I to him? I close my eyes, and the burn of tears fades as the light does.

I will get through this. Whatever I find on the other side of this black hole, it has to be better than the gaping emptiness I have now.

Droplets of water hit my lap. I open my eyes and look up to find Mason. His hair is wet and pushed back. Water glistens on his shoulders and chest, down his abdomen, and his pants are soaked. He holds out a hand. "Your turn, smelly."

I laugh through the air stuck in my throat and press my palms into my eyes. I slap my hand into his and pull myself up. He holds my hand briefly before letting my fingers fall from his.

"No watching me, forest boy," I utter, my voice raspy. I walk to the water's edge and peel the tunic from my chest, leaving my undergarment wrapped around my breasts. I slip my pants from my hips and pull them down over my feet, tossing the clothing onto a nearby branch. In only my undergarments, I glance back. Mason sits, bare chested, against the tree I was sitting at. He's watching me, his face serious, hands gripping his canteen.

"Hey!"

He raises a hand and pivots to face the other way, chuckling. I hurry into the deeper water and sink into it up to my shoulders. Moving my arms in wide circles, I wade toward the waterfall. Pure bliss hits my head and shoulders the minute the fast water rushes over my skin, and I stand, forgetting anyone is watching. I moan and let my head fall back, allowing the water to flood across my face.

I run my hands over my face and neck, cleaning away the dirt and sand from the last seven days. The rope burns on my wrists sting a little, not fully healed. I slip off my bottoms and rinse them in the flowing water before sliding them back on and walking out of the water. Mason is still sitting with his back to me. I pull on my clothes and wander over to where he sits.

"We should get going; two nights out here is enough. We don't want to be wandering around the forest longer than we have to," Mason says, shouldering his rucksack.

"Let's go then," I say, offering a smile.

He studies my face briefly before heading west.

So many hands touching me.

Women plead with me.

Their children are gone.

Taken.

Mason is cutting a path through the crowd of village people, asking them to wait. Every face is a mixture of worry and fear. Some are confused as to why I am not responding. I hang my head, grab Mason's hand, and push through the crowd to what I assume is my home. The crowd thins as we arrive at the door of the largest home in the village. Smoke billows from the chimney in the center of the woven roof. Mason pushes the door open and pulls me in behind him before closing the door on the confused, worried faces of the women who stand across the threshold. Some still pleading, some silent with gaping mouths, words lost to confusion and fear.

I turn and take in my surroundings. The home is big, a hearth to my right with an iron cooker. Beyond that is a curtain that separates a bedroom from the living area. A small table sits at the back of the home with two chairs. To my right by the door is a long, large table covered in papers, to my left a few walking sticks. Some bent, all worn with use and time. I pluck the oldest-looking one and run a hand down the smooth shaft. The wood smells like oils. A wrinkled fine hand gripping this stick, banging it on the floor flashes through my mind. She was bent over, her long grey hair wild around her face. Her eyes kind, loving, and all-knowing. I clasp a hand to my mouth. I close my eyes and smoke swallows my visions. A pile burning, a body wrapped in cloths.

She's gone.

I gasp and stifle a cry.

Mason appears at my side instantly. "What is it?" he asks, resting his hand on my shoulder. I spin to face him.

"This is my grandmother's home."

He nods.

"Do you remember who your grandmother was? Do you remember who Hanola was, Catori?"

"She was my family."

Was.

Meaning she is gone.

He nods, his hand falling from my shoulder. What? Was she not my grandmother? I distinctly remember her, just as I do my brother, Callian. I wander around the home, looking for other items or spaces to pull more memories back.

The cushions on the floor in the living room. I make my way toward them. I see her now, sitting there. She is humming; in most memories of her on these cushions, she is humming. I stop short of the rug they sit on.

A memory of Mason here flickers through so fast, I almost miss it. There are others sitting with us. My brother and three others, two women and a man with brown hair, brown eyes, and a wide smile. A woman with dark hair leans against his chest. Were these people my friends?

Is Mason my friend?

Logs thud over the floor near the hearth. Mason builds the fire back up to a roar, adding larger logs and kindling. Flames soar for a moment before settling over the logs. The crackle and pop of the burning timber is the only sound between us. He stands and dusts his hands on his pants.

"That should keep you going until morning, at least."

"Thanks. Mason?"

"Yeah?"

"Are we friends? I mean, before you found me, before I was taken away. Were we friends?"

He studies the ground for a long moment before returning his gaze to mine. "Yeah, we are friends. You should get some rest. It has been a long seven days. I will bring you some food in a while."

We are friends. I swallow the lump in my throat and nod. Mason pulls the door open and walks through. He hovers over the threshold and looks back. "If you need anything, I will be just outside."

"Okay," I choke out.

A small smile blooms over his face. The door latches shut, and I wander back to the cushions and crumple to the floor, shoving my face into my hands.

What is wrong with me?

Why can't I remember who I am?

Why am I so helpless?

I know, with every fiber of my being, this is not who I am. I loose a ragged scream and toss the cushions on either side of me at the wall. I lay down and grip a cushion in front of me and hug it to my chest.

I hate this.

Almost an hour later, a knock echoes from the front door. I push up from the floor and straighten my clothes, wiping the tear-soaked hair from my face with the backs of my hands. I pad to the door, opening it to find Mason holding a tray of food and drink.

"Oh, thank you." I hold the door open, and he walks to the back of the home, setting the tray between the cushions. It seems a lot of time is spent in that spot.

"Hungry?" he says.

"Yes, you?"

"I ate earlier. I thought you might want some space to get reacquainted with your house."

"Um, thanks, I guess."

Mason's gaze drifts to the scattered cushions by the wall. "Redecorating?"

I laugh and pick up a plate of fruits and meat. "Something like that."

He smiles at me, and my heart picks up pace. I toss a piece of fruit at him, and he catches it midair, popping it into his mouth. I laugh, letting the sound carry through my chest and upward out of my throat. He relaxes, leaning back on the cushion, and I follow the length of his frame. I swallow and imitate his position. He sucks in a long breath and stares at the floor between us. We don't feel like just friends. But until my memories return, that is the way it will stay. I have enough to work through without complicating things. I pluck another morsel from the plate and chew on it, watching his hand trace circles on the rug. Another knock on the door startles us both. Mason sits up and pushes to his feet, striding to the door.

"What is it?" He steps outside, leaving the door half-open. I stand and walk to the door, wiping my hands on my tunic before leaning on the doorjamb. Mason pays me a glance, his brows drawn with lines over his forehead.

Not good news then?

I push off the jamb and step up beside him. The man talking with him shifts his focus from Mason to me. "The blacksmith has been reported missing, Catori. His wife is beside herself with worry. She says he didn't return home yesterday after a supply run near the tower."

"I, um—"

"Thank you for reporting; we will start inquiries straight away," Mason says, waving the guard-looking-type man off.

"What tower?"

"The Chancellor's tower, attached to the barracks." He walks back inside and slumps onto the cushions and snatches up a piece of fruit.

I follow and sink into my cushion, staring at his face. He's worried. People are going missing. First the children, and now the blacksmith. We need to make a move on this before more happens.

"What can we do?" I ask.

"We don't have the manpower—sorry, people power—to do anything at the moment."

"What do you mean? What about Callian? There must be warriors or something?" My hands hover beside my hips.

"We don't know where they are." Mason's face is stone, but fear and sadness lace his blue eyes. He runs a hand through his hair. "Catori, I need to tell you some things. Things that can't wait."

I freeze.

With a long inhale, I shift in my seat. "Go ahead."

Mason stares at me, his jaw feathering, chest rising and falling in deeper cycles by the second.

CHAPTER 9

MASON

This is the hardest thing I have ever had to say. How do you tell the person you love more than anything in the whole world you lost her family? You have absolutely no idea where they are.

"I—"

Catori grabs both my hands and shuffles closer to me, her face inches from mine. My heart flings against my chest. The smell of her electrifies my entire body. I rub my thumbs over her hands and try to steady my breath.

"It's okay. I would rather know. Please, Mason."

Please, Mason.

Those words, the last time we were together, saw me undone. My breath is all but nonexistent. I swallow past the rock lodged in my throat. "Callian isn't here."

Her face falls. "Where is he?"

I grip her hands a little tighter in case my next words see her fly out the door. "I have no idea. When you were captured by the Guardians, they took your brother too. Except they didn't take him to the desert side or the tower. We can't find him."

We can't find Imani either, and I have been struggling with that. Imani is resistant, resilient, clever, and not able to be detained long. I should know. There has been word Harm is in the prison tower. But not a whisper about Imani or Callian—it's like they simply disappeared. Tears line Catori's eyes, but her face is composed.

"Is there something else?"

"I'm not sure who you remember; I don't want to confuse you or upset you."

"Just tell me what you know. I will process it the best I can."

I study her face for a long while and she nods.

"Harm is in the tower prison. We had word of that the day after you were taken. Miya and her team are in the desert prison in Etonia. Nirri and Marshall made it out. I saw them in Trindari, where you were on that pole."

Catori flinches.

I loosen my grip on her hands, and she stands and wanders over to the fire. "These people that I should know, that are important to me, some I don't remember. Miya, I can recall from the prison, her relationship to me I don't remember. My head feels fuzzy, like I am half-asleep in some moments. Too much information or having to try and remember some things is like falling into a hole in the ground—dark, damp, and deep, no way out. I want to remember. I *am* trying."

I stand and walk to her side. "It will come back; the healer said it will just take time."

She turns to face me. Tears run down her face. "How will I find Callian?"

"Honestly, I don't know. I have scouts out; they are all coming back empty-handed. There is only one other place the Guardians could have sent him and Imani, and we can't access it."

"Where?"

"The mountain wilds."

"The what?"

"We spoke about it a month ago, and with Hanola before she died." I watch for a reaction to the words about her grandmother. She stands tall and rests her hands on her hips, brows lowering slightly.

"Okay, so if they are in the mountains, can they get out? Can they come home? Will Imani help my brother?"

I huff a laugh, thinking about Imani and Callian together. "Believe me, if Callian is in the mountains with Imani, they will find their way back to us, sooner rather than later." I almost believe my own words. It's not that I don't believe Imani and Callian are a formidable duo, but the mountain wilds are home to ex-Guardians and savages. Neither of which are forgiving to intruders.

Catori pads across the room to the strategy table. She looks through the papers on the top of the table, picking up sheets, reading one and selecting another.

"So, where are the children?"

"In the tower prison. The forest children are, at any rate. The desert children are being held in the prison at Etonia."

"The Chancellor has taken all of the children, from both sides?"

I nod and her mouth gapes.

"And now he has most likely taken the blacksmith from this village also?"

"Yes."

"This stops now." She turns and faces me, her hands on her hips, looking more like the Catori I know and adore by the second.

"The only reason we have not brought them home yet is because we are missing half of our team. Callian, Harm, Imani, and Nirri were a big part of that team. Miya's team is also gone and warriors from other villages are still deciding if taking action will do more harm than good. Every decision we have made lately seems to end badly."

Catori leans against the table and hangs her head, hands gripping the edges of the table. I close my eyes against images of her on the table, hands behind my neck, legs wrapped around my waist. I rub my hands over my face and loose a strangled groan.

"What?" Catori's gaze burns into mine.

"I, ah, nothing." I make my way to the door before turning back to her. "If you need anything, I will be outside."

I haven't even taken three steps outside when Jeselle stops me in my tracks.

"Is she okay? Is Catori going back for Miya?"

"Jeselle." I hold a hand up and try to find the words. I know Miya will have three days once the Chancellor decides what to do with her. I also know that Catori is not able to help. Not for a few more weeks, maybe even a couple of months.

She folds her arms around her chest, hugging her small frame. "We are running out of time, Mason." Her voice notches up an octave.

"I know, Jess. But Catori has lost her memory. She has no idea who she is, let alone what to do or how to carry out her duties as a leader."

Jess's mouth opens and doesn't close, her eyes tearing up. "What about Callian? Any word on him today?"

"No. Nothing." I watch as she struggles to stay composed. Her hands clamp over her mouth. "I'm sorry Jess, I really am. As soon as I know anything, or if the other warriors arrive, we will move out. But Catori can't go with us."

She nods vaguely, staggering back toward the eating area of the village.

Everywhere I look, there are people struggling with loss. Tensions are high and they are scared and worried. Rightly so. The

Chancellor's cruelty seems to never end—things we once thought he could never inflict on his people, he has done without warning or ceremony. He is the most dangerous man alive. He also holds all the power, and that needs to change. Our world needs to change. We were getting so close.

Figures he would pull our world apart, scatter our people across the three sectors. If we can't find each other, if our leaders are divided, we can't fight. The oldest and most effective strategy known to man, divide and conquer. He has divided, we cannot let him conquer. Or everything is lost. We can't just outlive him, too many will suffer or die in the meantime. Something must be done.

The village center is busy with adults eating at long tables. I walk over to the side of the kitchen and grab a tray. The ladies behind the benches offer solemn smiles. I nod and walk to the front of the bench with the tray. One of the younger women piles food onto the tray, enough for two.

"Is she any better today?" the woman asks.

"Much the same. She doesn't say much. I think she is remembering little things. Everything helps, I guess."

"The parents of the children are getting distraught. I'm not sure how much longer they will wait for her to recover before someone takes things into their own hands." She looks behind her briefly. "There has been talk of the fathers banding together and storming the tower. With the way things are, that can only end badly for the men and the children. But people are desperate. Can the healer not help her to speed up the process?"

"I have spoken with the healer several times, and she assures me all we can do is wait."

The woman releases a long sigh and places a large chunk of bread on the tray that is now full.

"I guess you are right." She turns and walks to another bench, busying herself with chopping up more fruits.

The tray is heavy in my hands as I wander through the crowd of expectant people, every set of eyes tracking toward me at one point as I return to Catori's home. I wish we could hurry this remembering process along. Not having Catori even know who I am hurts, but to think we have lost what we had before—the bond we had made—the thought of losing that is crippling. By the time I reach her door, my knuckles are white around the edges of the wooden tray. I pry one hand off and knock quickly. A heartbeat later, she stands combing her fingers through wet hair, a towel wrapped around her wet body. My stomach flips over, sending my blood thundering through my veins. I clear my throat, dislodging the breath stuck there. She steps back, allowing me in.

"Lunch?" I offer, setting the tray down in the center of the cushions on the rug. It takes everything I have to not look in her direction, to not pull her against my body that responds to just the sight of hers. I flop onto a cushion and divide the bread. Without a word, she wanders into the bedroom, only separated by a curtain. I hear the towel hit the floor and grip the edge of the cushion, focusing on chewing the bread. I swallow and pop a piece of fruit into my mouth, analyzing the texture and flavor, trying desperately to keep my mind off Catori.

"Enough for two?" She sinks onto the cushion beside me. Her hair is brushed, her skin clean and fragrant. She wears the clothes from her dresser, the forest warrior green-and-grey fitted pants and tunic. Her shape is cut neatly into the clothes. I have missed seeing her like this. I hold out a hand, palm up, offering fruit. She smiles and takes all of it. Her eyes close as she takes her first bite. A little moan spills from her lips, along with juice from the fruit.

"The people are worried about their children. Tensions are rising in the village, and there has been talk of a group of men going to the prison to try and get their children back."

She stops chewing and opens her eyes. "That wouldn't be a

good idea. Not if what you tell me is true about the Chancellor and the Guardians. Despicable men."

I stop chewing.

My breath stops.

I force a swallow and meet her gaze. "Some are not."

"Really, after all you have told me about them? If anyone deserves to be imprisoned or executed, it would be every last Guardian. Starting with Williams from the desert. Disgusting man."

I drop the food onto the tray. I open my mouth to speak but can't even form a response.

A loud knock rattles the front door and I spring to my feet and make my way over to it. *Every last Guardian,* she said. Including me?

I pull the door open. Standing with feet slightly apart, faces of stone, and chests strapped with weapons, are five forest warriors. All around Callian's size and my age or older, they stand patiently as I take in their bulk and hordes of weapons strapped to their chests, arms, thighs, and some poking out from the tops of their boots.

"You came," I utter.

"It was decided that something must be done. To do nothing would send a very bad message. We will not be considered weak or afraid," the man in front of me says.

"No, that would be a mistake." I open the door further and they step through. "We meet by the strategy table, if you would like to wait there." I point to the long table covered in maps and papers. The man nods and the five of them wander to the table, looking at the papers.

"Some men are here to see you." I offer a hand to Catori, and she pulls up from the cushion and follows me to the table. They turn and watch her approach. They make a fist with their right hand and hit it to their chest just above their heart, nodding at Catori. She searches my face for the meaning of the gesture. How do I tell them their leader has no idea who they are, or who she is?

"We are here to do what you see fit, Catori; send us wherever you feel the need." The warrior looks at her, waiting for her response.

She shifts her focus to me. "Mason, a word please." She turns on her heel and stalks into the bedroom.

I follow.

Catori pulls the curtain across to separate us from the men and turns to face me, eyes burning into mine. "Is there something you forgot to tell me?" Her arms fold over her heaving chest.

I close my eyes and pinch the bridge of my nose. The healer told me not to tell her anything, to let her discover things for herself, so that memories can come back naturally. She told me not to force it. But that feels like a luxury we don't have now. I should have tried to tell her at least something when the village people came to her about the missing children the day we arrived home.

"Well?" she snaps.

I open my eyes and hang my hands by my side. "You might want to sit down."

"Mason, tell me what is going on. Why are they coming to *me* for their orders?"

The mumbles of the five men in the living room seep through the thin material. If I can hear them, they can definitely hear us. Here goes nothing.

"Catori, you are the leader of the forest people, as was your grandmother before you. The warriors are here for their orders because *you* are their leader. They are waiting for you to decide what to do next. The people of the village are waiting for you to bring their children home. Because that is who you are. That is the kind of leader you are. You do what it takes to make things happen, to make things right."

She stares at me, her hands trembling by her side. "What?"

"The healer told me not to tell you. She said you had to realize these things, and let your memories return at their own pace. But we don't have time, not anymore. Too much has gone wrong. Too many people need you now."

I need her now. It is like half of me is missing. But I won't burden her with something else she doesn't know how to give.

"Mason, if what you are saying is true, why don't I remember a scrap of this leader I am? Why can't I remember these people? My life? Who I am?" She sinks onto the bed, and her head falls into her hands. She groans before sucking in a long, harsh breath. Lifting her head and gazing back up to me, she searches my face, as if trying to figure out where I fit in all this. Where I fit in her life. My heart flings in my chest and I shove my hands through my hair and knit my fingers behind my neck. I can't tell her about us. But if that part never returns to her memory, I don't think I want to bother breathing any longer.

She stands and raises her chin, her face tensing with determination. "Right. We need to make plans. We need to bring the children and the blacksmith home." She flings the curtain back and strides into the living room.

"Catori, are you alright?" the warrior asks.

She meets his gaze. Her composure falters for a second, either from guilt of not remembering or from doubt in herself. Which, I don't know.

"I'm fine. Let's figure a way to return our people."

He nods and they filter around the table. I join them, taking a place beside Catori. She smiles at me quickly before returning to the maps. Her finger traces over the names of every village, then stops on the tower in the north. "We need to retrieve our people from the desert prison first. This way, we have greater numbers to bring home the children. So, first stop is Etonia, then to the tower."

"The tower prison is harder to infiltrate, being linked to the Guardian barracks," the warrior to my right says.

"I can get us into the tower. We can use the workers' entrance. If that is not accessible, then there are two other doors that the Guardians use, but they would be much riskier," I say.

He nods at me.

Catori watches me, her eyes soft, lips parted, her arms hanging by her side.

"Very well, we will train this afternoon, camp here tonight, and decide party numbers in the morning before making a start to the desert sector," the warrior heading the table says.

"Sounds like a plan," Catori says.

"Great. We will meet you in an hour to train. We won't be taking anyone who can't keep up with a blade." A warrior from across the table says, his eyes moving between Catori and me, suspicion furrowing his brows.

"Fair enough," I say, and they show themselves out and we return to our food. Catori is quiet, eating small bites, staring at various places around the home. First the back wall, then the strategy table, before her eyes linger on the bed in her room.

"Catori?"

She shakes her head and meets my gaze, as if she was a million miles away. She clears her throat. "Yes, I was just thinking."

"What about?"

Her face flushes and she drops her eyes to the tray of food. "Nothing much, just this house."

"Oh." I try to quell the smile that wants to split my face in half. She was looking at every place we were together, before. Hope flickers in my core for a second.

An hour later my blade smashes against the lead warrior's,

letting loose a deafening clang. Catori watches me from the side of the training ring. I sidestep and retract my sword, spinning to reposition my feet and thrust the blade at his ribs. He freezes and I step into his space from behind, raising a dagger to his throat.

"Very good. You are with us, Mason."

"Thanks." I look to Catori; she is grinning from ear to ear. Apparently, she is impressed.

"You're up next, Catori," he barks from the ring. I hand her my blades as we pass near the border of the training ring. Her hand hovers over mine for a heartbeat before she steps into the ring with the biggest warrior. I have seen this woman take down twenty Guardians alone; this should be a walk in the park for her. They nod at each other, and the warrior takes the offensive. Catori raises her sword to defend, her feet close together, her breathing erratic.

She staggers backward as he removes the pressure of his blades on hers. *Come on, remember your training.* She lunges at him, and he easily brushes her blade aside with his. She grunts and runs at him. He sidesteps her and raises his blade to her throat. She goes still, dropping the weapons from her hands. She doesn't remember a thing. It is like watching a scared little child try to take on a trained warrior.

"Sorry, Catori, you won't be coming with us."

She stands, jaw clenched. "That's fine. I will see you all at supper."

She stalks past me, tears welling in her eyes. My heart wrenches in my chest. How could I have let this happen to her? If I had stayed with her that day in the village, none of this would have happened. Instead, I wandered off, trying to be helpful, trying to... I don't know what. Now she has gone through so much and lost everything in the process.

I walk back to the village center to find Jeselle. She is inspecting a bundle of arrows the blacksmith fashioned before he was taken.

"Jess, I need you to do me a favor."

"What is it?"

"Can you stay with Catori while I am gone? Four days, five tops. We are going to the prison at Etonia to retrieve Miya and her team."

Her eyes light up and she hugs me tight. My arms hang by my sides, and I chuckle. "Can you do that for me, so I know she is safe while I'm gone?"

"Of course. I will sleep in the living room. Maybe some of her memories will return while you're gone?"

"They will return when Catori is ready. I don't want to push her."

"We are lucky to have you, Mason. I can't imagine what would happen if you had been taken too."

"I will be happy when all of us are home. Miya, Harm, Imani, Callian, and every last village person that has been detained."

"You should go and get ready. I will find Catori; I am sure she could use a walk in the forest. Maybe it will help her remember?"

"She would love that."

By the time I grab my rucksack from Callian's house and make my way to Catori's, she and Jess are heading to the forest. I walk into the house and to the bedroom. The last drawer of Catori's dresser is full of my clothes and belongings. I pull out a fresh set of clothes and shove them into the bag. I grab my canteen and matches, a small knife, and underwear, and pile it on her bed. I pluck my rucksack from the floor and drop it onto the bed. The drawer hangs open. I do a mental check I have everything.

"Why are your things in my house?"

I spin around at her voice. "I, ah—"

"Mason, why are your belongings in my dresser?" Catori stands with her hands hanging, her eyes searching my face.

I break my gaze from hers and shove my things into the ruck-sack. Jess appears behind her, mouthing *sorry*.

"I thought you went for a walk?"

"She remembered something. She wanted to tell you," Jess utters.

Catori is staring at me.

I step toward her. "You remembered something? That's great, what was it?"

She drops her gaze to the floor and stalks out of the room, out of the house, slamming the door against the wall.

"That went well." I run my hands through my hair and sink onto the bed. "I feel like every time I don't remind her of some-thing, I am lying to her."

"None of this is easy. None of us know what to do. Catori was..." She looks toward the door. "Catori has always been the strongest person we know. It is hard to see her any other way. None of us know what to do or say. Every choice feels weighed down with some underlying guilt or mistruth."

I gather my rucksack and stand. I will sleep at Callian's tonight. In the morning, I will be gone, and Catori will have the space she needs to figure out what she knows to be truth.

"Stay with her tonight."

"Mason." Jeselle reaches for my arm. I walk out the door, my heart breaking with every step back to Callian's house.

CHAPTER 10
CATORI

My blade wavers in front of me. Hands gripping the hilt tight, I block Mason's blow. He is moving slowly, like I have never done this before. But I must have; my body has felt naked without blades strapped to my hips, across my chest, and on my back. Today he retrieved my blades. They were found tossed into the forest outside a village to the north, closest to the tower. No one will tell me why they were there. But I assume that is where I was attacked—how else would they have gotten my blades from me? Something must have distracted me.

Clash.

Another blow. I falter backward and grind out a word he ignores.

I steady my footing and move toward him. "Again!"

He lowers his blades, sweat running down his corded arms, and he looks at me, blue eyes searching my face. He won't find anything. If I can't find one scrap of a memory, he has no chance.

"Maybe we should take a break?" His words are kind and empathetic.

I hate it.

"I said again!" I lunge for him, and he blocks easily with his two blades. Mason has been away for five days and back for one, and I still have nothing to say to him. I have nothing new to tell him. I haven't remembered anything. Nothing about myself. Nothing about him and me. Five days I have spent walking in the forest, visiting with the people of the village, going through every nook and cranny of the house, and it hasn't sparked one memory. Not a single damn one.

"Catori, you're exhausted." He holds me at bay, his body taut but steady.

"You will do what I tell you!"

His eyes widen and he stills.

Grey.

Grey shirt, torn.

Mason on his knees in front of me.

My blade pressing into his throat.

My chest heaves.

I close my eyes.

His face is gaunt, his body skin and bone, but it is him. In one of those grey uniforms. Guardian.

"Catori?" he whispers. His words are close; his smell wraps around me. I push my eyes open, letting the blades in my trembling hands fall onto the grass.

"What happened?" He holds a hand toward me, and I step back.

I can't be here.

I turn, faltering on the grass, and run, tearing into the forest.

Branches and shrubs thrash against my arms as I plow through the dense forest growth, choking through ragged breaths. He is a Guardian? Was a Guardian? How did he get so mangy? Did we do that? Did I do that? What happened between then and now?

I stumble to a halt and grip my hair in my hands.

I scream, loud and painful wails leaving my lungs, and I sink onto the damp earth between the ferns. Every tiny piece of memory I can grasp I pull to the front of my mind, hunting desperately for any memory I can find with Mason in it. He traveled to the desert and saved me from those hideous men. Has taken care of me and protected me when the people of the forest are desperate to have me do something I can't.

What did I do?! What did I do to him? My forehead hits the ground beneath me. I scream again and again. Chugging breath through my shredded lungs, I pound both fists into the earth. When my arms ache and my body trembles, I slump onto the ground and whimper through breathy cries. My chest aches, the tightness long turned to a vice grip, sending pain throughout my entire body like lightning with every shallow breath I take.

A twig snaps mere feet from my curled-up form. I don't bother opening my eyes. If something or someone is here to finish me off, I welcome the release. I am less than half a person right now. And I don't know if I have the strength to live through the next few weeks, waiting for something that may never return.

A soft thud lands next to me. His smell again. Two arms slide under me, lifting me from the ground. I open my eyes. Mason looks into the trees, his jaw set. I feel his heart hammering in his chest against my body. He takes a few steps back through the forest.

"Put me down."

He stops, his gaze meeting mine.

"Put me down, Mason." I don't deserve his kindness, or whatever it is he feels for me.

"I don't want to," he whispers.

His words are strained.

His face breaks and I pull in a breath, tears burning behind my eyes. I clear my throat and wriggle.

He lets me down.

I stand facing him, so close, his breath meets mine.

"I remembered you were a Guardian." I meet his gaze. He runs his hands through his hair and looks away from me.

"We should get back," I say, walking back through the forest.

He doesn't follow.

I meet Jess at the tables for supper, and she tells me stories of her and me with Miya. Miya, who didn't return with the warriors and her team when they came home. But there were rumors she was shifted to the tower prison. The warriors left for their home villages this morning; Mason gave the order to return home. Miya's whereabouts are unknown for the moment. I can see the way Jess loves her in the stories she tells, the affection she has for her, the fierce love and loyalty to her chosen match.

It must be breaking her heart, not knowing for sure where Miya is.

Mason drops down beside me. He selects a plate from the center and loads it with food. He doesn't look at me. I try to find something to say, but nothing feels like enough. I don't know what he knows, but I have an idea of what he feels now.

"Can you pass me the water?" I ask him.

He slides the jug and a mug over to me, eyes not leaving his plate. He is so close to me but never touches me. I guess he must be protecting himself, not knowing if I will ever return to the person I was before. I take a mouthful of water and push up from the bench. "I'll see you later," I tell Jess.

She smiles and nods, as if understanding I need to be alone. I walk home and push through the door. The house is empty, quiet. I wander to the cushions, hesitating. I pad to the window, where a small water jug and mug rest. The moonlight streams through the window, through the gaps in the canopy. And then I feel it.

Heat.

Hands spinning me around.

The whip of a memory of my naked body standing by the window drifts past.

But I am still alone. I am tired of being alone. I am tired of being helpless. I press my hand onto the wall, waiting for more memories to come.

No images, just a smell.

Mason.

Confused and worn out, I make my way to the bedroom and curl up on my bed. Flickers of my life from before have been haunting me all day. My brother's laugh. The girl with wavy dark hair, Imani. I remember her. Dancing with Mason, his arms around me, the feeling of being content, spinning around, the scowl on Callian's face as we move to the music. Harm, standing in the training ring, chest heaving, the widest smile on his face. Miya, her hair falling over her shoulders as she braces for a fight. These people are my family.

My friends.

I see their faces.

I feel their love, but I can't feel anything in return. What is wrong with me? I breathe through each self-deprecating thought, waiting for sleep to drag me under and save me from myself.

I stand in the training area, sword held high, arms shaking. Callian is watching as Mason lunges for me. I block the best I can, meeting my blade against his two. The vibration of the impact burns down my arms. I falter backward and trip over a log, landing on my back,

the air knocked from my lungs. I sit up and try to rise, but my arms are held back. Mason's hand covers my mouth, a smirk unfurling across his face. Hate laces his eyes. He leans down to my ear. "Your turn." His other hand grabs my hair, tugging it painfully, pulling my head back, my throat exposed. The air is too thin. I gasp and struggle against his hold.

My eyes fly open. In the grey light of my room, a dark figure hovers over me. His filthy hand is pressed over my mouth. I'd recognize the reek of his dirty, sandy body anywhere. Williams.

I slam my knee into his side. I scramble sideways and jump off the bed, grabbing his hair with my hand and sinking my knee into his gut. He collapses to the floor. The creak of wood sounds to my right. Jess stands in her nightclothes, bowstring taut, arrow aiming for Williams's head.

"Don't bother getting up," she snarls.

Plucking the lantern from my dresser, I light it and bend over Williams. He is still in his uniform. It's filthy and his face carries many days' worth of growth. I stand up and turn to Jess. But my focus goes to who now stands behind her.

Mason.

His face is drawn. He pushes past Jess and looks between me and the cowering Guardian on the floor.

"What happened?"

"Williams was paying me a visit." I set the lantern on the dresser and grab my dressing gown, tying it around my waist.

"How the hell did he find you?" Mason growls. He steps up to the Guardian and pulls him to a stand. "Cells, now." He shoves him around and walks him out the door, Jess following, arrow still nocked. I stand in the doorway until they are out of sight. I place my hands on either side of the doorjamb and sigh. If Williams found me here, does that mean Peaches and his men will also come? I glance to the small table at my side loaded with my weapons. Running a finger over one of the fighting knives, I pick it up and slide it into the tie of my dressing gown. I pad back to my bedroom, blow out the lantern, and lie back on the pillow, hands under my head, waiting for Jess to return.

Moments later, two voices enter the house. Jess bids Mason goodnight and curls up on the cushions, setting her bow closer to her than before. I track Mason in the grey light until he stops just inside the curtain of my room.

"You don't need to stay, Mason."

"Yes, I do." He lowers himself in the doorway, propping his head against the wall before closing his eyes. Is he going to sleep there for the rest of the night, sitting up? I pluck the pillow to my left and toss it at his head. He startles when it hits him, opening his eyes, but smiles and slides onto the floor, putting the pillow under his head. I close my eyes, holding back a smile, suppressing the urge to tell him he can lay next to me. I am still unsure if the feelings he has for me are real, or if I ever reciprocated. Until then, I will wait. I will wait for my memories to return. I want to have everything I lost back before I make a decision that big.

I wake to find the floor beside my bed empty. I get out of bed and pad into the living room. Jess sits at the small table, eating breakfast from a tray that looks like it carries enough food for about six people.

"Hungry?" she asks.

"Where—"

"He went home at dawn. I don't think it is easy for him to be around you when—"

"It's okay, Jess. It's fine. Let's eat." I drop onto the chair opposite hers, popping fruit into my mouth. I close my eyes, enjoying the textures and flavors of the fruit. Instantly, Mason's broken face from yesterday flies into my mind. I stop mid-chew and swallow before I am unable to. "Can you tell me something?"

"What do you want to know?" Jess says, looking up from her plate.

"I want to know what was between Mason and me, before."

She stops. Eyes widening slightly, she begins chewing again. "Are you sure? I thought you were supposed to wait until your memories came to you, not go searching for them. In case they get muddled up or something?"

I look toward the door, Mason's broken face still etched into my mind. I cannot keep hurting everyone else for the luxury of my own piece of mind.

"Start from the day I met him, until the day I was taken."

She puts her food back on her plate and clears her throat.

"What? It can't be that horrible, Jess."

"Oh Catori, it's not, but it's also not easy. You and Mason were —I mean are, or whatever you decide. You were intense, and he was—"

"What do you mean intense?"

Jess starts from the moment Imani had her blade to Mason's throat in my old house. She tells me of the days that followed. Mason was a Guardian. The prison cell I kept him in. The things we asked him to do. The training I made him undertake. The assignment in the tower with Imani that my grandmother sent him on. The sacrifices he made to get Imani home to Harm. The day I rescued him and killed twenty Guardians to save his life. The day my grandmother died, and he found me in the forest. The day I became the leader of the forest people, and he swore his oath to me. The nightmares he had that I held him through. The moment my friends and family knew we were together. The day we went to the village that was gassed.

I stare at her an hour later, tears burning their way down my face and dripping into my lap. My chest heaves, shards of glass ripping my lungs apart with every breath. I wipe my face with the backs of my hands, stand on shaky feet, and walk to the back wall of my house, pressing both hands against the wall. Flashes of Mason holding me against the wall flood in. In the bedroom. On the strategy table. I wander to the table where scattered papers cover its top. A memory splits my mind: my grandmother stands to my left, propped up on a stick, her wrinkled face smiling up at me. Callian, Imani, Nirri, Harm, and Mason stand around the table with Miya and Jeselle talking strategies, locations, and resources.

I grip the edge of the table.

I remember them all.

The desert children had been taken.

The villages had been gassed just like ours were the day before I was taken. Mason wandered through the haze, searching for people, searching for the children. The three Guardians were waiting for us, masked and armed. We didn't stand a chance. Callian falling. Mason screaming for me.

I slump against the table.

Jeselle appears by my side.

I turn to her, mouth agape.

"Catori?" she chokes.

"I remember, Jeselle. I remember them all. I remember everything." I hit the floor on my knees. Her arms wrap around me, and I sob into her chest. Breathless, aching sobs for everything that has happened. For everyone I have lost.

Hanola.

Myself.

"Do you want me to get Mason?" she asks softly.

I shake my head. "No."

"Catori." Her words are firmer.

"I just need a little more time to piece everything together. Please?"

I stand, and she releases me, rising to meet my gaze. "Whenever you're ready, Catori."

I nod and she grabs her bow and quiver and walks out the door, looking back with a smile on her face. It is so good to see some happiness at last.

A handful of heartbeats later, Mason walks in. I steady myself and suck in a breath, hoping he can't tell I have been crying.

"Morning," I offer.

"Morning," he says, not looking at me. His focus is on the maps on the table.

"Mason?"

"Yeah?" He studies the map in his hand. Still not looking at me. Still protecting himself.

I am supposed to do the protecting. I am the leader. Huntress of this sector of the wall. I have wasted enough time.

"We go to the tower in three days and retrieve the children. Send word to the other warriors and what's left of Miya's team. I am going with you. I am going to bring our children home, along with Miya and Harm."

He spins on his heel, map gripped in his hand, jaw feathering.

"No, you are not coming with us if we have to go to the tower. We will not lose you again. You stay here!"

I lean into his space. "That's an order. And is exactly what is happening," I grind out.

His eyes burn into mine. "And what happens when we fail? As we likely will, without your skill. What then? When another seven of us are captured by the Chancellor? Where does that leave our people?"

"We will not fail!" I can't tell him I remember. I don't even know if I can fight the way I used to. I need to train and find out first.

"You don't know that! The Chancellor is doing things we once thought far beyond his capabilities. Things have been going from bad to worse while you have been lost somewhere inside your own mind!"

I step back.

The air leaves my lungs and doesn't return.

"Catori." He holds up a hand before going slack, sorrow pulling at his brows. "I'm sorry. Please, I didn't mean that." He takes another step toward me.

I hold my shoulders back and set my jaw, willing my thundering heart to slow. I count each breath until I spin and stalk out the door.

CHAPTER 11
HARM

The wooden door to the cells opens. Three sets of boots march down the hall, dragging between them one forest-clad warrior. Her head lolls, wavy light brown hair spilling around her shoulders and freckled face.

Miya.

I jump to my feet and grab the bars, watching her limp body be moved into position at the shackles and strung up. Two of the Guardians attach shackles to her wrists before securing her ankles, while the third holds her up. After the last clasp is closed, he drops her weight, and her body jerks instantly when her weight hits her wrists. She lets loose a long, painful gasp, scrambling to steady her weight over her feet.

The officer who stands in front of her, mere inches from her seething rage, huffs a laugh as a smirk pulls over his face.

"Drop dead, filth," she hisses through busted lips.

"You first." He turns on his heel and nods for his comrades to follow. They chuckle, slamming the door behind them. One spins back and turns the key in the lock. They joke, scanning the cells as they leave. The heavy door thuds closed. I rush to the bars that separate Miya and me.

"Miya," I choke out.

She raises her head. "Harm. I wondered where you got to." She smiles but winces, letting her face fall.

"What happened to you?" But I already know the answer to my question. They beat her in the prison in Etonia before bringing her here. The fact that they moved her and didn't just kill her outright worries me. Heaviness sinks in my stomach with the dread of what the Chancellor has planned for her.

She looks around through puffy eyes. "Our children are here."

"They are." I release my tight grip on the bars, turning to look at the tens of children who sit stunned in the cells around us. They recognize their warrior, staring at her battered face. Some of the older girls begin to sob.

"Tell them I'm fine, Harm." Her words are soft but fierce. She pushes her shoulders back, standing a little taller.

I wander to my cell door. The face of every forest child is pulled tight in a combination of fear and sadness. The strongest woman they know stands before them, battered and chained. One of the older girls curls into the chest of the boy beside her, her sobs echoing around the large room.

"Hey, Miya says she is fine. She is strong, you know that. We will be okay." I almost choke on the words; I barely believe them myself. A few of the younger kids nod and the sobbing girl quiets. "She told you that?"

I swallow past the lump in my throat and find my firmest, most comforting voice. "Yes. She just told me. She looks worse than she feels. Now, so the younger children don't become upset, why don't you play a game?"

"What kind of game could we play in a cell?" one boy huffs, throwing me a dirty look.

"I spy? Guess the number? Follow-along stories? What do you play to pass the time when you can't go outside at home?"

"Sometimes mother plays and-then stories with us. She starts, and we have to think of what happens next whenever someone says and-then," a smaller girl offers.

"That sounds great. Who wants to go first?"

Their little bodies sit up tall, like at the village school, most of them eager to have a turn.

"Okay, you can go first, since you came up with the game," I say to the girl. She nods and starts her story. I turn back and walk over to Miya.

"We will get out of this, Miya."

She hangs for a moment, eyes closed. "Maybe, Harm. Maybe not."

I slide down the bars and sit on the floor, as close to her as I can get. "Was Imani in the prison with you?"

She turns and looks at me. Her breathing accelerates and my stomach plummets. *Please don't tell me she is dead.*

"She wasn't there, Harm. If they took her, and she is not here or back in Etonia, I have no idea where she could be." She moves in her bonds and winces, before sucking in a ragged breath. "Catori was there, but something was wrong. She didn't recognize me. Any of us."

"She lost her memory?"

"It seemed that way."

That is not good. If we had any chance of getting out of here, Catori and her warriors would have been our only hope. Without Imani and Catori, that leaves Mason and Callian.

"Wait, why would they have Catori? She wasn't with you in Etonia."

"They were intercepted at one of the gassed villages and taken by the Guardians. At least, that is what my team found out."

"Who was? Just Catori?"

"Callian and Mason were with her that day too. No one has heard the whereabouts of the boys. It is like Callian just disappeared. Nothing on Mason either, if he is still alive. The Guardians don't take kindly to traitors or defectors, as you well know."

In this moment, I am glad I'm already on the floor. I shove my hands on top of my head and loose a groan. Rubbing the heels of my palms into my eyes until stars burst, I grip my hair with both hands, eyes shut tight. This couldn't get any worse.

"The Guardians had both of us in Fletcher's office before Catori was moved to another location, and they didn't even realize they had the leader of the forest people in their hands. Their arrogance leaves them complacent."

"They moved her? Where to?"

"I have no idea. They don't exactly update fellow prisoners."

The wooden door opens again. Two Guardians march toward Miya's cell and unlock the door. One is carrying a chair and rope. I know exactly what that is for.

Please no.

Not in front of the children.

"Hey, whatever it is you think you need to know, why don't you just ask?" I snap.

The Guardian with the keys stalks to the bars, inches from where I now stand on the other side of Miya's cell. He looks me up and down briefly. "We don't take orders from the Chancellor's *pet*."

Miya pays me a sideways glance.

"I am nobody's pet. Leave her be; I will tell you anything you want to know." The words are out before I have even thought through how I am going to pull it off.

"And you are going to tell us what we want to know about the rebels and your little band of forest friends." The Guardian with the chair dumps it onto the stone floor. She shakes her head, eyes piercing mine.

"Whatever you need to know, I will tell you. Just leave her be."

Miya's eyes widen.

I will tell them half-truths and falsities, and by the time they discover my words are hollow, we will be long gone. At least Miya will be, I hope.

The two men remove the shackles from her wrists and ankles and bind her to the chair with the ropes. She grunts as they tighten the rope around her wrists.

"Does it have to be in front of the children? Don't you have an interrogation room or something?" I plead.

Miya closes her eyes just before the officer with the keys, now jingling in his pocket, lands a hand across her cheek. She doesn't make a sound, her breathing paced and eyes closed. She is somewhere else, working through the pain, as if disconnected from it. Part of her years of training, no doubt.

"I am going to ask you a series of yes or no questions. You will respond, or I will continue hitting you. Do you understand?" Miya stays still, eyes closed. She doesn't even give him that answer. He leans down, inches from her face.

"Do you understand?!" His voice bellows from his chest, his face reddening by the second. The whimpers of the children around us pull me back. I look to the oldest of the children and put my hands over my ears. Some do the same, the eldest of them covering the ears of the children too young to understand. All but a few close their eyes. A crack echoes through the chamber and I spin back to see Miya sway sideways on the chair. Blood blooms from her mouth, dripping onto the floor.

"Are there rebels still active in the forest sector?" he barks.

Miya opens her eyes, but her gaze stays fixed on something

across the room, in the distance. He turns, trying to see what she sees, but spins back.

"Are there rebels in your sector, girl?"

She doesn't respond.

He lands another blow, this time to the other side of her face. Miya spits out blood and retrains her focus across the room.

"Do they have plans to act soon?"

"You are wasting your time," I growl. Miya won't give them anything.

"Shut up, mongrel," he seethes.

The officer beside him looks to the ground before focusing back on Miya.

"Do you work together with the desert rebels?"

Nothing.

Crack!

Miya's nose starts losing blood. It runs down her chin and neck onto her tunic.

"Are you the leader of the rebels on the forest side?"

Nothing.

Crack! Crack!

Miya falters forward. She shudders through a breath and pushes herself back up.

"Are you the leader of the forest people?"

Nothing.

Miya's gaze stays fixed on the wall.

Crack. His fist connects with her ribs. Short breaths cycle through her gritted teeth.

"Are you the leader of the forest people?"

Nothing.

Crack! Crack!

Miya sways on the seat, her eyes half-closed. The officer cracks his knuckles before shaking his hands out. He walks in a small circle and utters to himself. His comrade watches for a moment before stepping toward Miya. He leans down and whispers something in her ear. Her eyes open and her face turns to stone. What did he say? I grab the bars, chest heaving, watching them torture my friend. Imani's friend. Miya is like a big sister to her. Miya is our family.

Jaw set, I can't pry my gaze from her face. Her loyalty to her family, her friends, and her people. Miya will not break. Having been on that chair more times than I wish to count, I know exactly what that takes.

The officer plucks a knife from his pocket and flicks it open. He grabs her hair, ripping her head back and presses the edge into her throat. My heart races, pumping blood through my veins, thundering through my head. She holds his gaze, and he leans closer.

"Are you the leader of the forest people and the rebels?"

Miya's gaze falters to mine for a heartbeat. "Yes."

My breath stops.

What?

Miya, no!

She's protecting Catori.

What the hell did the Guardian whisper to her?

"You are the leader of the forest people as well as the rebel leader in the forest sector?" he repeats, looking briefly at his comrade, making sure he hears the confession.

"Yes. My name is Catori. I am the direct descendant of Hanola, my grandmother and predecessor. I am the leader of the forest people."

I slump to the floor.

Miya doesn't flinch.

A sickening smirk curls over the face of the Guardian holding the knife to Miya's throat. He retracts the blade and flips it shut, sliding it into his pocket.

"That wasn't so hard, was it?"

He motions for the bonds to be taken off. The second officer unties Miya and removes the chair and ropes. They leave her sitting on the floor, head hanging and hair covering her face, and walk out of the cell, locking it behind them. Seconds drag by as they make their way out the door and close it.

"Miya," I rasp, edging closer to the bars, raising to my knees.

"What, Travesci?" she says finally.

I choke out a half laugh at her dig at me. "What did that other Guardian say to you?"

Miya raises her head and gathers her long hair away from her face. She releases a long, sorrowful sigh. "Either way, I am dead; just tell them something, and they may spare the children."

"He said that? What did they have planned for the children of the forest, then?"

She gives me an incredulous look and my gut twists.

Oh.

"If they think they have executed the leader of the forest people, Catori will be safe, at least for a while. Who knows if she will ever get her memory back. I bought her some time."

"Miya." I can hardly get her name past the stone lodged in my throat.

"Harm, can you do something for me?" She looks at me this time. Tears line her eyes and her jaw feathers.

"Anything."

"Can you make sure Jess is okay when this is all over?" She hangs her head, drawing up her knees, and sobs. As if she just realized the price she was paying. Losing Jess. Or Jess losing her. Her sacrifice is also Jess's. My heart breaks watching her fall apart, and tears streak down my cheeks. Her breathing turns ragged and mine follows. How is this happening? My thoughts turn to my own sacrifice; to never seeing Imani again. Never holding her. Never being with her. Never again hearing her laugh or her sarcasm. Her smile. Her hands on my face. Her lips on mine. Her body against mine.

Waves of grief suck me under. I sink my head into my hands and double over onto the floor. My hands turn to trembling claws in my hair. I curl up on the stone floor and pray the heavens send death for me before too long.

Nightfall arrives, leaving the cells to bask in the dancing flicker of flames from the lanterns flanking the room. The wooden door creaks open, bringing with it Fletcher and one of his officers. They all look the same to me now. In comparison, Mason stood out from them. It feels like he never truly belonged in the regime.

Fletcher stops at Miya's cell.

"So, you are the leader of the forest people? Catori?"

Miya meets his gaze and nods—a shallow, solemn nod.

"The Chancellor has given you two days. You have two days until your execution."

Miya stares past him, no longer bothering to waste her now-limited time on him or his words.

"I thought you would like to know." Fletcher turns to his officer. "Check the last cell doors on the left please; last week they were jamming up." The officer marches down the hall into the dim light.

"Miya, why are you taking her place?" Fletcher says.

Miya's head whips up instantly.

"How?" she murmurs, brows lowered, studying his face.

"I know a lot of things I don't tell other people. And I know you are not who you are claiming to be. What I don't know is why."

"You wouldn't understand, Guardian. Some of us are loyal to our families."

Fletcher looks at me briefly before taking in Miya again. "Not all of us were given that choice."

His comrade walks back over. "All good, sir. Nothing is jamming up today."

"Good, let's get back to barracks. I'm sure Catori would like to spend her last days with her people." He looks around at the children, gaze stopping on Miles, who now clings to the bars at his cell door. Fletcher walks over to him. Pausing briefly, he pats the boy's hand and pushes a small paper between the bars. Miles conceals it quickly and holds his composure. Fletcher gestures for his officer to lead the way out.

Miles unfolds the note and looks from the paper to me.

His eyes widen before his chin trembles.

CHAPTER 12
IMANI

The fire crackles, melting the snow around its perimeter. Callian is hunched over beside me on a fallen log, rubbing his hands together close to the well-used firepit in front of us. This cold never seems to leave your bones. Engulfed by the towering trees lined with snow, we huddle close, trying to block out the sounds of mountain lions and other animals I have no desire to encounter.

"If I never come back here, it will be too soon," Callian utters. Shivers cascade through my body, and he wraps an arm around me.

"I never thought I'd wish for the desert heat as much as I do now," I offer. A small chuckle leaves his chest and I tug my coat around me tighter. "I hope we can get some sleep without ending up supper for a pack of those mountain lions."

Callian's teeth chatter. "I can take the first watch, if you like?"

"It's fine; you rest. I doubt I will be able to sleep for a while yet. My stomach doesn't know which way is up right now." The dead weight that has been in my gut for days grows heavier the closer we get to the wall. I am terrified of what we may find. I am terrified we will be too late. My breathing turns ragged, and I sink my face into the warm fur of my coat.

"Hey," Callian says. The warmth slips from my face instantly. He bends his head to meet my gaze. "Imani, he is going to be okay. We will find him and bring him home."

"I hope you're right," I whisper and push up from the log. Hope; even *that* feels fragile right now. I trudge through the snow on stiff legs, searching for more firewood. If the fire goes out, I doubt we will bother waking up to die. The snow-covered forest is dark, but I manage to gather an armful of mostly dry timber. I turn back to the campsite and pick my way through the white blanket, its frigid fingers sinking through my boots and around my feet. The crack of a fallen branch taking weight sounds behind me. With arms full of timber and my blades twenty feet away, I'm defenseless. I stop, holding my breath.

I wait, straining to hear through the sounds of night goers in the heavily timbered forest. Another crack, and I turn back, searching the shadows between trees for the source of the noise. I huff a breath, and it curls into a cloud in front of my face. Something moves four feet from where I stand, poking toward me slowly, steadying their hands on trees as they go. I squint, trying to see better.

It's a man.

Hoping it's not one of those savages, I call out, "Hello?" The word bounces between the trees, and he slows.

"Imani?"

Luca.

I relax instantly, shivering.

He clears the last of the trees and takes the bundle from my arms.

"What are you doing here?" I ask, scanning his face.

His beard is gone, revealing the lines of his jaw, square like his father's. Like a younger version of Jonah staring back at me. He is so handsome. I had forgotten that. With the beard he had, he looked older, more rugged. Now, his face is clearly defined, and a broad grin spreads across his face as he watches me taking in his appearance, highlighting his hazel eyes.

"You look different," I murmur.

"Losing the beard was a strategic choice. Can't go over the wall looking like a mountain man." He winks at me and heads toward the fire.

"Over the wall? You are coming with us? I thought you said we were fools to try." I follow behind.

"Oh, you are. But I can't let you go alone. And besides, I figure I owe you."

He dumps the wood by the fire and Callian rises from where he was laying, his eyes widening when he sees Luca.

"Luca, what are you doing here?"

"Same thing you are, forest boy." He grins at Callian, who nods and picks up one of the logs, placing it on the fire.

I sit on the log next to my cousin. "How do you owe me? You saved both of us from freezing to death and took us in."

"You have been with my father for five years. I am glad he wasn't alone. I have you to thank for that, Imani."

"Well, if you're coming with us, you can see him yourself. There is no way you are coming this far and not going home." He doesn't argue, just stares into the fire. He picks up a stick and pokes the logs, embers flying into the air above us. I try again. "Jonah deserves his son home. After all he has gone through."

"Imani, I can't stay. After I help and visit with Pa, I have to return. Seb can't run this place on his own. It's a two-man job."

"I see. What about Jonah?" I feel heat rise in my chest, tracking up my neck. It would break Jonah's heart to have his son return, only to disappear again.

"Maybe he could come back with me?"

"I'm sure Enid would love that," Callian quips.

"I forgot about Enid. I don't know then. I will think of something." He bumps his shoulder into mine and offers a sad smile. "First things first, though. How do we get into that tower?"

"Servants' entrance," Callian grunts.

"Do you know the layout of the tower well?" Luca asks Callian.

"Well enough, but I guess we could use your help with the prison part, and the barracks, if need be."

"I remember most of that place. If he is there, it won't take long to find him. The problem will be the officers. We will need to get past them without drawing attention."

"We have done that a few times." I remember the time we broke in and donned grey uniforms to take Fletcher, and the look on his face when he heard my voice from behind the boys. Priceless.

"So, we go through the wall in the morning and head straight for the tower. Infiltrate through the servants' entrance and head for the prison section. The barracks are connected, so we don't want to go that way if we can help it. That would be literally walking into the lion's den."

"Been there too," I say.

Luca turns to me, raising an eyebrow. "What haven't you done, my fiery little cousin?"

"Not much." Callian chuckles and tosses a handful of snow at me. I return fire with a large chunk, and Luca's hearty laugh echoes through the trees all around us.

Hissing pulls me from my restless sleep. Luca stands pouring his canteen over the fire. Callian is ready, coat on, weapons strapped to

every part of his muscular body. He runs a hand through his blond hair, dislodging snow. "Morning, little sis. You ready for this?"

I sit up and swig mouthfuls of cold water from my canteen. Shoving it into my rucksack, I stand and pull my coat around me. "Almost."

I pluck my weapons from the log to strap and sheathe them one by one. Fighting knives across my chest. Long daggers on my hips. A dagger in my boot. A sword on my back. I pull my blue scarf from the large coat pocket and wrap up my hair. Ready.

Luca runs an eye over the countless weapons I have attached to my body. "We will have to lose the coats before we cross through the wall. One, we won't need them. Two, I can't risk the Guardians realizing anyone from this side has helped you—me being the exception, that is; I am more than willing. But I won't implicate any of my men."

"Let's go, then. The sooner we make it to the tower, the sooner we can find Harm and go home," Callian says.

Luca leads the way, winding southeast through the trees. We reach the wall in under an hour. We were closer than I thought. Luca shoves his coat off and dumps it by the large stone door that leads us into the wall and out the other side. The forest side. My heartbeat races—finally, we are going home. The few weeks we have been in the mountain wilds has felt like a year. A long, painful year.

Luca presses the stone to the right of the seam of the door and it grinds open, slowly. Callian and I shove off our coats, reapplying our swords before following Luca into the wall. The door thuds closed behind us, and darkness swallows the three of us before light slips through the cracks of the forest-side door. The piney scent floods the dim space, and Callian steps out first, sucking in deep breaths, like he's been underwater, struggling to surface. "Ah, it's so good to be back."

Home.

Luca looks around, wariness and curiosity warring in his expression, twisting his face. "I forgot how amazing the forest sector was," he utters. I rest a hand on his back, and he looks down at me.

"You can stay as long as you like. You're always welcome. My home is yours."

He swallows and sucks in a breath before nodding. The sounds of forest animals and birds ring out around us.

"I estimate it's about a half-day run to the tower from here," Callian says.

"Run?" Luca's gaze swings between Callian and me.

I lift my heel up behind me and grab my foot, stretching my leg. "In the forest, we run. No horses here."

"Try to keep up, mountain man." Callian chuckles, taking off at a run. I hold out my hand, indicating for Luca to follow, and he does. I take the rear position.

We slow to a halt mere feet from the tree line before the tower. My heart thunders in my chest. Luca is walking in circles, sucking in deep breaths. Callian crouches in the ferns, getting closer. A servant enters the tower, basket in hand. One of the ladies from our village. It looks as if she is going about her duties as normal. Are the children home now? I guess we are about to find out.

We wait a moment for Luca to regain composure and make our way to the servants' entrance, slipping inside the door. How many times have I been here, sneaking into this tower for one reason or another? The risk is always great. The fear I have to squash always gnaws at me. I grip the fighting knives on my hips and wait for

Callian to close the door. Luca stands beside me, still. How long has it been since he was here?

"We head to the prison. If we can't get there right now, we find somewhere to hide until roll call at midafternoon," Luca whispers.

Callian nods and I do the same.

Luca leads the way down the dim passageway. The last time I was here, Fletcher held my own blade over my chest. I shake the memory and continue down the hall behind Luca, Callian behind me.

Moments later, the sound of boots tracking toward us halts our progress. Luca presses against the wall. Callian and I do the same a second later.

"What now?" I ask.

"There are too many of them to get any closer to the prison," Luca utters.

"Maybe we can go up to the dial room. Nobody goes there," I whisper.

"Lead the way." Luca nods and I take off toward the stairs. I stop briefly, listening for movement above us. Nothing. I take the steps two at a time. The boys follow close behind, and we make it to the dial room without being noticed. Callian breaks the lock and pulls the door open. We slip inside and close the door. Luca leans against it and slides to the floor. Callian walks the room, hands gripping his weapons tight. I make my way to the window and push it ajar. The forest winds slip through instantly, melting my fear just a little. I take deep breaths and steady myself on the ledge, hands gripping the wooden window frame.

"It's only a half an hour until roll call. Every Guardian on site will file into the training yard for any business for the day. Then we can move back down to the prison."

"Good. The sooner we leave this place, the better," Callian rasps. But he isn't winded. He must be working his way through so much—Harm, Catori, Nirri. The rooms we just passed used to be her home. Evidence of her is everywhere still.

The call sounds for roll call and lines of grey uniforms pour into the training area, forming orderly rows. Luca comes to stand behind me, Callian filing in beside me. We watch as tens of officers stand, hands clasped behind their backs. Uniforms impeccable, bodies rigid. The Chancellor walks onto the platform a few feet above them, flanked by Fletcher. My grip on the ledge tightens. Callian nudges me. Luca sucks in a breath, not releasing it.

"Been a while since you've seen my father, I take it," I say to Luca.

He nods vaguely, eyes fixed on the Chancellor.

When every last Guardian has filed in, the Chancellor raises a hand.

"Today, we gather for a momentous occasion. The leader of the rebels on the forest side has been, as you know, detained by our regime. Today she will draw her last breath, and order over the forest sector will return."

Callian stills. His face is drained of color, eyes wide with horror.

Oh no.

Please, not Catori.

The door to the barracks opens and two officers flank a hooded prisoner. Bile rises in my throat as the breath in my lungs turns to glass.

Behind the Chancellor, a noose and two officers wait. The prisoner is moved to stand in front of the rope. Her hood is removed. Her long, wavy brown hair covers her face. She raises her gaze to the men assembled below her.

Miya.

Callian slumps against the wall by the window.

Luca's worried gaze travels over us both.

"This is not happening." I rip both blades from my hips and rush the door. A hand grips my arm and I spin back.

"No! Imani, if you go down there, you will die too." Luca's eyes plead with me. He maneuvers my stunned body away from the door. I pad to the window, my trembling hands resting on the panes of the window. Every too-fast breath shallows out, and I feel the prickle of fear and panic clawing me to pieces from the inside.

Miya stares down the snickering boys and men that stand in front of her. The Chancellor looks to Fletcher, whose gaze is vacant. He stands with his hands behind his back, like every other man in uniform. The Chancellor grunts and nods to the Guardians standing on either side of Miya. One places the noose around her neck. I whimper. Callian groans through each breath beside me. His large frame trembles against the wall holding him up.

The lever controlling the wooden platform slides forward easily in the officer's hand and the floor disappears from under Miya. Her body drops instantly and swings. She doesn't fight. Doesn't lift a hand to pull at the ropes. She has accepted her fate.

"No!" My scream is swallowed by the cheerful roar of the crowd of officers a second later.

"No! No! Miya!"

Callian slides down the wall.

Luca holds my arm again.

Fletcher's gaze tracks upward. I push the window open slightly, meeting his stare. I hold his gaze, chest heaving and tears burning down my cheeks, shaking my head.

"Imani. Now is the time to find Harm. They will be busy for at least another thirty minutes with other matters."

Luca's voice fades into existence. I turn, sluggish, toward him.

"Harm," I whisper.

"Callian. Harm." I tug on his arm.

He wobbles slightly but doesn't move. Doesn't stand. Luca

walks around me, grabbing Callian under the arm and pulling him to his feet. He follows, not seeing. I'm not even sure he's still breathing.

I slide my hand into Callian's and squeeze it. He eventually turns to face me. "We have to go, brother. We need to find Harm and go home."

He walks out the door behind Luca. I look back through the window. Miya hangs there still. My chin wobbles and I pull in a ragged breath, tears burning my eyes anew. "Goodbye, Miya."

I fly down the stairs after the boys, and we track to the prison with Luca's sense of direction. He nudges the large wooden door open, and I rush through the hallway, scanning every cell. In a cell in the middle of the rows, Harm is curled on the floor, his body shaking. Callian shakes his head upon seeing him, as if snapping from his daze. He slides a dagger into the lock and breaks the internal mechanism, pulling the door open. I rush to Harm, dropping onto the floor beside him. He is chugging through painful breaths. He must have been with Miya before they took her.

"Harm, sit up."

His eyes open at the sound of my voice.

"Hey, it's me. It's Imani. You need to sit up."

He turns to face me, releasing his arms from hugging his chest. "Imani?" he chokes out.

I nod and smile, tears slipping down my cheeks again.

"Come on. We are going home." I stand and pull him to his feet. He stands, wavering slightly. I place my hands on either side of his face, and he lowers his forehead to mine.

"Where you go, I go. Now let's get the hell out of here," I whisper.

A pained groan lines his next ragged breath.

Luca tracks to the wooden door and scans the hallway.

"Wait. We need to take the children with us," Harm says.

I look back. The cells are lined with children holding the bars, staring at us. One set of brilliant blue eyes holds mine. Miles.

"Harm, please take me with you," he cries.

I walk over to the cell and put my hand through the bars to ruffle his hair. "Imani! Where did you come from?"

"Hey, little man," I choke out, heart splintering in my chest.

"Imani, we have to go. Men are coming," Luca warns.

"I can't just leave him here!" I try to open the lock the way Callian did. My knife jams, and the door stays shut.

"Imani, let's go," Callian snaps.

"But I—"

"Imani, take me home to mother, please."

I retract my hand, stepping back. "Sorry."

His face twists in despair, and my chest all but cracks open from the blinding agony. But if we try to take the children now, none of us will leave this prison.

"I will come back for you, buddy," Harm says. He is nodding, trying to reassure Miles.

"Okay," Miles says weakly, hands sliding from the bars.

I join Harm and the boys and slip through the door. We turn into the hallway before taking the stairs up one level and entering the passageway to the servants' doorway. I hang back while Callian, Luca, and Harm make for the door, torn absolutely in half between leaving Miles and wanting to get Harm as far away from this place as possible. A set of footsteps rounds the corner before I have the chance to move. He stops abruptly in front of me, alone and looking disheveled. We stare at each other for what feels like an age.

"Why are you so hell-bent on destroying everything and everyone?" I snap.

"I see you have recovered from your last visit to the tower."

"He is your son!" I point to the level below us.

Fletcher's face hardens, but his jaw feathers. "He won't be hurt. I will make sure of it."

"Oh yeah? Why should I believe you? You trust the man who killed his own brother! I guess that's not so far from being the man who tried to kill his only daughter." Rage thunders through my body, heat flooding my face.

"You need to leave," he finally says to me.

"I am." But I hover before the threshold, too stunned by his demeanor, by the events of the past hour, to know what to do next. "Why are you letting us go?"

"I can't do this anymore."

"Do what, Father?"

His eyes widen and he drags his gaze from somewhere in the distance behind me to meet mine.

He waves his hands around. "This."

"You just executed my friend, and you expect me to believe you are tired of the regime? What the hell am I supposed to think?"

"It won't matter soon anyway. They plan to execute the children and anyone who comes looking for them. Everything is coming apart. The Chancellor, he..."

"He what?"

"So much death. Nothing is as it used to be."

"You are not exactly helping the situation." I throw my hands up.

"Imani, I don't have a choice. I never have. I don't make the rules; I don't set the outcomes. I definitely don't make the orders! *He* does that. I am solely responsible for carrying them out."

"You always have a choice!"

Footsteps, multiple sets of them, echo toward us through the hallway.

"Go home. Go home and enjoy what time you all have left."

"What?"

"Go home, Imani," he says.

The thunder of boots draws closer. "Go!" he grinds out.

I spin on my heel and sprint to the door, busting through it and flying into the trees. Harm and the boys wait for me. Harm stands shaking, his arms held by Luca and Callian, one on either side.

"What were you doing? We were about to go back in looking for you!" Callian hisses.

Luca throws him a warning look, releasing his hold on Harm.

"I'm sorry, I—"

Harm envelops me in his arms, crushing me to his chest. Sobs chug through each breath he takes, and my breath turns ragged.

"I'm sorry, I was coming. Harm I—I was so scared I would be too late," I whimper into his chest. I wrap my arms around him and whisper that I'm sorry, over and over. His heart gallops under my ear.

Crunching from mere feet away sees the four of us turn. We see the shrubs move, but not who moves between them. A heartbeat later, the bright-green eyes of Catori find us. Mason files in behind her, studying us all, his gaze stopping on Luca before his brows lower. Five forest warriors hang back just beyond them.

"Callian!" Catori runs to her brother, wrapping her arms around him. He lowers his head, closing his eyes before tears streak down his face, dripping from his jaw. His arms fold her in close, tight. Callian chokes through a few breaths before Catori extracts herself from his hold. She looks between Callian and me.

"Where's Miya?"

CHAPTER 13
HARM

Catori's painful cries ring through the trees. Imani sobs in my arms, and I sit with my face buried in her hair. Mason breaks through the shrubs, drying his face with the backs of his hands. He slumps to the ground by a tree, lowering his head onto his hands, pulling his knees up. Halfway home now, we have taken a break from running to eat and drink, but nobody has touched any food or water. Luca watches us, occasionally chatting with the forest warriors that came with Mason and Catori.

"We should get moving. It won't take long for officers to realize Harm is missing," Luca says, walking toward Imani and me. She pushes off my chest and turns to face Luca, wiping her face with both hands.

"Luca, this is Harm. Harm this is Luca, Jonah's son. My cousin."

"Son? I don't understand. Jonah told me you were dead?"

"I was selected the year I turned fourteen but didn't exactly become the most obedient officer. They sent me over the wall to the mountain wilds after twelve months."

I turn to Imani. "You were in the mountain sector?"

"It's a long story, but yes. Callian too."

I track my gaze to Callian.

"Terrible place. Nothing but ice and snow and packs of vicious overgrown furry things," he mutters, brows lowered.

Luca pats Callian on the back. "You survived, forest boy."

Mason stands from his spot at the foot of the tree. "He's right, we should move."

I slide my fingers through Imani's. We walk a little further through the trees before taking off at a run. A groan comes from Luca, and Callian takes the rear. Imani, Luca, and me are in the middle. Mason leads with Catori, who is silent the entire way home.

When we finally break through the tree line near the training grounds of the village we call home, Luca doubles over before walking in tight circles, chest heaving. A crowd of village people stands on the opposite side of the training grounds. Catori curses under her breath and walks over to them. She says something we can't hear, producing cries from some of the mothers.

"What's going on?" I ask.

"We were going to the tower to bring home the children. And you, of course. And Miya. They were expecting their children to return home," Mason says flatly, walking over to Catori.

"I guess we ruined their plan," Callian says, running a hand through his hair. We move across the training grounds and stop just behind Mason and Catori. Luca watches as Catori settles her people with promises of another visit to the tower soon.

I step up beside her. She looks at me sideways for a moment and looks to Mason, who nods slightly.

"The children have not been harmed. They are fed and together," I offer, trying to help Catori in a difficult situation.

"Harm!" Petria's voice comes from the back of the crowd.

"Harm! Did you"—she pushes past the last of the women, breaking through to the front—"did you see Miles and Ima—"

Her hands fly to her mouth, and she rushes to Imani, wrapping her daughter in a brisk hug before pulling me into her hold too. Petria sobs, hanging between us.

"I was so scared I would never see either of you again."

"You can't get rid of me that easily, Mother," Imani says.

Petria touches her hand to Imani's face and smiles through a torrent of tears. "What are we going to do, my girl?"

"We will get Miles back, Mother. I promise."

Petria nods, crushing Imani to her chest again.

After Imani is released from her mother's grip, she gestures to Luca. "Mother, you remember Luca? Your nephew?"

Petria's eyes widen, her mouth falling open. She takes a small step toward him. "Oh, my heavens." Gripping his hand with both of hers, she gasps as he pulls her into a hug. A small laugh leaves her chest.

"Hello, Aunty Tria," Luca rasps.

Petria pulls back, holding him at arm's length. Her gaze runs over her lost nephew. "Your father is going to have a heart attack, young man. Just look at you! You're the spitting image."

Tears stream down her face and she smiles, her eyes moving between her daughter, her nephew, and me. At least we made one person a little happier.

"Callian, can Luca bunk with you?" Imani asks.

"Sure."

"Actually, there's no room left at Callian's house. But Nirri's house is free," Mason says. Callian's jaw feathers. Why is Mason bunking back at Callian's? What did we miss? I track my gaze to Catori and then to Mason. He stands beside her, but not close like he usually does. Something's not right.

"Anywhere is fine," Luca says, looking between Mason and Callian.

"I'll show you where it is," Callian offers, gaze burning into Mason's.

The village people filter home one by one, leaving Imani, Catori, and Mason standing with me.

"You want me to take you home?" Mason asks Catori.

Okay, that's new.

"Yes, please," she utters, her gaze on the village center.

He turns to walk back with her, and I grab his arm. He spins to face me. "Mason, what's wrong?"

"Long story. I can find you later, okay?"

"I could use a walk," Imani says, walking after Catori who hasn't realized nobody is with her yet. Odd.

"Mason?"

"Catori lost her memory. She has no idea who most of us are. When I found her in the desert sector, she was strung to a pole. They must have hit her over the head. Hard. She only remembers Callian and Miya so far. No one else. Although she did relax when we got home to the forest. So, she must partially remember that too."

"Did you take her to the healer? When will she get her memory back?"

"They don't know. Just that it has to return by itself. We can't try and force it."

"That's why you're sleeping at Callian's? She doesn't remember you? Who you are to her?"

Mason's face twists and he looks away. His Adam's apple bobs, and his jaw feathers. Finally, he nods.

"Oh, man. I'm sorry. I can't imagine what that is like." I watch as Imani walks slowly with Catori toward the village center.

"Jess and I have had to fill her in on a few things. Her leadership depends on it. But other than that, everything else—her personal life, the rest of us—she has forgotten."

Of all the things to happen, this I never would have suspected. Life is beyond unfair.

"So, now you just have to wait?"

He nods and starts to walk toward the village center. As if he doesn't want to let Catori out of his sight. Maybe he is afraid something might happen to her. She was the most formidable person I had ever met. Now, she has to be chaperoned around like a child. It breaks my heart. I hope she recovers. For her sake as much as Mason's. And for everyone in the forest sector. She is an incredible leader; to lose her would be a huge blow.

"You can't say anything about us to her, okay?" Mason says as we almost catch up to Imani and Catori.

"I won't."

I offer him a sad smile as we file in on either side of the girls. Mason walks beside Catori. I lace my fingers with Imani's, and she looks up at me with the sweetest smile. I can't imagine losing that. Losing her. So many times, I have thought I had. So many times, my heart shattered with the pain of losing her.

And every time she put it back together.

Every. Single. Time.

I press a kiss to her forehead as we walk.

Every breath I take is for her.

Everything I do is for her.

And, I realize, it always has been.

And that will never change.

CHAPTER 14
IMANI

Catori sits across from Harm and me at the long table in the center of the village, staring at her plate of untouched breakfast food. She pushes food around with her fork under the concerned gaze of Mason. He came to see us last night, after everyone had settled back into their homes. Catori has lost her memory. She only remembers a few people, mostly Callian and Miya. Jeselle has been with her since Mason found her and brought her back from the desert side. Mason has instructed us not to talk about anything related to their relationship with Catori, claiming that the healer said she has to let the memories return of their own accord.

He is devastated.

Catori has been his lifeline, and now she has all but disappeared on him.

"Hey, you want to train? I could use the practice," I say to Mason.

He looks from his plate and forces a half smile. "Sure, Imani."

"I have to talk with Callian and Luca before training. I'll meet you two later on," Harm offers. Mason meets his gaze briefly but returns his focus to his food, mostly uneaten.

"Can I watch you train?" Catori asks.

Mason's head pops up. "If you want."

She smiles at him. "I do."

"I have to duck home for my wrap; I forgot it. I'll meet you in ten?" I say to Mason, and he nods.

I push up from the table and wander back to the kitchen, handing over my empty plate before walking home.

The door opens easily under my hands, and I stand for a moment, taking in the home Harm and I made. The table and chairs; the full, warm hearth. The neat dressing area and my dresser full of clothes and wraps, scraps and undergarments. Such a thing, a dresser full of clothes feels like such a luxury after being in the mountains. I run my finger along the top of the dresser and tug the top drawer open. Plucking out my blue scarf, I wrap it around my hair, tying it up. I wander to our bed and sit next to my pillow. The canopy of the bed Harm made for us creaks, and the sheer cloth draped over the long, slender beams between the head and foot of our bed moves, sending a wave down the curtains.

I trace a hand over the stars in the headboard and suck in a breath. How many times have we been so close to losing everything? I have lived through days of being told he was dead. The strength it took to still believe he was here was enormous. I can well imagine how Mason is feeling right now. I hang my head and say a small prayer that Catori finds her way back to us. Back to Mason.

Sighing, I push up off the bed and walk out the door, closing it firmly behind me.

I make it to the training area just after Mason does. Catori isn't here. Odd. He stands in the sparring ring, running a hand over his blades. Probably checking to see if he needs to sharpen them.

I step into the ring with him. He looks up from his weapon.

"You ready, Rayner?"

He lunges at me, the blade in his right hand coming at me fast.

I defend and spin away from him. He stalks me, his gait harsh. I sheathe my fighting knives and pull the sword from my back to give me better range. I will need it against the anger and hurt he is channeling through his blade. He connects with my sword with one hand and pulls a second blade from his chest. The tip pierces my shirt at my ribs, just below my heart. With no hands free I stand my ground for a heartbeat before ripping my sword from his dagger and stepping back.

Blood trickles down my stomach under my shirt.

He won.

"Nice move, Rayner."

He stares at me for a moment, stunned. "Sorry, Imani. I—"

"It's fine; don't worry about it." The blood seeps through my shirt and his eyes widen.

"Dammit, Imani. I didn't mean to hurt you."

"Mason, I said it's fine." I make no move to stem the blood.

"No, it's not. Nothing is fine." He sheathes his weapons with shaking hands.

I walk to him, wrapping my arms around his shoulders and hugging him tight. His arms wrap around me, sobs falling from his chest a heartbeat later.

"You haven't lost her, Mason. She is Catori. She will find her way back. You have to know that."

His sobs turn to ragged moans.

My heart cracks, and I hold him tighter, tears burning behind my eyes. I have been here before. I know every type of pain that is tearing him apart right now.

"It's okay. It's okay, Mason. You will get through this. You both will."

He pulls away and wipes his face with his arms, one at a time.

"Is this what you felt like when you and I went to the tower and Harm thought you had betrayed him?"

"Something like it." I swallow past the lump in my throat at the thought of those weeks. I was terrified I would lose Harm.

"Come on, let's go find the boys. I'm sure they are concocting some plan that we are going to have to participate in," I say, bumping his shoulder.

He huffs through a wobbly laugh.

We find Harm, Luca, Callian, Jeselle, and Catori standing around the strategy table. Silence fills the room when we walk in. Harm's gaze meets mine before trailing down my shirt to the blood. I give him a warning look, and he returns to his chatter with Callian.

"So, your husband is dead set on taking Luca home. Thoughts, Imani?" Callian grates out.

I look to Harm. "You're taking him home?"

Where he goes, I go. *We* are taking Luca home. If Harm has decided this is our next move, then it is.

"Yes, I think it is only fair. Plus, the desert side of the rebellion needs the numbers and the inside knowledge that only ex-Guardians have."

"When do we leave?"

"First light tomorrow."

"Great. I'll pack for us if you want to keep this discussion going." I wave a hand between Harm and Callian.

"Imani, you really think going back is a good idea?" Callian snaps, his eyes wide. I drag my gaze to his, and he continues, "We only just got back. We only just regrouped, and now you want to split up again? We can't afford any more setbacks. Not to mention you two are not safe on that side of the wall. I will not lose any more of my family!"

My chest aches with the weight of losing Miya. Swallowing, I force the stone forming in my throat back down. I meet his fire with my own stare. "Then come with us, brother. The choice is yours."

Callian's mouth gapes and he shakes his head. "Fine, first light tomorrow."

"You never know; you might even get to see Nirri." Harm hooks an arm around Callian's neck and rubs a fist into his messy blond hair.

Callian's face reddens, and he rolls his eyes. "Hey, I said I'll go, alright?"

The cool forest air winds around my feet as we wait for the others to meet us on the village's eastern outskirts, just inside the ring of trees surrounding the village. Harm wraps his arms around me from behind and nuzzles my neck. I lean into his warmth and pull in a long breath, languishing in his smell and tight hold.

Callian and Luca appear beside us a moment later.

"Let's get going, you two." Callian snorts, a grin splitting across his face.

Harm unfolds from around me and takes off running. I follow, Luca behind me, and Callian as our back runner.

After two days traveling through the trees, we stand in front of the wall that separates us from the harsh, hot sands on the other side. Harm presses the stone, and the wall grinds open. We step inside. Callian hits the stone for the desert side, and moments later the blinding sun splits through the widening doorway.

Luca takes a tentative step onto the sand and goes still. Harm stands beside him. Two desert men. I step up beside Luca. Three desert travelers. Callian chuckles and walks into the dunes. With a long look at me, Luca follows Callian. I can't suppress the smile that stretches across my face. Harm nudges me and nods sideways after Luca and Callian.

"Where you go, I go, Harm."

"And I you, Imani."

I tie my hair up, securing the wrap around my face, and stride into the sands after my cousin and big brother, Harm close behind. The warmth of happiness fills my core.

I stand in front of the door of Enid's southernmost home, fist hovering at the door midair. My heart thunders in my chest.

Callian leans over my shoulder and knocks on the weathered door, throwing me a crooked smile.

I huff out a laugh.

Luca and Harm stand behind him. Luca must be so anxious.

The door cracks open, and Enid appears from behind it.

Instantly, she gasps, pulling me into a tight hug. I wrap my arms around her, and she pats my back before I push away.

"My goodness, what are you all doing here?" Enid looks over the four of us, her gaze landing on Luca. Her brows lower and she shifts back a half step, her hand clapping over her mouth. Eyes still trained on Luca, she says, "Harm, my boy. Come here."

He steps into her hold and bows his head to wrap around her, embracing his grandmother with every fiber of his being. I smile at the two of them. Harm releases her and steps aside.

"Callian." She gestures for him to enter. He does and she rests a hand on his cheek briefly before returning her gaze to Luca.

"Imani? Is this who I think it is?" Enid breathes.

"Enid, this is Jonah's son, Luca."

Tears fill Enid's eyes. She steps over the threshold to Luca, raising her head to study his face. He stares back at her.

"Where is Jonah?" I ask.

Enid clears her throat and turns back to me. "He isn't here, my girl. He went with the gypsies last time they passed through. Trying to rally more men."

Luca deflates before us all, and my heart lurches in my chest.

"Where and which way are they traveling?" I ask.

"Toward Trindari. It is one of the few places we haven't gotten to yet."

Trindari.

Numbers must be bleak if he is hoping to find help in that damned place.

"How long ago did he leave?" Harm asks.

"Two days ago. He would be somewhere east of Perendi by now. Or maybe not quite that far; the caravans travel slower."

"Right, let's head that way." Callian crosses the threshold.

"Oh, please be careful. You know what happens to the two of you if you are caught on this side." She looks between Harm and me.

"We know, Enid. I promise we will be careful," I offer, grabbing her hands briefly before hugging her goodbye. She forces a smile and hugs Harm tight.

Callian drops a kiss on her cheek and waves with a smile as she stands in the doorway, watching us go.

Wraps around our faces and hoods pulled down, we track north-northwest.

Luca has been quiet all day. The sun falls to our left, the last amber rays of light turning the dunes a brilliant gold. With four days traveling through the sand under our belts already, we are tiring. I hope we reach the caravans soon.

Harm trudges up a monster dune, Callian beside him. I hang back, walking with Luca. The sands weigh heavily with every step up the enormous mound. Movement in front of us stops. Callian gasps. Harm stills beside him.

I push up the mound faster, praying it is not Guardians we have just found.

I make the crest of the dune and my breath stops.

Before us, in the valley between monster dunes, sit the flickering lanterns of the gypsy camp. Luca files in beside me.

"Will you look at that?" he murmurs.

"I think we just found your father," Harm quips.

My heart races a million miles a minute. I fly down the dunes, sending sand up around me. Cream-colored tents are dotted between the caravans. People wander around, their colorful clothes lit up by the fires that sit between caravans. A large communal fire blazes in the center. Lanterns, their stained glass consumed by the flames that dance inside them, line a path from the camp to the south. Another path lays on the opposite side, leading north. Another to the east and another to the west. Calling travelers home.

I slide to a halt in the sand and look back. The boys wade down the dune, Luca last. Above us, sweeping in from the east, is a dark velvet blanket that carries shining points. The strip of white starlight that spans north to south above us is sharp on this clear, cool night.

Harm and Callian pass me, not stopping. Luca comes to stand by me.

"You ready?" I ask.

"As I'll ever be," he whispers.

"You want me to go first?"

His jaw feathers.

I walk between the lanterns, following the path to the camp.

We wander through caravans toward the center fire. Luca follows a few paces behind, his hood still down. Harm has already found Indie, who is looking around for me as she hugs him tight.

"Imani!" she calls and runs to me. I meet her halfway, hugging her tight.

"Where's Jonah, Indie?"

"He's by the fire." She points to a group of men talking by the fire. His back is to us, his hands moving as he talks. I grab Luca's hand and pull him toward the fire. Harm and Callian hang back with Indie.

Stopping a few feet behind my uncle, I hesitate. Tears burn behind my eyes. I release Luca's hand and straighten up; I need to do this properly. I clear my throat. One of the men looks away from Jonah, meeting my gaze.

I take a step closer. "Jonah?"

He turns and jumps up at my voice. He wraps me in his arms and sways with me in his hold. "I missed you, my girl."

I choke through a laugh, and the tears fall.

He holds me at arm's length. "Let me look at you." He sighs, shaking his head. "You shouldn't be here."

My chin wobbles and his brow lowers. "Imani, what is it?"

"I—" I swallow, steadying myself. "I brought you something."

"What could you possibly need to bring me that you would risk being on this side of the wall?"

I grab his large hands in mine, squeezing them tight before stepping to the side.

Luca pushes his hood back and steps forward. "Hello, Pa."

Jonah's face goes slack.

His breath stops, gaze swinging between Luca and me.

Tears torrent down my face and I let them fall to the sands.

"Luca?" Jonah rasps, his chest heaving.

"Yes, Pa."

"I don't understand. I thought—" Jonah starts, staring at his son.

Luca closes the space between them and pulls Jonah into his arms, closing his eyes. His jaw feathers and tears streak his cheeks.

Indie comes to stand beside me. "Luca?" Her eyes are wide as she watches her cousin hold his father for the first time in a decade. For the first time since the day he was taken by the Guardians.

"Where did you find him?" she chokes out, her voice thick.

"Over the wall."

She wraps an arm around my shoulder. "You never cease to impress me, Imani."

I lay my head on her arm and smile. Family. My family never ceases to overwhelm me, in the best way possible. Harm's gaze meets mine from the other side of Jonah and Luca. He smiles at me, love, adoration, and something like pride filling his eyes.

After an hour of emotional tales and tight hugs, Luca and Jonah finally sit side by side near the fire, sharing a meal. Harm sits beside me, Callian on the other side. I realize in this moment that this is what we are fighting for. For our families. For every person who has been affected by the Chancellor and his rigid, tyrannical rule. Our children are still imprisoned. Our sons are taken. We are broken as a people. We desperately need to be whole again. My father told me to enjoy the time we had left. What did he mean? What does the Chancellor have planned this time?

Harm stands and drops a hand to help me up. I take it and follow where he leads.

"Indie has given us a tent for the night," he whispers into my hair. He pushes back the tent flap and walks inside, pulling me along. Once inside, his mouth falls over mine. I grip his shirt, twisting it in my hands. The warmth of his chest is like fire on my cool hands.

He breaks away, eyes burning into mine. "We should bring Fletcher home."

"What?" I shake my head, releasing my hold on his shirt.

"Your father, your family. You all deserve your life back too, Imani."

"You are talking about Fletcher, Harm. Even if we wanted him back, he doesn't want us. He left my mother for his position as commander. He never even came back."

"I know all that; I just don't think we should give up on him. When I was in the prison, he was not the same as last time. Something is different. He has lost his determination, or something. He left a key where we could reach it. He talked to the prisoners. He talked to me. Mostly about you."

I stand frozen to the spot. "What do you mean?"

"I mean he was in awe of what you have done. What we have done for each other. He spoke to Miles. He looked tired, Imani. Like he is over the whole thing. Just like we are. I really think if we gave him another chance, he would want to come home. He would want his life back."

My father's face as he let me leave the tower only days ago reflected everything Harm is saying. But it leaves an uneasy feeling in my gut. Maybe his shift in demeanor is just another one of his ploys to reel us in? I don't know anymore.

One thing I do know is that this man in front of me has the biggest heart I have ever known. His capacity for forgiveness is magnificent and never waivers.

Harm removes his boots and lays on the blankets. He pats the space beside him, and I kick off mine and crawl to where he lays. I shake my head, dislodging thoughts of the *maybes* and *what ifs* that run through my head about my father. Harm lies back, hands under his head, watching as I sit beside him. I lay kisses over his face and neck, and he pulls me on top of him. A wide smile covers his gorgeous face. This is my home. Wherever he is, I am home.

I sink into his kiss and explore his body with my hands. Happiness is what this feels like.

The flap to our tent flies open, and Callian walks in. Safely under blankets, I snuggle into Harm's side, and he releases a groan. "This better be good, brother."

"I'm heading to Donterra."

Harm sits up, letting the blanket fall. I grab it, shoving it around my naked body. Callian pretends not to notice. But a half smile breaks over his face before he clears his throat and huffs out a laugh.

"What do you mean you're going to Donterra? I thought we were sticking together and going home?" Harm says.

"I was talking with some of the other travelers last night. I found Nirri. She is working with Felicity in Donterra. That's where I'm going. You two go home. I will be a week behind you."

"You sure you don't want us to go with you?" I ask.

Callian smiles and looks between Harm and me. "No, this is something I need to do on my own. I'll see you two soon enough."

He retreats from the tent.

"Well, then. Let's go home," Harm says, dotting a kiss to my forehead.

CHAPTER 15
NIRRI

Gregor waves goodbye as I stand in the doorway of the healer's shelter. It has been a rough few weeks, but he is in a good place, and Felicity let him go home, finally. She is a fine healer, and one day maybe I will be as good as her. While she is good at healing broken bodies, I seem to be able to reach broken minds. I credit that to the endless hours my grandmother and Hanola spent together treating people's minds that I watched as a child. There is great value in helping people overcome what others cannot see.

The desert sun shines through the doorway of the shelter, lining the floor with golden light. I pull the bedsheets from the bunk and toss them onto the rolling cart. The creaky wheels squeal through the center of the shelter as I head for the backroom. I toss the sheets into the wide iron washer. Its low flame boils underneath, cleansing anything that meets the steaming water. I spin around and pluck fresh linen from the shelves and wander back out to make up the bunk for the next villager in need of the space.

Linen neat and pillow changed, I gather up Gregor's bowl and spoon from this morning. A shadow moves over the door to the shelter, and I turn, bowl in hand, to see who is causing the dimness. My eyes adjust slowly to the robed figure covering most of the doorway.

With one hand, he brushes the hood from his face. My breath stops.

The bowl in my hand slips, smashing on the floor.

Callian.

His eyes find mine, and a grin wraps across his sweet face.

I drag in a breath, wiping my hands on the sides of my apron. Too stunned to move, I stand as he wanders over the threshold, stopping a few feet from where I stand with only the shattered bowl between us.

"Callian," I whisper.

"Hello, Nirri." His eyes are lit up, breath coming fast.

"Wha—what are you doing here?"

He tilts his head to one side, and his smile fades a little. "I came to see you. I needed to see that you're okay."

"I am. I mean, I'm okay." My brow lowers. "You came all this way to check if I was okay? Didn't Mason tell you I saw him?"

Instantly, I remember Catori's state the last time I saw her. Something was not right. Callian's face gives nothing away.

"How is Catori?" I blurt out.

"She is fine, I guess. Her memory still hasn't returned. But she is home and safe. Thanks in part to you." He shuffles closer.

Relief washes over me. Thank the heavens Mason found her when he did. "I didn't do much; Mason was the one who saved her from those horrible men in Trindari. I can only imagine what they had planned for her." My gaze hits the floor. I shouldn't have said anything. I don't want Callian to have to wonder about any of that.

His hand lands on my arm. "I have you *and* Mason to thank for returning my sister to me."

I smile but don't look up.

"Nirri, is there some place we can talk?"

"I have to clean this up first." I wave to the floor covered in porcelain shards of the broken bowl. "I'll grab a broom."

I make my way to the backroom and grab the broom leaning against the back wall. For a moment I just stand there, both hands gripping the wooden handle, willing myself to breathe.

Callian crossed the desert to see if I was okay.

I have missed him. Just having him around. Hearing his laugh. Sharing his table. Being a part of his family. I have missed them all so much.

I shake off the sentiments, grab a pail from beside the door, and walk back out with the broom. Callian is on his hands and knees with most of the bowl already picked up, resting in one of his hands. He dumps the broken pieces into the pail, and I drop beside him, picking up porcelain from the floor. This close, his scent overwhelms me. I shuffle away a little, grabbing a farther-off piece. Standing, I sweep the remaining chips into a pile and collect them in the pail. Callian stands and waits for me to take the mess back to the storage room at the back.

What does he want to talk about? He knows I can't go back, not yet. I need to find my place after all the change that has happened. He knows this. He let me go, willingly. I wander back to where he stands and meet his gaze.

"Let me grab my robe. We can talk outside," I say.

He nods, looking around the shelter as if assessing this part of my life.

I grab my robe from the front door hooks and walk into the midmorning sun. Even in the morning, the sun is harsh. I shield my eyes for a moment and step into the sandy village center. Callian appears by my side. I try to think of something to say to him, but everything seems insignificant. He traveled across the desert alone to make sure I was safe and well. To talk about mundane and everyday things fails to measure up to what I expect he wants to talk about. We walk in silence to the southern outskirts of the village.

"Did you want to keep walking?" I ask, gaze set on the dunes in front of us.

"Sure."

His voice is steady, and the sound of it flips my stomach.

I trudge up the closest dune, reaching the top. Out of sight of most of the village, I push back my hood and let the winds tangle through my hair. I close my eyes and tilt my face to the sun. Its warmth blushes my cheeks instantly. A low chuckle leaves Callian's chest.

"You seem happy, Nirri." His voice is raw.

I cycle through a handful of deep breaths before opening my eyes and lowering my head to meet his gaze. "I am." I smile, and he beams back at me. His is the happiest face I have ever known. His energy and kindness have always surpassed mine. "What did you need to talk about so badly that you had to cross miles of desert to do so?"

He glances at the sand briefly before swinging his gaze back up to me. "I was with Harm and Imani, actually; taking Imani's cousin home. He is Jonah's son. An ex-Guardian."

"Oh." Not just here for me, then.

He grabs both of my hands, stepping into my space. I raise my chin to look up at him. His blond hair falls around his face, blue eyes piercing my own. Here it is; he came all this way to tell me something I already know.

"Nirri, I—"

I press my finger to his lips, and he stalls out on the unsaid word. "Stop."

"But I—"

"No, don't say anything, please. I know why you came. And I can't go back with you, Callian."

"How do you know that's what I was going to say?" His eyes are lined with mirth, but his hands squeeze tighter around mine.

"Why else would you cross all that ridiculous sand?"

His forehead meets mine and he closes his eyes. "I would do it over a million times to get to you, Nirri. Please know that."

"I can't come with you," I whisper, and my chest aches more with each word.

"I just wanted to check that you were okay. After everything that happened, it was killing me not knowing."

"I should have sent word, but then I ran into Mason. I thought he would relay the message that I am alive and well." I force a half smile. But the thought of not trying to contact Callian earlier sends heat through my body. I should have known he would be worried.

He stands back up and tugs me into his chest, wrapping his arms around me. I pull in a deep breath, calm washing over me. Callian wrapped around me feels so grounding. Like home. But I am not ready to come home—not yet. I won't be going home until I have found my inner peace. My place.

"Nirri!" The tense voice of Marshall drifts over the dunes. He will be worried something has happened to me, I guess. Ever since the prison, when Harm instructed him to protect me and Flick with his life, he has taken that order rather literally. Callian releases me and I step back, sheltering my eyes from the sun.

Marshall stands on the edge of the village, robes flicking around his lanky frame, his curly brown hair waving in the torrent of warm air rolling off the dunes.

"I should get back. Marshall will be anxious if I am out of sight for too long. Apparently, Harm's orders are akin to that of the regime." I pace down the dune, sand falling in around each step.

Callian huffs out a laugh and walks down the dune beside me. "He is keeping his word; can't blame a man for that."

I roll my eyes at Callian, and his hearty laugh follows.

I missed that sound.

After last rounds for the day, Flick and I leave the people in the shelter in the capable hands of the night healer. I wander home, thinking about dinner and the supplies I have left in my meager but sufficient kitchen store. Sitting on my patio are Marshall and Callian, both rocking in the chairs that were donated to me after my arrival. With neither of them robed up, I usher them inside.

"It's okay, Nirri, the last of the Guardians left an hour ago," Marshall explains.

"Still, what if one of the villagers realizes who you are? I don't think it would take much to get you handed in to the Guardians. Then who will be my constant shadow?" I ruffle his hair as he takes a seat in the only lounge chair in the front room of my house. "Feel like stew again tonight?"

"Anything you make is good with me." Marshall beams. He is like a little brother, and I am grateful for his company. Callian stands just inside the doorway, gaze flickering between Marshall and me. I pull a pot from under the bench and pour water up to halfway.

Callian doesn't move.

I shift the pot to the cooker. Pulling the door open, I stoke the embers and throw in two logs. Flames creep over the timber, licking its sides. I shut the door and slide the vent fully open. From the kitchen store cupboard by the sink, I collect some root vegetables and a handful of herbs before closing the door. I loose a squeak.

Standing where the door was a second ago is Callian. His chest heaves, hurt filling his eyes.

I hug the ingredients to my chest. My heart flips against my ribs. I can imagine what he is thinking. Me playing house with Marshall. It's nothing like that.

He takes the food from my almost limp hold and drops it onto the bench.

"Nirri." His voice is gravel.

"Callian," I mutter past the stone now lodged in my throat.

"What are you doing?" he murmurs, his eyes burning into mine, brows drawn down.

"I—I'm making you supper." My hands hang limp at my sides.

"Hmm, that wasn't what I was talking about."

"Oh, this—I am being a good big sister." A meek smile cracks over one side of my mouth. Callian tilts his head and swallows.

"I am here to find myself, to find my place." I stand a little taller and fold my arms over my chest. "You know that. What did you think was happening?"

He blinks and steps back. "Nothing. I didn't think anything. I'm sorry. Call me when supper is ready." He turns and wanders down the hallway to the back door. It bangs shut and I loose a breath, closing my eyes. I pull a knife from the drawer and chop the vegetables up before shredding the herbs with my hands and dropping the lot into the pot. I unwrap some dried meat I was given by the village boys this week. *In exchange for helping out at the shelter or something,* one of them muttered as he handed it to me, his cheeks flushed.

Women seem to be outnumbered in this village. Is that what is getting at Callian? I toss the meat in and stir it with a wooden spoon. Placing the lid on slightly ajar, I leave the stew to simmer. I wipe my hands on the cloth by the sink. Marshall sits reading in the lounge chair. I smile at him and pad toward the back door.

Callian stands on the back patio of my home, gazing at something in the distance. The shooting range Marshall made for me sits across my sandy backyard. The quiver with a dozen arrows hangs by the back door.

I stand beside Callian for a moment in silence. It feels surreal to have him here. In the desert, in this little home I have made my own.

"Would you like to have a shot?" I ask, breaking the silence.

Callian clears his throat and looks between me and the small archery range, half dusted with golden sand.

"Sure."

He plucks the quiver from the back wall and walks to the furthest point from the round target Marshall built. With a steady hand, he lines up the bow, nocks an arrow, and lets it fly.

Bullseye.

He nocks another.

It sails toward the target.

Bullseye.

"You're making me look bad." I nudge his arm and take the bow from him. He watches as I nock an arrow and hold my arm steady, focusing my line of sight toward the center of the target. I pull in a lungful of air. Releasing my breath, I let the arrow fly. It lands just off-center. Dammit. Still no bullseye. I practice every day. Ever since I was a girl, I wanted to own a bow and arrow. But living in the tower and barracks with the Guardians, there was never room for an archery range. Grandfather would have never allowed me to partake in such unladylike pastimes, regardless.

But he is not here now. I am free. Finally. And I am not giving that up for anyone.

I look up to Callian. He smiles at me, taking the bow from my hands. He walks back to the back door, replacing the bow and quiver on the hook.

"Nirri," he says, his back to me.

I stand waiting, but don't reply. He turns around and I walk into his space, lifting my head to meet his stare.

"I can't come back with you, Callian. I have work to do here. I'm finding my place, finding what I'm capable of. I am finally free. Please don't ask me to give that up."

His Adam's apple bobs. "I wouldn't."

"Good. Let's have supper."

He takes my hand and presses it to his lips, closing his eyes.

"Whatever you decide and whenever you decide it, I am here. I will always be here."

"I know that. You have been my friend since we were eight, Callian. You will always be a part of my life."

His face tightens. We are friends. I can't imagine a day without some kind of thought about Callian in it. Without him in it. And when I am finished here, I will find my next adventure and maybe he can be a part of that too.

Breakfast always makes me nervous. I guess it stems from my grandfather always feeling the need to announce his latest plan or regime order to grandmother and me in the mornings at the breakfast table. Callian stirs his porridge like there's a desert viper in his bowl and not grains and goat milk.

"I have to go back," he says.

My spoon hovers suspended between my bowl and my mouth. "Okay."

His pained gaze meets mine. "Please, promise me you will be careful."

"I will be fine. Marshall will make sure of that." I grin, but it feels off.

Marshall nods furiously and Callian spits out a small laugh.

"The children are still being held by your—by the Chancellor, and we are not sure how long they will keep them fed and housed before he changes his plan and starts doing something we can't fathom."

"Of course."

"I had a week, and that has already been and went. Harm will be getting restless if I don't return soon."

"If you need my help from this side, send word and I will do anything I can."

"I will." He rises from the table and pulls on his robe and rucksack. I stand and pad toward the door where he stands. The air feels heavy in my lungs, my stomach turning to knots as I swallow.

Marshall meets us at the door, gaze alternating between Callian and me. "I will make sure she is safe, Callian. You have my word."

Callian slaps a hand on his shoulder and smiles. "I know you will."

Marshall ducks back to the table. Callian strides across the threshold and I follow. He shuts the door behind us. "Nirri, no matter what happens, if you need me, send Marshall or anyone with word and I will be back here in a heartbeat."

"I will be fine. I'm making a difference here. You are all better off with me out of the picture. Arthur thinking I am dead or disappeared is better for you all."

He wraps both arms around me, crushing me into his chest. I wrap my arms around his waist.

He holds me for a handful of heartbeats and releases me. "If you ever need anything—" The words get stuck in his throat.

"I know." I push out of his hold, and he nods, turning away from me.

He throws his hood up, winding his way through the rings of homes toward the south. The ache in my chest grows as he fades further away with every step. Tears burn and I choke through a breath. The door cracks open, and Marshall appears beside me. He offers a sympathetic look and rests an arm over my shoulders. I laugh through a strangled whimper and dry my face as my chin wobbles.

"If you ever want to go home"—he nods in the direction of Callian's shrinking figure—"just say the word."

I smile at him, and he hugs me tighter.

CHAPTER 16
CATORI

Mason leans on the table beside me on one hip, his arms crossed, eyes fierce. If he thinks I am going to let him and the others go into that tower and infiltrate the Guardians without me, he has another think coming!

He studies the faces of the three other warriors around the table. Their gazes drop to the table one by one. I may be a little off, but I am still their leader. And Mason knows it. His eyes soften, and he drops his arms by his side with a sigh. The warrior closest to us clears his throat and meets my gaze.

"Without Miya and yourself, we have neither the numbers nor the skill to pull off a rescue with that many children. The chances of getting out are almost impossible, Catori."

Mason's attention swings back to me.

My gut flips.

They are right.

They are all right. But I am still torn between the odds we have paired with better judgment, and the suffering parents and children who are separated and have been for weeks now. How did we let this happen? I have to do better. I haven't even been their leader for a full cycle of seasons, and we are already up to our eyeballs in disaster.

"We can reconvene in an hour. I think we all need a break," I offer.

The three warriors nod and file out of my house.

One thing I know is the overwhelming pull I feel to Mason. I should tell him... something. That my memories are back. That I know exactly who he is to me. That he is desert boy, not forest boy. Not that there is anything about him that is *boyish*. I take a step toward him, and he looks up from the papers on the table.

"Mason, I—"

The door opens, a damp breeze fluttering the papers beside us. Imani walks through the door, Harm close behind her. They pull their robes off, tossing them onto the hooks by the door. Imani's gaze finds mine and she smiles. She looks to Mason and grins. He pads over to where they stand, and Imani wraps her arms around his shoulders. Mason chuckles and Harm watches them, eyes fixed on Mason. His jaw feathers slightly as he watches his wife embrace her friend. They may have traveled a long and rough path to get there, but Mason and Imani are friends, and good ones.

My brother. He didn't come back?

"Where is Callian?" I ask, the words short and panicked.

"He is fine. He had a detour to make to see someone," Harm says.

"Who could he possibly need to see on the desert side?"

"Nirri," Imani says, a smile blooming over her pretty face. I keep mine static to not give away the memory of another person I am not supposed to have yet. Of course he did. My little brother will never stop loving her. I hope one day Nirri sees that.

"So, what mischief have you been up to while we were gone, Rayner?" Harm says as Imani releases him and walks over to me.

"Not much has changed, Travesci." He snorts and rolls his eyes. Harm follows Mason over to the strategy table.

Imani stands in front of me. I know she is trying to determine if I remember her. Her face falls when I don't react.

"Hey, Catori," she says, schooling her face. My heart cracks for her.

I pull her into a tight hug. "Hey, Imani Fletcher—or is it Travesci now?" I whisper.

She pushes back, her face lit up. I hug her again, my lips almost on her ear. "Please, don't say anything. Not just yet. I just need a little more time." She nods against my cheek, and I squeeze her tighter.

We join the boys at the table and watch as Harm's face grows harder by the minute as Mason explains that with our current warriors, the loss of Miya, and my apparent loss of skill, we don't have the force to make rescues of the size we would need to bring all the children home. It would have to be simultaneous, both prisons infiltrated the same day—the same hour—or we would likely lose one side's worth of children to the Chancellor once he got wind that we were moving to take them back.

Imani's gaze alternates between Mason and me as she tries and fails to suppress a smile. I hold back the laughter that bounces up my throat and throw her a stern look. She cackles, and bends over, gripping her knees. Heat floods my face.

Mason and Harm stop mid-discussion, staring at Imani, who is trying to compose herself with strangled breaths. I've never seen her this elated over anything before. She is a good friend to Mason, and I am glad he has her.

"Imani?" Harm asks.

She clears her throat and huffs out one last chuckle. "Sorry, I needed that. Been an intense few days."

"Okay..." Mason says, grinning with a raised eyebrow.

"I'm fine; sorry, go ahead," she says, flattening her face back to seriousness. The boys go back to studying the map in front of them. She bumps into me, looking up with those stunning blue eyes, now lined with silver. I swallow past the lump in my throat, gaze settling back on Mason.

The light recedes from the living room and Harm calls it a day. They must be exhausted.

Mason waits for me at the door, ready to head to supper. "Hungry?"

"Yep, you?"

"Yes, for a while now." His eyes burn into mine as I stop in front of him by the door. We stand frozen for a minute before he gestures for me to lead the way. I step through the door, and he pulls it closed behind us. The tables are lined with the same faces I see at every mealtime. Faces that are drawn out with worry, people who are missing half of their families. Missing the most precious part of their lives, their children. The village is too quiet. Too somber. Too grey without the laughter and happiness, noise and mischief the children bring.

Mason sits, and I grab two plates and pile them with food, placing one in front of him as he talks to the man beside him. They chat about supplies and the last downfall of rain. I pick at the food on my plate. Mason loads up his fork, shoveling food into his mouth between the banter.

Imani and Harm arrive, only to load up two plates and disappear home again. A woman sits down across from me, chatting away as if I am supposed to know her. I don't say her name, just return matching pleasantries and half-baked, vague responses. She smiles at me after a time, rising from her place to return to her home.

"Mason?"

He turns back to me. "Yeah?" Light-blue eyes search mine.

"I'm going to turn in." I stand, grabbing my plate. I walk to the kitchen and hand it to the ladies. Their sympathetic smiles twist something in my stomach as I walk across the damp, grassy village center toward home. Mason falls in beside me.

"You can stay if you want," I say.

"I was just killing time, honestly."

"Oh? Waiting for something?"

He stops and I turn back to face him.

"Catori." He goes still, then runs a hand through his sandy blond hair, his arms flexing under his sleeve. "Do you think we should go back to the healer and see if she has any other ideas about getting your memory back?"

My breath stops.

The desperation in his face, lined with sorrow, sends my heart pounding against my chest.

"Maybe tomorrow?" I say, finally.

His body sags. For a moment, I think he is going to turn and walk the other way, but he steps closer, resting a hand on my arm. "Come on, let's get you home." He forces a smile.

My chest tightens. We're so close I can feel his heat, smell his skin, and yet I feel miles away. I turn in his hold and walk beside him. Once over the threshold, I excuse myself, padding into my bedroom. With the curtain drawn behind me, I collapse onto the bed. I shove my head in my hands, suppressing a groan. For weeks I didn't know what was what or who was who. Now, my feelings are so intense, it is hard to be around Mason and not be close to him.

That is my truth. Mason is my truth.

The last tiny ember of doubt melts away as I replay the pain in his eyes when he thought I was still indifferent to him. That single moment could break my heart, if I let it. If I don't fix this... My hands tremble, heart stammering along as I peel myself off the bed. I rise and push back the curtain.

The candles that were lit when we returned home are blown out. The only light comes from the subtle fire in the hearth. Mason is lying down, hands behind his head and eyes closed, on the cushions in the living room. Always here.

"Mason?" I whisper.

His breathing is steady, but he doesn't respond.

I slide the curtain closed and step backward toward the bed and move to the dresser in the half-lit room. The top drawer is full of linen nighties. I pull one out and toss it onto the bed. Peeling back my clothes, I stand bare, caressing the thin, soft fabric of the nightie. I slide it over my head and pull back the bedcovers. Sliding under a thin blanket, I roll onto my side.

Now, I process every moment I remember about Mason. Every moment we had together. A weight sits on my chest, pressing down harder with every memory. I close my eyes tight and grip the pillow with both hands.

Half-asleep, I roll over to see Mason standing with a hand on the curtain, looking in. He sucks in a breath before moving to the hearth, rubbing his arms. The air has cooled, and I sit up, pushing my hair from my face. I swing my legs over the side of the bed and move to the doorway, leaning on the frame. A shiver runs down my body. Walking back, I grab the blanket from my bed and return to the doorway.

The night is quiet, only the few sporadic sounds of night birds and the distant call of the forest nocturnes drifting through the open window of my home. The cushions Mason has been sleeping on are scattered, as if he had been tossing and turning. He is squatting in front of the hearth, placing logs onto the embers. Sparks fly as he shuffles the logs around to make room for another.

"Feeling the cold, desert boy?"

His hand stills over the pile of logs. *Desert boy*, not forest boy.

He turns his head to meet my gaze and stands. I push off the door frame and take a step toward him. His jaw feathers and his breaths deepen.

My body shakes, and I tighten my hold on the blanket.

"Catori," he breathes, but hovers where he stands.

Rooted to the spot, I whisper, "Come here."

He takes a step, then another.

"Don't make me wait for you." Each word is ragged.

He steps closer until he's in my space. His breath lands on my face; his warmth flushes against my skin.

His brows lower. "What's wrong? Are you okay?"

"Mason," I murmur, resting a hand over his heart. It thunders under my fingers, and I choke back a breathy cry.

"What is it? Did you have a nightmare?"

I pry my gaze from my fingers moving to the rhythm of his heartbeat and meet his gaze. Tears burn my eyes.

"Not a nightmare. A memory."

He huffs a laugh as if he doesn't believe me.

"Mason Rayner, I have lots and lots of memories," I say as I move closer still, pressing my forehead against his, "of me"—the blanket hits the floor—"and you."

Eyes wide and searching my face, he huffs through a choked breath. He takes my face with both hands, his mouth slamming into mine. I wrap my arms around his neck, and he tugs me closer with a hand on the small of my back. He breaks away, finding my gaze before closing his eyes. His forehead meets mine. "I thought I lost you," he rasps.

I pull in a wobbly breath, holding the cool air in my lungs. Every inch of me is alive. "Never."

Tears slide down his cheeks, and my chin wobbles. "I'm here, Mason."

He opens his eyes, pulling away slightly.

"I am yours, always," I whisper, running my hands through his hair, searching every inch of his gorgeous face—his slightly crooked smile, his angled jaw, his eyes that burn into mine, full of love and pain and desire.

His breathing is erratic as he picks me up, one arm under my legs, one behind my back. I pull his face back to mine, kissing his mouth, wanting to be closer still.

"I missed you, so damn much," he growls, walking into the bedroom. He stands next to the bed, mouth hungry over mine. Slowly, he lowers me to the bed. I sit up.

"What's wrong?" he rasps.

"Nothing, it's just..." My gaze goes to the wall, and memories flood in of us up against it. I stand on the bed and take his face in my hands. I kiss his mouth, pushing him backward as I step down off the bed.

"Where are you taking me?" he utters.

"To the wall."

His mouth claims mine as he groans. The sound travels down my throat into my heart. The fibers of my body are lit up like never before. I pull at the hem of his shirt, and he raises his arms. We break apart briefly, and the shirt hits the floor. Mason nuzzles my neck, dotting kisses down my throat, his hands gripping my hips.

"Mason." His name is barely a whisper.

"Mhmmm."

I close my eyes and let my head fall backward. "Closer. I need you closer."

A second later, my nightie is around my shoulders, and I let him lift it over my head before he tosses it to the floor with his shirt. I undo the fastener on his trousers, and he steps out of them as they fall. His mouth finds my chest, nipping kisses around each breast. His tongue finds my nipple and my breath stops. I almost go limp in his hold. He picks me up, one arm under my bottom, one around my back, and I wrap my legs around his waist as he spins to face the wall.

"Dammit, Mason."

"Are you sure?"

"Absolutely, more than you could ever know."

He slams me into the wall. "I have a pretty good idea." His lips curl into the sweetest smile.

I devour his mouth with mine, one hand in his hair, a finger of the other trailing down his chest, down his abdomen. "I missed you too."

He stops. Confusion tightens his eyes.

"Some of my memories came back a few weeks ago. I knew who you were. But I—" I suck in a breath, searching his eyes. "I didn't know for sure how much, how far you and I—"

"Catori," he whispers and brushes a piece of hair from my face, tucking it behind my ear. "It's okay."

"No, it's not. It was killing me, not telling you that I remembered who you were. And the most precious memories came back so slowly, in bits. I didn't want to pressure you into something you might not want anymore."

"Heavens, Catori, there will never be a day I don't want you or need you."

A strangled cry leaves my mouth as I crush my lips to his. His hands find my skin, the rounds of my breasts, the peaks of my nipples, the flesh of my throat.

"Mason," I rasp.

He lifts his head, meeting my gaze as he presses his forehead to mine. My chest tightens, the air in my lungs burning.

"I love you, so much it hurts." Tears streak down my cheeks, hot and fast.

"I love you too, Catori. Every day without you was torture. Don't ever leave again, promise me."

"I promise." The words are breathy, and I mean them with every inch of my soul. Mason thrusts me against the wall. I moan as he fills every part of me that was empty. His hands grip my hips tighter still as our cadence intensifies. The warmth that pooled in my core when he stepped into my space moments ago shatters through my center, electrifying its way through my body. I whimper into his ear, and he moans so raw, it steals the last of my breath.

He nuzzles against my neck, spent and shaking. I cradle his head in my hands and kiss the top of his head. After a handful of heartbeats, he takes me from the wall to the bed. Kneeling as we descend onto the soft mattress, he kisses my mouth before we part and lays beside me. I roll into his chest and his arm tugs me closer, holding me tight. I run a finger over his collarbone and up his neck. Laying here, wrapped in Mason, I pull in a long, slow breath. I never want to forget this. I never want to forget Mason, ever again. If I am lost, this is the only place I ever want to find. This is my home. He is my home.

"Now do you remember why my things are in your dresser?" he asks, and I can hear his smile.

"Yes, I remember exactly why your clothes are in my home." I look up and he loosens his grip around me. "Our things are in *our home*."

CHAPTER 17
MASON

The dawn's earliest light just splits through the canopy, sneaking its way through our bedroom window. Catori lays beside me, her hair draped over her pillow. It's past her shoulders now. Every time I look at her, she takes my breath away. She is sound asleep, so I close my eyes and sink into the grey oblivion of hazy morning slumber.

What feels like a second later, but as is evident by the light outside is not, I crack one eye open. Catori lays propped on one elbow, staring at me. She smiles and slides over me until she is straddling my hips. The sunlight isn't much brighter than before; it is too early to get up yet.

"Can't sleep?" I ask.

"Something like that."

She lifts from my hips and crawls backward, disappearing under the blanket. Her hands trail down my stomach, stopping shy of my now-throbbing hardness.

"Cat?"

From under the blanket, she huffs an amused laugh. "Yes, Mas?"

I groan through a smile. I like that, Cat and Mas.

Her mouth takes me in, almost the full, hard length of me, and I grip the bed with both hands. Every movement she makes sends me higher.

"Cat," I rasp.

She doesn't respond, still under the blanket. Her movements intensify, and I hold my breath, swallowing past the emotion in my throat. Her fingers trail up my thighs, around the base of the full length she now has in her mouth. My body vibrates with every inch she moves.

"Cat."

She continues, and I grip the bed harder.

"Catori." Her name growls past my lips. I release the bed and reach under the blanket. Hands under her arms, I pull her up to me. She crawls the last few inches to meet my face and devours my mouth with hers. After a moment, she pulls back and trails kisses down my neck, over my chest, and down my abdomen.

I grab her and lift her over me until she is straddling my hips again. "Nope." Bracing my feet on the mattress, knees up, I wrap my arms around her and flip us over. A giggle spills from her gorgeous smile. She takes my face with both hands and kisses my mouth. I sink into the kiss and take her hands, resting them above her head, holding her wrists. Her legs wrap around my waist, drawing me into her. I kiss her harder before trailing kisses down her neck. Her hips lift off the bed, and I meet her need with my own.

"Mas," she says, so softly.

"Hmmm."

"I love you."

Every breath heaves through my warm, tight chest. "I love you too, Catori. You are everything to me." Her hands find my face again and silver lines her eyes. I kiss her forehead and her nose, her chin and then her lips. "I'm yours, always, I promise you that."

She pulls in a ragged breath. "And I yours."

Her words are barely more than a whisper.

Harm and Imani sit across the breakfast table, looking as happy as I feel. It is so good to have everyone home and settled. Almost everyone. Callian should arrive back today, hopefully. Then we can get on with whatever comes next with plans to overthrow the regime and oust Arthur. Everything seems to take four times as long as we plan, and every plan comes off slightly askew. Imani and Catori banter back and forth about numbers and training, and Harm eats his food quietly. This is the first time we have lived in the same village and not been at each other's throats. We have Imani to thank for that. I have Imani to thank for many things.

I glance at Catori as she chuckles at something sarcastic Imani says.

"Well, I don't know about you, but I could use a trip to the sparring ring," Harm says.

"I'd be more than happy to oblige, Travesci, but I have a sparring partner today." I look at Catori, and the girls stop talking mid-banter, staring at me.

"Are you sure you're up to it, Catori?" Imani asks.

"Yep. I have my memories back. And that includes my training." She looks around the table as if gauging our reactions.

Imani jumps up from the table. "Right, let's get into it, then!" She leads the way, followed by Harm. I take Catori's hand and she rises from the table. We amble toward the training area, winding our way through the homes.

"You sure you want to fight me?" she mutters.

"I think I can handle it, mostly."

She laughs and squeezes my hand, bumping her shoulder into mine. Her hair is down around her shoulders, her green eyes lit up. Happiness beams from her beautiful face and my heart aches like it never has before. The overwhelming feeling of love for her threatens to close over my throat.

I swallow and focus on the sparring ring. Harm and Imani have started already, and we sit on the grass near them, watching Imani dance around Harm, her fighting knives drawn. She is his match in every way.

For as long as I can remember, Imani has been a part of my life, in one way or another. The day I met her, when she staggered in from the sands to the outskirts of Amondo where I was tending goats, she was the first person in a long time to hold no judgment. She trusted me. I know she was around when Harm was thrown in the well. She had been on the regime's radar for a while, despite being Fletcher's daughter. Then she took every beating the officers gave her to protect Harm. I swallow, my stomach flipping at the memory. I still wonder if Fletcher would have made me go through with her hanging if Harm hadn't turned himself in.

I think I would have committed treason myself if it had come to that.

Then I held her against her will, to keep Fletcher happy; the offer to be Blended with Imani from Fletcher was as much for my benefit as it was for hers. I wasn't thrilled with the idea, but I wasn't going to let her die either. I guess Fletcher thought he was protecting her in his own way. Possibly it was the only option he had left, after the Chancellor got wind of her actions against the regime. He is a hard man to read, her father.

The day I followed her over the wall was the first time I felt unsure about the way things are. After weeks in the forest prison, I was hardly a shell of a man. The first time I saw Catori... I will never forget that memory, her standing, hands on her hips, barking out orders. I look at her now, her gaze following Imani as she lunges for Harm again. He blocks with a swift move, and she spins out of range.

The look on Imani's face brings back memories of the two of us in the tower, pretending to be Blended, pretending I had taken what Fletcher had offered me. The devastation she carried, thinking Harm would never forgive her, broke my heart. I have never seen a person so tortured as I did that morning. I hope I never do again. Those two have been through more than the rest of us all put together, and they never waiver. Hanola was right about them; they are one of the strongest bonds.

The clashing stops, and I look up to see Harm standing in front of me, chest heaving, sweat dripping from his face. Imani drops to the ground, and he sinks beside her. Catori jumps up and offers her hand to me. I take it and push to my feet, following her to the sparring ring. I take the right side of the ring and draw my daggers. Catori shakes her body loose and widens her stance. I pull in a long breath and wait for her to move.

Catori stalks toward me, swinging her hips, a grin wrapped across her elegant face. Her hair bounces around her shoulders as she tugs twin swords from her back. I step into her space, and she draws her blades down on me. I meet her metal with my crossed daggers above our heads. Catori growls. I snap my teeth at her. Her grin widens.

Imani bursts with laughter, tossing her head back and clapping her hands over her head. It is good to see her so happy. It's so good to see Catori back to herself. In this moment, we are all happy.

Harm chuckles to himself and wraps an arm around Imani. I lower my blades. Catori drops hers to the ground. Pressing her body against mine, she hangs her arms around my neck as her mouth finds mine. I take her face in my hands, thumbs trailing over her soft cheeks.

"Well, that's a new technique, sis; don't know how effective it will be with the Guardians," the voice of Callian booms, the smile on his face carrying in his words.

Catori releases me with a peck on the lips. She jogs to Callian, hugging him tight. He folds his arms around her and hangs his head beside hers. Harm and Imani stand to greet him. I wander over, hanging back slightly. When all the hugs and hellos are done, everyone moves to the side and Callian steps up to me.

His stare wanders over my face for a moment, his mouth drawn to a thin line. I glance at Catori, but she stays watching her brother, face hopeful.

Callian grabs me and hugs me tight. "Nirri says hello."

I huff out a strangled laugh and pat him on the back tentatively.

He releases me and stands tall. "Thank you for saving my sister."

"I—"

"I'm glad you're part of our family. And I'm sorry if I haven't been very accepting of you before." Callian's gaze swings between Catori and me, his face tight, serious. Very un-Callian like.

Harm smiles at me and Imani sucks in a wobbly breath through a crooked smile.

"I would do it all again a million times over, and I am grateful to be part of your family, brother." I glance at Catori. Her hand covers her mouth. Harm wraps an arm around her, and she leans on his shoulder, closing her eyes briefly.

Callian grabs my shoulder and squeezes it, jaw feathering, and nods.

Imani jumps between us, an arm around each of us. "Since you two have finally kissed and made up," she starts, "Catori and I have a plan, and it's a good one! Let's go and iron out the details."

Callian's hearty laugh fills the damp air. Catori files in beside me, grabbing my hand. She leads me home, the others following a step behind.

The five of us sit on the cushions on the living room floor, like we have done so many times before. But this time, things feel different. Better. The only person missing is Nirri.

"So, we know our numbers and skill sets are low, and this is the only thing preventing us from rescuing the children. But what if we could source the warriors we need from each village and still meet production quotas for the Chancellor, so he doesn't realize anything has changed?" Catori says.

Harm and Callian glance at each other.

"The crops and harvest still need to carry on, so supplies are not interrupted. But what if we train the women to fight? Without the children here right now, we have the chance to train the women, which will give us the numbers we need to storm both holds and take the children back."

Callian raises a brow. "What happens when we get there, and they have only had a few weeks training? What if they get there and they freeze, or panic."

Catori continues. "They won't. These are their children we are talking about. The Guardians are holding their life and blood. Their babies. Their motivation will be the highest it has ever been. They can channel that, similar to how Imani channels her energy into a force that can take down up to one hundred Guardians. We will have the numbers to infiltrate the prisons on both sides simultaneously and get back home. After that, if Arthur makes a move or goes for full-out war, we have just added almost two hundred and seventy warriors to the ranks of the rebellion. Making *our* side of this fight the stronger side. Plus, we have weapons, at least—a lot more than Arthur has. This will work."

Callian looks at me. "What were the final numbers for the Guardians before you left?"

"Around fifty in the Etonia prison, another fifty at least patrolling the central and northern villages. About thirty in the tower itself, if you count Arthur's personal guard. Lastly are the main barracks here, attached to the tower, that house up to two hundred men."

"So, they have around three hundred and thirty. We have about two hundred on the desert side; the warriors here, so another twenty-odd; us, that makes five; and if we go with this plan, an extra two hundred and fifty women to fight." Harm runs a hand through his hair, making him look younger than the years he has lived through. "That's four hundred and seventy-five to fight. This could work. But, signing up must be voluntary."

"Agreed," Imani says.

"I don't think we will have a problem with that," Catori says.

"I think so too. This is our best shot. And with a little bit of luck, after we bring the children home and the Guardians realize we outnumber them almost two to one, they may reconsider waging war," Callian says.

"Let's hope," I say. The plan is simple and optimistic. Something sinks in my gut. Arthur doesn't take defiance lightly. If this is going to work, we need to stand together. And Harm needs to change that dial very soon after, or the Chancellor will retaliate. The consequences of going against him are always far too high.

"I can go around to the villages and get volunteers and bring them back with me," Callian offers.

"No, that would draw too much attention. It would look like we are amassing an army, which we are. But surprise is the key element to getting the children back in the first wave. Train them in their own villages. We assemble them the morning of the raid," Harm says.

"I agree with Harm—things need to look as per usual, or this will just blow up in our faces," I say.

"Settled, then. Callian, you visit each sect of warriors for each village and fill them in, stay for the selection process, then give the orders to your men and move to the next village," Catori says.

"My men?"

"Yes. Without Miya here, you are head warrior, brother."

Callian's gaze sticks to his sister's, but he nods, rising from his cushion.

I rise and hold out a hand to Catori. She waits for Harm and Imani to follow her brother out the door before sliding her hand into mine. I tug her up and into my chest and she nuzzles into my neck. I fold her in my arms and drop my head onto her shoulders. I don't want things to change. We just found a little peace and happiness, and I have the uneasy feeling that it is all about to be taken away.

"We should get some lunch before we start the selection process here," Catori whispers in my ear.

"Hmmm, lunch sounds good."

She trails kisses up my neck, finding my mouth.

"I was thinking about food." I chuckle.

She nips my ear. "I wasn't."

I groan and lift her to my hips. She giggles and tugs her shirt off, tossing it onto the floor. Kissing her collarbone, I trace my mouth over one soft breast and then to the other, the heat in my core growing more intense by the second. I walk toward the wall by the hearth, and she moans as her back meets the wood.

"Mas."

"Uh huh," I moan past the peak between my teeth, and she squirms up the wall.

"You have far too many clothes on."

I chuckle and pull my mouth from her nipple, letting it slide through my still half-closed teeth. She whimpers, her hands pushing and pulling their way through my hair.

A scream rips through the air from the center of the village.

I still, my face inches from Catori's. Another scream pulses in the damp air, and she loses her hold on me, landing on her feet. I spin and find her shirt. She holds her arms up as I slide it over her head. We rush over the threshold, jogging toward the rising ruckus of harried yelling and crying. We round the last home before the training area, and I stop dead in my tracks. Catori slams into me and we stand frozen. Gasping, she grabs my hand.

I don't even believe what I am seeing.

CHAPTER 18
IMANI

Harm's hands are firmly around my shaking shoulders. My father stands two feet from me with Miles sitting on his shoulders. Blood soaks his left leg, and his grey uniform is torn everywhere, covered in mud and green debris. The blacksmith that gave me the fighting knives—whose wife, Carol, worked in the tower—stares at me. He too wears a Guardian uniform that sports multiple rips, blood caked on his right hand, and a darker crimson patch covering his left shoulder.

The village people stand as one, unmoving. The commander of the Guardian Regime sways in front of their tired but happy children. They are not frightened. They are home.

"Miles!" The scream of my mother pierces my haze as she pushes her way through the dazed crowd. Sobbing, she steps up to my father, extricating her son from his father's shoulders. Fletcher staggers forward with the movement, chest heaving. He meets her gaze, and she stays standing mere inches from him. His breathing is ragged, and his eyes glaze over.

"Daniel?" she whispers.

"Petria," he chokes and sinks to his knees. His face ashen, he tries to stand, but collapses onto the damp earth.

Mason appears by my side. Harm offloads the child from the blacksmith's back, his gaze tight on Fletcher the entire time.

"Imani?" Mason asks softly.

"Get him to the healer's shelter," I say, turning on my heel. I stalk every step of the way home with my fists tight in my hair. I circle the ground in front of the door to my house over and over. He came back. He did something good. And not a *small* good thing. A big, *enormous* good thing. I choke back the tears that threaten to steal the air from my lungs. Harm rounds the last house, jogging toward me. Pounding my fists on our door, I barrel over the threshold and pace the floor near the hearth.

"Imani, this is good."

I rest a hand over my thunderous heart and force each long breath through my lungs. "I know."

He walks over and stands to block my pacing.

"Do you know how many times I begged him to come home from the regime when I was young?" The words are mangled and choked. The tears that were burning my eyes now travel down my cheeks, dripping onto the floor.

"Your father is stubborn, my love. He gets it from you."

I huff a laugh and bury my head in his chest. His hands rest against the back of my neck, in my hair. I sob, hard. I know it is a good thing he came home. But the wound that has been open for years is going to take time to close. Time I don't know if we even have now. If things turn out for the worse with the Chancellor, I have just gotten my father back to lose him all over again.

I pull in a burning breath and push away from Harm. "I wish Jonah was here. He would know what to do. How to mend such things. I have no idea where to start." I think of Luca and Jonah. After so many years, they got another chance.

A real chance.

I want that more than anything, if I can get past the hurt and anger toward my father I have housed for so many years. But he is going to have to prove his worth this time around.

I hover in the door to the healer's shelter. We are supposed to be gone by now. The others have surely left already. We have no time to spare to retrieve the desert children, with Fletcher—my father—bringing the forest children home. Arthur is sure to be doubling his forces around the Etonia prison now if he hasn't already.

"I am right here, Imani. And have no qualms with punching his smug face if he says the wrong thing." Mason stands to my left, Harm to my right.

"You can do this. Where you go, I go, remember," Harm whispers, and I close my eyes to savor his voice. My body reacts automatically when Harm is anywhere near my father. I take a step toward the bunk the ex-commander of the Guardian Regime lays on, eyes closed, breath steady. Four forest warriors guard the room before me, standing with weapons in hand, ready for any wrong move he may make. They track my every step.

I stop next to the wooden frame, and he opens his eyes and pushes to sit up. "Imani?"

"What are you doing?" I hiss.

"I'm helping you."

"Why? Why start now?"

His gaze hits the floor. I hold my stare square on his face. The stubble he arrived with has been shaved.

His blue eyes find mine. The same as mine. The same brilliant blue, as Harm calls it. His leg is bandaged. His face is pinker now, not the ashen shade it was when he arrived. He'd lost too much blood, the healer told my mother when she came to see him. She hasn't been back since, or so Harm tells me. She is probably trying to process this, just like I am. I fold my arms over my chest. I wonder what Miles thinks of all this. Who he thinks carried him all the way home. Maybe mother has told him. I would know the answer if I went to see her, but I haven't.

"I never—" he starts, the words choking out in his throat.

"Never what?" I snap.

"I just wanted to keep you safe. That's all I have ever wanted."

Jonah told me that once. I didn't believe him. Why would a man join a regime that damns its people to save his family? That's just ridiculous.

"How is torturing and killing innocent people keeping me safe? Or anyone else, for that matter?"

"That's not how it started; you know that."

"Well, it's how it ended; and you made every choice leading up to it." I huff a low breath. My heart flings against my ribs. Harm steps closer, and Mason does the same.

My father's gaze swings between them before returning to me. "If you would let me explain. Tell you everything that happened around the time you were in the gallows, maybe—"

"Save it. I am not interested in your twisted games." Heat rises through my core. Even the slightest memory of Harm after the gallows makes me nauseous with anger. He did that. And I will never forgive him for it. I spin on my heel and stalk toward the door.

"Imani Fletcher, don't you dare walk away from me again!" The pain in his voice cuts like the sharpest blade.

I turn back, slowly.

Again.

I have walked away before. Ran, actually.

The memory of the day I screamed in his face and ran away

from home floods back. The rage and the hurt. The look he gave me, full of anger and disappointment. Devastation. Why couldn't he just quit the regime? Why couldn't he see what it was making him do? I couldn't stomach it any longer.

I walk to where he sits. He looks up at me and I level my gaze to his, tilting my chin upward.

"It's Travesci."

His face twists, and he swallows.

"My name is Imani Travesci, and just because you came crawling home does not mean I will forgive you any time soon." My body shakes, my heart thundering so fast it deafens out the ragged breaths that push my chest out in unsteady bouts. I march over the threshold and down the stairs, the ground blurring under my feet. He calls my name. I barely hear it. Sobs spill from my throat and I run through the village and past the tree line. I make it to the forest undergrowth before I hit the muddy earth on my knees and scream so wild and so painful, I am sure my throat will peel out of my mouth.

The markets in Etonia are busy. Harm stands beside me, hood down and wrap over his face. Enid, Jonah, Luca, and Christopher were supposed to arrive this morning. So far, we haven't found them. I crack the door to the hideout in the wall beyond the markets and slip into the dim light. Harm follows closely, closing the door on silent hinges. The lock clicks, and I sweep back my hood, unwrapping my face, thankful for the cooler air in the damp sanctuary of the wall's innards.

"You okay?" Harm asks, sliding down the stone as he pulls his canteen from his rucksack.

"Fine."

He raises an eyebrow and offers me a crooked smile. "Yeah, you sound fine."

"Why would you want to try with Fletcher? After everything?"

"Because I know what it is like to lose your family. And I would give anything to have Amaya and my parents back. Your father, Mason, and every other Guardian is just following orders. They don't make them."

"Thanks for the update." I roll my eyes at him, and he grabs my hands and pulls me down to him.

"Imani, you are getting a second chance."

"What if he doesn't want us back? What if we don't want him back?"

"If he wasn't interested in being with his family, he would have stayed in the barracks. At least you now have the choice." He pulls me onto his lap. I tilt my head, looking at him with a twisted face of sarcasm.

He's right.

His capacity for forgiveness is endless. For me, it is more like an uncomfortable stretch. He takes my face in his hands. "I will fight for your family. Whatever it takes."

"You're too nice. You know that, right?" I murmur.

He chuckles and kisses my forehead. "Only when it comes to you."

"I'm pretty sure it's hereditary. Your grandmother would do anything for you. It's my guess that your mother was that way too." I press my forehead to his, nudging his nose with mine.

"She was." His words are quiet.

I kiss his mouth and hold his face. I turn to straddle his lap. He shoves the robe from my shoulders and pulls my tunic open, laying kisses over both of my collarbones, gripping my hips with his hands.

"Harm," I rasp between ragged breaths.

He doesn't respond, mouth wandering over my chest now. He hardens under my center, and I rock into him. His groan sends electricity through my body. With every move he makes under me, I tremble.

"Look what you do to me," I whisper.

He chuckles, mouth around one of my peaks.

I tug at his shirt, and he lifts his arms. I pull it up and over, throwing it onto the ground beside us. He pulls my tunic over my head and drops it onto his shirt.

"Imani, I need you. So damn much." His voice is raw, low.

I stand, kick off my boots, and wriggle out of my pants. Harm shuffles out of his trousers and reaches for me. I sink onto his lap and cover his mouth with mine. His heat finds mine, filling me entirely. The sweetest groan spills from his chest. My chest tightens, and I swallow past the emotion in my throat. My breathing is erratic at thoughts of being on this side, at having him so close to the Guardians and the Chancellor again.

Harm in chains.

I can't breathe.

I can't breathe.

My fingers sink into his shoulders.

No, no, no, no, no.

"Imani." Harm shifts under me, pushing me back a little, trying to meet my gaze. "Imani!"

I can't breathe.

I can't breathe.

I can't breathe.

My hands tingle and my body stiffens.

Harm hugs me, holding me tight to his body.

"You're okay. I'm right here. Breathe. Please, breathe."

He chokes through a sob.

And I shake in his hold.

I can't do this again.

I can't lose him again.

Dammit.

I groan through the waves of sobs that strangle their way up my throat.

"Imani. It's okay. It's alright. Breathe, please breathe, my love."

I pull in air, and it burns all the way down. I wail through another lungful before pushing off Harm's chest.

His hands travel my face, brushing my tear-soaked hair from my cheeks and forehead.

"What is it?" His face is twisted in pain and worry.

I whimper and close my eyes, forcing myself to take air in and pushing it out again.

I grab his hands in mine. "I can't lose you. Not again."

He shakes his head violently. "You won't. Never again. You hear me?"

I nod vaguely but sobs choke back up, closing my throat. I slump, my forehead resting on his chest.

"Imani. Listen to me. I am not going to let anything happen to either of us. Where you go, I go. No matter where that is, you hear me? Whether that is in this life or the next. You are—" Tears course down his face as the word chokes him. He lifts my head up, hands gripping my jaw.

I drag a breath in. My body shakes on his. Tears drip from my jaw, hitting his bare chest.

He tilts his head a little and blows out a breath. "We do this together. We go home together. There is no other option."

I steady my chest and close my eyes. "We go home together." The words are wobbly, but they are ours.

"Look at me." His voice is a low growl.

I open my eyes to find his. His face is stone, his eyes fire.

"Imani Travesci, you are mine and I am yours and we will never be apart. Never. Again."

"Never again," I echo.

He pulls my mouth to his, hungrier than before. My hands search his face, then run through his hair. I lift up, and he moves under me. I sink onto his lap, and he growls, low and deep. I lift again and slam back down, desperate to be so close we can't be parted. I lift again and, this time, lower down ever so slowly. Electricity flings through my body and I lay my head back. Harm's lips find my peaks and I lose every last bit of self-control as beautiful agony floods my body. Harm follows me over the edge on the next lift of my hips. When the fire ebbs, we stay huddled and spent, holding on for an hour, not willing to let go.

Dressed again, with my head on Harm's lap, we banter about the things we will do once the regime is overturned. Harm's ideas, of course, are all to help other people. I just want to live in peace with the people I love and not have to look over my shoulder, not be running from something or someone, and have a home I can grow old with Harm in. Catori and I have talked about the roles we will all have once things change, and so far, she has me pegged to take her place as forest huntress. But I have a feeling Harm won't want to stay in the forest, especially when the desert side needs so much to redeem it from the ruination the Chancellor has caused.

The door to our wall hideout rattles under the hand of someone outside. I sit up, and Harm checks his weapons before walking to the door.

"Who is it?"

"Your father's only sibling." Christopher's voice drifts around the door.

Harm turns the latch and pulls back the door. Four figures slip into the space before the door thuds shut. Each one of them removes their hood and wrap. Enid finds me first, wrapping her arms around me.

"How have you been, my girl?" she whispers. I hug her back, tight.

"I'm good, Enid. Keeping safe?"

"Yes, your uncle sees to that." She rolls her eyes. I have never been prouder.

"Imani." Luca pulls me into a hug and releases me. Christopher stands beside Harm, gaze fixed on my face.

"Hello, Christopher."

"Hello, Imani."

Jonah wanders over to my side and wraps an arm around my shoulders. "My girl, I have missed you."

I beam up at him and he winks at me. His face falls and he turns to face me, resting his hands on my shoulders.

"You ready for this?"

"Before we go, there is something I need to tell you."

"Oh, what is it?" He shifts on his feet.

"Fletcher. He—"

I glance at Christopher and Harm briefly. Jonah leans in. "What did he do this time?"

"Nothing. I mean. He came to the village."

"Your village in the forest?"

"Yes, but—"

"What did he want? What were they there for?" Christopher asks, brows lowering.

Harm is trying to school his face. I huff out a breathy laugh.

"He didn't want anything. He brought the children back. Him and one of the other men who was taken weeks back, the blacksmith. He brought them all home."

Jonah's jaw hangs from his face. "He did it."

"What do you mean?" Christopher spits.

"He got out. Finally, Daniel Fletcher got out of the regime." Jonah walks in circles, glancing at me briefly.

"You knew he was going to do this?" Harm asks.

"No, not knew. I had a hunch, when he let you go last time you retrieved Harm from the tower. Things have really changed. Even he can see that." He walks over to me and grabs my arms. "I have known your father since he was five years old. Perendi was a small village back then. If there is one thing I know about Daniel Fletcher, it's that once he has set his mind about something, he always follows through. He is stubborn, just like someone else I know."

"So, what, Fletcher is on our side now?" Enid chokes out.

"Not exactly. He is still under guard in the forest village. It is up to Catori if she trusts him. And that is not going to be an easy feat, believe me," Harm says.

"Still, with him out of the picture, Arthur has lost one of his major assets. This is only good news for us," Jonah says.

"Then why do I have a bad feeling about this all still?" I ask.

"Imani's right," Christopher says, meeting my gaze. "If Arthur loses too much at once, he is going to get desperate, and desperate men do terrible things."

Right now, I don't know if he is talking about Arthur or my father. Guilt tugs at my core.

"We need to move, then. Now," Luca pipes up.

Enid wraps her face and pulls her hood down. "Agreed."

We don our robes and wraps and stalk through the sand to the spot where Saraya's stall stands. We pull up short.

It's gone.

The small door is boarded up.

We have no way in.

CHAPTER 19
NIRRI

Flick holds my gaze, but all I want to do is run away. Breath stopped, I stand rooted to the spot, letting her words sink in. I thought he was better. That we had worked past the trauma from the past that had haunted him. The torture he withstood from that low-life filth in Trindari had been healed. At least, that is what I had believed. But the still body draped in a sheet on the bunk before me is real. Gregor's blood spots the edges of the cloth.

"You gave him so much, Nirri. You helped more than you know. This is not your fault." Flick hugs my shoulders again and again.

I can't move.

Air lodges in my throat.

"I—"

She turns me away from the bunk, pushing me into familiar arms. "Come home, Nirri. I'll get you some stew." Marshall ushers me out the door and toward home.

"No, I need to—"

"Flick needs to finish preparing him. You can go back tomorrow."

"Okay," I utter as he guides me into the lounge chair in the living room. I stare at the wall. Wishing I could turn back time. Wishing I could have visited him sooner.

The moment replays in my head over and over. Knocking on his door. Opening it and walking in to find Gregor, my first *real* patient, grey and lifeless on the floor, eyes unseeing. I know in this moment I will never forget it. I will never forget the hot bile that clawed its way up my throat. The knot that filled my stomach and the scream that pierced my ears, spewing from my own mouth.

Heat travels into my chest and up my neck. My mouth waters fast. "Marshall!" I crumple to the floor, losing my stomach over the mat. With trembling hands, I hold my hair back.

A warm hand lands on my back as Marshall drops beside me. Why did I think I could do this? I can't help anyone.

This world is ruined.

Every small thing turned sour.

Nothing but devastation survives in this desolate, sandy place. For the first time in weeks, I just want to go home. I just want to see Callian's smiling face. I want to feel his warmth wrapped around me. I want to laugh with Imani and spar with Catori. I want to feel alive. Not weighed down by stupid helplessness, the way I have my entire useless life.

Dammit.

Sobs choke their way out of my throat. Marshall sits on the floor beside me, hugging me to his side. I would be lost without him. My little brother—or at least, the closest thing I have ever had to a sibling.

As the light fades from our small living room, Marshall helps me up, walking me to bed. I lay where he settles me, blanket over my body, pillow under my head, and stare at the ceiling, pondering the uselessness of everything we hold dear. The stars pop from the darkness, one after the other, as I watch the wisps of clouds travel past my window. Never big enough for rain. Just enough to block out the sun's rays from time to time. Heaviness drags my eyes shut, and I roll over, letting the darkness claim me.

The blood on the floor is not mine. That I know. I checked. My hands shake as I turn them over for the third time to look at the perfectly unmarked skin. Gurgles come from behind me, and I force my feet to turn. My body follows. The room is familiar; I have been here before, I think. A woman is screaming at me. Asking. No, demanding I save her brother. I can't. I can't help anyone. I step backward and hit the wall that wasn't there before. She appears from behind the curtain. Her face is stretched with panic.

Catori.

No. No, no, no.

I rush the curtain, flinging it to the side. Callian lays on the bunk, his face white, his blue eyes searching the ceiling, as if what can save him floats above. The line of red across his neck bubbles with each labored breath.

Firm hands grip my arms.

"Save him! Help him!" she screams.

Catori is screaming, her face mangled by fear and desperation.

I can't help him.

It's too late.

I'm too late.

I'm useless.

I'm not what he needs. He needs a real healer. A real person to fix that gaping line on his neck.

"No, I'm sorry," I sob.

She growls, lunging for me. Her bloody knife stings against my throat.

I sit up gasping, hand around my throat. Heart flinging around in my chest, I suck in deep breaths and force my mind to count the objects in the room. The feel of the blanket, of the breeze that drifts through my window. Slowly, my body settles. Shoving my head in my hands, I whimper through every thought, every moment I had with Callian. And, for the first time, the realization that I could end up without him hits me. The weight of it caves my chest in. If this is freedom, I don't want it. Not without Callian.

A figure hovers in the doorway to my bedroom. "You okay?"

Even in the dim light, the lines on Marshall's too-young face are visible. At only fifteen, he is one of the kindest, most stable people I know. He reminds me a lot of Harm.

I pat the bed beside me and wipe the tears from my face. He wanders in and sits beside me. "You were screaming in your sleep, Nirri."

"I bet I was."

"Nightmare?"

"More like a defining moment. Let's go home, Marshall."

"Are you sure? Flick said it wasn't your fault, you know."

"I know that. I can't save everybody. I wouldn't even know where to start. But I do know where I belong."

"Back to the forest we go, then." He smiles at me and gives me a tight hug before padding back to bed.

Back to the forest we go.

I have one stop to make on the way.

The lights of Trindari flicker over the dunes before us. Marshall stands on the crest of the dune next to me, robes flapping around his legs as mine do. The village seems quiet enough. But I know looks are deceiving with this place. The last time we were here, the leader of the forest people hung from a pole.

Nothing good happens here.

And I am about to add to the long list of unpleasant things that happen to the folk of Trindari. Conscious of being recognized, we pull our hoods down and pull the wraps tight around our faces. I stride into Trindari with the fire of every drop of Gregor's blood that spilled over his sandy kitchen floor. Marshall says nothing as we make our way to the tavern.

I hesitate outside the swinging half doors of the building.

"Remember the plan," I whisper.

Marshall nods, eyes fire.

I push through the doors and walk to the counter. A bald man, ruddy and in need of a long bath, runs his eye over my robe, finally landing on my face. I pull the wrap down slightly as a sign of trust.

"I need a meal and board. One night," I say, gaze fixed on his.

"We don't take travelers here." The man glances at Marshall's wrapped-up face and returns his stare to my chest. "But we may have a bed out the back you can sleep on for the night." A smirk grows across his face.

Marshall shifts on his feet beside me. I can feel the anger blooming in his veins from here.

"That won't be necessary. Is there somewhere else we can bunk for the night?"

"Only one place. But it's not exactly friendly toward women, if you know what I mean."

Marshall's hand shifts to his hip, where his knife is concealed.

"Fine, where is it?" I ask, knowing all too well where the brothel is located.

"Three doors down. You will need something to barter with to get in."

"Thank you," I say, mustering the most insincere smile I can.

Marshall stalks through the front doors, and I follow him.

I walk toward the building three doors down but duck down

the alley before it. Marshall slides down the building to sit on the sand. I plop beside him. Now we wait. Wait for word of a naive girl wandering about their infamous village.

Sure enough, moments later, three men travel toward the building. Peaches and his posse. That was just too easy.

"I'll see you on the other side of the dunes," Marshall says and stands, walking back the way we came. I wait until I smell smoke, then poke my head around the corner. A tower of smoke billows up from behind the closest dune to the village. Men run out toward the smoke, yelling about travelers. I hope Marshall stays well-hidden like we planned.

Peaches and his lot run past the alley, and I follow, hood down and wrap around tight. I double-check my quiver and count the arrows behind me with quick fingers. Some men turn back, deciding the small fire is not worth their time. Peaches sprints into the sands, most likely eager to rob whoever was stupid enough to camp that close to Trindari. He disappears over the dune as I reach the outskirts of the village.

Yelling drifts back, and I break into a run. *Please don't have Marshall.*

I follow the boot indents in the mound of golden sand darkened by the night's light. Cresting the dune, I see Peaches and his men. They are the only men left out here now. And they have a firm grip of Marshall's collar. My stomach plummets, my breath hitching.

I stand on the top of the dune, mere feet from them below me. "Let him go."

Peaches rips his attention from Marshall to me. A smirk grows over his face, and his men snigger. I untie the wrap from my face, letting it hang over my shoulders, then push back my hood. Blonde curls whip around my shoulders and face in the dry desert air.

"Oh, this is going to be good," Peaches says, releasing his grip on Marshall. His men move closer to my little brother, tugging him hard to regain their hold, and I barely manage to reign in my temper.

"Yes, Peaches, it is." I pluck an arrow from my quiver and nock it so fast, shock barely registers on his smug face before the arrow sinks into his heart. His men drop Marshall immediately, staggering through the sand to either side of me, trying to run back to the village. I nock another and let it fly. It finds its home in the neck of the man to my left. The last man stumbles down the dune, begging me to spare him. I nock another, and a second later, it's shaft-deep between his eyes.

I walk across the sands, stopping at the limp body of Peaches. "That was for Gregor. And Catori. And Imani. And Harm. And every other person you tormented, you filthy ingrate."

Marshall clears his throat. "Remind me never to get on your bad side, sister." He is smiling, an eyebrow raised.

"You could never do that."

I just hope Gregor is at peace.

Wherever his soul ended up.

He hugs my shoulders, and we trudge through the sands toward the southeast. In four days' time, I will be able to breathe.

I will be home.

CHAPTER 20
IMANI

"What happens once we get the children out?" I ask.

"There are people waiting east of the closest rocky outcrop with the caravans, ready to take the children home," Jonah says. He turns back to the barred door and grunts.

"Wait here," Christopher says.

"What are you doing?" Harm asks.

"I will make a distraction, then you three get that door open."

Jonah nods and Christopher jogs toward the prison.

We hover by the door, waiting for who knows what. Harm stands beside me, watching the movement of every person in his line of sight.

Boom!

The loudest sound I have ever heard ricochets around the prison walls, a tower of smoke billowing up from the entrance. The clatter of falling stone follows instantly. A heartbeat later, screaming penetrates the smoky air.

"That's our cue," Luca says, grabbing the wooden boards and tugging at the top one with both hands. Harm files in beside him, pulling the other end. The wood splinters, and they rip the broken board from its anchors.

Jonah steps in, and the last three boards suffer the same quick fate. With a quick hand, Harm flings the door open. It hangs on its twisted hinges, and we slip into the dim, damp space. Luca, the last to enter, pushes the door shut, leaving the barring board swinging beside it. Christopher will need to get in too.

We take off running, following Harm upward along the sandy tunnel toward the cells. Time drags in the crowded space, and every breath we take seems louder than the last. The tunnel winds up to the right, and Harm slows, holding up a hand. We hover behind him as he pushes a panel in the wall ever so slightly to one side. Light spills through the slim opening. Enid stands by my side, wiping sweat from her face and neck with a cloth.

Footsteps echo up the tunnel from the way we came. Enid freezes beside me. Harm and I take our stance in front of the group, drawing our blades and scanning the darkness. Waiting. The footfalls grow slower, steadier, and Harm braces, weapons turning over in his hands.

The desert robe and hood come into view first, and I let out a short breath. Harm relaxes, sheathing his weapons. I slide mine home and turn back to see Enid, face lit up with wonder and pride.

"You two are really something, you know that?" she says, a hand on each of our shoulders.

Harm chuckles and gives me a sideways look, his gorgeous face wrapped in a smile so wide he steals what's left of my shallow breath. I huff out a laugh and look to Jonah. He scrunches his face at me and winks, wrapping his arms around both of us. I roll my eyes at him, and Enid stifles a laugh.

"Time is of the essence, people," Christopher interrupts our small huddle.

Luca stands holding the panel open as we slip into the corridors of the prison. Harm takes the lead. I hope the children are still in the same place. We need to get in and out as fast as possible. We turn left and find the wooden doors to the holding cell shut. Luca and Harm draw their arms and I push the door open, one hand on the hilt of my dagger.

The room is empty.

"Dammit," Harm utters.

We turn back and continue down the corridor. Luca tries the next door.

Nothing.

Finally, we turn the corner and find two large wooden doors open. Inside, the large room is flanked by cells. Full of children. Boys on one side, girls on the other. The smaller children sit huddled with the older ones. Some are playing, some are sleeping. They look fine. We step through the doors and an older girl gasps.

Enid presses a finger to her lips.

Instantly, the children stand and crowd the cell doors, silently. As if they know what they need to do. Luca slides his blade into the lock, smashing the mechanism and pulling the door open. Harm does the same on the other side, and in mere moments children are pouring out of the cells. I turn to Christopher, and he tilts his head to the wooden doors. Jonah hangs in the hallway, keeping an eye out for any movement. I beckon the children to follow, and we make our way toward the panel leading to the tunnel.

I turn back and grab the arm of the oldest girl in the group. "You need to run down this tunnel and wait for us inside the exit door. The men will get you to the outcrops. Your people are waiting there to take you all back to your own villages. You must be quiet. Understand?"

She nods and I wave them through the door. Luca and Christopher catch up, going through the tunnel as the last of the children pour through the corridor toward the secret exit. Jonah walks alongside them, hushing them as they go. After the last son of the desert has made it through the panel, Enid steps into the dim space, followed by Harm. I slip inside and pull the panel shut tight.

That was almost too easy.

I turn to find Harm hovering behind me.

"Why did that feel way too easy?" he says.

"My thoughts exactly."

"Come on you two, count your blessings and let's get out of here," Enid presses, hurrying off after the children. Harm jogs to follow the crowd. I check the panel again and take off after them.

Harm walks with the smaller boys, guiding them over the uneven ground, talking to them about everyday things, keeping everyone calm. Enid and I watch as he rounds the corner with them, and we fall into step.

So far, so good.

"Imani," Enid starts.

"Enid?" I look at her as we move through the dim space, trailing a handful of steps behind the others.

"I wanted to tell you—"

Shouting comes from behind us, faintly reverberating through the tunnel walls. I stop and raise my hand.

Enid stills.

The clatter of hurried footfalls presses in on us.

"Go!" I whisper. With my hand on her shoulders, I turn Enid on the spot.

"No, you need to run too."

"I will buy us some time. Go!"

She staggers forward, face twisted with fear.

"Go, now!" I hiss, drawing the twin swords from my back. Enid rounds the corner and I take up fighting stance. Feet apart, shoulders open, hands loose on the hilts of my blades.

Inhale.

Exhale.

Inhale.

Exhale.

I think of Miya.

Of every moment the Guardians stole from someone we loved. Of every person the regime crushed, every family it destroyed.

I make out at least five or six voices, jeering each other on as they draw closer to my position.

Inhale.

Exhale.

Harm's beautiful family he will live without for the rest of his life.

Inhale.

Exhale.

Mason's family.

Mason's life as a Guardian.

The men discarded to the mountain wilds.

The forest people, killed to satisfy Arthur's anger.

Inhale.

Exhale.

The first glimpse of grey I see flies at me, and I spin out of his path, slicing through his throat with my right hand. The remaining officers halt as their comrade drops onto the sandy ground at my feet. They take a moment to gather their composure while I stand, waiting.

Eleven are left standing. The oldest officer's eyes burn into mine, hate pinching his rugged features. I glance to the lifeless body at my feet and raise both blades.

"Wait," a younger officer says, holding up a hand in defense. "That—that's the commander's daughter. She is dangerous."

They are afraid of me. Good; they should be. The older, hate-filled man steps forward. "I am not afraid of some half-witted flake of a girl."

I step forward to meet his gesture. "Your mistake."

Lunging, I slice his arm, crimson soaking through his grey sleeve. He growls and rushes me with his cane, and I meet him with my swords crossed. He leans through my crossed blades and snarls. "Filthy traitor."

He spits in my face and smirks.

The spittle runs down my cheek and drips from my chin. I grit my teeth, holding my weapon against his. If he thinks he can intimidate me, he is a fool.

"That the best you got, Guardian?"

He huffs, pushing me backward. I spin and ready both blades. His comrades step up around him and move closer, like predators circling their prey. Something in my gut flips. I haul up every piece of training Miya put me through. It's eleven against one. Catori once took on twenty and won, spectacularly.

I can do this.

"Your speed is your greatest advantage, Imani, never forget that." Miya's words play over and over in my head. I swallow past the lump in my throat that tightens my chest with the memory. I sheathe my swords and pull both fighting knives.

This is how I win a fight—with speed, accuracy, and at close quarters.

The Guardian huffs a disinterested laugh and tosses his cane to the ground. All at once, every officer pulls out two daggers. Twenty-two cutting edges against my two.

The officer grunts at one of the men to his left, and the boy lunges at me like a harried animal, the whites of his eyes showing. He must be terrified. Just some village boy, taken from his home and commanded to fight against his own. I end his fear quickly, and he drops to the ground behind me when his momentum dies out.

Again, their superior grunts, this time signaling two men to attack simultaneously. Between them, I turn from side to side, matching their easy swipes before sinking my blades into both of their necks. The horror of their fates is scrawled across their faces. I whisper a prayer for them, hoping that their souls find peace after their life without freedom and choice.

"Her leg," the young boy from earlier pipes up. "The commander once broke her leg. It's her weak spot."

I keep my gaze trained on the officer spelling out the orders. Defense is the fastest way to lose a fight. I fly at him, darting to his side before sinking a blade through his ribs. He folds and staggers away. I spin back and slit the throat of the younger boy. Who has a weak spot now?

The older officer straightens, walking back over. I still as one blade points into my back, then another. A heartbeat later, the officer lowers his gaze, raising his blade to my throat. "A fitting end for a filthy traitor, just like her father."

So, they know the regime is without a commander. He must think if he does enough damage, he can replace Fletcher.

Firm hands grip my arms, pushing me to my knees. The officer stands closer, so he is standing over me. Someone grabs my hair, ripping my head backward. Pain shoots through my scalp and I force air into my lungs, meeting his gaze.

A gasp sounds from by the corner.

Enid stands, both hands over her mouth.

I shake my head, willing her to run. She tilts her chin, lowering her hands by her side. Finally, she steps away from the corner and holds her head up, fire burning from her gaze into the eyes of the man whose blade has now drawn blood from my throat.

"You leave her be," she snaps. Her hands shake against her sides.

"Run, Enid," I rasp against the blade.

"Never, my girl."

Three of the men leave my side and surround Enid.

Air chokes its way up through my throat, fear clawing its way over every inch of my body. I close my eyes briefly.

"Finish off the old lady, and then we take this one to the Chancellor to hang alongside her father," the officer at my throat says.

"No! No, let her go. I won't fight. I'll go with you. Just let her go, please!" I beg.

Enid's gaze finds mine.

Tears fill her light-blue eyes and her mouth pulls up into a wobbly smile.

"I will go with you. Take me. Let her leave; she hasn't done anything wrong."

"We don't take orders from traitors."

He slams his remaining blade into my bad leg. The scream that flies through my throat feels like fire. Stars invade the sides of my vision. I shake my head, trying to dislodge them.

"Get on with it."

The words my father used so many times.

No. No, please no.

The officer holding her moves his arm quickly. Gurgling fills the dank space and Enid sinks to her knees.

Each breath I loose is a scream.

I will her to stand up.

I scream at her to stand, to stand back up and fight.

"Enid!"

The blade digs into my throat harder. Blood trickles down my neck, soaking my tunic. Fire has engulfed my entire bad leg and my body trembles.

"Enid!"

Heat floods my core, lighting up my chest. I growl, so pained and haunting that the men holding me lose their grip momentarily. I spin in their hold and knock two off me. The blade at my throat disappears. I stand on wobbly feet and roll back my shoulders. I rip the swords from my back and stalk toward the main officer. He stumbles back, mouth gaping, before he recomposes himself and meets me halfway across the space. His blood will cover this ground if it is the last thing I ever do.

Shuffles from down the tunnel echo toward us. He looks back at the sound quickly, and I lunge. I hold my sword above my head in both hands and slam it down into his chest. It finds its mark, but he spins out of line, and I stumble past him. I steady my feet and turn back to face him. He walks around me in a small circle. I glance at Enid's limp body and limp toward her protectively.

He stalks into my space, and I stand over her, unmoving.

"Enjoy your last breaths, filth," he spits.

"After you," I snap, ripping a dagger from my side and finding it a home in his chest.

Harm appears around the corner the second I pull my blade from the Guardian's chest.

Splinters of white swallow my vision and I collapse to the ground, my blades thudding on the earth on either side of me.

My breath stops and doesn't return.

The beat of my heart echoes through my head like a clanging bell.

Harm's tortured scream pulls at my chest just before darkness swallows me whole.

CHAPTER 21
HARM

The thunder in my ears blocks out the screams of the men I cut down. The two most important people in my life lay lifeless to my right. My body goes through every movement automatically, as if killing men is just another mundane chore I undertake mindlessly. My blades find a home in every last standing Guardian in the dim space. I stand shaking for a heartbeat before the blood-soaked blades in my hands fall, hitting the ground.

Every breath burns.

Time stands still.

I refuse to turn around.

To see Imani and my grandmother lying on the ground.

Gone.

Blood covers most of the ground around me. The grey, limp bodies scattered around are evidence that what just happened is real. I cut down half; Imani, the other half. The air leaves my lungs and doesn't return.

I stagger backward and fall to the ground, crawling over to where they lie. Sobs swallow every breath.

Imani lies next to Enid, as if she was standing between her and the Guardians. Fire to the end, my girl.

I press my head to hers, then turn to Enid. Taking her head in my hands, I wail, dropping my head to her chest. The smell of stew, herbs, and home still lingers on her shirt and robe. I curl both hands around her robe.

Her body rocks like a dead weight in my arms as I cradle her, whispering everything I have ever wanted to say to her.

I love you more than you know.

You have given me so much.

Goodbye, grandmother.

The lump in my throat burns as I lay her back to the ground and turn to Imani.

No, no, my sweet, fiery love.

My Imani.

I take her face in my hands and kiss her lips, brushing her hair from her face. Blood and dirt are woven through her gorgeous dark waves of hair. Her blue eyes are sheltered under ivory lids. Her face is warm in my hands.

She is still warm.

Agony squeezes my chest so tight, my heart cracks.

I scream, sending the tortured sound around the space and down the tunnel.

Over and over, I scream.

"Imani, please. Don't leave me."

I bang on her chest with my fists.

The memory of the boys in the well, years ago, flickers through my mind. I thump her chest again. And again.

"Imani Travesci, don't you dare leave me."

Thump.

"Please... Come back."

Thump.

"Come on!"

Hot tears spill down both cheeks, burning their way to my chin and dripping onto her tunic.

"Imani, where you go, I go. You hear me? Come back!"

Her body jostles under my fists again.

"No! Please. Imani. Imani." I cradle her head in my hands, drifting my thumb over her lips.

I groan, rocking back on my heels, every breath a whimper.

"Don't leave me, Imani. Don't go. I'm begging you, please. No."

I kiss her forehead and drop my head to her chest, shaking her shoulders. Throwing my head back, I roar. Every last thread of agony from my shattered heart splits the air around us.

Her body shudders in my hold.

I snap my head down, scanning her face.

She jerks upward, gasping through ragged breaths, eyes wide.

I sit back, stunned.

I pull her into my arms as she screams into my chest. Her hands grip my arms, clinging tight. She is terrified. Devastated.

I thought I lost her.

I almost lost her.

Dammit, Imani.

I nearly lost you.

Breath shatters through my lungs like glass. I push her back, sobbing through deep breaths, hands exploring her face. Her pained, twisted expression falls to Enid.

"No!" she wails, head tilting to one side. "Harm—" My name dies in her throat as she chokes for air.

I cradle her close and rock her back and forth. She screams into my chest endlessly. Blood trickles from her leg, soaking my lap. I release her and rip my wrap from around my neck, tying it around her leg tight. She winces and whimpers as I take her face in my hands.

Remembering where we are, I rest my forehead to hers. "We need to leave, now."

She whimpers through a nod, and I help her to her feet. She wobbles in my hold, and I wait until she is steady before turning back to Enid.

For a heartbeat, I don't believe what I am seeing. The woman who raised such strong women, who led a rebellion and protected everyone she loved for decades, devoted her life to healing others, lays lifeless at my feet.

"Harm," Imani utters. "We can't leave her here."

I bend down and pick Enid up. Her head flops back over my arm, and Imani stifles a sob with her hand.

I take a step toward the corner of the tunnel and adjust to her weight. The wound at her neck gapes, and bile rises in my throat. Imani limps beside me, lifting Enid's head in her hands. The wound closes as Imani holds her steady, cradling her every step down the long, now painfully quiet tunnel.

After what feels like a lifetime of walking to the end of some empty place flanked by darkness, we reach the group of children. Luca, Christopher, and Jonah wait with them.

Luca spots us first and rushes to where we stand. Enid lays limp in my arms. Imani trembles at my side, tears coursing down her cheeks.

"Pa," Luca murmurs, eyes tight with sadness and worry.

Jonah rushes over.

His breath catches as his eyes land on Enid.

"Hell." Christopher groans, turning back to the children, ushering them toward the door.

I kneel and lay Enid on the ground.

Jonah tumbles to his knees beside her, mouth gaping, eyes

scanning every inch of her frantically.

"Enid, no. What happened?"

"I—" Imani starts and chokes into tearful sobs.

"There were eleven of them," I say, finally meeting Jonah's gaze as if my heart is not cracked all over.

His jaw feathers, his head shaking. "Enid, what have we done?" Jonah whispers, his calloused hands caressing her face before hovering over the long wound on her neck.

"Pa, we need to get out of here."

"How many of the eleven got away?" Christopher asks.

"None," I say. Imani meets my gaze and closes her eyes.

Luca studies Imani's clothes, noting the bandaged leg. "Well, at least that's something. Let's move." He stands next to his father, trying to get him to move. Gazing off into the distance, Jonah sways on his knees.

I lift Enid from the ground and carry her, following the crowd. Imani hangs back, waiting for Jonah. Luca helps me with Enid, and we move through the door, letting the children file out before breaking off into smaller, less noticeable groups. The chaos at the prison entrance is still causing a good distraction, with officers running around, trying to pull men from the rubble, yelling for healers and volunteers and finding few willing to help.

Once out the door, I turn back. Imani stands beside Jonah, hand extended to help him up. Her weight is on her good leg, although her body sways—most likely from exhaustion and shock.

"We need to move," she says to him.

He looks past her. I have never seen Jonah, the man who has led us through some of the toughest times in our lives, so shaken. Imani bends down, wincing. Her hand rests on his cheek. "Please. We can't lose you too, Jonah."

He looks up at her and nods vaguely. His big hand finds hers, wrapping around it as he wobbles to stand. She keeps her hold on his hand and leads him out the door, walking in front of Luca and me.

An hour later, we hang around the rocky outcrops as Christopher sorts out the children and packs them into the caravans, ushering them off. When the last caravan has slipped over the dunes, Luca turns to face me. "I can carry her home, Harm. You two should make your way back to the forest. Stay there until we send word our side is ready. It shouldn't be long now."

He stands and extends both arms as if accepting a great honor. I release Enid to him, and he huddles her into his chest. Jonah, with a pale face and vacant eyes, stands beside him. Imani hobbles to where Jonah stands, wrapping her arms around his shoulders. He lowers his head to her shoulder as if moving automatically, and she sobs something into his ear before kissing his cheek and turning back to me.

Jonah's chest heaves as he walks into the dunes.

"I'm sorry for your loss, Harm," Luca says, tears lining his eyes as he turns and watches his father trudge through the sands after the last caravan. Emotion clogs my throat. I nod and take Imani's hand. He is right; we need to leave. For so many reasons, we need to leave. I watch as he turns and walks into the sands, carrying my grandmother in his arms. My chin wobbles. I drag in a painful breath. Imani rests her hand on my chest.

"Let get out of this place before we lose anything else," I say, the words like glass in my throat.

Callian's hard stare burns into Fletcher, dressed in plain forest clothes, no grey in sight. He looks younger, softer than he did in uniform, as if the hold the regime had over him has been wiped away, and the real man, the husband and father version of himself, is the only part of him we see.

Catori rolls her eyes and slams a fist on the table. "We are not going to get anywhere if half of us are holding grudges and acting like imbeciles! Not now, Callian. You can be at each other's throats later. We are running out of time."

Callian drags his twisted glare from Fletcher's face and meets his sister's raised eyebrows with a grunt. The four forest guards shift on their feet, as if uncomfortable with the whole ex-commander-helping scenario. None of us are fine with this; but like Catori said, time is running out, and we need options.

Imani stands at the table, across from her father and me, her gaze almost vacant.

"What about the leader of the desert rebellion? He will need to be informed," Fletcher says, searching our faces.

"She..." I start, swallowing past the lump in my throat. "We lost her a few days ago to the regime."

"What? How? She should have been protected," Fletcher snaps. Heat rises in my core, flowing to my neck and face. My hands ball to fists at my sides. Imani sways beside me before walking out the door into the village center.

"How the hell did that happen?" Fletcher grinds out.

Mason stiffens, and Catori's arm lands on his. The sight of Imani limp on the ground, lying beside my grandmother, scrapes through my memory. I lunge at Fletcher. Grabbing his shirt by the opening, I slam a fist into his face, hard. He waivers but doesn't retaliate. I land another, and another. Fletcher takes every blow I throw down on him. Blood leaks from his nose and mouth before he grips the table beside him with one hand.

"Harm!" Catori shouts.

I push him backward into the wall near the hearth and slam his body into the wood. He stares at me, eyes vacant, but still doesn't raise a hand.

"Enough!" Catori barks.

Mason and Callian appear on either side of me, a firm grip around each arm. They tug me backward, and Fletcher slumps against the stone.

I stand, seething, fists in hard balls, splattered with his blood.

"Imani almost lost her life trying to protect Enid," I rasp.

Fletcher looks through the empty doorway.

"She fought eleven of your men, trying to defend my grandmother. She killed five of the mongrels, until they got the better of her." I shake off the hold of my brothers. "She wasn't breathing. They almost killed her." Every word is like fire. "You did this to her! They knew about her injuries, and where to hit her to bring her down. It is your fault we almost lost her."

Mason and Callian stand rigid, faces paled. It is the first time I have been able to talk about it. The first time Imani or I have told anyone what happened in that tunnel. I almost lost Imani. They almost lost a sister.

"What? How—" Fletcher starts.

Catori's gaze burns into mine before flicking to Fletcher.

"Those Guardians knew about her leg, the one you broke in the tower when her and Mason tried to escape," I growl.

Fletcher's expression is blank as he searches our faces.

"Get him out of here," Catori says to the guards.

Fletcher goes willingly, looking back at me as he crosses the threshold, confusion and devastation pulling at his face.

Mason steps in front of me. I try to explain what he just heard and why I hadn't told any of them. But his face is kind, and he places a hand on my shoulder.

"Harm, Fletcher doesn't know what you were talking about, because he most likely doesn't remember that part of the event."

"What are you talking about?"

Catori appears by Mason. "The regime uses mind control, a sort of hypnosis to control the effectiveness of its officers. It's how they carry out such atrocities without even blinking. When their minds become overwhelmed—like I imagine they do, following the Chancellor's hideous orders—the hypnosis kicks in, and officers act on orders, not impulse, emotion, or feeling."

I remember Mason's face that day at the well. His expression flickered, like he was another person. I saw his struggle; for a second, he was fighting it. That also explains the vacant gazes on every officer on selection days, at executions, during every brutal punishment they carry out. Mason's face and the way he seemed to snap out of a trance the day of the gallows when he stood on the platform with Imani.

"So, how do we break it?" I ask.

Catori looks to Mason. Her face twists, and he sighs.

"That's what Hanola was doing with me when I first arrived here. It's not pleasant," Mason says.

"And Hanola's gone, so there is no hope for them now?"

Catori's gaze lands on Callian, and he shifts on his feet. "Not exactly," she says.

I stare at her, waiting.

"Nirri knows the technique," Mason offers. Callian's jaw feathers and he walks back to the strategy table.

"Can she do it, help officers that defect?" I ask.

"Or survive the war," Mason adds.

"That too. She could break Fletcher's mind control." I pace around Catori's living room. "If Fletcher doesn't remember everything that went on in the tower, he doesn't remember breaking Imani's leg, then one of the officers that were with him must have remembered."

"That's the only way it would have gotten around, that it happened," Mason says.

Callian stands staring at the maps on the table, both hands gripping the wooden edge.

"Surely, Fletcher must have heard what his officers were talking about," I say.

"Possibly. Maybe he didn't want to believe it. Imani recovered well; maybe he assumed it was the men exaggerating," Catori offers.

"At any rate, he doesn't remember almost running his own daughter through. That is a good thing. We need him. Believe it or not, he is one of our greatest assets at this point," Mason says.

"I have villages to visit." Callian stalks out the door.

Mason moves, but Catori rests a hand on his chest. "Let him go."

"I highly doubt Callian is going to let Nirri anywhere near Fletcher," Mason says.

"It's not his decision, Mason. It's Nirri's," Catori says.

"I'll speak with Nirri about working with Fletcher next time we are in the desert," I say.

"Harm..." Mason starts.

I walk out the door before he can finish his train of thought. I find Imani wandering the village toward Petria's. She hesitates at the front door, hand raised to knock. She turns back, and I lean against a building to watch her. She shakes her head, walking toward home. I catch up with her and slide my fingers through hers. She offers me a sad smile.

I wrap an arm around her shoulders and kiss the top of her head. She sighs, and we walk in silence back to our home. Once inside, I stoke our fire, tossing another log onto the pulsing embers. Imani sits on the bed, staring at her hands. I pad to where she sits and drop onto the bed beside her. The cushions jostle, the carved stars of our headboard just visible between two of them. The breeze that carries through our window plays with the sheer curtains tied neatly to each post of our bed, framing the space I treasure most. The space where it's just Imani and me. Where the rest of the world, and all the heartache in it, disappears for a little while, her body against mine. Her heart and soul, tangled with mine.

A plop breaks the silence between us, the wetness of her tear spreading on her pants.

"I'm sorry I couldn't save her," she sobs, her hands wringing together, over and over.

Tightness claws at my chest. "It's not your fault." I force the words out on burning breath.

"I told her to run, I told her to go. But she—"

"Hey." I turn to face her and take her face in my hands. Pain etches its way over her beautiful features.

I rub the tears from her cheeks with my thumbs. "You did everything you could. This is not your fault. You fought hard, Imani. Enid would have been so proud of you. *I* am proud of you."

Her head hits my chest and sobs turn to wails, her hands tightening around my arms. My chin wobbles and I hold her tight, letting the tears I have been struggling to hold back for days loose over my face. I am so grateful I didn't lose Imani too. And I have been counting that blessing since the day Luca walked away with Enid in his arms.

I hold Imani until she pushes away from my chest. Her face is red, her eyes swollen.

"How about I run us a bath?" I offer.

She nods and wipes her face dry. I walk to the bath and scatter some dried herbs and petals that we were gifted on our Blending day into the tub. That day feels like another lifetime ago now. I fill a bucket with water and hang it over the fire. In no time, the water is steaming. I pour it into the large wooden bath and stir it around, testing the temperature.

Imani walks over, peeling off layers of clothing as she crosses the floor. I tug the shirt from my back and toss it onto the changing screen. Her hands find the fastener of my trousers, and I lower my mouth over hers. She pushes the pants over my hips and removes her own. I slide my fingers around her neck, one hand in her hair. She moans into my mouth, and heat fills my core. I pick her up, and she wraps her legs around my waist as I step into the bath. Sinking into the warm water, I sit with Imani on my lap. Her mouth explores my face, my neck, and then down my chest. I lay my head back and close my eyes. She sinks below the waterline, her hair floating around her shoulders above her. Her mouth finds my hardness, and I groan. A few heartbeats later, she emerges from the water, takes a long breath, and disappears again. I chuckle, watching her naked curves move in the water. Another few languid movements of her mouth, then she emerges again, the sadness in her eyes replaced with cheekiness.

She stands, water coursing off her body, her nipples tight peaks and eyes burning into mine. I move forward in the water until my mouth is at her center. Her hands find my hair the second my mouth meets her wetness. Her fingers tighten in my hair with every stroke of my tongue over her throbbing center.

"Harm," she whispers, breathy and low.

"Mhmmm," I growl, knowing exactly what that sound does to her.

"No more playing around. Please," she begs.

"Who's playing?" I suckle her center and she whimpers.

Her legs tremble. I grab her thighs, holding her steady. She pushes from my grip and turns to face the edge of the bath. I stand and move behind her. She bends over the bath, looking back with a hunger like I have never seen in her before. She parts her legs, her back curved so her bottom is up. Her center is soaked. I grab her hips and lay kisses along her spine.

She moans. "Please, I need you. Now."

I sink into her, slow and steady. The sound that leaves her mouth is the most beautiful thing I have heard. I pull out and take her again. She trembles against the edge of the bath, throwing her head back, waves of dark hair fling over her back and shoulders. Water sloshes against my legs, stroke after stroke. Every sound she makes drives me higher. Heat prickles low in my spine, intense bliss building with every movement we make.

"Harm," she cries, and her core tightens around me. I explode inside her with a low growl. After the lightning in my body peters out, I rest my head on her back, breathing hard.

Imani wriggles out of my hold, sinking into the bath. She rests her head on the side of the wooden tub and closes her eyes. I drop into the water on the opposite side of the tub and watch her chest go from deep cycles to a steady rhythm. Finally, she opens her eyes and finds my gaze.

"Come here," I rasp. She wades through the water on her knees, stopping over my lap, straddling me. I drop my head onto her shoulder.

"I love you, Imani Travesci," I whisper into her neck.

"And I love you, Harmen Travesci," she breathes, nipping my neck.

CHAPTER 22
NIRRI

The forest is brimming with life around us. Marshall, ever vigilant, walks ahead of me along the path that leads to Catori's village. Another night under the canopy and we will be home. Ever since the night with the wolves, before my time in the desert village, being out in the forest makes me nervous. I hug the strap of my quiver tight, double-checking the blades hanging off both of my hips. Marshall insisted I be well-armed—he has taken such good care of me. I will have to tell Harm all the ways he has helped me, protected me, and just been there for me. Marshall should be proud; he is growing into a wonderful young man. I'm proud of him.

The last of the light ebbs from between the timbered trunks of the trees around us as we reach the small clearing the villagers use for a campsite. Marshall drops our rucksacks and wanders off to find food and firewood. I roll out the sleeping mats and busy myself with finding dry sticks for kindling. I pluck a few handfuls from around the base of the larger trees, bundling them in my shirt. I drop them by the fire as Marshall returns, logs in one arm and his other hand holding his shirt up, which I imagine is loaded with pickings from the generous forest around us.

As the calls of the birds wane and the nightlife settles into its quiet rhythms, hissing grows to our northwest. The waterfall. I could use a wash. I don't really want to traipse through the dark by myself though.

"Can you come with me to the waterfall? I really want to take a bath, but the wolves—"

Marshall rises, gathering his weapons, and nods. "Lead the way."

"I won't take long, I promise."

"Take your time, sis."

We plod through the dense undergrowth. Something snaps in the distance—perhaps other forest travelers. *Heavens above, please don't be wolves.* I quicken my pace and Marshall does the same.

We arrive at the waterfall. Its hissing drowns out every other sound. The area opens up. Stars hang above the craggy ledge the water pours from like moving, fluid stars. It takes my breath away. Marshall slides down the trunk of a tree, sitting on the moss that flanks it. He turns to face away from the water, and I move behind a large bush and peel off all my clothes save my tunic.

I wade into the water. It's cool and like the smoothest cloth against my skin. I walk deeper until it laps over my chest and lay my head back, drenching my curls. I plunge my head back further, until the water is inches deep over my face and the stars above me are nothing but watery dots. I release my breath and watch the bubbles rise and fade in the ripples of the water moving around me. Just as my lungs begin to burn, I push up out of the water and suck in a long, exquisite breath. The curtain of water in front of me is so enticing. I tug my tunic over my head and let it float on the water beside me. I walk into the waterfall like a woman entranced. The pressure of the waves of wetness that flow over my skin, my head, shoulders, chest, and back is magnificent. I stay there, mouth open, taking shallow breaths as the water washes every inch of my tired body. Tired from trying so hard. Tired from the brutal place we live in. Tired from wanting someone so much that it hurts just thinking about it.

I step back from the forceful sheet of water and drop into the water. Arms stretched out, I lay back and float, studying the shimmering stars above me. So permanent, so stunning. The ribbon of cloudy light that wanders over the sky waivers as the trees dance with the breeze.

Someone wading in the water from behind me startles me. I grab for my shirt, now a few feet away from me, and miss. What is Marshall doing? I lunge for it and drape it over my chest.

"I'm not done yet, Marshall. Just a moment." I sink into the water until it covers my shoulders, hiding my body, and turn to face the water's edge. It's not Marshall wading across the water toward me. The large form, so familiar, lowers into the water more and more with every step toward me. I hold the tunic tight over my chest and back up toward the waterfall hissing at my back.

Callian.

He runs a wet hand through his wavy blond hair, his stare burning into mine before his gaze tracks to the tunic at my chest. My heart thunders against my ribs. It's as if I conjured him by merely thinking about him. I shake my head, sure this is some sort of fatigue-induced mirage. Grandmother once told me of men in the desert who found themselves in trouble because of what they *thought* they saw.

I step back again, and the waterfall stings my back. Its harsh flow feels like a thousand hands pushing me forward, toward Callian. "What are you doing here?" I rasp.

"I was on my way to the next village over. I heard voices from my campsite. Then I saw Marshall." He tilts his head to where

Marshall still sits at the foot of the tree. When he looks back at me, his face is wrapped in the brightest smile. The stars above pale in comparison. My stomach flutters, sending my heart racing.

"Oh," is all I can say.

He steps into my space.

"Where are you going, Nirri?"

He needs to hear me say it, I assume. I stand a little taller in the water, my grip on the tunic releasing slightly. "Home."

"And where is home, exactly?" he says softly, pressing his forehead to mine.

My breathing shallows and I study his face. His eyes are fire, his body hard against mine. "I—" I want to say it. I do. I want to take what I want, regardless of what anyone else needs or thinks. But I can't. "I don't know exactly yet."

Callian moans, releasing me. I step back, letting the waterfall swallow me. Tears burn behind my eyes. He deserves better. A girl with no purpose is a burden. I don't want to burden anyone, least of all Callian.

I should explain; I owe him that much. "Callian?"

He moves through the curtain of water, stepping through the torrent. I glance down, making sure my tunic is in place and my body is covered by water. His hair hangs wet around his face. Water courses over his shoulders, running down his defined chest and stomach.

"I don't want to be a burden to you," I say, the words barely audible over the roar of the water.

"Nirri," he starts, moving closer so his body is touching mine. "You are not a burden. To me, or anyone."

I lift my chin and meet his gaze. "Maybe one day, when I have a place on this side of the wall."

"The desert wasn't your thing, I take it?"

"Not really. Plus, I wante—"

"Wanted what?"

"I wanted to be back here, with you all. I missed you all."

"Everyone?"

I know what he is asking. He wants to know if he was the one I missed the most.

He was.

He is.

Every moment near him feels too short. Too far away. Not enough. But I need to find myself first. Then I will be able to give everyone my all. Give Callian my all. And still, I don't know if I am good enough for him—if I am his best option. He deserves so much, and I don't know if I am it.

"Like I said, I missed you all." I wade past him, acutely aware I only cling to a tunic against my chest. He doesn't move, still facing the waterfall. I stumble out of the water and duck behind the bush, pulling my clothes over my wet body.

Once mostly dry and dressed, I round the bush and offer my hand to Marshall. His face is lit up with a grin so wide, one grows over mine automatically. "So, you saw Callian then?" he asks.

"Yes. Thanks for the warning," I groan.

"I thought it would be a welcome surprise?" His brows lower.

"It was; he was. Come on, let's get back to camp."

"You're not going to go with Callian?"

"No, I need to get home and talk with the village healer. I have things to do. And I am sure Harm is needing his right-hand man back."

He nods and slaps his hand into mine, pulling himself to his feet. He hugs my shoulders like he has a hundred times before and we make our way back to camp. Even at sixteen, he towers over me. My big little brother. We settle down on either side of the fire, and Marshall tosses another two logs onto the embers. I lay back on my mat, glimpsing the stars through the moving gaps of the canopy.

"Nirri?"

"Yeah?"

"When we get back to the village, can I keep living with you? Even if it's just for a while?"

"Most definitely. I don't know what I would do without you around."

He laughs and slides his hands under his head.

"Nirri."

I chuckle and turn to look at him. "Yes, Marshall."

"Please don't be afraid to be happy." His eyes burn into mine. He's talking about Callian. I loose a wobbly breath, half for the love Marshall gives me—unconditionally, the way family should, like nothing I ever had from my grandfather, only from my grandmother. And half because he knows my heart so well. But I'm scared. Scared that if I take too long to find myself, I will lose the one thing I want most.

I force a smile and turn my gaze back to the canopy. For a moment, I let the sounds of the night lull me before closing my eyes.

The village is bustling with children and busy villagers. Smoke drifts through the homes, and Marshall and I walk directly to Catori's house. I am so excited to see them all, my hands are shaking, and Marshall wraps an arm around my shoulder. He is my constant companion, reading my emotions sometimes before I even recognize them myself. Catori's door swings open, and Imani flies at me. Marshall drops his arm a second before Imani plows into me, arms hugging me tight. I giggle through a sob, and she kisses my cheeks before holding me at arm's length, assessing me from head to toe.

"You know, for a sand rat, you're looking pretty healthy," she says with a wink.

"I will never be a sand rat. That place is a disaster."

Imani laughs and steps aside as Mason makes his way over to me, pulling me into a long hug. Marshall chats to Imani about the Trindari incident, regaling her with the tales of "Nirri the Archer," as he has been teasing me about for days.

"So, you found your weapon of choice, then?" Imani asks.

"I guess so."

Mason releases me and steps aside. Catori stands with her hands by her side. My friend since childhood. Her eyes are lined with silver. I pad to where she stands.

"I am so sorry about Miya," I rasp.

"Me too," she says, her words barely a whisper. "Thank you for helping me, Nirri."

I look to Mason, and he smiles.

"She killed all three of them, Catori; they won't be stringing anyone else up on that pole anymore." Marshall pipes up.

Catori's eyes widen and she finds my gaze. "Nirri!"

"It's the least I could do."

"Callian. You just missed him. He left two days ago," Mason says.

"Oh, we found him." Marshall grins. I slap his arm and he winces, giving me a playful dirty look.

"We were camped near one of his stops. I saw him yesterday," I offer.

Imani raises an eyebrow. Mason stares at me, and Catori looks at me as if I need to explain.

"It's okay, he knows where I was going."

"But you came home? Does this mean...?" Imani asks.

"It means I am here to work. Whatever happens between Callian and I, well—"

"Is that the girl from the tower? Our fearless desert-crossing Nirri?" Strong arms pick me up from behind. I squeal and wriggle from his hold. I turn to see the happy but pained face of Harm. Marshall beams beside me. I fly into his arms, and he wraps them tight around me. "It's so good to see you home, little sister."

I choke through a breath, nodding my head.

"And you. I hear you are quite the devoted companion," Harm says to Marshall.

"You gave me an order, and I followed it. But to be honest, she was kind of a pain in the butt." Mirth lines his words, his eyes crinkled with cheekiness. Marshall dodges the fist I send toward his ribs. Harm pulls him into the hug for a moment before releasing us both.

Imani watches the three of us, eyes lined with silver.

"Come on, let's get some lunch. I'll bet you've only had desert rations for days. We can fix that," Catori says, taking Mason's hand and walking toward the village center. I hover on the spot for a moment, taking in my friends. The love they have for each other. For me too. They are my family. And I will use everything I know and have to keep them safe. To fight until we get to keep this freedom and our family.

Harm and Imani sit across the table from Mason and Catori and Marshall, and I slide in beside them. Catori hands out plates to each of us and Mason starts loading a little of everything that each of us likes onto our plates. Harm smiles at me, but his face falls.

"Nirri, there is something I need to ask you."

"Ah. If it's about Callian, I would rather not talk about it."

"No, not Callian. It's about Fletcher; and all the Guardians, really."

"Fletcher? What has he done now?" Marshall asks.

The four of them exchange looks.

"Fletcher came home. To the village. A handful of days ago," Harm says.

I look at Imani and then back to Harm. "What do you mean, he came home?"

"He defected; he has left the regime and joined the rebellion," Mason says.

My breath stops.

"It was a hard fact to swallow for all of us. But he risked his life to return the children and one of the village men who was taken. He arrived with the children and the blacksmith," Harm says.

"Oh, that's—that's good, I guess."

"Yes and no. It means one of Arthur's main assets has been removed. But he..." Harm looks to Imani. "Fletcher needs your help."

"What kind of help?"

Mason's eyes hit the table, and Catori stiffens beside him.

They are talking about the mind control technique. On the commander of the regime. That could take days.

"We need you to break the hypnotic control Arthur put in place during his training."

"That was over a decade ago, Harm," I warn.

"I know, but if he is going to be fighting with us—if he is going to be able to help—he needs to have full control of his mind. He is no use to us if we get into battle and he zones out and starts attacking our side."

"I guess I could try."

"How do we know when it is been broken?" Imani asks.

"They feel fear again. You can see it in their eyes." I look to Mason, and he nods solemnly.

"How do you test that?" Imani asks.

"Do something to make them afraid," I say.

Catori's face slackens.

"What did Hanola do to you?" Harm asks Mason.

"Catori, she—" Mason starts. Catori pushes her plate away and rises from the table, walking home.

Mason pulls in a breath. "She made me afraid. It worked."

"And then?" Harm asks.

"Then I attacked her, like a mad man," Mason utters, shifting on his seat, "and I remembered everything. Everything I had ever done."

"You remember the things you did under the mind control?" Harm says.

"Yes. Every last act; every last person." His eyes well with tears, his hands shaking around his cutlery. My heart thunders in my chest, watching the two boys stare at each other.

"I'm sorry you have to live with all that, Mason," Harm rasps. Imani's hand slides through his on the table, and he leans into her.

"Me too. For everything, Harm," Mason chokes and rises, following Catori home.

Imani offers Harm a wobbly smile and he kisses her forehead. Even if I can break the mind control on these officers—of which there are hundreds—that means we will be left with villages full of men who are haunted by the acts they carried out. That kind of trauma isn't always survivable. And I wonder whether it is kinder to leave the hypnosis in place.

Another impossible choice forced upon the people of the sands by the Chancellor. Every part of my soul is lit with hatred for my grandfather. He may be my blood, but he will never be my family.

Never again.

I finish my plate and excuse myself, heading for the healer's shelter with Marshall following close behind.

There is much to be done.

CHAPTER 23

IMANI

Islam my blade into his with every morsel of anger I have been carrying around for the last eight years. He staggers slightly backward but regains his composure and pushes back. His bright blue eyes burn into mine. His jaw feathers, and I rip my steel from his, spinning out of range. He staggers to where I stand, his stance open and fingers loose around both sword hilts. My father is tiring at a concerning rate.

No one else trains with him. I don't want him hurting anyone else I love. And if someone must train Daniel Fletcher to wield a blade, it is going to be me. The insignificant bit of training Arthur issued when the Guardians started carrying daggers is laughable. They would barely last minutes in a real fight with a forest warrior. Not that it's a problem since he is fighting with us and not against us now. Harm and Mason sit on the sideline, closer than usual. Their focus hasn't wavered, not for one second. The bruises from Harm's fist still cover Fletcher's face, and I have no doubt he would flog him again for the slightest slipup. The kindness that used to hold him back has waned in the last few months. Now, he is formidable. I glance at Harm and warmth rises in my chest.

"Again," Fletcher rasps.

His body is dripping with sweat, his hands trembling around the handles of the blades that hang between his fingers. I imagine every breath burns.

"Again!" I fly at him, both blades angled down. He tries to side-step me and falters. I press the tip of one blade against his ribs, the other at the now rapidly pulsing great vein in his neck. He wobbles to a stop and pulls in a breath, slamming his eyes shut.

"You're not fit enough to fight for very long."

He opens his eyes and winces. The tip of my blade twists between his ribs. I hold the pressure for a moment before dropping the sword to my side. "Maybe you could go running with the boys every morning. Get some general fitness before you start training any harder."

He nods and stands taller.

Three figures appear behind Harm and Mason, now standing. I glance over Fletcher's shoulder and find the familiar face of Jonah. He stands with Callian and Christopher. His gaze meets mine and he offers a small wave and a smile, that large grin that lights up everything around him. Instantly, a smile blooms over my face. My father notices the change in my expression and turns to find the source.

"Oh," he utters. The word is raw. It is the first time he has seen Jonah, his brother-in-law, in months. And now, as just an ordinary man. I can only imagine what is going through his head at this moment.

Jonah's mouth gapes, his gaze flickering between Fletcher and me. I hold out a hand, and Fletcher places his blade into it. I toss the weapons onto the rack and replace the shackles around his wrists. Just until his mind control is broken. He agrees it's the safest option for everyone. He has been staying in the prison under lock and key, instead of residing with my mother as Catori suggested.

Something about reintegrating him back into society to speed up the transition process. She sounds so much like Hanola; I am so proud of her. But I do worry about Fletcher around Mother and Miles.

I walk to Jonah, and he wraps both arms around me, his gaze never leaving Fletcher.

"Imani, what is this?"

"We are training him. He can't go into battle defenseless."

"I see," he utters, releasing me.

Fletcher appears just behind me. "Hello, Jonah."

"Daniel." Jonah swallows before looking at me.

"Fletcher," Christopher grunts.

"Christopher."

The air between the three men is like cold steel, dense and unbending. Jonah and Christopher both already knew Fletcher defected and joined the rebellion, but I guess it is another thing to see it with their own eyes. I am still not used to having my father around. It takes everything I have to suppress the anger and the multitude of unsaid things each day.

But this is bigger than any one of us. Much bigger. I can deal with the fallout of my relationship with my father when this is all over.

"Right, well, we have a ceremony to prepare for," Harm interrupts the heated gazes and confused looks.

"Yes. Yes, we do," Jonah says, his face falling.

"I'll take him back," Mason offers, stepping up to Fletcher.

"Thanks," I utter. They walk toward the prison keep, two defected Guardians of the regime. Two of the highest-ranking officers the Chancellor had, both now part of the rebellion. I can't decide if that makes me nervous or full of pride. I guess time will tell.

"I missed you, my girl," Jonah says, pulling me into a hug beside him as we walk to the village center.

"I missed you too." I mean it. I haven't stopped thinking about Jonah since we lost Enid. And I hope having Luca home eases his loss, even if just a little.

"How's Luca?"

"He is well. Went to Donterra to do recon and a head count. He is staying in the healer's shelter, so as to stay out of sight of the Guardians. His idea. Apparently, they don't bother the sick like they harass the village people. So that's his cover. But he should be home by the time I return."

"Nirri has just come from there. She was working with a friend of Harm's, Felicity. Flick, he calls her."

"Well, hopefully she will keep him out of sight if they do come around."

"I'm sure she will."

"Where is that adventurous friend of yours?" Jonah asks. Callian walks silently behind us.

"At archery training. She is getting great with a bow and arrow."

Callian walks off without a word, heading for the archery range. We reach the village center, where the space has been transformed, similar to the day Harm and I were Blended. Lanterns hang from every available point above us. Tables are in neat rows. Flowers from the forest line the center of each table.

The path between tables is lined with large forest leaves and fronds, like on the day of Catori's inauguration. At the end of the path sits a table with a handful of items, petals scattered around them, candles dotted between the items. I walk with Jonah and Christopher to Catori's house. I knock, and Mason pulls the door open a moment later.

We arrange ourselves on the cushions. Callian is already sitting on the floor. No Nirri. Jonah sits across from Harm and I, next to Mason and Catori. Christopher lounges in a chair near the window, staring out at the canopy. I almost forgot this is his first visit to the forest. I remember the awe and wonder of seeing this place for the first time.

"How is Fletcher reintegrating?" Jonah asks.

"Well enough. But we do have the issue of the mind control to deal with," Harm says.

"Enid told me of the process once. It is not pleasant," Jonah says. All eyes land on Mason.

"No, it's not," he says. "But it is worth it. At least in my opinion."

"Right. Well, as soon as we can, let's get that done for Daniel," Jonah says. Hearing him call my father Daniel is strangely comforting. As if we can leave the man Fletcher behind and have Daniel, the version we need and want, instead.

"Nirri can do it. I have spoken to her about it," Harm says.

Callian shakes his head, gaze burning into Harm's.

"So, let's make this quick; the ceremony starts in an hour," Catori says, throwing a glance to her brother, a warning to behave.

"Last count, we had enough men to match the current regime, just. But if Arthur pulls something last minute, the fight won't be in our favor," Christopher says.

Jonah nods.

"Right. Then we need to increase our numbers, along with our training and strategies," Harm says.

I watch as they talk tactics and numbers and lose track of the discussion, my mind wandering back to the women of the village who signed up to fight. They have their children back now. Are they still willing to fight? From what I can gather, the men here are not counting them in the final numbers anymore. If they were, we would outnumber the Guardians by around a hundred warriors.

"What about the women? We asked them to fight, they should still be able to do so, if they choose," I say over the chatter. The conversation halts, and everyone turns to me. "If we count the women who agreed to fight. We have enough."

"They have their children home now. That was when you were desperate, Imani," Christopher says.

"No, she's right. Arthur won't expect it. It gives us the numbers advantage and it would be a true revolution," Harm says.

"If we asked the women of the forest sector to fight and they agreed, why can't we ask the desert women also?" Mason asks.

"You are asking them to fight their sons and brothers. That isn't likely to happen," Jonah says, worry creasing his face.

"Who says they need to be killed? What about just uncon-scious long enough to give us the chance to get to Arthur and change the dial?" Catori says, more and more like her grandmother as the days pass.

"You are telling me that you are going to go into battle with the intent of not killing anyone?" Christopher snaps, his stare piercing Catori's. She sits, returning the gaze, unbending.

"Nothing about this is conventional. And Jonah is right, they are our brothers, cousins, sons. If we can spare them so they can recover after this is all over, we must at least try. The only person who must end up in the ground is Arthur," Harm says.

"You saved me and intend to save Fletcher; why not every boy and man that was taken against his will for the regime's sake?" Mason offers quietly. Catori leans into him.

"And I suppose you expect Nirri to work on every last one of them?" Callian breaks his silence.

"Maybe, maybe not. She can train a team of mind healers. It will be much quicker that way, and leave less chance for problems to arise," I say, feeling hope blossom in my chest. I think of the life Mason has had since he defected. There would be hundreds more like him, hundreds more who could be saved, could get to live a full life and make homes and families. Hundreds more who could be productive members of society. The chance to create a world where we all thrive seems a little closer right now.

Christopher takes in every face around him and grunts before standing.

Jonah watches him go before turning back to us. "The last two decades have been hard. For some more than others. I think you have a good plan. We take prisoners over killing outright—as many as we can without compromising the rebellion ranks. As for the women of the sands, if they understand they can bring their sons home, I think you will find a very willing audience. Luca, Christopher, and I can handle that part. But you are going to have to buy us another month to get around to every village."

"We can do that," Mason says.

"Right. First things first. Let's give our loved ones a proper farewell before we launch into another fight," Callian says.

"Agreed," I say, standing. I extend a hand each to Harm and Callian and they take them. I almost topple over from the boys pulling up to their feet.

Jonah chuckles. "This right here is what we are fighting for. Every single one of us. Our family."

"Damn straight," Callian says, punching Harm in the arm.

Mason rises to his feet with a breathy chuckle. "To our family." He wraps an arm around my shoulders and pulls Catori into his chest. Harm's laugh, so hearty, splits the air around us. I almost forget we are all gathered to say farewell to two of our most loved people.

Every last soul in the forest sector has filed into the village center. There are as many people here as there were for Hanola's funeral and Catori's inauguration. Miya was so very loved. My chest squeezes around my heart, banishing the breath from my lungs. Harm stands beside me, his arms around my waist, chin on my head. Chanting starts. Low, slow, and long, like the smoke that now drifts through the crowd of hundreds of forest people and a handful of desert dwellers here to say goodbye to Miya and Enid. He hugs me tighter as the first sob leaves my chest.

Catori stands at the front of the crowd, dressed in her traditional robes. The large amulet Hanola passed down to her hangs from her neck, bobbing on her chest with every breathy word she says as she remembers Miya. She talks of her bravery, her loyalty, her fighting skills, and her compassion for every single person she met. Tears stream down my face, and I grip Harm's hands tight in front of my waist.

Callian stands beside us with Nirri at his side, her face wet with tears. Callian shakes, his chest plummeting with every breath. Mason stands next to Catori, close. His face is twisted with pain as he watches her pull air into her lungs over and over, words clawing their way through her trembling lips.

"Miya was a warrior to the end. Her love and unwavering loyalty to her people was so strong. She will be missed, every day," Catori says. She lights the pyre to her right and steps back. The fire crackles and hisses, consuming the heady oils the rags are soaked with. Mason pulls her into a hug and kisses her forehead. She sobs into his chest.

Sobs and whimpers carry over the crowd as Jeselle stands and walks to where Catori just stood. She lays a green wreath of forest vines and flowers on the small table. Dropping to her knees, she grips the edge of the table and wails. Her pain, sharp like a dagger, weaves around every one of us and lingers. A warrior from Miya's team steps over to Jeselle and helps her stand, guiding her back to a seat at one of the long tables. She turns into his chest, loosing a long chain of whimpers. He rubs her back and holds her close.

Catori looks to Harm; it's his turn to speak about Enid. His hold tightens for a moment. I turn in his hold and cup his jaw with my hands. Tears flow down his face, his jaw feathering.

"Hey, where you go, I go," I whisper and he closes his eyes, nodding. I take his hands and lead him to the front of the crowd. He stops and turns to face the people. I pull in a ragged breath and stand beside him.

"Enid was the leader of the rebellion on the desert side," he begins, his grip steady on my hands. "She was a talented healer."

He freezes. His Adam's apple bobs, and he groans. I squeeze his hand, and he looks down at me, chin wobbling.

"She was a selfless woman who put others before herself always. That made her a great leader and an even better grandmother. She will be missed, by so many," he finishes and looks back at me.

"Miya and Enid," I say, raising my right hand over my heart, the way the forest people did at our Blending ceremony. Every last person raises their hand to their heart. Catori and Mason step up beside us. Mason slips his hand into Catori's. The chanting starts again; this time, it is a fast rhythm.

A happy farewell.

Our loss is their freedom.

Until the next life, Miya.

Until the next life, Enid.

I lead Harm back through the crowd, Mason and Catori following close behind. When we reach Callian, he is almost breathless. Nirri stands unmoving, her face broken as she watches him. Catori folds into her brother for a hug, and his arms move slowly around her as he drops his head to her shoulder. Jonah pulls Harm into an embrace, and they stay there for moments. They have both lost someone so special. Mason wraps me in a hug. "Dammit, Imani, this is hard," he whispers.

Callian untangles himself from his sister and moves to sit on the closest bench. He wipes his face with the backs of his hands. Nirri wanders over to where he sits. He raises his gaze to hers, and she hesitates before stepping closer. He grabs her around the waist and pulls her onto his lap. She sits rigid, staring into his sad eyes for a moment.

"Nirri," he chokes.

Her chin wobbles, but she stays where he put her. A minute later, Callian's head falls onto her chest, and she wraps her arms around his neck. "I'm so sorry, Callian," she whispers.

Each one of us watches the way those two need each other, fight for each other. It is torture waiting for them to make the choice to take what they both want so badly. Right now, I want more than anything for both of them to be happy. Life is far too short under this regime.

It would be devastating if they lost the chance when they could have had it so many times over already. Nirri's shoulders shake as Callian sobs into her chest. She looks so small with him wrapped around her. But she holds him tight through every pain-filled sob.

Catori stares at her brother for a moment then turns on her heel, heading for her home. Mason follows. And as the village center loses the crowd slowly, I wait for Jonah.

He finishes his conversation with one of the village men and turns back to me. His eyes are red and puffy. He wobbles on his feet as he reaches me.

"You should stay another few nights," I say.

He shakes his head. "We have to head back. Time is not on our side right now."

I snuggle into his chest, and he drops his head onto mine. "I love you, Imani."

"I love you too, Uncle Jonah."

"You never call me uncle." He chuckles as he tugs me into his side and walks with me to Catori's house, Harm by our side. I wish I could have done things differently. I wish I could have run with Enid instead of stopping to fight. I wish she wasn't gone. Now, because of the choices I made, the two people I love the most in the world have shattered hearts.

Heat prickles behind my eyes and I suck in a long breath to stave off the tears. We have to win this. Because I don't know how much more we can take before the people I love start falling apart at the seams.

CHAPTER 24
NIRRI

I sit close to Callian on Catori's floor littered with colorful cushions. They almost feel inappropriate right now. Callian takes shallow breaths. One last meeting before the men return to the desert side. If time had allowed, we would have waited another day. But time is as much our enemy as my grandfather is. The door opens, and we all look up. Fletcher enters with two forest warriors. They usher him to the cushions and retreat to the door. He sits on the floor beside Harm. His shackles clink as he adjusts his weight on the cushion. The irony is not lost on any of us.

"Take them off," Harm says.

The warriors look to Catori. She nods, and one of them steps over. Bending down, he unlocks the shackles and removes them from Daniel's wrists. His face, static and neutral, doesn't change as he rubs his wrists.

"Right, well. What are we waiting for?" Mason says.

"The plan so far: do another round of recon, this time including the desert women in the talks and numbers. Both sides will assemble for the battle in around a month's time. We change the dial and take out the Chancellor, trying to spare as many

Guardians as we can for rehabilitation." Catori's words are clear-cut, no emotion spared.

Daniel tilts his head. "You are going to try to win without killing officers?"

"That's the plan. We would rather try to rehabilitate the sons and brothers of the desert than murder them." Harm's voice is flat, but his eyes burn into Daniel's.

"That is very altruistic of you, but it's risky," Daniel says.

"It is a risk we think is worth it, if boys of the desert side that were taken can be spared and returned to their families," Mason says. I watch him stare down his former commanding officer.

"Fair enough. I am in no position to argue, considering what you are willing to do for me. But I do think there will be some that will be a problem for you. Don't give them the benefit of the doubt, or you will end up on the wrong end of their blade." Daniel searches Imani's face.

"We will be careful. Anyway, you will be with us. You will know who is worth saving and who is not worth the effort, Father," Imani grinds out. Her face is twisted between knowing and annoyance.

"Yes, I will. Any news on that front, Miss Nirri?" Daniel asks. Callian stiffens beside me, his hands balling into fists.

"Yes. I can start your rehabilitation tomorrow. But it is going to be hard for you; please know that."

"I am aware of what it takes," he says, his gaze briefly flickering to Mason.

"And Daniel, please call me Nirri."

He forces a smile and nods.

Callian uncurls his hands, and I slip one of mine into his. He turns to face me. The warmth in my chest settles low in my belly. I lean closer, our shoulders touching, and breathe him in. Heavens above, the things he does to me.

"What about the dial? When are you planning on changing that? Before or after Arthur?" Daniel asks, looking to Harm.

"We plan on doing that during the battle. Hopefully, he will be distracted enough that the majority of his men will be away from the tower. We change it, then we take out Arthur," Harm says.

"Solid plan, but why not wait until the battle is over?" Jonah asks.

"Contingency plan. If we fail, at least the dial has been altered. So even if he wins, he can't change it back. The weather will remain as I set it—back to normal patterns and seasons. The remaining people will have a fighting chance if they can grow crops and have viable work, not like it is now in the desert sector," Harm says.

"I like it; forward thinking," Christopher says. "You could also render the dial useless from that point, if you were willing."

"I'll consider that. There is a small risk that I will get the setting wrong. If I destroy it, it can't be changed again." Harm and Christopher hold their gazes steady, as if communicating something the rest of us aren't privy to.

"Well," I start, and every head turns to meet me, "you will need the power source to do any of that. We must get that first. Without it, you cannot change anything. The dial won't work."

"Callian and I can retrieve it," Mason says.

"It would be better if more of us went," I say.

"Why?" Imani asks.

"There are six crystals that make up the power source. You can activate it with only four, but six is optimal. And they are not small; each one is at least the size of Callian's arm." Every head glances to Callian's arm, his fingers still intertwined with mine. Heat rushes into my neck and face. I clear my throat.

"If six of us go, we can carry one back each. Even if..." I pause. I don't like my next words, but they have to be said. "Even if only four of us make it back, Harm can still change the dial."

"So bottom line, Harm and four of the crystals must make it back? Is that what you're saying, Nirri?" Daniel says.

"That's correct," I say. The words are steady, but my heart thunders in my chest.

"From my calculations on the time it took last time and the supposed location of these crystals, it will take us ten days to travel to the place where they are stored," Callian says.

"And ten days back. That's almost three weeks. That's cutting it fine before the rebellion assembles. If something goes wrong, we may only just make it back. Or we miss the fight, and the odds are even worse for our side," Mason says.

A string of knocks thunder at the door, and Catori jumps up to answer. Her two warriors move aside, clearing the space, and she opens the door. Three breathless warriors I recognize from one of the more northern forest villages stand panting just beyond the threshold. Catori's hands drop to her sides.

"What is it?"

"Movement at the tower and the barracks. It appears the Chancellor is readying for some sort of mass gathering. Maybe extending the regime in one big wave. But whatever he is doing, it doesn't look good. And the infrastructure he is assembling is big enough for a couple hundred more men."

The pit of my stomach flips and sinks. I swallow past the stone forming in my throat. A full-frontal attack. My grandfather used to tell me about war strategies. I studied them for half of my education. As if I would be the one ordering them when the time came, and not him. He is assembling now because his back is to the wall. Surely, he has realized by now that Daniel has joined the rebellion. The deaths of ten Guardians at the prison and the explosion that would have taken out tens more has only inflamed the situation, and the tipping point is coming. I can feel it. We are not ready. Where would he get another couple hundred men? The desert side is all but picked clean of able boys and men now. I don't like this one bit. I tighten my grip on Callian's hand, and he shifts beside me. My breath accelerates.

"We need to get that power source. And now," I growl.

"I agree. We should leave at first light," Imani says.

Harm looks at each of us. "Whatever is going on, it won't be pleasant. The sooner we get the power source and return, the better. If anything happens in the meantime, can you hold off the Chancellor?" He looks to Christopher.

"We can put a dent in his plans, if that's what you mean."

"Good, at least that will buy us some time. We should all get some sleep. We leave for the mountain wilds at first light," Catori says.

"I can start your rehabilitation when I return," I say to Daniel.

"What? Are you mad? The men on that side are barbarians!" Daniel's face is stricken.

"Is that what you call the men you shoved over the wall, Commander?" Mason spits.

"For the record, the Chancellor made those calls, not me. And you haven't seen what the natives are capable of over there."

"Imani and I returned from the mountain wilds just a few weeks back. Some of the men tossed out of the regime were less then amicable, but we made a few friends over there." Callian looks to Imani.

"Seb will be happy to see us, I'm sure," she drawls and Callian laughs. Some sort of private joke, no doubt. Whoever this Seb is.

"You were in the mountain wilds?" Daniel is staring at Imani now.

"Yes, Father." Imani rolls her eyes at him.

"It appears I have been underestimating my daughter," he utters.

"You think?" Catori snaps.

"My Luca was one of those that were tossed over the wall into the wilds, Daniel. You'd do well to remember they are our sons and brothers too," Jonah growls.

Daniel's gaze tracks to Jonah's face set in stone. "Sorry, there is a lot to take in. But I will help wherever I can."

"Good; that's settled. Now, time for some shut eye so these kids can run off into the mountains and get themselves into heaven knows what trouble tomorrow," Jonah says. He sucks in a breath and looks at Imani. "You just make sure you all come home. You hear me?"

Imani crawls to Jonah, smothering him in a hug. "We will be right back."

Daniel's gaze hits the floor as his jaw feathers. Hurt and regret flash in his eyes briefly.

Jonah pats Imani on the back and she releases her hold, returning to her spot next to Harm.

Mason stands and offers a hand to Daniel. He holds Mason's gaze for a moment before slapping his hand into his. We all stand, helping each other up before bidding our goodnights.

"Can I walk you home?" Callian asks.

"Sure."

We step into the cool night air and pad toward my house. I'm in no rush to return to my house. After today's events, half of me wants to curl up with Callian wrapped around me. The hour is late, and Marshall will be sound asleep by now. Callian stops, and I look up to see my front door.

"This is you," he whispers, moving into my space.

"This is me."

"Nirri, I—"

I press a finger to his lips. And it takes everything I have not to drag it down his neck and cover his mouth with mine. He chuckles, and the sound sends vibrations through my finger, through my hand, and into my chest. My breath turns ragged again.

"Remind me again why we do this?" he murmurs.

"Do what?"

"Fight every part of us that needs each other." His words have turned as patchy as my breath.

"We don't fight it. I fight it. It's just not the right time. I may not"—I lift my gaze to his, and it feels so heavy—"I might not be your best option."

Even now, the vicious words of my grandfather taint my thoughts. The unworthiness of my female existence.

Callian's head tilts to the side. "You can't be serious, Nirri."

"I—"

He grabs my arms, tilting his head lower to mine.

"No! I am done with the self-doubt and the *you deserve so much better* rubbish. I don't deserve better than you. You are the best thing I have ever had in my life. And it is ripping me apart watching you doubt yourself, watching you choose everything else except me. Dammit, Nirri! All I want is you! You're it for me. How—"

He turns away with a growl, then swings back around. My heart thunders in my chest. I grip the hem of my tunic with trembling hands.

"How am I not the right person for you?"

"I didn't say that," I utter. Sobs lodge in my throat.

"You didn't have to."

Callian stalks off into the darkness.

I hug my arms around my chest and stagger around to push through the door. Ripping my belt and boots off, I crash onto my bunk face down. I slam the pillow over my head and scream into the mattress. Marshall murmurs in his sleep but doesn't wake.

Dammit, what the hell is wrong with me?

I toss and turn, hating every word that has ever left my mouth.

Replaying every moment of my life that included Callian. The memory of him kissing me in the tower the day Mason and Imani came to infiltrate the tower sticks on repeat. His hands on my face. His lips on mine. His body against mine. The light in those blue eyes—hope, love, and longing. I roll over to study the ceiling. When my breath finally settles, I close my eyes and run through everything I would give him. Everything I plan to give him when all of this is over. If I can get past the worthlessness that has sunk into my soul from growing up with Arthur's constant taunts.

Finally, I let the night take me, falling into the dark depths of unconsciousness.

The tall, timbered, snow-lined ancient trees surround us in every direction. Imani walks beside me. Harm and Mason behind us, Callian and Catori in front. The stone building that shows signs of weathering sits unceremoniously between the frosty trees.

It's quiet.

Too quiet.

Mason sneezes again. Catori gives him a bothered look and Imani suppresses a giggle. Harm points to the doors, chained shut and locked with two padlocks. My grandfather's favorite mode of protection—locks and chains, if death isn't an option. The snow crunches under Callian's boots as he moves ahead of Catori slightly, shielding his sister from whatever is lurking in the blinding whiteness that covers everything.

I hear the whistle of the arrow before I see it. The sound multiplies. I rip an arrow from my own quiver and nock it. Callian throws up a fist and we halt. An arrow sails past to our left.

"Scatter and hide!" Catori yells.

A heartbeat later, arrows rain from the trees around us. Some bury in the snow up to their feathers, some lodge in trees. We cower behind the overgrown trunks and fallen logs until the arrows stop. Harm stands and surveys the treetops. No more arrows come.

"We need to get into that building, now!" Mason calls.

Callian stands and pulls both blades from his back. He takes off toward the building. Catori moves out of hiding and pulls her own twin blades, her back to her brother. Callian rushes the door, slamming a sword into the first lock. It shatters onto the icy ground at his feet. He takes out the other lock the same way. He turns back, waving us in. We move out from our hideouts and crunch through the snow, crossing the span between us and the building, Callian in front of it, smiling.

He sheathes his weapons and calls out to Harm. The whistle of an arrow stops me dead in my tracks. But I feel nothing. With slow movements, I track the sound. My gaze falls to Callian's face, and I watch as his smile fades. He looks down at the arrow lodged in his chest. His arms lift out from his sides as he hits the ground on his knees. Blood trails down his chest from the entry point.

"No!" I scream, snow flying from my boots as I scramble to where he kneels in the snow.

Red snow.

Leaching further around him with every heartbeat. My hands wander fanatically over his chest. Catori appears at my side.

With every second, Callian's face pales.

"Nirri," he gasps, hands gripping my arms.

"No! No! Please, Callian, no!"

I scream until I no longer recognize my own voice.

I jerk up in my bunk.

"No, no, no, no. Dammit," I choke through a ragged whisper. I toss the blanket from my body and run through the door, into the dim village center. Callian's house sits in the silence of the night, five houses down from mine. I run on bare feet to his door. I grip my tunic at my chest and push his door open. He is asleep on his bunk with only pants on. His shirt hangs over the chair beside his bed. I walk to the chair and look at the wooden seat. He breathes steadily beside me, his blond hair messy around his gorgeous face.

I sit on the bunk beside him, closing my eyes. But all I see is his stricken face, red snow around him. I choke back a sob, and he moves on the bunk beside me.

"Nirri?"

I open my eyes, and he sits up.

"What is it?"

"I can't lose you," I sob, tangling my fingers in my tunic.

He takes my hands and holds them in his. "You could never lose me." His words are thick, and he swallows.

"I could. We could lose each other before we even have a chance to—"

He presses his forehead to mine. "No one is losing anyone. I'm sorry I snapped at you."

"Don't be, I deserved it."

"Nobody deserves or doesn't deserve anything; there is just what is. And what is, is the fact that I can't live without you. Even if you never feel the same way I do, I couldn't bear to not have you in my life. If friends is all we can be, then friends is good enough for me."

"Callian," I utter.

I don't want to be just his friend. I look at Harm and Imani and Mason and Catori, and that is what I see for us too. But how do we get there when I second-guess everything I am and do? I search his face, like the answer is written across his jaw, his wide smile, his burning blue eyes.

"All I want to do is kiss you," I whisper.

His hands cup my face, and he covers my mouth with his. My body all but goes limp. A heartbeat later, I run my hands up his neck and through his hair.

Worthless girl.

Just a burden to everyone who ever bothers with you.

I suck in a breath and jerk backward at the memory of my grandfather's words.

"What's wrong?" Callian whispers, confusion filling his eyes, darkened with everything he wants right now.

"I'm sorry, I can't." I shuffle off the bunk and stagger backward.

"Nirri, please don't do this. Just talk to me."

I sob and fly out the door. The cool grass of the training area covers my feet as I stalk in circles, pulling at my hair. Pain aches through my scalp as I try to rationalize the thoughts and memories that haunt me, that have haunted me since I was thirteen years old. The day my grandfather discovered I couldn't manipulate the dial was the day I lost his respect and his adoration. I guess I never had it all along. I was just a means to his ends. Just like he was going to entrap Harm to turn the dial for him for the next two decades.

But Harm told me he couldn't turn the dial until he was eighteen. My grandfather mustn't have known that if he tried it when I was only thirteen. So maybe now I can? Eighteen for me was just a few months ago. I could be Harm's backup plan if he can't get to it, or worse. I push back the horrible thought of another one of my friends dying and stop dead in my tracks.

Callian stands at the edge of the training area, arms crossed over his still bare chest, watching me. I walk to where he stands and push my shoulders back. "Goodnight, Callian." I walk past him, and lose no time getting inside, slipping under my covers, and dumping the pillow over my head.

The next thing I know, the dawn's light is poking under my tired, half-closed eyelids. I swing out of bed and toss clothes and weapons into my rucksack. I walk to Marshall's bunk and tousle his hair with one hand. He opens his eyes, blinking at me.

"I'll see you in a few weeks," I say, smiling.

He sits up and pulls me into a hug. "Be careful, okay?"

"I will." I straighten as he releases me, and I wander out the door. Harm, Imani, Mason, Catori, and Callian stand on the other side of the training area, ready to go. I jog to where they stand and bid them good morning. Imani hands me a chunk of bread and cheese.

"Morning, Nirri," Catori says.

Callian stares at me, the heat in his gaze sending a prickle up my spine.

Every one of my friends—I guess they are more like my family—watches as Callian and I exchange awkward greetings.

He shoulders his rucksack. "Right, let's move," Callian snaps.

This is going to be a long three weeks.

CHAPTER 25
HARM

I love my brother, I really do, but he is a stubborn ass sometimes. Nirri and Callian have been at each other's throats for half the trip so far, the other half refusing to speak to each other. Imani has rolled her eyes at them so many times, I'm pretty sure she's made herself dizzy. And, to be honest, my patience with both of them is wearing thin.

Six days of tension is getting to all of us. Catori refuses to get involved. I understand that. Those two are usually the happiest, most optimistic two out of the six of us and right now, they are hell to live with. Nirri is absolute with her resolve of not letting anyone help her, saying she won't be a burden and can make her own way. Callian watches with a pained face as she clambers over logs and through freezing water, too stubborn to step in and help. Or maybe he is just giving her the space she asked for. Either way, it is killing him.

Mason is the only one who doesn't seem to be bothered by them. Maybe it's because he grew up with rough parents, or maybe he knows it's just a patch they have to go through before they figure it out. Either way, I wish I had his calm. It is entirely possible that I am too close to the pair of them. Callian is the closest thing I have had to a sibling in a long time. And Nirri reminds me of Amaya so much, with her curly blonde hair and fierce independence.

"Right, that's far enough for today," Catori says as we file into a small clearing between the trees. I check the map and estimate the distance we have traveled by the landmarks high around us, only just visible through the dense forest. Six days of traveling. I run a finger across the map. The mountain range in front of us marks us at almost halfway. We are too slow. At this rate, it will take us more than three weeks to get there and back. And we don't have that kind of time.

Imani drops onto a fallen log, groaning as she stretches her lower back and neck. Another two logs border the small makeshift fireplace in the snow. Mason and Catori claim one, leaving one for Callian and Nirri to share. Or Maybe Callian and me. I doubt Nirri will sit with him at this point.

Nirri hovers at the edge of the clearing, waiting for everyone to sit. Imani glances at Callian's face of stone and pecks me on the cheek before rising and walking over to where Callian sits on the log. She dumps her rucksack at his feet and drops onto the log, nudging him with her shoulder. Nirri makes her way to where I am and sits on the fallen tree trunk beside me. Mason kneels by the fireplace indent in the ground, brushing away the snow. Catori disappears. I pull out my canteen and guzzle water. Even with the extreme cold, we are still becoming parched. The air is crisp, and we sweat under our many layers despite the freezing temperature.

Nirri hunts through her rucksack, pulling out a rolled-up parchment. "Here. We can study the dial while we travel to save time."

I take the paper from her and unroll it on my lap. She leans closer and points to the array of foreign symbols. "These are the elements the dial controls. By selecting the right combination, you can reset the entire mechanism to either one weather pattern or to the naturally occurring ones. See here"—she points to a wavy circle —"this here is a high wind pattern. If it is chosen with the wriggly lines with the angled line through it, that makes desert conditions. No rain, all wind."

I stare at the chart, stunned by the way the elements of the weather are just symbols on an ancient stone dial, free for anyone with the ability to mess with. To mess with the lives and livelihoods of everyone in that sector. It's insane. That is far too much control for any one man or woman to have.

"How do we get the dial to reset to the naturally occurring seasonal patterns across each sector?"

"You must choose all four symbols at once. That is the way the dial was originally set. When my grandfather messed with it, his ability was not strong enough to manipulate more than two elements at one time. Hence, we are stuck with either too much rain or none at all in the three sectors."

"You're telling me Arthur had no idea what he was doing, and he did it anyway?"

"Pretty much. The more I learned about the dial in my studies, the more I realized he didn't understand. It was reckless and arrogant of him to touch it in the first place. But that sums up my grandfather to the mark."

"You would have made one hell of a Chancellor, Nirri."

She smiles but shakes her head. "No one person should have total control; that's never going to be in the best interest of the people. You and Catori should lead. You were both born to do it."

"So were you," I say, watching her gaze.

"I doubt that. I was just another pawn in my grandfather's hideous plans."

"You are like a sister to me, Nirri. You know that right?"

"I do. You already feel like my big brother. You have ever since that night in the forest when Elijah—"

Callian tosses a stick larger than his arm into the fire. Embers shoot into the air above us. His gaze pierces Nirri's. That night, when she ran away, convinced she didn't belong with us, Elijah found her before Callian and I did. I still remember the terror in her eyes, and the rage in Callian's, as Elijah tried to force himself onto her. He is lucky Callian didn't snap his pathetic neck right there and then.

I wrap an arm around her, and she lays her head on my shoulder. "I will always be here for you. We all will," I say, the lump in my throat almost strangling my words.

Catori breaks the moment. "How is our progress?"

I sit up straighter. "It could be better. We aren't even halfway, and we have used half of our quota of days already."

Nirri sits up and rolls up the parchment, sliding it back into her rucksack.

"Can we make up time somehow?" Mason asks.

"Well, if we head straight over the mountain ridge instead of going around like we originally planned, we will cut off two days of travel, getting us back on schedule. But—"

"So, we do that then," Callian snaps.

"It is a much harder trek, brother." I track his gaze and catch it with mine, holding firm. "The shorter path leads us closer to the first savage camp. That is more potential for setbacks and more risk."

"We can manage it," Imani says.

"It's decided, then. We go straight over," Catori says.

"Up and over," I say. But the weight in my gut twists as I look around our small circle. Each one of these people is my family. The shorter way is much more treacherous. For more than one reason.

And for the first time on this cold, frigid trek, the feeling of unease settles into my core.

The ledge above me spits a shower of snow and dirt as Nirri finds her footing. The straight path we chose has us climbing up steeps and scaling almost cliff-like rocky patches. Callian took the lead a few hours ago. I am the rear, on constant look out for savages and anything else that may decide we're fine prey. The mountain lions Imani told me about cling to the front of my mind with every shaky, unstable step I take upward. The sooner this part of our journey is over the better. The thought of having to go this way home and scale down these patches sends my gut plummeting. And pulls up the memory of Imani falling in the crevice back in the sands when we were running from Mason and Fletcher.

Daniel.

He is Daniel now.

A hiss leaves Nirri as she readjusts her grip around a sharper rock, propelling herself up the face of the mountain. A second later, Callian calls from the top of the ridge, bending down to help up Mason, then Catori, then Imani. Nirri reaches the top and he holds out his now-red and calloused hand. She ignores him, scrambling over the edge.

"Nirri," he growls.

She ignores him, swinging her legs up onto the edge. Pushing up on her arms, she rolls onto the top of the ledge by his feet. He steps back and offers his hand again. She pushes to her feet, brushing off her trousers and tunic, and stalks past him. His jaw feathers as he closes his eyes briefly, with a low breath. I reach the top and grab his hand. He pulls me up and over the edge.

"Thanks, brother."

"At least someone will let me help them," he grumbles.

I choke out a laugh as Imani checks me over. She steps between my legs and pulls me to my feet. I slide a hand behind her neck and kiss her forehead. She hugs into my chest. Her skin is cold, and I run my hands over her neck before cupping both her cheeks with my hands. She leans into my touch and a moan rumbles from her throat.

"You are so warm. How is that fair?" she murmurs.

"I will happily warm you up once we find camp," I whisper in her ear, and she laughs before nipping my ear. Her hands drop and curl around the opening of my fleece-lined coat.

"I'll see that you keep that promise, Harmen Travesci."

I can't help the wide smile that stretches over my face. She dots a kiss onto my lips before slipping away to follow the others. I track after her, my center much warmer than before. The way I respond to even her lightest touch, that will never change.

By the time the light starts to fade, Mason and Catori are mulling about making the start of a small fire. The wind on the top of the ridge is erratic and frigid. Snow drifts on its tumultuous waves, plastering everything in its path with powdered white. Imani shivers beside me, and I tuck her in close.

"Maybe we should go deeper into the forest to get out of this wind. You're never going to get a fire started in this," I say.

Mason grumbles in assent and gathers up the firewood Catori just dropped by his side. We stalk through the timbered surroundings until the forest thickens enough to block most of the wind's brutal assault. The light almost gone, we stumble across another clearing, slightly larger than the last, and settle onto the forest floor, huddled away from the wind. Catori makes short work of the fire and has a blaze going in no time. My body aches from more climbing than I would have liked, and Imani lays her blanket out for us to recoup on. I lie beside her and pull out the fleecy blanket I brought, throwing it over the both of us. I am far too exhausted to be hungry and wrap Imani in my arms, pulling her up against my chest before closing my eyes. She shivers against my body for an age before she finally settles, and her breathing slows. Mason and Catori are tucked in tight like we are. Callian rolls out his bedding and huddles under his fleece. Nirri sits by the fire, poking the coals, watching the embers float to the canopy above her. She pulls her coat around her neck tighter with one shaky hand and drops her face into the fleecy opening. Her teeth chatter.

Callian watches her, a frown plastered over his face. "Nirri, come and get warm."

"I'm fine," she utters through chattering teeth.

"Suit yourself," he says rolling over and giving her his back. Why he doesn't just pick her up and wrap her in his blankets, I'll never know. We all know he wants to. They both do. Whatever has them constantly going around in this cycle of hostility must really be something. I have never seen them *both* angry at each other for more than a few hours, let alone for days.

I grumble into Imani's hair and close my eyes. When Imani's face is finally warm, I loosen my hold around her. She rolls away slightly, and I let sleep drag me under.

Smoke twists around my blurry vision. My right side is warm, still under the blanket. To my left, the blanket is folded back. The space beside me is empty. Cold. Snow coats everything around us, including the snuffed-out fire. I shiver and sit up. Mason and Callian are still asleep. Nirri and Catori are gone as well. The girls are up early. I clear my throat and shuffle closer to the fire. Mason wakes, rubbing his face with both hands. He startles and swings side to side, panic flooding his face.

"Catori? Where's Catori?"

My stomach flips.

"What do you mean? They must have got up early. Probably off looking for breakfast."

Mason twists in his blankets before stumbling to stand. He bends down and scoops up a belt of weapons. "Without their weapons?"

His stricken gaze finds mine. A stone lodges in my throat. I search the area behind me. Imani's weapons and wrap are still where she put them down. My heart thunders in my chest.

I jump up and rush to Callian, shaking him awake.

"Okay, okay, I'm awake already." His jovial tone falls flat when his eyes meet my face.

He bolts up. "What? What happened?" He flings the blankets from his body and twists back and forth, searching.

"They're gone." I shove my hands through my hair, turning in a tight circle. "The girls. They're gone!"

A tangled moan rips from Mason's chest. He wanders the perimeter of the campsite looking as panicked as I feel.

"Dammit!" Callian grinds out.

"We shouldn't have come this way," I snap. Swaying on my feet, I search the faces of my brothers. We stand frozen for a moment.

Callian's face turns to pure thunder. He rips his weapons from the ground, slapping them on faster than I have ever seen before. "Mason, track them. Now!"

CHAPTER 26
CATORI

Imani shivers, hanging by the wrists from to pole to my right, Nirri to my left. The clothes we were sleeping in are far from enough to stave off the cold. We shiver so violently that I'm sure each of us has injuries from just hanging here. Both Nirri and Imani are still out; whatever our captors used to render us unconscious is still affecting them. The village in front of me is nothing like I have seen before.

The people, mostly men, are dressed in furs, weapons dangling from their waists. The smell of rotting innards from a recent kill tangles in the air that blows from the south, behind me. The air is thin, just like at our camp last night. So we can't have come too far.

Smoke plays around the rough-built huts, where a handful of women and children alike work, preparing the limp bodies of the latest slaughter. Some work with knives, shaping wood for whatever they are building. From where we hang, I make out that we are on the southern edge of the village. Not much lays behind us, save a few smaller huts and the waste piles. A mangled body sits on the top of the pile.

Nobody in the village pays us heed—not the men, not the

women, not even the children. Either having outsiders strung up is a regular occurrence, or someone has these people locked down with severe punishments for disobedience.

Imani stirs beside me. Her eyes fly open as she twists where she hangs, fighting at the ropes that bind her.

"Imani. Shhhh. Don't draw attention."

Her gaze snaps to mine and her face screws up briefly. "What the hell happened?"

"Somehow, they dragged us here. Who knows what for. But I doubt it's for anything good." I nod to the pile of dead remains behind us.

"Nirri," I whisper. Her head hangs, arms stretched above her. She jerks awake, whimpering as fear floods her face. She whips side to side like a harried animal in a trap before her gaze finds mine and she settles.

"Cator—"

"Shhhh." I tilt my head toward the village center where people mill about their daily existence in this rotting place as if we don't exist, strung up on the poles.

"How did they take us without the boys waking up?" Imani asks.

"Maybe they knocked them out too. I don't know. But I do know we are not going to wait around for whatever it is they have planned for us."

"How do we get down?" Nirri says.

I work the rope around my wrists back and forth over the iron loop holding me up. The fibers burn my wrists with every pass. Imani does the same, pushing her feet flat against the pole for support. We hang, running our ropes across the loops until the burn turns to a sting and the tang of blood reaches my senses. I groan and look up. Blood trickles down both my wrists. I clench my jaw tight and keep going.

A ruckus from the village center sees the three of us freeze where we hang. Four men, dressed in furs with weapons hanging off their hips, swagger toward us. Imani curses. I tilt my head up and pull in a long breath. They stop a foot in front of the posts, studying each of us. The man in the center moves to Nirri before wandering past me and then Imani. He turns on his heel and faces the younger man now in front of Imani.

"Which one will it be lad?" The older man grunts before a smirk wraps across his face.

The younger lad stares at all three of us in turn before shifting his gaze back to the older man. "The curly-headed one." His gaze moves up and down Nirri's body slowly, from head to toe. My stomach turns, a sick feeling clawing up my throat. The way his eyes darken as he takes in Nirri's curves, pausing at her chest and wandering across her face, tells me more than I want to know.

"She will make a fine hedge wench, son. Good choice. The men will be happy," the older man says, turning back for a brief glance between Imani and me as he leaves with his son. The other two men move into Nirri's space. She kicks at them, and they laugh at her.

"Leave her alone!" I scream at them.

Imani is working her ropes like her life depends on it. It most likely does.

"Shut up, woman, or you'll be next. And we will leave your pretty, dark-haired friend for last."

Nirri's terrified gaze meets mine. "Catori," she chokes.

The man to her left slices through her ropes with a blade, and she falls into the groping arms of the man in front of her. She struggles and screams. Imani bucks on the post, blood trickling down her arms. I tug at the ropes, hoping the knotted twine will snap.

It doesn't.

Grunting, I work the rope fast. It splits a little and I pick up the pace.

Nirri is screaming as she is dragged between the two men toward the main hut on the opposite side of the village. The woman and children don't look up from their tasks. Their heads remain down. Their hands keep up the pace of whatever they were doing before Nirri started screaming. My heart flips against my ribs.

Hedge wench.

They intend to use her for their own release. One after the other.

The disgusting thought has bile sliding up my throat. Nirri would be terrified and hurting. The damage to her mind would be irreversible. If they intend to let her live after.

Callian would be devastated.

Imani stills. "Catori, what the hell is a hedge wench?"

I study her face and her expression moves to match my pained one. "The men take turns. With her body."

Imani's breath turns ragged. "Dammit." She pulls down hard on her ropes. Her hands turn pink, then white. Tears fall down her face. I do the same, and we wrestle with our bonds until the sunlight starts to fade over the horizon. I stop, straining to listen to what is happening in the village, trying to hear anything from the main hut. But everything seems quiet. I haven't heard any screaming since they took Nirri away.

Please let her be untouched.

Unhurt.

Imani's head thuds against the pole behind her. Her eyes are closed and her chin wobbles. "For once, why can't something just go as planned? Why does everything have to end up with someone we love getting hurt? I am so sick of this!" A low, raw groan rumbles from her chest and she yanks on her wrists, harder than she should.

I look up at my own fraying ropes. I need more weight. I drop my feet from the small wooden platform under my feet. The rope bites into my wrists and I grind out a whimper. Using my entire body strength, I grab the ropes at my wrists and saw from side to side, swinging with every movement.

The light is almost gone and the firepit in the center of the village roars and crackles as children toss more timber into the waiting fiery jaws of the hellish, growing flames. The rope on my peg creaks. I swing harder.

Snap!

I plummet to the frigid, hard ground. Wind leaves my lungs, and I struggle to my feet and gasp to get a solid breath. Without waiting for the burn in my lungs to subside, I climb up to Imani's ropes and try to untie them. The knots are so tight from her pulling on them I can't get it to budge.

"There is a knife in my boot," she whispers. Hope fills her dirt-covered face, now littered with the tracks her tears carved. I reach into the boot she wiggles at me and find the small hilt with my fingers. I pull it out and look back to the village. No one seems to have noticed. If they have, they haven't bothered to alert anyone. I slide the blade under the rope around her wrist and slice it in two. Her arm drops by her side, and she shakes it. I release her other wrist, and we drop onto the freezing ground and duck behind a group of bushes. Time is not our friend right now.

"We need to get into that main hut and sneak Nirri out and then run like hell," I say.

"Agreed."

I stalk around the side of the shrubbery and creep, bent over, to the first hut. We flatten ourselves against the home. Voices drift through the slightly cracked window. There are about a dozen makeshift huts between us and the main hut. We make it past five huts before the commotion starts.

"Hell." The word is a choked whisper.

"Faster," Imani hisses.

I pick up the pace, leaving caution on the hard, cold ground behind us. Men pour out of their homes and into the village center. We lean against the wall of the last hut before the main one and watch as they hurry to the empty poles.

"Time is up," I snap.

Imani nods and we round the hut, filing into the main building. Nirri sits huddled in the corner of the large room, her wrists and ankles bound, a gag around her mouth. That's why I didn't hear any screaming. My stomach plummets. Imani rushes to her side and I lean against the door, keeping watch. The yelling is still moving away from us. Imani rips another blade from her other boot and releases Nirri with two quick moves. Nirri rips the gag from her mouth and flies into Imani's hold. Imani hugs her tight for moment before pulling her toward the door.

I lean out to check the area. A blade hits the wooden wall beside me, missing my face by mere inches. I duck back inside.

"How are we going to get out?" Nirri's voice is strained.

Imani searches for another exit, finding nothing. "We can't fight our way out without weapons." I look around the hut for anything to fight with. There isn't anything useful. Hand-to-hand is not my strength. Miya was always so good at that; I was mediocre at best. The doorway darkens as the large frame of the older man from before fills the space. Three men file in behind him. The annoyance on his face turns to amusement when he takes in the three of us standing in what I presume is his hut.

"Well, isn't this a convenient turn of events. Look at this, boys! Not only do we have one wench—we now have three!"

My hands ball to fists by my sides. If I could just get a weapon, this would all be over very quickly. Imani steps up beside my right. Nirri flanks my left. The men laugh at us in unison. The blood in my body turns to thunder.

"And what do you three think you're going to be able to do against the four of us?"

"Why don't you give me a weapon and find out?" I hiss.

"Not likely," he snaps and nods toward Nirri. The three men behind him move to where she stands and grab her. She struggles against them, and a fist strikes her cheek. She stumbles on her feet, blinking before the tears fill her eyes.

"What do you want with us? You have plenty of women of your own to harass," I grind out.

"It's how we welcome outsiders in these parts of the mountains. You really shouldn't have ventured this far north," he growls, stepping into my space. His unwashed body is inches from me. His dank breath lands on my face.

"Get out of my space, you filthy ingrate."

"Oh lass, it's my space now." He inches closer and shoves a thin stick between his teeth, chewing on it as his gaze drifts to my chest and then to my waist.

I step back and he steps forward again. Another step backward. He steps forward.

His eyes light up. "I am more than happy to chase you, lass."

My heart flings against my ribs.

"Don't you dare touch any of us. Or it will be the last thing you and your pathetic posse do," Imani snaps.

Her back is to the wall just behind me. The man steps closer to me again, and my back hits the wall. They have Imani and me cornered. I track my gaze to where Nirri stands in the grip of the men. Her head is held high, but her hands tremble, balled into fists. She is terrified, and they haven't even done anything to her yet. I close my eyes, sifting through every tactic and strategy Miya ever taught me. Hand-to-hand is the only option I have left until I can get my hands on a weapon. Maybe if I play along, I can get close enough to the man to rip one from his belt. At least then I will stand a chance. We all might.

I push back the stone that has lodged in my throat and wait for the twisting in my gut to settle. I open my eyes and study the older man's stubble-covered face, his hazel eyes still wandering over my face. His hands land on either side of my head, and he leans closer until his face is almost touching mine. He turns quickly and spits the stick onto the floor. I tilt my head slightly and allow him to lower his face to my neck. I close my eyes again and Mason's gorgeous face is all I see. I force myself to stay where I am.

"Catori," Imani chokes.

I let my gaze settle on hers, and she stills. He groans and presses his body onto mine. I suppress the shudder when a prickle runs up my spine and I press my shaking hands flat onto the wall behind me. I pull up every happy memory I have of Mason and me, turning them over in my mind to stave off the panic that is writhing up my body. Every second longer in his revolting grip loosens his guard around me. Every second I wait buys me a better chance. He tugs at my blonde hair and releases it from the cloth I had wrapped around it. It falls around my shoulders and he groans again, pushing me against the wall.

After a moment of flattening me into the timber he moves away and pulls in a long breath. "Come with me, lass."

I hesitate.

All I want to do right now is be curled up in my bed at home with Mason around me.

Imani's gaze turns feral.

Nirri gasps. "No, Catori."

I push off the wall and drag my stare from Imani. I imagine I look much calmer than I feel. I move on shaky legs to follow the man to a space with a pile of furs and blankets. He nods to the blankets, but I don't move. My breath is so erratic, every one too shallow, and my lungs burn. I just need to go far enough that I can get to his weapons.

He palms the front of his trousers and nods to the pile of blankets again. This time bile makes it into my mouth.

"Now, lass. Or all three of you will be back on that pole."

I take a step forward. His belt holds two daggers and one curved blade. Whatever he uses that for, I don't want to imagine. So vicious. He pulls the curtain across behind me and loosens his trousers. They slip to his knees.

"On your knees, lass."

"Which way?"

"Facing me first."

I hold back the whimper that wants out of my tight throat and kneel in front of him. His weapons dangle in my face as he frees himself and shoves his hardness toward my face. I wince and jerk back, and his hand slaps my face.

The sting burns.

I press my shaking palm to my cheek and drag in a long breath. He fists my hair and I close my eyes. Mason's wide smile pops into my head and I choke out a sob.

"Hold it and get on with it."

I raise my hands. They tremble. I push my shoulders back. The daggers on both sides of his belt only hang by twine. I grab both blades and tug, hard.

He teeters forward. "No, you don't!"

I toss the blades in my hands and rise to my feet, taking a step back. He grapples with his pants before reaching for the curved blade. "You stupid little bitch!"

I wink at him.

His face turns sour as he realizes he was played. Heaven knows that was far too close for comfort. Just thinking about where I was moments ago makes my stomach drop.

"Now, you have two choices. You can let us all go, or I will chop it off."

He grinds out a curse and lunges for me, blade swinging.

I meet his curved blade with both of mine. I spin mine on his, knocking it out of his grip, and it hits the floor to his right. He bends down to pick it up and I move into his space to press both blades to his neck. "Bad idea."

He shoulders me and I stagger backward, tripping on the pile of blankets. I tumble backward, landing of the softness. Before I have time to roll away, he lands on top of me, a knee on either side, his curved blade now against my throat.

Dammit.

A scuffle starts in the main area. The curtain is ripped back. Mason stands wide-eyed and furious beside the hanging cloth. "Get off her!"

The older man startles and I shove a fist into his nose. He flails backward, blood running down his chin. I roll off the blankets and fly into Mason's arms. He wraps them tight around me, dropping his head into my neck. "Don't ever do that to me again." His words are wobbly. His whole body trembles. I look over his shoulder. Harm is holding a man against the wall as Imani dons her weapons beside him.

Callian stands in the doorway with both swords drawn. He stares at the men still holding Nirri. *Hell, brother.* This is going to get ugly by the look of complete and utter rage on his face. He stalks toward where they stand with their hands around Nirri's arms, one holding her head back by her hair, a blade against her neck. One man starts to shake his head and releases Nirri, stepping away from her with his hands in the air.

Callian pays him no heed.

"Back off, boy," the man at Nirri's side snaps.

"Let. Her. Go."

"We don't take orders from you, pup."

"Too bad." Callian sheathes both blades and rips a dagger from his chest, lodging it into the retreating man's chest on Nirri's left. He drops and hits the ground face-first. The blade against Nirri's neck digs in further as the man holding it stands taller. He takes a step backward, dragging Nirri with him.

She whimpers softly.

Callian's face turns to stone.

Nirri's captor is a dead man.

Callian pulls another dagger from his chest and throws it into the man's leg. He screams but holds his ground. Callian pulls another dagger. It buries deep in the man's upper arm. The grip on his blade slips, and Nirri steps out of his hold. Callian pulls his swords from their sheaths with a long, cruel whine. The man holds his hands up in an X, shading his face, the dagger in his arm wobbling as he shakes from head to toe.

"Put your arms down," Callian says, words like ice.

The man lowers his trembling arms.

Fool.

Callian raises both blades in an X formation. A second later, the man's head hits the floor. The older man behind me starts murmuring something. His murmurs turn to yelling.

"Time to leave," Harm says.

Imani grabs Nirri, pulling her out the door after Harm. Mason and I follow. Callian stands for a moment before spinning and stalking after us. Tens of men run toward the main hut. The older man inside is still yelling, cursing, and crying out in a language I don't recognize. We clear the village and sprint into the forest. After half an hour or so of running through the thick, harsh mountain woods, we stop. Scratched up and out of breath in this thin air, we huddle around a pile of rucksacks. The moon is high in the sky, the cries of the mountain lions echoing in the distance. We are in no position to slow down now. Mason hands out the rucksacks. I help Nirri buckle on her quiver and weapons belt.

"Thank you," she utters, her eyes locked on my brother. He meets her gaze, and his jaw feathers. He moves out. We make a line following him and trek through the timber toward the north, knowing full well we just made another enemy.

CHAPTER 27

MASON

The building stands ancient and proud amongst the woody timbers with a slight clearing around it, dense debris bordering every side. The entrance is boarded up by wooden planks nailed into stone. The tree line flanking us on either side is still.

Too still.

Not even the birds make a sound. The dawn's light pokes over the horizon to our right. Exhausted and on edge, the six of us stand trembling from the abysmal cold, just staring at yet another obstacle. We have come this far. All any of us want to do is go home.

Callian moves, and Catori throws her fist in the air, ordering him to hold his position.

"Something feels off, even for this place," Imani whispers.

Knots tie frantically in my gut. She's right. Everything about this feels wrong. I study the spaces between the timber trunks, searching for anything that would pose a threat. Nothing moves. Not in the undergrowth, not under the canopy. Catori lowers her hand, and Callian moves forward, blades drawn. Harm follows his lead, trailed by Nirri and Imani. Catori steps out of the tree line with me and we move with slow steps, constantly scanning the trees around the small clearing. Harm walks up the three stone steps and onto the landing. Pulling his sword from his back, he slams it between the wood and the stone building, tugging backward. The timber splinters but doesn't budge. I pull the sword from my back and slam it into the other end.

"One, two, three!" Harm says. The board breaks in half, and we make quick work of the four remaining. The double doors that had been barred for protection all but fall from their hinges as I shove my hand into them. Dust and cobwebs tumble from the doors, and we step inside. Inside sits a wooden rack in the center of an otherwise empty room. No windows stud the grimy, dark walls. The ceiling is lower than it appeared from outside, and Harm ducks to get to the center of the room. I crouch and follow him, scanning the area for any signs of booby traps or items left behind. The crate, held together with metal straps, is covered in layers of dust—years' worth, from what Nirri tells us.

I lean down and blow the dust away. Instantly, my lungs are full of the filthy stuff. I cough, waving a hand in front of my face, like that will help me breathe. The dust settles around my feet, and Harm continues to wipe away the rest of it with both hands.

"It's like the treasure in the books Amaya and I used to read at night." He chuckles softly and runs a hand over the opaque white crystals. Nirri was right about another thing—they are big. I'd say slightly bigger than Callian's forearm, if I was to go by her method of measurement.

"We need to get these apart and hand them around. One is all we will each be able to carry back over that sharp terrain," Harm says, pulling on the latch that has held the crate together for so long. The rusted metal all but crumbles in his hands, and he flings it off the wood. The crystals shake, falling without their metal stays. I grab two before they tumble and smash on the floor. Harm stabilizes the last four with both hands. I shove one in my rucksack and one in his before taking another two. We exit the eerie building, loaded with crystals. Callian and Catori meet us at the door, and I shove a crystal in each of their waiting hands. Imani and Nirri stand watching the perimeter, weapons drawn. Imani holds both fighting knives, while Nirri has an arrow nocked, her bow strung tight.

We hear shrill calls. Before we can locate the source, arrows rain down around us. Imani screams, "Run!"

The swishing sounds thud into the ground all around me. Harm sprints beside me, eyes firmly on Imani. I track Catori, who runs beside her brother, both swords drawn. Imani and Nirri clear the tree line and into the dense forest before the rest of us make it to the center of the clearing. Imani spins back, screaming for Harm to hurry. Catori and Callian slam through the trees after them, arrows barely missing them. The breath in my lungs burns, heart smacking against my ribs erratically as Catori dodges an arrow to her left. She spins back and scans the space between me and her.

An arrow sinks into my upper leg and blinding heat turns to pain. I lose my grip on the crystal in my hands and plow knees-first into the debris-covered ground.

Catori screams. The painful sound rips through the trees.

Harm is by my side in seconds, heaving me to my feet. He pulls my arm over his shoulders, and I limp as fast as I can. Another arrow finds my shoulder and I hiss through a groan.

"Dammit," Harm grinds out.

I shove the crystal into his chest. He shakes his head, pulling me along faster. A moment later, Catori is under my injured shoulder.

"Go, you two! Take the crystal," I rasp.

"Not happening, brother," Harm says.

Catori doesn't speak, her face set in stone.

We reach the tree line without another arrow poking holes in my half-limp body. The pain in my leg is agony. The arrow in my shoulder bobs with every step. I clench my jaw tight. The ground sways under my feet, and I am lowered to the ground. Nirri's blonde curls bounce around my periphery as something tugs at my leg. Fire rips through my thigh. A half-muffled scream rips through my lips. Two hands wrap around my face. The blurry outline of Catori's sweet face moves in and out of focus.

"Hey, don't you bleed out on me, Mas," she whispers, her hands trembling around my cheeks. "Nirri is fixing things. You will feel better very soon."

The stick in my leg moves, tugging upward. My mouth waters and bile burns my throat, choking out my shallow breaths. Catori curses and tilts my head to the side. Warm liquid spills from my lips. Another burning tug and warmth gushes over my thigh. A moment later, firmness takes over, wrapping around my leg. The burn peters out to a throb.

"The bleeding should stop now. But he lost a fair bit of blood," Nirri says.

"What about the shoulder arrow?" Harm asks.

Nirri's hands move from my leg to my shoulder. "I can pull that out too, but maybe we wait until he is out. It's not that urgent."

A weight settles on my chest. I open my eyes. Catori's forehead rests on my chest, her hair splayed around my shirt. I lift my hand and stroke her hair. She huffs a wobbly laugh. "I am supposed to be comforting you."

"You are," I utter and close my eyes again.

Inhaling a long, slow breath to steady my racing heart and the pain that is stabbing my shoulder, I open my eyes and find Nirri.

"Who's the burden now, hey?" I force a laugh.

She frowns. "That's not funny. You could have been killed."

"You are the furthest thing from a burden, Nirri. I would have bled out if not for you. If you won't believe Callian, then believe me. I am nothing if not objective. I wouldn't tell you something if it wasn't true."

She stares at me for a handful of heartbeats and hangs her head.

"Hey." I find her hand and wrap it in mine. "Thank you."

"You're welcome, brother." She rises and walks into the forest. Catori smiles at me and kisses my lips before settling in beside me while Harm and Callian talk strategy to get us out of this mess.

Another slow day's trek through the snow-ridden woods, and we make it to the base of the mountain ridge. My leg is functioning, but it is painful. And we are too slow. Catori walks beside me, taking in the beauty of the white-frosted forest, so similar to ours yet still so different. Callian and Nirri walk in the lead. It is the first time in days that they have been amiable. I wonder what happened to cause that?

Harm and Imani take up the rear behind us, weapons drawn, still on edge about the savages and the mountain lions. Imani has sworn not to take either presence lightly. Pure fire, that sister of mine.

"So, do we go over or around?" Callian says, glancing at my bound leg.

"Over," I say.

Catori opens her mouth, but Nirri holds up a hand. "It will be fine; I can rig up a brace to help him climb. I did one similar in Donterra with Flick."

"Fine, that's settled," Harm says.

Imani lowers her brows. "Mason."

"I am not going to be the reason we miss the fight. No way in hell."

She schools her face to straight business. "Right then, up and over. Let's hope this time we make it without the drama."

We climb up the terrain with new determination. Callian is strung tight, hands hovering over his weapon hilts every time he slows to catch his breath. When we reach the steepest part of the climb, Nirri calls for us to stop. She orders Callian to find three lengths of wood and starts ripping cloth for the splint for my leg. She ushers me to sit. Callian returns with the wood she asked for, and she gets to strapping it around my leg. Now, it has less movement.

"Are you sure?" I ask.

"You will be able to put weight on it now. It gives you strength, and you will need that to haul yourself up that cliff face," she says, tilting her head toward the intimidating rise of rock. "Stand up and try it."

I stand and hover for a moment before Catori releases her hold. I put weight on both my feet. An ache spreads through my thigh, but I can stand and walk independently. We should have done this in the first place.

"Thanks," I utter, and she forces a smile before heading back to Callian. She studies his face briefly before making her way to the cliff. One foot after the other, she scales higher as we watch her. Harm and Imani take their footholds and climb. Catori stays by my side as I test my footing and push upward. She climbs at my pace, her brother a few feet below, as if he has been instructed to catch me if I fall. By the time we reach the first ledge, my leg is heavy and burning. My breath is ragged. Catori runs a hand over my forehead, frowning constantly. I grab her hand and pull her down to where I sit on the frigid, snow-coated dirt.

"I'm fine, stop worrying."

"Nope, can't do that." She suppresses a small smile, her green eyes wandering over my face.

"Let's just get home. I so want to be home right now, Cat," I whisper into her neck.

"Same," she whispers back, but rises, leaving with a wink. I scan the expanse around us. So high up, the ledge feels inadequate to keep us from plummeting to our deaths. I push onto my feet.

"Ready to move?" Harm asks.

"Get me as far away from that edge as possible."

Imani rolls her eyes at me, and I chuckle. Catori appears by my side again. We move out, our pace slightly faster than before as the fading light to our right chases us higher.

Back in the same camp spot we used last time we crested this mountain range, I settle next to the fire, glad of the reprieve from walking on my aching leg for hours. This time, Harm and Callian take watch while the girls and I get some sleep. We will be up and gone by dawn this time, leaving less chance for the savages to make a move. The fire crackles, warming the air around us. The calls of two mountain lions startle Imani and she sits up, shuffling closer to Catori and me.

"I promise I won't let them eat you," I chuckle. She tosses a small piece of kindling at me before curling into her fleecy blanket, pulling it over her head.

"We will take watch next," Catori says. I grumble a response, eyes closed, tugging her closer to me under the blanket. She presses her cold nose into my neck. I kiss her hair and she relaxes with a sigh.

My body shakes; something firm grips my arm. I jerk upward

and Harm's face, his finger over his lips, comes into focus. Imani is dressed and packed beside him.

"The savages have found us. We need to move," he whispers.

I shake Catori awake. One look between Harm and me and she is up and donning her weapons, rucksack, and coat. We move out, leaving the fire burning, not wanting a plume of smoke from dousing it to give away our position. Nirri and Callian run along behind Catori and me. I awkwardly skip along with the help of the splint, faster than I thought I could. Harm and Imani rush through the undergrowth ahead.

The calls of the men chasing us are closing in. Harm slides to a halt and waits for us to catch up. "We need to split up. They can't chase all six of us."

"Being alone out here is not a good idea," Catori says.

"Okay so we split up in our pairs and meet back at the wall," Callian says.

Nirri's gaze hits the ground.

"I can go with Nirri, if she wants," I say. Catori's gaze burns into mine.

Nirri's eyes alternate between us. "I can't ask you to do that. It wouldn't be fair, after everything you two have been through."

Callian stares at me like I will be next to lose my head. I hold up both hands. "Sorry, I just thought I might need her to help me with my leg."

Callian grunts and looks back the way we came. I meet Nirri's gaze, and she suppresses a smile.

"We need to move, now," Harm barks.

"Head south, but in slightly different directions, for half a day. Then track straight to the wall. We will meet up there. Make sure I see all of you again," Catori says.

The brush behind us cracks underfoot and we all turn, splitting off into pairs. Harm and Imani head directly south. Callian and

Nirri set off to the southwest at a run. Catori and I plow through the timber to the southeast. I fight back the panic in my chest, forcing every breath until my legs are numb.

Please, Hanola if you can hear me. Let us all make it back. Every single one of us must make it to that wall.

Make it home.

After everything we have been through, surely, we are owed that much.

CHAPTER 28
NIRRI

Callian thunders through the dense undergrowth in front of me, both swords drawn. The men behind us are mere feet away now. Of the three sets of tracks to follow, they chose ours. My heart flings so rapidly in my chest, I am almost sure it will burst through at any moment. Callian looks back every few seconds. I am keeping ahead of his big stride the best I can. The crashing footsteps at our backs gain on us every second.

I push my way through the thick, frigid snow. The tips of my boots are wet through, and my toes are numb now. My foot slips on a frozen patch, and the ground slams into my back. The canopy blurs above me as I gasp for air. None comes. Tears prickle behind my eyes; my body is stiff. So much so that it is hard to move, hard to breathe. Callian's face appears above mine, his eyes pained, face twisted with something like fear and agony. With one swift movement, he scoops me up and plows through the snow. I curl into his chest tight, trying to make myself smaller, lighter. My bow digs into my back, and I know it must be digging into his arm. With the crystal in my rucksack pressed hard against my spine, I cling to his coat with rigid fingers. His steps slow after what feels like an hour.

I wriggle and he lets me down onto my feet. I adjust my coat and pull my bow off, checking it briefly. It looks fine. Some of my arrows must have fallen out when we were running, but I still have four left. I tighten the string at the opening of the quiver. I can't lose any more.

The sound of gushing water steals our attention, our breaths steady. To our south, down the path about a hundred feet, a river cuts its way through the tall timbers. The surface is chaotic, ripples and streams of water twisting and turning around each other, fighting to go first. Debris is tossed atop the raging silvery mass.

"Please tell me we don't have to go through that?" I ask.

Callian holds my gaze for a moment. "We do."

"There is no other way around? The river we crossed last time was shallow and calm."

"We must have gone too far west. We are closer to the mountain range than we were last time. We could follow it southeast, but that takes more time and pushes us closer to the savages' first camp. We go across." Callian shifts his rucksack to the front of his chest.

"Get on, I'll take you over. Climb on my back."

"What?!"

"Get on."

"Callian." My hands shake in my pockets. I watch the rapids on the river, my stomach now matching their turbulent waves.

"Fine, but I can walk until we get there."

He nods and strides for the river. I tighten the straps on my bow and quiver; the rucksack on my back I tighten to the point of being uncomfortable. Callian stands on the water's edge, gaze following the current downstream. Two hundred yards along, the water disappears over what I assume is a ledge. There is no way of knowing how long the drop over that is.

Callian crouches beside me, and I hesitate before climbing onto his back. Even through his cumbersome coat, I can feel his warmth. He stands and folds his arms underneath me, then wades into the water. Hissing from the sharp cold, his chest cycles deepen with every step further into the water. I drop my head onto his shoulder, trying to give him more warmth.

The water splashes against my feet before swallowing them whole and instantly, the pain from the intense cold shoots up my legs. Callian keeps walking. The cold climbs higher up my body, reaching my waist. It burns my skin through my fleecy layers.

"Hang on, Nirri. I will go as fast as I can." His teeth chatter with each word.

By the time his body is chest-deep in the water, he shivers so violently I almost lose my grip around his shoulders.

The water pushes me with so much force, the grip I have with my almost immovable fingers isn't enough. I open my mouth the cry out, but no sound comes. I try to get Callian's attention by shaking his shoulder, but my movements are numb on his skin. The water drags me away from his body. I barely feel it when my legs swing downstream. I slip from his hold and the water clambers up my chest, stealing the last of my breath.

A strangled cry leaves my heavy lungs. Callian jerks in the water. The current tugs me down hard and my fingers slip from around his neck. Desperately, I try to pull in a lungful of air. I get a small pocket before the water slaps over my head, and everything turns to a muddle of grey movement. Bile rises in my throat as spots fill the sides of my vision. I search for something solid with my feet, grabbing at nothing with both stiffened hands. The voice of my grandfather echoes through my head. *Useless girl, see what you have gone and done now?!*

Lungs burning, I drift in the water, paralyzed. My side bumps into something solid, but I don't reach for it. I close my eyes tight and find Callian's wide grin in my memory. A smile pushes up on my rigid face, but I barely feel it.

Something else solid brushes against my arm. I imagine every moment we could have had. A normal life with our family.

A home of our own.

Blending.

His body over mine.

I choke through a ragged cry and water floods my lungs.

Something tight burns around one arm, then the other. The dark water lightens, shimmering above me. The surface rushes toward me.

Warm air touches every part of my face. Sunshine makes me squint. Gasping through watery breaths, my eyes focus. Callian's terrified gaze finds mine. He slams me to his chest, his hold so tight I cough up water.

He makes for the water's edge, faster and more determined than mere moments ago. By the time the water shallows, he has me cradled in his arms, muttering into my wet, matted hair. I press my cheek to his warm neck and close my eyes, shivering violently. He lowers me onto the forest floor and kneels beside me, crushing me in his hold before sitting back on his heels.

"I'm fine, Callian." My teeth chatter painfully.

His Adam's apple bobs, and he hangs his head.

"Dammit, Nirri." His words are choked.

I wrap my arms around his neck, hugging him tight. "We're okay."

His arms wind around me. His heartbeat thunders through his neck. Water pours from our coats with the tight squeeze. I breathe through a shaky laugh. My teeth chatter before the shiver takes over my body completely, and he releases me.

"I'll get a fire going," he says, pulling off his weapons and coat.

No rucksack.

"Callian, where is your rucksack? The crystal?"

He looks downstream. "Somewhere over that edge by now, I guess. It came loose when I was trying to get to you."

My stomach plummets. We need at least four, and now we are down to five and, by quick calculations, none of us are near the wall yet. He walks into the forest in search of timber, and I peel off my waterlogged coat. I rub bluish fingers up and down my arms to entice some warmth and feeling back.

Callian returns with an armful of timber in his trembling arms. He gets a small fire going with the flint from my rucksack. I peel off all but my last layer and drape my clothes over nearby logs, hoping they will dry quickly. I huddle by the fire, letting the warmth dry my last layer of clothing and return color to my skin. Callian is down to just his pants. His clothes hang over the logs beside mine. I stare into the fire. My stomach rumbles. My food is all wet and ruined. Apart from birds, I haven't seen too much smaller game here. They are either very well hidden or low in numbers, no doubt from the mountain lions and the continuous freezing conditions.

"Nirri, I—" Callian shifts on his seat beside me. "Never mind. Forget it."

"What is it?"

"I want to understand what's holding you back." His voice is thick with emotion.

"From what?" I know very well he is talking about us.

"This"—he gestures between us—"you and me."

"I told you. I don't know who I am yet. And I don't think you should settle for anything less than someone amazing."

His brows lower and he cycles through a handful of breaths.

"I know who you are," he whispers and leans closer.

"I'm not looking for other people's opinions of me; I want to make a life I can be proud of. I don't want to be useless."

He leans backward, shoving his hands in his hair. He stands

and stalks toward the trees. And I push to my feet and follow him. This time, he will hear me.

"Callian!"

He stops, then turns back slowly.

"You'll freeze without your clothes." I lower my brows, taking in his goosefleshed chest.

"You know what, Nirri? I don't care!" He stalks into the timbers. I traipse after him, teeth chattering.

"I care! Come back to the fire, please!"

"You go back, stay warm and undecided!"

I gasp at the words tossed back at me. *Undecided.* I jog to catch up to him, my once-warmish hands turning blue again. "Hey."

He keeps walking.

"Hey!" I grab his arm. He stops.

I slide to a halt just shy of slamming into his back. "Listen to me."

He turns, eyes burning into mine. His entire body shakes with cold. I think.

"I am listening, Nirri." His words are quiet, but his face is stone.

"I just think you should think about all your options. So you aren't stuck with someone you will regret later on." The fire I felt a second ago has all but abandoned me when his blue eyes find mine.

"For the last ever-loving time," he growls and steps into my space, "I don't want options, Nirri. I want you."

His breath is warm on my face, and I crave everything about him. His touch, his gaze, his hands on me, his lips on mine. Those corded arms around me. His warm body against mine.

"Fine," I utter.

He flinches, leaning back from my face. "What?"

"I said, fine."

His jaw feathers, eyes tightening. Hurt blooms across his face. "Who's settling now?"

He brushes past me and walks back to the fire. Damn this from the heavens to the depths of hell. My gut drops. The hurt on his face rips a sharp pain through my core and into my chest. My breathing quickens as the prickle of tears spreads behind my eyes.

I turn and wander back to the fire. Dropping next to Callian, I open my mouth, but nothing comes. No apology for the misunderstanding. No true feelings. Not the words that show him how much I want to be his. And he mine. Not the way I have loved him since I was a little girl. His friendship, his laughter, his smile, his hugs, his gorgeous face, his arms around me, enveloping me in his smell.

Instead, I glare into the fire, hating myself for being such a coward. Part of me really wants him to find someone amazing. But most of me just wants him, regardless of what's best for him.

And I am fighting it. I have been for years. Elijah was a good distraction. An easy option, being a Guardian and practically living in the same building as me. But there was never this overwhelming pull like what I have with Callian. It has a life of its own. I don't even have a choice. But I will try my hardest to make sure whoever he ends up with is worthy. He is the greatest man I have ever known.

I wake tucked under a warm, dry fleece blanket, closer to the fire than I was when I fell asleep last night. Callian sits on the log where our clothes were, dressed and armed. I sit up and run a hand through my wild curly hair.

"Morning," I murmur.

Callian stares at me and stands. I stifle a sigh and pull on my layers before adjusting my bow and quiver over my back, followed by my rucksack. The crystal is hard and heavy in the pack. *Please let the others still have theirs.* I check the placement of the sun and start trekking through the snow-coated timbers. Callian follows a few footsteps behind. My legs ache after only a half hour through the dense snow, boots soaked again. My feet numb, again.

We keep the pace up, not wanting to run into any more problems, and by dusk we have made significant progress. But the calls of the mountain lions that started just before the sun started to sink over the horizon draw closer. Callian has taken to walking beside me now, weapons drawn. I nock an arrow, and we both scan the spaces between the trees as we walk. By the calculations Harm explained to me, we should only be a day or so from the wall. Despite our setbacks with the savages and the river crossing, we have made excellent time. I hope the others are faring well.

Callian grips my shoulder and I freeze. Double-checking the woods around us, we stand still, listening to every tiny sound. A twig cracks to my left. Another to my right. Callian puts his back to mine, and we wait, weapons raised, for the hellish beasts we imagine the mountain lions are.

In a flash of white-and-grey fur, a fanged overgrown cat the size of a billy goat leaps from a branch above. It flies through the air, claws outstretched, toward me. I release the arrow and it sinks into its long, pale fur. A knife thuds into its neck beside my arrow, burying deep, and I spin back to glance at Callian. Twin swords occupy his hands, his chest rising and falling in quick succession. I spin back as the cat on the ground at my feet jerks with a last shallow breath. Crunching snow to our south snags our attention.

I see her blue wrap before anything else.

Imani.

CHAPTER 29
IMANI

I break through the trees, my second knife still in my hand. "That was close, little sis! Nice shot!" I call to Nirri.

Harm steps up beside me, sword drawn. Callian all but sags behind Nirri. She tosses her bow to the ground and flies into my arms. I chuckle and hug her tight. Harm tousles her hair before slapping Callian on the shoulder.

Nirri pushes back from my hold. I beam at Callian, and he pulls me in for a hug. "Hello, brother," I mutter into his chest. It is so damn good to see them both.

Callian releases me.

"So, you two still have both your crystals?" Harm says.

"No, only one with us," Callian says, frowning.

My mouth gapes, and I turn back to meet Harm's gaze with a twisted face.

"What is it?" Nirri asks.

"We lost one of ours on the cliff face."

"Just great," Callian says.

Please, heavens above, let Mason and Catori have both of theirs. We collect ourselves and head south. If Harm's estimates are correct, we are only a day from the wall. A day from getting back to the forest sector.

Home.

I have had enough snow for one lifetime. It takes another hour of walking through the white powder before we make it to the last campsite before the wall. The boys set about making a fire, and Nirri and I rummage through the forest floor for anything edible. Having lost Callian's rucksack and used up most of our supplies, our meal will be light tonight.

We find a handful of roots and berries that Nirri assures me won't kill us and head back to the fire. She is distracted. Not herself.

I wonder how much of that is Callian and how much is because of what is coming. Arthur, even though he is the reason so many suffer, is also her only family left.

"Nirri?"

"Hmmm?" she says, dividing the food into four piles.

"Are you worried about the battle? About what that means?"

She stills and looks up from the food, meeting my gaze. "Not really."

"Are you sure?"

"Yes, I am sure. Natural justice doesn't bother me, Imani. Others suffering at the hands of one selfish person does."

Well, there you go. I feel foolish for underestimating her. I move closer and wrap an arm around her shoulders. She smiles at me, but it doesn't meet her eyes. My gut sinks. "We are always here for you. You know that, don't you?"

She nods and looks down at the berries.

"We are your family. Always will be."

She swallows, a tear streaking down her cheek and splashing onto the berries. She wipes her face with her hands. I pull her into a hug.

"Can you come for a walk with me?" she asks, her words wobbly.

"Sure."

We stand and brush off the snowy dirt, making our way into the forest. Harm watches us go and I wave to him. He smiles back and turns back to Callian, who seems to be elaborating on something with a mountain of zeal.

We walk for a few minutes before Nirri drops onto a fallen log. She shoves her head into her hands and groans. I sit beside her and pick at the bark of the log. She'll tell me when she is ready, whatever the cause of that sigh is.

"How did you—" She starts and stands, walking in a tight circle in front of where I sit.

"What is it, Nirri?"

"I want Callian to have what you and Harm have," she says, slapping a hand over her mouth like the words weren't meant to come out.

"I want that too. But Nirri, he wants that with you."

"I know."

"If you don't feel the same, you need to tell him."

"It's not that." She pulls in a ragged breath and meets my gaze. "He's all I think about. But I just know he deserves so much better." Her face crumples.

I jump from the log and pull her into a cuddle. She sobs into my shoulder, and I rub her back. What horrible things has she lived through with that hideous man who calls himself her grandfather that she would think she is not worthy of the one thing in her life that she wants and needs so desperately?

The sooner the Chancellor stops breathing, the better. Her sobs wane and I release her, wiping her face with my hands.

"Callian knows exactly what he wants, Nirri. He is waiting for you."

She whimpers and looks toward the fire, where the boys sit. "I'm scared, Imani. What if we start something and he realizes I'm not who he thought I was?"

"Callian is the one person on this earth that knows you better than anyone. He knows who you are, Nirri. We all do. We are just waiting for *you* to realize who you are."

Her eyes widen and find mine. I tilt my head and smile. "We see it every day—the capable, strong, courageous woman you are. And Callian saw it first, little sister. He loves you like nothing else. The choice is yours."

She stares at me, eyes wide, mouth slightly agape.

"You have what Harm and I have. It's there; has been for a long time," I say and look toward the boys.

She grabs my hands and pulls me around so I am shielding her from their view. "Imani, how..."

"What?" I ask softly.

"How do I give him... everything?"

Ah. I suppress a chuckle. "You just let your love guide you and follow your instincts." I grin at her, and she blushes. "If you ever want to talk about anything, you have me, okay?"

She nods and releases my hands. With a quick peck on the cheek, she whispers "thank you" and strides toward the fire. But to my surprise, she sits on her blankets and pulls out the parchments about the dial. Harm notices and falls in beside her. I wander over to Callian and sit beside him in silence. He bumps my shoulder with his and I smile up at him.

"You two okay?" he asks.

"We are now. That cliff face was a long day. We lost the crystal. And almost the both of us. I can't wait until this is over and we can all just go home. Hopefully, Mason and Catori are close behind us."

"Hopefully." Callian turns to call out, "Harm? What's our timeline look like?"

"We are a day ahead at the moment."

"Good. We wait for Catori and Mason one more day, then."

"Solid plan, brother," Harm says and goes back to the parchment between him and Nirri.

"So, bad river crossing?" I ask.

Callian stills and meets my gaze. "I thought I lost her, Imani." His jaw tightens. "She was under the water. I couldn't find her. It felt like a lifetime."

His chin trembles. My heart breaks for him. I tousle his hair and lay an arm over his bulky shoulders. These few months have been long and hard. Miya. Enid. Catori's memory. Harm in the prison. In and out of trouble. I let my gaze wander over Callian's face, trying to judge when enough will be enough, at what point the six of us may break. Because to me, it feels like things are getting more brittle by the day. And I just pray that we make it out the other side of this war with the six of us still standing. Any other option is not acceptable.

A stick cracks to our northwest. Harm flies to his feet, grabbing for his sword. Callian moves into position beside him, both blades drawn. The drag and crack of something heavy closes in on us. I pull both fighting knives and come to stand between the boys. Nirri nocks an arrow and takes position high up a fallen tree behind us. The stance we make would be enough to frighten off even the most insidious savage.

A chuckle rattles through the timber before we see the source. I drop my weapons into the snow and take off crashing through the undergrowth toward that familiar laugh. Moments later, I launch myself into the waiting arms of Mason, Catori beaming next to him. He staggers backward, splint scraping on the ground. "It's good to see you too, Imani."

I push out of his hold and check him over.

"I took good care of him for you." Catori winks before wrapping an arm around my shoulders and rubbing her knuckles into my hair. Mason laughs at the two of us. His rucksack hangs from his shoulder.

I straighten. "Do you both have your crystals?"

"Yes, do you?" Catori raises an eyebrow.

"We lost two," Callian says behind me.

"Hell," Mason growls.

"But we have four. We only need four," Nirri says, standing next to Callian.

"Right; let's have some supper and a well-deserved sleep, then I reckon it is about time we went home," Harm says, taking Mason's rucksack from his shoulder.

After an hour of talking and regaling each other with survival stories from our trips to get to this point, we curl up beside the fire. Mason and Catori disappear under their blankets, and Harm and I do the same. Callian slides under his blanket, tucking it around him tight. Nirri cuddles into hers by the fire, her teeth chattering.

I tuck under Harm's chin and press against his warmth. He groans into my hair, hands running over my neck and into my hair. Nirri's teeth chatter so loud, I'm sure every mountain lion in this sector knows our location. I poke my head out of the blankets. She lays curled up in a blanket by the fire, trembling. I look from her shaking form to Callian.

"You know, Callian can probably fix that noise," I whisper to Harm.

He chuckles. "Is that what you two were talking about in the trees earlier?"

I nod.

"I see."

Nirri shivers through a loud bout of chattering.

"Callian, you want to fix that noise, brother?" Harm calls.

Nirri stills in her blankets for a moment before the shivering overwhelms her again. I watch as Callian tosses back his blankets and walks to the fire. He unrolls her and scoops her into his arms. A few strides later, he lays her inside the blankets and settles in beside her. She lies next to him, studying his face for a moment. He tucks the blanket around her shoulders, and her hands rest on his jaw. Callian presses his forehead to Nirri's. "You're safe. Close your eyes, Nirri."

She nods, lowering her head to press her cheek against his neck. Her chattering teeth settle, along with Callian's breathing. I touch Harm's face and he opens his eyes. I nod toward Nirri and Callian. Harm smiles, kisses my forehead, and hugs me close. My heart swells, set to burst in my chest, and I exhale through a wobbly chuckle.

This.

This right here.

My family, happy and together, is what *I* am fighting for.

The morning air nips at my face, and I roll over, closer to Harm's warmth. He groans and rests a hand on my stomach. What I wouldn't give to be in our bed at home right now. He cracks an eye and watches as I roll toward him. "Morning," I say.

"Hello to you too," he whispers and shifts onto his elbow, dotting kisses down my neck. Giggles escape me and I press my lips tight, squirming under his touch.

A throat clears next to us. Harm sighs. I cup his face with both hands and peck a kiss to his mouth before pushing him onto his back. I sit up and find the amused face of Mason. "Get some sleep?" he asks, flicking up an eyebrow.

"Yes," I drawl.

"Slept like a rock, after Callian took care of that noise," Harm says.

We all look to where Nirri and Callian lay. Callian's deep, steady breaths are audible over the crackling fire. Nirri is tucked into his side, his arm around her still. Finally, they have found some reprieve. At least, I hope.

Catori tosses a stick at her brother. It bounces off his shoulder, and he mutters in his sleep before squinting at the four of us. He rolls toward Nirri and groans into her hair.

"I will never get used to sleeping on the ground," he says, sitting up.

Nirri wakes, moving out of his hold to stretch. "Morning."

I school the smile from my face. "Hey." The smile grows before I can hold it back. Nirri blushes and leans back into Callian's chest.

"Well, now that that is sorted, maybe our trip home will be more pleasant than the trip out?" Harm winks at Callian.

Catori tosses a stick at Harm.

"Ouch, hey!" Harm laughs, holding his hands up in surrender. I punch his arm and Nirri shoots him a mock-offended look. We all holler with laughter. It sounds so good. My heart bursts with love, pride, and happiness.

After a meager breakfast, we pack up camp and head south to the wall. Our steps are light and quick, like the conversation between us. The snow is thinner near the wall, and we make good time. By late afternoon, the wall comes into view. The banter between us has died down, the weight of what comes next taking its toll.

An hour later, we approach the wall. Catori raises her fist, and we halt in line.

Two figures hover near the door in the wall, wrapped in bulky coats and well-armed. I squint, but the figures don't come into focus. A voice calls out. They have seen us.

Callian shifts on his feet, tilting his head. Another "hello" resounds in our direction. He straightens and looks back at me.

I know that voice.

Seb.

"It's okay," Callian says, walking past his sister. I follow after him, eager to see Seb. We track past the snowy tree line and walk toward the two men. Callian waves and I do the same. Seb waves back but holds a wary stance.

We stop a few feet in front of him. His gaze travels over our filthy clothes and faces.

"Well, you pair look a little worse for wear. But all things considered, at least you're alive."

"All things considered?" I say.

"We heard about your run-in with the savages. News travels fast in this sector. Especially when it involves the commander's daughter." Seb smiles at me.

"Ex-commander now."

"Heard that too. From Luca."

"Luca sent word?"

"Nope, he's here. Well not here." He waves around himself. "Back home."

"He left the desert sector?"

"Just for a short stint; he was back to manage some things."

"Oh, I see." I hope he doesn't stay away from Jonah too long. Jonah has lost enough.

As if Seb read my thoughts, he meets my gaze. "Don't worry, he is going back in a few days."

"Good. That's good. Is everything okay?"

"Yes, he sent us here to wait around for you, and if you didn't show in the next few days, well..."

"Well, what?" Callian says, folding his arms over his chest.

"He wanted us to start looking for you."

I smile and look to Callian. The others have filed in behind us now, and Harm wraps an arm around my waist. Seb catches the gesture and nods at Harm with a tight smile.

"Seb, this is Harm, Mason you may know of, Catori, and Nirri."

"I have heard quite a bit about you all." He looks at Harm, then Nirri.

"Well, we need to get home. Unless you want to join the cause too?" I say to Seb.

"You know how we feel about that, Imani."

I suppress a sigh and roll my eyes at him. His head tilts, his mouth making a thin line.

"Yep, I remember, Seb."

I slap him on the shoulder and walk toward the door but keep my gaze on him. He turns, watching me go. Filing past him one at a time, the six of us come to a halt at the door. Mason hunts for the stone brick to depress with a wandering hand.

"Imani," Seb calls.

I spin back and meet his dark eyes.

"What, Seb?"

"Just, be careful, please."

"You too."

He holds my gaze. His Adam's apple bobs, and he hesitates before turning and walking back into the timbered forest, his comrade following a step behind. The door grinds open behind me and I spin back to the waiting faces of my family. Callian has an eyebrow raised. Mason's are drawn down, his light-blue eyes filled with worry. Harm stares at me, but a smile kicks up on one corner of his mouth.

I rest a hand on his chest. He bends and dots a kiss on my neck before straightening. His finger lifts my chin up and I watch his brown eyes darken slightly. "Let's go home."

"You don't have to ask me twice."

I wrap my arms around his neck and cover his mouth with mine.

Home is wherever Harm is.

Where you go, I go, Harmen Travesci.

CHAPTER 30
MASON

I pace back and forth outside Harm and Imani's front door, heart snapping against my ribs. I want this more than anything. I have just spent the last half an hour trying to convince the healer to Blend Catori and me. Her response was kind, but not what I wanted to hear. Only leaders can bless two people and perform the Blending ceremony. Catori *is* the leader, so that only leaves Harm. He and I have come a long way since Amondo, but my hands still tremble as I wring them together.

The door cracks behind me and I spin around to find Imani watching me, leaning on the half-open door. She raises an eyebrow, crooked smile stretched over her elegant face, and a wobbly laugh leaves my chest.

"You waiting on someone or something, brother?"

"I..."

"Huh?"

"I need to talk with Harm."

"In that case, you ball of nerves, you better come in." She extends a hand to me, and I close the gap between us. She hooks her arm around mine and drags me through the door. Kicking it closed with her foot, she holds me on the spot as she waits for Nirri and Harm to look up. They sit at the small table by the hearth, both absorbed by the parchments in front of them.

"So, to activate the dial, blood is required," Nirri states, looking from the text in front of her to Harm.

"Okay, like how?" he asks.

"Not much, a small amount in the center depression. It looks like a seven-pointed star. See here?" She holds up the rolled-out paper and points to the marking at the center of the drawn dial.

"That shouldn't be a problem. Just remind me to take a knife." He smiles through his words.

Nirri huffs a laugh and slaps his arm. "Pretty sure your sword will be sufficient." She shakes her head at him.

Harm tracks his gaze to his wife standing beside me, her arm still hooked in mine. He smiles at her, and she scrunches up her nose playfully. "Mason has a question for you."

"Shoot, brother."

I shift on my feet and look to Imani. She withdraws her arm, giving me a quizzical look.

"I was wondering..."

Nirri's head snaps up, her gaze falling onto my face. I swallow past the stone lodged in my throat, shoving my hands into my pockets.

"Mason, what is it? Is Catori okay?" Harm asks, rising from his chair.

"She's good. Actually, that's what I came to ask you."

"Go ahead."

"Would you be able to Blend Catori and me?"

Harm stills and studies my face. My heart picks up pace again, breaths shallowing out. He tracks his gaze to Imani briefly before returning to me.

"No. Sorry, brother," he says, his face unreadable.

My gut sinks like a stone in river rapids.

Imani's face drops, mouth agape, eyes burning into Harm's.

"I just don't think I'm the right person for the job," Harm utters.

I pull my hands from my pockets and wrap them behind my neck, steadying each inhale. "Right." I turn on my heels and push out the door.

"Mason, wait," Imani calls.

I stalk through the village toward home. I know we haven't always gotten along, but I thought we had moved past that. We are like brothers, for heaven's sake. I don't know who else I can ask to perform the ceremony. Surely Catori's mother would have hang-ups about Blending her only daughter.

Deep down, I really wanted it to be Harm. It would mark such a milestone for us, the two remaining sons of Amondo. We have been on opposing sides most of our lives, and this was a way to leave that in the past. To seal the friendship and brotherhood we have had of the past twelve months or more. I walk into our home. Catori stands by the strategy table with two warriors, talking supplies and weapons stores. She looks up from the table. Instantly, her face twists with concern as her gaze meets mine.

"Hey, what is it?" she says, coming over to me in a few strides.

I stop pacing, pulling my hands from where they are cradled tight behind my neck.

"Mas?"

"Nothing, forget it."

"Okay, well, Daniel will be here in a few minutes for his last treatment. You good?"

I forgot about that. It took me multiple treatments with Hanola, but Nirri is phenomenal with minds. This will be Fletcher's—Daniel's—third and last treatment. I would be happy for him, if I didn't know what he was about to live through. Catori is still standing in front of me, eyes studying my face. She rests her hands on my face and gives me a small, crooked smile.

"I'm fine. I promise. Let's get the space ready for Daniel."

She leans into me, brushing her lips over mine. "I love you, you know that, Mason Rayner." Her bright-green eyes find mine.

"I know you do," I whisper, running a thumb over her lips.

"Later, Mas." She winks and returns to the strategy table. She looks back and smiles when she gets to the table's edge. Heaven knows the lengths I would go to for her. If I have to scour every inch of the three sectors to find someone to Blend us, I will.

The door rattles under a knock.

"Enter," Catori barks.

Daniel enters, flanked by his two constant forest guards. If today is a success, this will be the last time he needs their company. I pray, for his sake, it works. But my gut twists with the memories of my own transition.

Harm, Nirri, Callian, and Imani follow the three men through the door, and everyone takes up a spot on the cushions in our living room. The two guards wait by the door, and Catori dismisses the two warriors to their tasks.

We all sit, waiting for instructions from Nirri. Daniel sits in front of her, chest moving through deep cycles, his gaze moving between Nirri and Imani.

"Imani, I have a feeling you will need to wait outside for this session," Nirri says.

Imani looks to her father before nodding and rising from her cushion. She pushes through the front door and hovers by the wall of the next home. The guard shuts the door, but I see her pace by the window every few minutes.

A stone lodges in my throat watching her worry herself over her father. The commander of the Guardian Regime, officer of the fourth rank, the highest-ranking man of all three sectors, is about to be reduced to the sum of his broken parts. I shudder at the memory of my last session with Hanola.

Catori laces her fingers through mine and bumps my shoulder with hers. Warmth spreads in my chest. I would do it over a thousand times for her.

"Okay, everyone else needs to be still and silent. We can't have any distractions," Nirri says. Each of us nods.

"Daniel, I am going to get you to settle into a lower state of consciousness, then ask you some questions. Just answer the best you can or respond the best you can. When I snap my fingers twice, you will come back to full awareness. Okay?"

"Okay." He swallows, shifting on the cushion.

My heart thunders in my chest. I sit, watching the man who led me and so many of my comrades to carry out sickening punishments wait for a torture of his own. The only thing I feel right now is overwhelming sadness for him. Years of actions he carried out under the glazed facade of unknowing indifference are about to surface to his conscious mind. He will remember and relive every single one of those moments. Every single life. Every single face.

And I find myself wondering which ones will haunt him the most.

"Close your eyes and listen to the rhythm I make," Nirri says.

Daniel closes his eyes. Nirri starts her humming incantation, similar to what Hanola did for me. It lulls all of us into a peaceful state, and I make sure my eyes stay open. After a couple of minutes, she taps Daniel's knee. He doesn't respond. He is under.

"Daniel, can you hear me?"

"Yes." His voice is gravel, as if he is trapped under the weight of a deep sleep.

"Good. From this point on, I want you to control everything you think, say, or do. And when the feeling of overwhelm starts to pull on your senses, feel it. Feel your emotions, feel your instincts, and act accordingly."

"I will."

Nirri shifts on her cushion, moving closer. Her smaller frame and tousled blonde curls look childlike and innocent next to the hardened man in front of her. Callian jerks and Harm slaps a hand on his shoulder, holding him back.

"Open your eyes, Daniel," Nirri says.

He opens his brilliant blue eyes, the same as his daughters. He stares into Nirri's gaze.

She snaps her fingers twice.

He twitches, eyes widening, mouth curling up on one side.

Nirri pulls a blade from her hip, pressing the sharp tip into the hollow of his throat. His mouth pulls into a thin line and his eyes tighten.

"Fletcher," Nirri grinds out, twisting the blade into his skin.

His eyes glaze over.

Hell.

He jolts toward her. His hand swings up, grabbing her by the throat. She stiffens, pushing her shoulders back.

"Daniel, let me go."

His eyes remain glazed.

She retracts the blade.

It didn't work.

Callian strains against Harm's hold, both of Harm's hands keeping him down on the cushion. Nirri snaps her fingers twice and Daniel sits back, hand falling from her neck and into his lap.

Nirri looks to Harm. "It didn't work. I have another tactic left, but it's a much crueler method. And any one particular memory can override all of them, if it is painful enough."

Harm finds my gaze, and I work through a handful of breaths before nodding.

"Do it, Nirri," Harm says.

Catori moves closer to me and rests her head on my shoulder. I close my eyes for a heartbeat and drag in another burning breath.

Nirri starts again, humming through a short melody of oscillating notes.

"Daniel Fletcher, can you hear me?"

"Yes."

"Daniel Fletcher, you are hereby accused of the following crimes against humanity: The wrongful deaths of Arlo, Arlo's family. The mass murder of the village people of Amondo. The deaths of the Milfrey family. The torture and attempted murder of Harmen Travesci. The mass murder of the people of the village of Slenbir. The deaths of Rupert Barlow, Matthew Onnerhall, Nathaniel Brimmerstone, and countless rebels from the desert sector. The abduction of hundreds of children from the desert and forest sides. Lastly, you are accused of the attempted murder of Imani Fletcher on two separate occasions.

"These are your crimes. From this point on, you will remember and relive each and every one of the lives you have affected. From this point on, when you feel overwhelmed, you respond to the instincts it triggers, and act accordingly. Do you understand?" She rises to her feet.

"Yes."

"Stand," Nirri orders. Silver lines her eyes, but she stays steady, gaze burning into his face. Every one of those crimes, he was carrying out orders. None of those lives he took were his choice. Every last Guardian has been the pawn of the despicable Chancellor. Every emotion I have had in the last ten minutes converges into heartbreak for him. He will never recover from the things he has been forced to do. Never feel peace, not for decades—if at all.

He wobbles to his feet. She looks up at him. His larger frame towers above her. Nirri's gaze flicks to Harm, and her face bunches with sorrow. Her eyes plead with him a little, as if saying she is sorry for what she is about to do.

She snaps her fingers twice.

Daniel opens his eyes, meeting her gaze.

We all rise to our feet and step back, giving them space.

Nirri presses the blade to the hollow in his neck again. The caked blood from moments ago slides away with a trickle of bright red. His eyes and face contort with fear and pain.

He lunges for Nirri and grabs her throat again, his large hands tight around her soft neck. Callian's body is trembling, held steady by Harm's tight grip.

But Daniel's eyes are clear.

Instincts fully intact.

She holds her ground.

Callian sways and Harm readjusts his grip, only just keeping the warrior back. Callian grasps Harm's arm with a harsh grip. They are hanging on to each other like both their lives depend on it. Brothers to the end.

"Daniel, let me go," Nirri says calmly, her blade still digging into his neck.

He doesn't move, wide-eyed and shaking hard. His grip around her neck tightens.

"Daniel Fletcher! Let. Me. Go."

He jerks, tilting his head to one side, a groan spilling from his twisted mouth. He looks around, taking in the people in the room, as if he has just realized where he is and who stands in front of him. Nirri raises her head, pushing her shoulders back again.

His hand falls from her throat, and he staggers backward, staring at the floor, hunched over.

Nobody moves.

The silence is deafening.

The only movement is my thundering heart.

He screams, a jagged and raw sound, and every heart in the room shatters. Each of the loving faces of my family is flooded with intense pain. We knew it was coming, but nothing could prepare us for this.

"Imani! No. Imani. Imani!" Each word is coated with terror and pain.

Harm gasps for air through sobs.

Callian wraps an arm around his shoulder, pulling him close, watching his brother unfold before his eyes.

Releasing another soul-crushing, agonizing cry, Daniel slumps to the ground, hands ripping at his hair.

"Imani! Ahhh. No, no. No. Oh god, my baby girl. What have I done? My sweet girl."

Callian stands stunned, rigid, holding Harm. Tears stream down Harm's jaw, dripping onto the floor. I lose the last hold I have on my resolve and huff out a sob, my cheeks now wet too.

Ugly, growling sobs rip from Daniel's twisted face, echoing around the room. He calls her name, over and over.

"Imani, I am so sorry, my girl. Papa is so sorry," Daniel whimpers, now curled up on the floor.

Movement at the door steals our attention. Imani stands with her hand over her mouth. Heaven knows she has waited long enough to get him back. Pain wrecks her face.

CHAPTER 31
IMANI

My father lies, curled and broken, on the living room floor. Groans choke through his erratic sobs, sending tears over his stubbled face. Every part of my body trembles. Agony streaks through flesh, heart, and soul.

I can't breathe.

The air is too thin.

The room is too small.

My heart kicks outward at my ribs, stomach twisting and sending a wave of sickness up my throat. I stagger closer, my eyes fixed on the writhing, devastated man on the floor.

Instantly, memories arise of him swinging me up over his head, the both of us laughing. The tight hugs he gave me when I was small. The pride and love in his eyes when I started school. The way he held my mother as they watched me play in the sand, dancing around as free as the desert sands on the warm breeze.

Tightness consumes my chest. I close the gap between us. He doesn't notice. Rocking on the floor, he's still curled up, choking for air through whimpers and wails.

I kneel beside him, taking in the grief and pain etched across his usually stoic face and racking his body to a trembling mess, ripping him to shreds where he lay. I rest a hand on his shoulder. He slows and cries out my name. Now, sobs rattle from my throat. Tears stream down my cheeks, hitting the floor between us.

"Father." The word is no more than a jagged whisper.

He doesn't respond, still working through breathy groans. I lay down on the floor next to him on my side, facing him, and take his hands in mine. His shattered heart pierces right through his tormented gaze.

He stills slightly, gasping for air.

His eyes close.

His scream splinters the air around us. I grip his hands in mine. "Father?"

He groans something I can't understand. I release one hand and rest it on his cheek.

"Papa?"

He sobs and opens his eyes. "Imani."

"I'm here, Papa."

"What have I done," he wails.

"It's okay." I wriggle closer, pressing my forehead to his. "It's okay, no one can make you do anything anymore."

His chin wobbles. "I have already done too much. I have already hurt you."

I suck in air, struggling to find enough. The years of anger and resentment I have carried fall away to nothing.

"I'm okay too. I just need you to be alright." I stroke his cheek with a trembling hand. "I just want my papa back."

He sobs hard, pulling me into his chest. I grip his shirt, letting my sobs chug through each exhale. The light footsteps of my family recede through the doorway, and I press harder into the familiar smell of my father, a smell I have missed for so long. It's as if every year that went by without him, every moment I needed my father, comes crashing in all at once. Breath leaves my lungs and doesn't return. I struggle for air. He pushes me back, sitting me up. Whimpering, he wipes the veil of tears from my face with his thumbs.

"I am so sorry, Imani. For every single thing I ever did to hurt you. For not protecting your mother, or Harm, or Miles. For dismissing your worries and pretending to know better. For not having the courage to stand up for what is right when I should have. Heaven knows I had enough chances to do all of those things."

"What's done is done. All that matters is changing what we can, now that we have the chance."

He nods and pulls me back to his chest, stroking my hair.

Dammit, I missed him so much. I missed his strong arms around me, keeping me safe. I missed his love. I missed him. I missed him for so, so long.

"I don't expect you to ever forgive me," he chokes into my hair.

I remember Harm's words when I came home from the tower, and they sit well in my chest now.

"Already done, Papa." The words burn on their way out, not because I don't believe them, but because I have waited so long for my world to be whole again. And having my father back fills the hole in my heart that has been ravaged with anger and hurt and contempt for his actions for years. I do forgive him. I have to; it's the only way forward, and more than anything I want a life with my family.

Him included.

I pour the steaming tea into the mug at my side and refill my father's water cup. The herbal tea I have been taking since the week before Hanola Blended Harm and me has become one of my favorite small pleasures. He watches as I sit opposite him at Catori's small table at the back of her home.

Having recovered from our moments on the floor, I have questions for him. And I want him to be honest.

"Did you Blend with Mother because you loved her?"

He stares at me. His brows lower for a second before he takes a sip from his cup. Placing it back down. "Yes, very much."

"You expected me to forgo that? Having someone that I loved?"

He tilts his head, eyes confused.

"You matched me with Mason after the gallows. Or did that slip your mind in all the chaos?"

He huffs a laugh and sets his cup down. "Love was not a luxury you had at that point in time, Imani. The Chancellor was well aware of your actions. The only thing that kept him at bay was my loyalty to his regime."

"You promised me to Mason when you knew what Harm and I were. How could you do that?"

"It was the only way to keep you safe. Running around the desert with Harm, you weren't exactly making it easy for me. Being Blended with Rayner, you would have been protected."

I scrunch my face up and take a mouthful of tea. "What about the gallows? Was executing your daughter the Chancellor's idea?"

"You really think I wanted that? Your consequences were fast leaving my hands. It was a gamble, but it worked, and you lived."

"What are you talking about?"

"The Chancellor wanted you both to hang, Imani. I convinced him you were more useful to us alive. Actually, Rayner helped with that also. So, we used you as bait. It's not something either of us were proud of. But it was a far better outcome than seeing you both hanged."

"Oh."

"You know Harm gave up his life for you in the prison before you burst in and saved his skin. He offered to work the dial for the rest of his life and remain a prisoner if the Chancellor would grant you immunity. And he did."

I sit searching his face, my heart flipping at pace. I swallow. Harm has always protected me the best way he knows how. To put himself in danger's path so it can't find me. I drag in a lungful of air and exhale slowly.

"He deserves you far more than I do, my girl."

I release a wobbly, strained laugh and shove my head into my hands. His chair scrapes the floor and a warm hand lands on my back. "Imani, I will do everything I can to make sure all of us survive this war."

I clear my throat and straighten. I throw back the last of my tea, burning my throat, and we stand. Father looks down at me; his blue eyes meet mine.

"Can you do one last thing for me, though?" I ask.

"Anything." His words are breathy, tears lining his eyes again.

"I will hold you to that. Follow me."

I walk through Catori's front door and track toward the last of the homes by the training area, my father beside me. He doesn't speak. I imagine he can guess where we are going.

I round the last home and stop just short of the door. He comes to a stop next to me, his hands trembling. I knock on the door and watch his face contort with hope and fear. A moment later, my mother opens the door. Her gaze alternates between Father and me.

"I brought you something," I say to her through a strangled breath.

"Imani? What's going on?" she says.

Father's breath turns choppy beside me. My mother glances at his wrists, and her mouth gapes. She slaps a hand over her mouth, muffling a sob.

"Just as Harm promised; your husband is home."

Father turns and looks at me, his face stretched with shock. I tilt my head and offer him a wobbly smile. The bounds of Harm's kindness never cease to amaze me. And this time he truly has delivered in the best way possible. His belief in my family and in the power of forgiveness never wavered. And for that I will be ever grateful. Forever is never going to be long enough for me to love Harmen Travesci.

As if my thoughts were intercepted, two strong arms slip around my waist, and a kiss presses into my cheek. I lay my head back onto his chest before spinning around. His face is streaked with tears.

"Does this mean...?" Mother utters.

"It does. He's all yours, Mama." I haven't called her that since I was five. It feels nice. Right.

"Daniel!" She flies into his arms, and he sobs into her neck. They hold tight for so long. Miles sits on the floor, playing with his toy, staring at his mother and father.

Mother pulls the both of us into the hug. A moment later, the corded arms of my father envelop the three of us. Something bumps into my leg. I look down into the excited blue eyes of my little brother. Miles jumps up and down, happiness exploding all over his face. Father releases us all and scoops up Miles. He tosses him into the air, catching the wriggling boy with both hands under his arms. Miles squeals and his laughter swells my weary heart, filling it with so much joy. Mother slides a hand around the back of my neck and tilts her head until my forehead is touching hers.

"Thank you, my girl. You are the strongest woman I have ever known. Don't you ever forget that, Imani Travesci."

I laugh through a tight chest.

"I love you too, Mama."

She kisses my cheek and releases me to Harm. Her eyes tighten again, tears flooding down her face.

Our strategy table is littered with maps, parchments, and scribblings by Harm and Catori. Miya's handwriting even covers some of the older maps. The six of us and my father stand around the worn table, maybe for the last time. The air is tense and too quiet. Nirri watches as Callian drags a hand over the map, tapping the nearest clearing by the tower. "This is a good spot to intercept the Chancellor's men, if we can draw them to this area. Our archers can be hidden in the canopy at that point. I can place three battalions north facing. One head on, one on either side of that. This is our rendezvous point," he continues.

Catori folds her arms over her chest, leaning against the table. "Solid plan, little brother. Divide your men and women and give them the run down. How are the women coming along with the training?"

"Almost ready. We test them out today. My second will be sorting them into ranks," Callian answers.

"Good. Harm, you ready for this?" Catori asks, shifting her gaze.

Harm's gaze flicks to Nirri before returning to Catori. "We have been ready for a long time." He turns to Mason.

"We got this, brother," Mason says, holding up a fist. Harm bumps it with his. A smile breaks over Mason's face, and Harm slaps his shoulder playfully. For two boys who grew up hating each other, they sure work well together. I am counting the days until this is over, and we can all have a chance at a normal life.

Mason's bright gaze finds mine. Father watches the two of us as we exchange silent sentiments, pride filling his clean-shaven face, and my heart warms.

"So, as far as we can tell, then, we are all ready," Nirri says. Her face doesn't carry the determination and excitement every other face in the room does, and my heart breaks for her. We are about to wage war on her grandfather. Despite all the inhumane things he has done, he is the last of her family. Her last living relative. She and Harm have lost everyone they loved, save their matches. It feels like too high a price to pay for simply carrying an ability the rest of the population does not. My breaths turn shallow, watching her straighten under our collective gaze. She holds her head high and pulls in a long, purposeful breath.

"To a better world," she says, taking Callian's hand. She hesitates a little before sliding her hand into my father's. He takes Catori's, who takes Mason's. I grip onto Mason as if that will keep my heart from shattering after watching Nirri. Harm laces his fingers through mine and slaps a hand into Callian's waiting palm.

"We do it together. We get it done," Catori says.

"Where you go, I go," I say, drifting my gaze across each person who I call my family in this room.

Every last set of eyes meets mine. Mason squeezes my hand and Harm tugs me closer.

The door bursts open, startling the seven of us. We release our holds and turn to find one of Catori's warriors standing breathless over the threshold. He has been running hard.

Catori rushes to where he stands, Mason close behind her.

"What is it?" Catori asks. Her hand rests on the warrior's quickly moving shoulders.

"At least a hundred of them. Rough-looking men, filing into the makeshift building the Chancellor erected."

"Dammit," Mason mutters.

Rough-looking—what, like savages? My heart kicks up to a

thundering belt. The only men more dangerous than Catori's warriors are the savages. If Arthur has sided with them, our chances just got a whole lot less favorable. I swallow past the growing stone in my throat. Harm moves to where Mason stands.

"What do you mean, rough?"

"They have beards, big coats, some had nasty-looking weapons. Nothing I have seen before and certainly don't want to be on the wrong end of." The warrior all but pales as he uses his hands to show us the size and shape of some of the weapons. My gut sinks, sickness clawing its way up my closing throat.

Heavens above.

"We need to warn the rebels and get organized. A surprise attack is the only tactic left to give us some kind of advantage," Father says.

"I agree, but we wait until our numbers are gathered. No going in with half our battalion. That would be suicide," Callian says.

"Fine. Move the rendezvous forward by two days. Gather both sides, and let's get this over and done with. Harm, you lead your side to the rendezvous point or organize someone who can. Either way, we rendezvous at the point in six days," Catori says. Her words are harsh and, for the first time since I have known her, they are laced with fear. Her gaze is stuck on Mason. None of us want to do this. None of us want to lose another person. But we are fast being backed into a corner, and there is no way Arthur wins this time. Whatever we must do, his reign is over.

"We need to move," Harm says, his gaze almost vacant.

"Nirri and I will come with you halfway to the wall, then break off to round the last few forest villages," Callian says.

Harm nods.

We walk from Catori's home back to ours. I lace my fingers through Harm's. He tugs me into his side and presses a kiss into my hair. Moments later, we are packing our rucksacks. I toss in my blue wrap, Hanola's tea, clothes, nuts, and jerky from the table and pluck my canteen from the hook by the door. Harm throws his rucksack over his shoulder, and I toss his canteen to him. He catches it midair in one hand and slings it over his shoulder. I step into his space. He is lost somewhere deep in his thoughts. I place my hands on his face, and his gaze falls to mine.

"Fancy one last adventure through the sands?" I ask.

His chin wobbles, but a smile kicks up one side of his mouth. He lowers his lips to mine, and we stand lost in each other for a handful of heartbeats. He breaks from the kiss and rests his forehead on mine. "Where you go, I go, remember?"

I huff a small laugh and peck a kiss to his nose before dropping my hands from his face. I take his hand and lead him out the door, praying to anyone who will listen that we come home.

Hanola, Enid, if you can hear me, please keep my family safe. Please let us all come home together.

And soon.

CHAPTER 32
NIRRI

Imani walks beside me, quiet and lost in thought. It's not like her to be so quiet, but we are all trying to cope with the possible outcomes of the coming days. I know they all think I am upset over the Chancellor dying, and I guess a small part of me is sad. But what worries me the most is losing any one of these people I have come to love more than anything else in the world. The first people who accepted me in as long as I can remember.

Callian. I cannot lose him. Tears burn the back of my eyes at the thought of life without him in it. I grip the strap of my rucksack and blow out a long, hard breath. My fingers tremble around the weathered cloth strap.

Imani notices and rests her hand on my arm. I stop and track my blurry gaze to hers. Instantly, she pulls me into a hug. "Oh, Nirri, I wish things could be different."

"I don't. And I just want this to be over and everyone to be safe."

Imani releases me and holds me at arm's length. "Are you upset about Arthur?"

Her words are kind, the traits of her husband having rubbed off on her over the last couple of years.

"It's not that." I glance at Callian, and Imani tracks my gaze. "I cannot lose him." I gasp through the next breath.

Her face cracks, and she grips my face in both hands. "We all come home, you hear me? No matter what it takes."

I nod, tears dropping from my face to the forest floor. She wipes my tears with her thumbs. "We are all scared. But the life we can have on the other side of this is worth it. I truly believe that."

"So do I," I manage to rasp.

"Good. Now, you see that hunk of a warrior, walking away from us? You find your mettle. For him. For yourself. For the life you want for the both of you. Alright?"

I nod, swallowing back a fresh torrent of tears.

She releases me.

"Now stop that, before you make me bawl, little sister." She loops her arm through mine and tugs me forward. We walk through the forest arm in arm for a while before jogging to catch up to the boys.

As the sun reaches its apex on our second day, we reach the clearing where we will split up. Callian and I are to go to the last two villages in the forest and bring back the tested and ranked warriors, ready to join the main group that will be filing into our village.

We drop to the soft, mossy floor, and I reach for my canteen. Callian sits next to me, studying my face. The light in his eyes when he looks at me floods me with so much love every single time. And I have been dying to get closer to him for days. He shifts his rucksack to the forest floor, his corded arms moving with the action. My breath turns shallow again, for the second time today.

"I guess we will see you two at the rendezvous point in a few days?" Harm says, breaking my stare from Callian's body.

"You sure you will be okay on your own?" Imani winks at Callian.

Heat rises up my neck and into my face. Callian clears his throat and glances at me. "We will be okay, little sister; no need to worry about us." His smile is so wide it must make his face hurt. Happiness personified, my Callian is. Heaven knows he turns my head and heart to a puddle.

I suppress the urge to cover his mouth with mine.

Harm swallows the last of his jerky and follows it down with a long swig from his canteen. Imani packs her food away. She pulls a small brown packet from her rucksack and hands it to me. Its contents feel loose, and I raise it to smell the strong fragrance it carries.

"Tea. Make sure you drink a cup of that every day," Imani says softly. Harm gives Callian a strange, crooked smile. What did I miss? I nod in thanks and shove the packet into the front pocket of my rucksack.

Imani pushes to her feet and lowers both hands to me. I grab them and pull myself up. I hug her tight and she whispers in my ear, "Make sure you drink the tea each day. It stops you conceiving."

"I will."

She leans back a little and rubs her belly. Heat floods my neck and face. "Or else." Scrunching her face a little, she takes my hand in hers, silver lining her eyes. "I love you, Nirri."

"I love you too. Both of you."

Harm wraps an arm around my shoulder and whispers his goodbye. Callian slaps a hand into Harm's and pulls him into a tight hug. With a fist bump like back in Catori's, Harm and Callian part ways, and Imani and I follow them in separate directions. My heart feels like it is being ripped from my chest as she and Harm walk into the forest. Imani turns back and waves, tears streaking her face.

I've been lost in my head for the past couple of hours when hissing falls in around us, bringing me back to the present. I stop when Callian stops in front of me and turns back. The hissing has turned to gushing, and I realize where we are. The waterfall.

"You want to go for one last swim?" His eyes are soft, his lips parted.

"That would be nice," I say, stepping toward him.

He dumps his rucksack to the ground before pulling mine from my shoulder and dropping it with his. I step into his space and grab the opening of his shirt with both of my hands. The water cascades in spectacular fashion only ten feet away. I grab the clasp of his weapons belt over his chest and fling the metal open, pushing the leather straps back over his shoulders. It thuds softly onto the ground.

His breathing turns ragged to match mine. He slides his hands behind my neck and claims my mouth. I close my eyes and sink into his kiss. Every inch of my body vibrates with need. With both hands, I tug his shirt upward. He leans back for a moment, letting me lift the shirt up over his head, and I toss it to the ground. His chest rises and falls, and I rest my palms on the heady movement.

"Nirri," he rasps.

I look up. His blue eyes pierce my gaze, holding me to the spot, darkening further with every too-shallow breath he takes.

"Yes?"

He lowers his mouth to my ear.

"Last one in the water is a rotten egg." He takes off, diving into the water, and I loose a chuckle. Love doesn't begin to describe how I feel about Callian.

He emerges from the water, rivulets running down his hard body, over his defined stomach. I wander to the edge of the water, unbuttoning my tunic further with each step. He watches every move I make, his arms floating outwards, fingers playing in the waist-high water around him. I slide the tunic off one shoulder, and his Adam's apple bobs. The next sleeve falls, and my tunic hits the grass at my feet. All that covers me are my supports, now stretching with every heaving breath I take. I slide my fingers inside my pants at my hips and push them over my bottom and past my knees.

Standing in my undergarments, I watch as his gaze turns almost feral. The fact that I can do this to him makes my chest swell until it bursts with adoration. I step into the water and wade in until I am up to my waist and standing in his space, my chest touching his. Callian groans, low and raw, and smashes his mouth over mine. I run both hands through his blond hair and pull him down closer to me. He moves closer, his hardness pressing into my stomach. My breath leaves and doesn't return.

"Nirri, I am burning up here," he says, his voice gravel.

"You have no idea," I utter between breaths.

He grips my hips and pulls me up onto his. I wrap my arms around his neck and my legs around his waist. His lips find my neck, and I tilt my head to one side, trying to find my breath. His arms hold me up. One under me, one behind my neck.

"Callian, please."

His mouth finds mine again. I grip his face in my hands and meet his movements with my own. Something needs to happen before I ignite. *Heavens above.*

He lowers me back into the water and I stand on shaky legs as he gently removes the wrap holding my chest in place. His fingers graze my hard peaks, and a whimper leaves my mouth. His hands are so warm as his fingers slide between the fabric of my undergarment and my hips. A handful of heartbeats later, they are in his hand with the rest. He bundles up the supports and tosses them onto the grass near our rucksacks. I stand, breathing heavy as his eyes wander over my chest, and he swallows. His hands tremble on my hips. He pulls me closer and touches his forehead to mine. A moment passes before I realize that he still has too many clothes on. With slow movements, I find the fastener for his pants. His breath stops and I meet his gaze.

"You sure, Nirri?"

"About you?"

He closes his eyes and nods. My heart squeezes in my chest, as if it is not already strung out enough.

"Since I was about ten," I whisper.

He huffs a laugh and opens his eyes. "Me too."

I have made him wait a decade. My stomach flips with the thought. This man, this warrior, who could have had whoever he wanted so many times, has waited that long.

For me.

I tug his pants away from his arousal and push them down his thighs.

"Wait just a second longer," I utter, dropping into the water as I submerge. The clear water rolls around me, the current playing with my hair. I push his pants to his feet, and he lifts them one at a time as I pull them off. I let the pants bob to the surface, staying in the quiet serene water for a moment, biding my time as my heart flings against my ribs.

A heartbeat later, Callian's face appears in the water in front of me. I laugh, and bubbles fly to the surface. He pulls me into him and covers my mouth with his. Water floods in. I float, arms waving at my sides. Eyes closed, his arms wrap around my waist. The heat of his kiss is barely subdued by the cool water.

I wrap my legs around his waist. He trembles from head to toe. When the last of my air runs out, I tap his shoulder, and he rises, taking us out of the water. He stands waist deep, water running off us both. He shakes his head, spraying water from his messy hair. I giggle and hold my hands in front of my face. My laugh peters out and I sit on his hips, every breath heavy yet shallow.

With nothing left between us, he adjusts me over himself. His lips find my neck, then trail down to my chest. His warm breath hits my peaks. A second later, his mouth covers one hard peak.

I can't breathe.

Oh heavens.

I moan, so deep it rattles through my throat. Callian moves under me, so his hardness presses against my aching wetness. I whimper, and he lifts his head to meet my gaze. His blue eyes have never been so dark.

I shove my hands through his hair and pull his mouth over mine. I choke for breath past the stone in my throat.

"Nirri, I love you." His words are raw and soft.

"I love you, so much Callian; I always have."

His face breaks, and he lowers me onto him. A sharp sting gives way to warmth at the stretch of him inside me. I whimper a cry. *Oh god.*

He smiles at me, but his face returns to sweet agony as he pulls me back up. My core vibrates with every inch of him and every small movement we travel together.

His hands grip my hips hard, as if holding me is his only life-line. I hold on tight, fingers splayed around his neck. I tilt my head back as he lowers me again. His mouth finds my peaks and my core lights up, legs trembling around his waist. His teeth tug at my breast.

Everything inside me shatters at once. My ragged cries echo around us, blending with the roar from the falling water behind him. Callian groans and slows the pace of my rise and fall, his arms flexing with my weight on every upward pull. He throws his head back and sucks in a raspy breath before meeting my gaze.

"I can't hold off much longer, Nirri."

"Then don't." I tighten around him, and he tugs me up hard before letting me fall. Another cry shatters from my chest, then another, and my core lights up again, sweet agony ripping through my center and trailing outward along every limb. Callian groans into my ear as his grip on my hips intensifies. He growls into my neck. Heat fills my core as he finds his release. His body shakes, chest heaving. He hunches, almost curling around me, still standing.

I release my legs from his waist and stand in the water. His forehead meets mine. I hold his jaw with both hands and kiss his mouth as he comes down from breathlessness back to a steady pace. I sink into the water and pull him down with me until the water is at our shoulders.

"Lay back," I whisper. He does, floating in the water. I move so his head is cradled against my chest.

"Close your eyes," I say.

He does.

"Every kiss I give you is a thousand times I love you," I whisper into his ear. He smiles, so wide, so bright across his gorgeous square face. I dot kisses over every inch of his face, and he chuckles with each one. His hand finds mine under the water. I lace my fingers through his and cover his mouth with mine. He moves out from under me, eyes still closed.

"Nirri, when this is all over?"

"Yes?"

He opens his eyes and looks up at me, still floating in the water beside me. I step around to his side, so I am the right way up for him. His gaze follows.

"Promise me one thing," he says.

"Anything." My heart kicks up its pace. What could he want me to do? I would give him anything.

"You'll let me love you," he whispers, rolling over in the water. He finds his feet and looks down at me and continues, "the way you deserve to be loved. Nothing less."

I can't breathe, again.

His hand rests under my chin, and he tilts my head to meet his gaze. "Promise me that, Nirri."

"I promise."

"No more doubting yourself, or thinking you are a burden."

"Alright."

The last forest village lies just beyond the tree line we stand behind. Callian's home village. His parents live here still. He takes my hand, and we step from the trees and make our way to the village center. People stop what they are doing to greet him. Old ladies tug him down for a hug, kids slam his hand with high fives. He catches my gaze and shrugs. I punch his arm, and he laughs, heartily. I will cherish that sound until the day I die.

A man and woman walk through their front door, and Callian stops in his tracks. His parents.

"You ready?" he asks.

"For you, I am always ready."

He chokes through a laugh and crimson covers his neck. We walk toward his parents. His mother opens her arms for him, cradling her son in her embrace. I drop my gaze to the ground. Shoes appear in my line of sight. I look up.

"We have waited a long time for you, Nirri," his father says. His face is an older version of Callian's. I huff a nervous laugh, and he folds me in a warm hug, his strong arms similar to his son's.

"Who has waited a long time?" his mother says, slapping her husband's shoulder.

"Okay; Callian has waited for you. But to be honest, we knew you two were a match by the time he was ten. You have no idea how long I have had to wait for grandchildren," he jokes.

Heat flushes my neck and face as my mind wanders back to yesterday at the waterfall.

"Oh Enzo, now you have gone and made the poor girl blush. What am I going to do with you?" She shakes her head, and Callian suppresses a laugh. I see now where he gets his happy disposition from. He is just like the both of them. And, the best part, he is all mine.

Later that night, after supper and Callian's rounds for numbers, we sit in the living room. I sip on the tea that Imani gave me. It took me a few goes to get the portion right. But by the third cup, putting twice as much in as I initially thought to, it actually tastes nice.

The fire crackles in front of the four of us. Enzo yawns and Anya nods to the hallway.

"You're right, my love, it is definitely bedtime for this old man," he grumbles, rising from his chair.

Anya presses a kiss to Callian's forehead and steps to where I sit beside him, arm wrapped around his. She bends down and cups my face in her hands. "Goodnight, sweetheart. We are so glad you are here."

I smile. "Goodnight, Anya."

Callian watches me and his mother, the sweetest smile wrapped across his cheeky face, before she wanders down the hall after Enzo. After a moment passes, he stretches, hands turning to fists over his head. His chest sinks with a long sigh. He is happy. I watch his face relax as he closes his eyes and rubs his thumb over my hands.

I move off the chair and straddle his lap. His eyes open. "Hello, beautiful. Not tired?"

"Not really." I trace the border of his jaw with a finger and watch as his lips curl into a smile.

I lower my head to his neck and kiss my way from the base of his throat to his jaw. His breath shallows out, and his hardness grows underneath me. Heavens, I could do this forever. His large, warm hands slide under my tunic, and he makes quick work of tugging my supports from my chest. In one move, he has both the tunic and supports on the floor. The fire crackles behind me, flames licking the glowing timbers in a dance of heat and hunger.

His shirt hits the floor next. He slides a finger into my pants. I stifle a whimper as he finds my wet heat. He swallows and lays his head on the back of the chair. I rise on my knees, nipping his ear before dragging my teeth down the column of his throat. He groans into my ear and sinks two fingers inside my core. I bite his shoulder to hold back the moan that rattles against my teeth.

Callian shifts his head forward, and his eyes find mine. "You want to go to bed?"

"Here is just fine," I rasp.

The corner of his mouth kicks up, and he removes his hand from my pants. I whimper at the loss. He tugs at my pants with both hands. I stand and he slides them over my hips, taking my undergarments with them. I pull my hair from its ties, and it bounces around my bare shoulders. Callian's eyes darken as he traces a finger around my stomach, circling my belly button. His finger tracks downward, and I hold his gaze. The heat in my core is so intense, I need to move. I fumble with his trousers, and he lifts his hips for me to slide them down to the floor. His hard length stands, waiting. Just looking at it makes my entire body burn.

He smiles and tugs me back onto his lap. I kneel over him. I plunge my tongue into his mouth, and he devours me. I wriggle my hips over him, and he groans so loud I am afraid his parents will come out to see what the noise was. I still for a moment, hovering over him. Waiting for movement in the house.

"I don't think they are going to come out here, Nirri."

I suck in a breath and track my gaze back to his tortured face. Bringing him to this is addictive. Seeing the beautiful agony on his face is one of the best things I have ever done. I promise from this day forward that Callian will always feel loved and wanted, and I will do everything I can to see that face he makes when he is in heaven, every day.

"Callian," I whisper.

"Hmmm," he all but groans.

"I don't want this moment to end."

He opens his eyes and smiles. "We can have millions more, Nirri."

I grip his face in my hands and cover his mouth with mine as I sink onto him. The moan that leaves his mouth rattles all the way into my chest. I adore that sound more than anything. I rise, moving all the way up, until he is at the entrance of me again. Over and over until his breath is so ragged, his face so wrecked with plea-sure, that my heart wants to burst. I whimper, and his mouth finds my chest, clamping around a peak. Instantly, release tears through my core. I ride each wave, tightening around him with a long steady stroke upward. His forehead hits my shoulder as he growls through his own release.

I sit hovering over his lap with nerves alight, dotting kisses over his face and neck and trailing my lips over both hard, molded sides of his chest. His hands wander through my hair. He sighs and lays his head back on the chair, letting his eyes drift closed.

"You can't fall asleep here," I say.

"Who said I was sleeping? Just don't want to leave heaven, that's all."

Heaven.

Why did it take me so long? Now, it's just days until the war. What if this is all we get? My hands shake on his chest.

"Open your eyes, Callian."

He does and finds my gaze. Tears burn as they well in my eyes, and his hands reach for my face. "Hey."

I sniffle back a sob and let a tear slip down my cheek. "I cannot lose you."

"You are never going to lose me." He sits up and wraps both corded arms around my bare body. "Never, Nirri." His body trembles. "Never." The word is no more than a choked whisper.

He holds me for a moment before I compose myself and push off his lap. He stands and pulls up his trousers, fastening them around his hips. I pluck my clothes from the floor. He scoops me up in his arms and I giggle.

"I need to get dressed."

"Nope. You don't need clothes, not tonight. Not around me."

He walks us down the hallway and turns into his bedroom. The double bunk is lined with furs and pillows. It smells like Callian. I breathe it all the way in. He lowers me to the bed. I don't care if I never sleep again.

CHAPTER 33
HARM

Imani's wavy dark hair drifts in front of my gaze. I swallow past the growing stone in my throat and slide my hands around her waist. The sun is fast disappearing to our left. The birds call impatiently before the dark forces them to roost high in the canopy above us.

We settle down next to the fire I made moments ago, and Imani pulls her food from her rucksack. I watch her—her pink curved lips, the way her hair hangs beside her face, her hand pushing it behind her ear. My stomach flips at the possibility of losing her.

She is trained to fight, but she stands a solid six inches shorter than most men. I flex my fingers from fist to stretch, over and over. As if she can read my worried mind, she looks at me, still chewing, and offers a soft smile.

I shuffle closer and wrap an arm around her waist. She offers me some of the jerky and cheese she is nibbling on. I shake my head. She swallows and drops the food in the cloth on her lap, brows lowering. "What is it?"

I tamp down the need to pull her into my chest, safe and sound, never to be in harm's way again. But that would be like plucking the wings off one of Charlie's elegant, free-soaring butter-flies. And I could never do that. Imani holds her own. She lives to make our world a better place. One of the many reasons I am hopelessly hers until my last breath.

"Nothing, just tired."

Her eyebrow raises. She doesn't believe a word I say. I chuckle to myself and shift closer still. The trees surrounding us fade in the mist that rolls in, cloaking everything it touches with its wet fingers. She shudders, and I pull my robe from my rucksack to lay it over her shoulders. I am rewarded with a soft kiss to the mouth.

She goes to move back, but I hold her where she is. A smile grows on her beautiful face, blue eyes burning into mine. The sky above us growls, mist swirling around us, the fire hissing in protest of its new watery threat.

Both hands holding her face, I smash my mouth into hers, and she meets me with equal hunger. My breath turns urgent. Her hands slide behind my neck and up, gripping my hair right above the small birthmark that started this journey of ours so long ago.

Emotion clogs my throat, and I falter through a rough breath. Imani sits back and stands. The air turns heavy around us as the sky groans under its weight. Lightning flashes to our north, lighting up the forest around us for a second. I sit on the damp ground as she loses the robe, then her tunic. She fumbles with the fastener of her pants for a moment before they also slide onto the grass.

In nothing but her undergarments, she watches me, her blue eyes turning to liquid slate. With one hand, she peels back the supports around her chest. My mouth goes dry as my breath stops. I will never have enough of my wife, for as long as I live.

Keeping her gaze steady on mine, she slides two fingers into the undergarment at her hips and pushes it off, letting it float to her feet. She pulls the wrap from her hair, and it tumbles down around her shoulders. Bending over a little, she steps out of the pile of her discarded clothes. Lush, round breasts hang in front of me.

The fire in my belly now fuels the almost painful hardness in my pants. "Dammit, Imani, you are so beautiful."

"And you, my sweet husband, have far too many clothes on." She kneels in front of me and tugs at the hem of my shirt. Half-dazed by too-shallow breaths, I let her remove my shirt. Her fingers trace the contours of my chest, leaving a trail of sparks as she goes. She rises and pulls on my hand. I stand, and she moves into my space. I slide my hand around her waist, tugging her into my chest with one hand. The other finds the lushness of her chest. She whimpers into my mouth, and heat rushes my body.

Raindrops scatter through the curling mist, landing on our skin. I feel every drop. I feel every inch of her skin on mine. Her hands tangle with the top of my trousers before they fall from my waist. Her hand wraps around me, and I almost choke on the groan that follows, heart flinging in my chest. Thunder cracks over-head, and I pull us to the ground. Imani kneels, waiting for what-ever I choose to do next. I want her where I can see her. Where I can watch her face and cover her with kisses and affection. I sit on the grass and tug her into my lap. She chuckles and takes my face with both hands. Her mouth finds mine. I run my knuckles over one peak and then the other. She squirms on my lap. Moaning, low and rough, every inch of me burns for her.

Her breathing has long turned shallow. I trail a finger between her breasts and down her stomach, stopping just short of where she wants me. She leans back and grips my hair in her hands. She growls at me. I force back a smile. Turning Imani Travesci feral is my absolute favorite pastime. I lower my finger to her throbbing, budded apex. She whimpers as her head falls backward.

"Harm," she whispers, my name a plea.

"Yes, my love?"

Her chest rises and falls quickly, her grip in my hair tightening. "Please, don't make me wait."

I grip her hips and raise her up so we meet up where we need it most. The soft pitter-patter of the rain turns heavier. The fire hisses to embers beside us.

Her eyes find mine.

I lower her down, ever so slowly. "Never, Imani." The crooked, cheeky smile on my face earns me a small growl.

A breathy cry rips from her lips, and she trembles in my lap. I raise her up, this time letting her fall back down. Her moan sends fire through my core, the swell of heat gathering at the base of my spine. She tightens around me, burying her head in my neck, laying kisses from the base of my throat up to my ear. Lightning snaps across the sky, blasting light finding its way through the gaps in the canopy. I groan into her hair, hands tight on her hips. Breathless and shaky, I pause for a moment to hold off. Thunder crackles directly overhead. The tingle of approaching release spreads through my body. She finds my mouth with hers, coaxing my willing mouth open. Her elegant curves move under my hands, and she rises and falls, taking me higher with every move she makes. I break from her mouth. Her hair, now wet from the rain, covers her chest, and I move it aside with both hands to find her peaks with my teeth. Rain trickles down her face, her neck, and her chest.

Her sweet cries echo through the forest for a handful of heartbeats before she shatters altogether. Keeping her cadence, she takes me with her. Reluctant to take my gaze off her broken, stunning face, I close my eyes as the blinding light of my release flares. The rain's steady hush turns to a roar, pelting down on us. I force my eyes open after a breath, determined to watch her through the veil of the rain. Droplets hit her face, sliding over her mouth, split by another sweet sound that sings through her lips. Her cries settle to moans before her trembling hand touches my face and she opens her eyes, a happy, satiated smile lighting up her face. We sit, mouths open, breathing heavily through the rain. She runs her hands through my wet hair and laughs, the sound so free and so loving that my heart aches.

When the last of our heat leaves our ragged bodies, Imani rises, sending a shudder through my body at her absence. She stands, arms open wide, head back, and mouth open in the pouring rain. The smile that grows at her absolute happiness in this moment consumes my face. I stand and take up the same pose. Naked, arms out wide, head tilted back, and mouth open. And in the handful of heartbeats that follow, I realize that this is a moment I will remember and cherish for the rest of my life.

Harsh, brilliant golden sunlight slips through the widening crack of the stone door. Our last trip to the desert side. And, if everything Nirri and I have worked for plays out the right way, it will be the last time we step onto desert sands, void of all moisture, packing a stinging heat few can survive. I place a foot into the glittering sands and glance sideways to where Imani stands beside me. Where she has stood all along. Where she goes, I go. No matter if that means this life or the next, as Hanola would say.

After two days of traveling through the day and half of the night, we arrive at the front door of my grandmother's house in Indori, east of Mareya. The home I recovered in after my prison stay with Fletcher. When we thought we had lost Imani.

I knock on the weathered wood, glancing around the sandy village. Imani's wrap is firm over her face, only her eyes visible. Her hand hovers over her hip, where her concealed fighting knives hang.

Footsteps from inside drift toward the door, light and elegant. My gut flips. Has Jonah moved on? Does someone else live here now? With Enid gone, maybe staying here was too hard for Jonah, and we have come to the wrong place.

The door creaks open slowly. The face that greets me is not one I expect. Her wavy light brown hair is tied and pulled to one side, her round face and kind hazel-green eyes lighting up as she realizes who I am.

Flick.

"Jonah!" she calls behind her. "Quick!"

Mumbles and the hurried steps of the heavier, slower man I was expecting shuffle toward the open door. He pauses just before the threshold as his gaze drifts from mine to Imani's.

"Courtesy of the south winds," I joke, remembering the night I met Jonah, when we had come from the north to his gypsy camp. He pulls the both of us into a rough hug before dragging us through the door. Flick shuts it behind us. Jonah holds Imani at arm's length, as he always does, and inspects her over. She releases a hand from his and unwraps her hair and face. Her smile beams, and Jonah pulls her into another tight hug. I turn to see Flick smiling at the two of them. Why is she here? What did I miss?

"Who is it, Flick?" The voice of Luca comes from the back door. Ah, now I understand. They must have found each other when Luca was hiding out in the healer's shelter in Donterra. Good for them. But I didn't think Flick would leave her post as healer for Luca. Not permanently.

As if my face had altered to match my thoughts, Flick rests a hand on my arm, nodding to the living room. Unwrapping my head gear and dumping my rucksack by the door, I follow her. Luca bounds through the flimsy wooden screen door toward the living room. His face lights up the same as his father's did moments earlier as he meets my gaze.

"Harm!" His hand slaps over my shoulder. I return the gesture.

He sits on the larger lounge chair, and Flick drops beside him, tucking her feet under her lap.

"It's good to see you both," I say.

Luca beams at Flick, and she blushes before clearing her throat.

"Flick tells me you two grew up together," Luca says.

"Yep, we did."

Flick scoffs and pushes Luca's arm. Ah, so she already told him she and I were matched years ago. I am so glad that turned out different from how my parents intended. And, by the looks of things, so is Flick. Imani walks in, followed by Jonah, and drops into my lap, leaving one chair for Jonah to sit.

"Well, you're here. Does this mean the forest dwellers are ready?" Jonah asks.

"We are. Rendezvous is in four days," I say. Imani hops up from my lap and walks to the rucksack, pulling out the map Callian sent with us. She unrolls it as she walks back, resting it in Jonah's lap and pointing to the mark on the map that shows the rendezvous point.

He studies the paper for a moment before meeting my gaze. "Seems like a sound place as any. Your warriors are ready?"

"Yes, with the women and the existing trained warriors from every village. The forest dwellers are ready and two hundred and fifty strong."

"Luca?" Imani asks.

Instantly, the happiness falls from his face. "No help from the mountain side, I'm afraid. The cost was too steep for most of the men. I can't say I blame them, but I am disappointed—after all the Chancellor put most of them through, I really thought at least half would step forward. I only returned last night. Seb is taking care of things for now. Sorry, Imani."

"Don't be; you can't make people do things. None of this is

anyone's fault. The Chancellor has controlled everything for so long that free choice has become a foreign concept," she says.

Jonah eyes her and his gaze wanders to me. "Listen to you two. You are fast becoming leaders that deserve the title."

Imani shakes her head and flops into my lap. "I don't know, Jonah, but anything has to be better than the way things are now."

"I agree," a gruff voice interjects from the doorway. When did Christopher get here?

We stand and watch as he removes his wrap and robe just beyond the threshold, letting the sands fall to the ground outside the house.

Imani steps toward him. "Hello, Christopher."

"Hello, Imani. How's your father coping?" Christopher has always held more of a soft spot for the ex-commander than the rest of us.

Imani's face twists with a wobbly smile, silver lining her eyes. "He is doing just fine."

"I am glad to hear that. Regime aside, the past eight or so years have been particularly rough for him." Christopher steps into her space. "But I had a feeling the two of you would work it out. After all, a man who loves his daughter enough to join a regime that would bend him to his breaking point, to keep his only daughter safe? Nothing could come between that, not even the two of you stubborn Fletchers." His deadpan face cracks under a meek smile.

Jonah stands and claps a hand on Christopher's shoulder. "She is a Travesci now; you're stuck with her, Uncle."

Imani feigns an offended face, and Luca chuckles shaking his head.

"Come on," Flick says to Imani, rising from the chair. "I bet you would love a hot bath."

"You have no idea, Flick."

I smile, watching as the girls walk down the hall of Enid's

home. It seems that in her home we are always welcome. Her spirit lives on in the people around us, and still, if she were here, she would be fussing over us, loving and protecting us with everything she has. Warm baths included. I look to the heavens and whisper a silent thank you for all she has done for Imani and me.

Jonah's heavy arm wraps around my shoulders and I look between him and Christopher, who seem to have found their peace.

"How is Maryanne?" I interject, worried I may have missed something crucial.

"She is well, with some of our friends two villages over. Safe from the goings on of the current moment." He hesitates, drawing in a long breath. "You ready for this, my boy?" His gaze tracks to the hall where the girls just were before swinging back to me.

"Yes and no, if I'm honest. I'll never be willing or ready to put Imani in danger. Or anyone, for that matter. But I know it has to be done. I realize it may get worse before it gets better. I just keep reminding myself: what waits on the other side of this war is worth it."

Jonah nods as if the words he wants to say are lodged in his throat.

"Never have I heard a more accurate word," Luca says, pushing out of the deep lounge chair.

"But on a more practical level, we are ready, more than we have ever been. Our chances are good," I offer.

Christopher grunts in assent. I swallow at the words that need to follow. They don't know about Arthur rallying the savages. I search both Jonah's and Christopher's faces, my brows lowering, mouth tight in a thin line.

"What? What is it, Harm?" Jonah says.

I suck in a steadying breath. "The Chancellor"—I cast my gaze to Luca—"he has rallied the savages. Our numbers are not going to help us like we thought they will now." My stomach almost twists inside out with the way the three men's faces fall, mouths slightly agape.

Jonah staggers backward and sits in the chair. Christopher runs both hands through his hair, releasing a chain of hissed curses. Luca stands frozen, face paling.

"The forest warriors sighted them just two days ago; that's why we are here earlier than expected. We need the element of surprise now," I say, my voice gravel with the burden of the news I carry.

After moments of silence, Jonah snaps his head up.

We all stare at him, waiting.

"So be it. It's now or never. Be damned with what the Chancellor thinks he has. We are fighting for family. That is stronger than any makeshift, paid-off army he could gather."

Christopher shifts in his seat, eyeing Jonah for a second before he slaps the arms of the chair and nods. "Agreed. We follow through. But we double up on tactics to hone our strategy. Losing is not an option."

"You have no idea of the cruelty those savages are capable of, Pa. They are vicious. Nothing with them is a fair fight," Luca says, his hands balled to fists on the arms of the lounge chair.

"We fought and won against some of them once. Catori and Callian know some of what they are capable of and have adjusted accordingly," I offer.

Luca's devastated face doesn't shift. Flick walks into the lounge and stops short when she takes in the look on Luca's face.

"What did I miss?"

"The..." Luca starts, forcing a wobbly breath.

"The what?"

"The Chancellor has rallied the savages from our sector for the battle."

Her face pales.

She too must know about their methods, and I have no doubt Luca has told her many things about his life in the mountain wilds.

"Oh," she utters, falling onto the chair beside Luca. She stares at him before taking in the faces in the room around her.

Imani appears at her cousin's side. I hold out a hand, and she studies every silent face before settling on my lap. "You told them, I take it."

"Yep." I slide my arms around her waist and bury my head in her fragrant, damp hair hanging down her back. With a swift inhale, I wish we were anywhere but here. Anywhere but about to go to battle with the most ruthless, depraved humans to walk the earth.

"This changes nothing," Imani says. "We have one thing they will never have."

Jonah lifts his face to hold her gaze, as if asking for the answer to her rhetorical statement.

She lets a small smile push up on her face. "We have each other. We are family."

"Like hell you are going through that wall without me! I am not waiting here without you!" Flick snaps at Luca. She is sounding more and more like Imani by the second. And I feel we have spent decades underestimating the women in our villages.

Christopher tamps down a smile as he packs his rucksack. Imani stands and folds her arms, fierce blue eyes burning into her cousin's now-wavering front. He stands taller than both women by half a foot, easily.

He doesn't stand a chance.

"You cannot seriously expect Flick to stay here while you're risking your neck on the other side of the wall!" Imani hisses.

"If something happens to her, I am the one who will have to live without her!" he grinds out, scrubbing both hands behind his neck.

"And what if she has to live without you? You stubborn ass!" Imani fires back.

Apparently, judging by the stony expression that folds over Luca's face, it's hereditary. I know this scenario well. I have been fighting this internal war since the moment Imani's brilliant blue eyes first met mine. I know all too well the heaviness in your gut that comes with watching your loved ones near danger. But I bite my tongue with the knowledge of what trying to control others for our own benefit, to ease our own discomfort, does to the other person. Imani huffs, shifting her feet in the face of her hulking cousin.

"She won't be left behind. She can travel with the rest of the healers in a days' time and stay away from the battle lines. This is not up to you, Imani. It is between Flick and I," Luca bites out.

"That's right, Luca; we both get a say. And there is no way you are going over that wall to a potential death sentence and leaving me with a broken heart. If you are going, so am I." Flick shoves her belongings into his rucksack. He rips them out and puts them on the kitchen table to his right.

"Fine, I will pack my own bag, you infuriating man!" She stalks down the hallway to their room. The old spare room. Once my room, then Marshall's.

Jonah appears by his son's side. "Don't make a choice you will regret, my boy. Let the woman make up her own mind. It's not yours to command."

Luca's jaw feathers, but he nods, fear and love tearing his stoic square face apart with every shallow breath. He has met his match. And I know how he feels. The thought of Imani being anywhere near those savages guts me. But as Jonah said, it is her choice, not mine. I have learned slowly over the last year to turn that part of me off when we are fighting. It doesn't serve either of us well to be distracted by the other.

"If it helps, she will be tending the wounded behind the battle. Not actively part of it," I offer.

Luca frowns and ties up his rucksack. Flick waltzes to the front door, robe on, hood up, wrap hanging around her neck, and rucksack over her shoulder. She gives Luca a cheeky smile before landing a brief kiss on his worry-twisted lips. I smile at them both. His arm slides around her waist, and he pins her to the wall by the door.

"That's our cue," Christopher says, stepping outside as if they have been living around the desires of Luca and Flick long enough to know when it is time to take a walk.

We follow the two older men outside, and I shut the door behind me, leaving Luca and Flick behind for a moment. Imani bumps her shoulder into mine. "Remember when we were like that?"

"Remember? You're still like that."

"Don't you forget it, Harmen Travesci," she says with a wink, wriggling her hips and walking a few paces in front of me.

Christopher chokes on a laugh. "Well, I guess there will be no dull moments with you two around."

Jonah's laugh fills my weary heart. A few heartbeats later, the door behind us shuts again, and Luca and Flick jog to catch up, flushed but smiling. I am glad they are both here. We are going to need all the help we can get. Luca is a born fighter, hardened by living in the mountain wilds. Flick is a talented healer, and with her team and supplies arriving the day after us, her presence is invaluable. I track my gaze to the defiant hips striding into the sands in front of me. A wisp of her dark hair escapes her wrap. I hasten my step and catch up to Imani. She glances my way with a soft, loving smile. Our last walk through the sands, if we're lucky. If we can best an army pieced together with soldiers and savages hell-bent on wiping us from this earth. If we can get through that, the rest will be easy.

That's what I tell myself as I lace my fingers through Imani's. She dots a kiss on my neck and squeezes my hand.

My heart tightens.

I have absolutely *everything* to lose.

CHAPTER 34
CATORI

The clash of steel reverberates through the canopy swaying above our makeshift rebel camp an hour from our final rendezvous point. Each forest warrior takes a turn to fine-tune their skills, some of them have been honing them for years, some only months, and the pit of my stomach turns to rocks. *We are ready*, I keep telling myself. Everyone has done their utmost best. But the growing weight in my chest has been second-guessing every decision the six of us have made over the last year. The decisions I have made since Hanola left us.

Callian finishes up yet another round of twin sword work with one of the newer warriors and calls it a day. Having taken over from me at lunchtime, he is drenched in sweat. He must be exhausted. Tomorrow, we rest our tired bodies before the day of the battle. We will need every minute of rest to recover enough to fight with power and clear heads.

I walk to where the new warriors are now draining their canteens. "How did you lot go?"

They look up at me, red faced and breathless. They left nothing behind in the sparring ring. My brother wouldn't allow them to.

"I think we are ready, Catori," one woman says with a brief smile. I search the faces of the others who sit on the grass around her. They nod sporadically, out of breath, their bodies alive with the harsh strain of fighting. I can't help but wonder how many of these brave souls we will lose. How many will live past the next forty-eight hours to return to their families. But we have little choice now.

War is never fair nor is it pretty, my grandmother used to tell Callian and me when we were younger. I used to think she was saying it for his benefit. But as I look around at the people willing to fight for what we believe in, for a better future, I realize now, as her heir and leader of the forest people, her words were for me.

Death is not a path you choose. It finds you one way or another. So, if we are to face it soon, let it be for something worth fighting for.

Mason appears by my side. His fingers wrap around mine, and I press a kiss to his lips. He leans his head on mine briefly, squeezing my hand. I want to tell him so much. He is what I am fighting for. For the things he has suffered through. For the future I want for us. But when his gaze catches mine, silver lined, I see that he already knows. My match in every way.

"We are ready." I nod to the last of the warriors in the sparring ring on the other side of the makeshift training area.

"I see that," he says, his voice low and gravelly.

"Any sign of Harm and Imani?"

"Not yet, but they will be here soon."

"I hope so. Yesterday would have been better. Being split up like this makes me nervous."

"You, nervous? Leader of the forest clan?" He leans into me.

"Yes; I have the same emotions as the rest of you. I'm just mostly better at controlling them. Something Hanola taught me."

"Except around me?" He raises an eyebrow.

"You will always be my exception, Mason Rayner."

The widest smile lights up his face, and my heart skips a beat.

The next beat sees my throat close over as it dawns on me that I could lose the most important person in my life in the next few days.

I push the hideous thought from my mind and spin into his space, crashing my mouth over his. He sinks into the kiss, hands curling around my cheeks.

A hearty laugh breaks the humid air behind us. "You will have plenty of time for that after the battle, you two." I turn toward my brother's voice and see the humor fade from his eyes, as if he just had the same thought I did seconds ago. Not all of us may make it to the other side of this. And if we lose, chances are none of us will live very long.

"Come on, let's check in on Nirri. She is running herself ragged in the healer's tent getting ready," Callian says.

He stalks toward the makeshift healer's tent, the biggest tent in our temporary camp. He flings back the tent flap and holds it open as Mason and I follow him into the space.

Rows of roughly made bunks line the walls of the tent. Three trolleys are loaded up with a few of each necessary item for wound care, sitting patiently in the long, narrow space between the two rows. Nirri looks up from the bunk she is making up with clean linen and finishes tucking it down before moving around it toward my brother. Callian closes the distance between them and presses her to his chest, kissing her wild blonde curls, now escaping the cloth she has tied over her head to keep her hair out of her face as she works. They fit together so well, needing each other like the earth needs the sun.

"This looks great, Nirri," Mason says.

She moves from Callian's hold. "It should suffice—as long as we are not inundated and the rest of the supplies arrive with Flick."

With the rest of the desert side and Flick coming tomorrow, I feel some of the weight in my chest lighten. But not enough.

"We should settle in and get these hungry warriors some supper before they start running on fumes. I doubt that would work out well for any of us," Callian says. A true leader, my brother. Becoming head warrior has truly seen him thrive. He is no longer a boy. My little brother is a man. A selfless, caring man.

I stem the prickling at the back of my throat that is surely to come with tears and suck in a breath. "Yes, I'm starving."

We walk slowly toward the village center. There are no tables here. We eat on the ground or in our tents, saving the manpower for carrying weapons and other crucial supplies. The small kitchen the women set up is busy, and I get to work handing out the hearty portions of food. Every warrior will need proper fuel to carry them through the next two days. With every plate I hand out, a set of grateful eyes meets mine. And before long, my face hurts from smiling back at them as they nod with thanks, taking the plates and settling on the grass to eat.

I turn back to pick up another two plates. The line shuffles behind me, and I spin back, plates in hand, to see what the fuss us about. Harm and Imani stand in the line, grins stretching their faces, each holding out a hand toward me.

Tension lifts from my shoulders like a bird taking flight. I drop the plates and round the bench, barely getting halfway before Imani envelops me in a hug. Mason chuckles from a few feet away, meeting Harm's gaze before walking to where we stand. Imani releases me and Mason folds her into his chest. Those two will always be inseparable.

Harm stands to my side and wraps an arm around my shoulders. Our greetings after being apart are always so familiar. He squeezes me into his side. "Hey, Catori. How's it looking?"

I blow out a deep breath and scan the camp before meeting his gaze. "I think we are ready." My words are solemn, and he catches the tone, frowning.

"The rebels will be here around lunchtime tomorrow, hopefully. As long as they don't run into any trouble. Also, I brought a few extras with me." He nods to Luca and a girl I have never seen before. I study her face as she stands with Luca, fingers laced in his. Harm tracks my gaze.

"That's Flick. Marshall's cousin. Nirri's mentor from Donterra."

Oh, she is young. But I guess, when I think about it, we all are. Too young to die, but old enough to fight. *That* particular irony will never be lost on me.

"How about that food?" Harm nudges my hip with his.

"Sure, I could use the distraction." I grab two plates from the girl who took over serving when I was intercepted by my family and hand them to Harm and Imani. Two more plates appear in the girl's hand. Mason takes them for us, and we follow Imani as she picks her way through the groups of hungry warriors to a clear patch of grass. Dropping to her seat, she instantly starts eating. I guess five days of mostly jerky and cheese will do that to a person. I sit beside her and offer her a smile. She beams back at me. I am so glad she is home. I know Mason misses her and Harm. I do. The six of us are like a fixed entity these days. And being split up has never served us well.

We eat under the flickering light of the fires burning on long sticks sunk into the earth all through the camp. Their shadows play around the small groups of people chatting and eating happily. Nirri and Callian join us after seeing to the last few people, ensuring each warrior had been given supper before they took their own.

Nirri rests her head on Callian's shoulder and closes her eyes, her hands gripping her plate in her lap. She looks exhausted, and the fight has not even begun.

"Good to see you, brother," Callian says to Harm. Nirri's eyes open and she mutters her greeting, a smile lazily pulled up over her pretty face.

"Good to be back. I see you have made some good progress since we left. The camp and the warriors all look ready to go."

"We still have that one loose end to tie up before battle," Callian says, eyes burning into Harm's as he winks.

"Oh, I haven't forgotten." Harm smiles, tearing off a chunk of meat and chewing on it.

What are they talking about? Everything has been planned out and executed. What could we possibly have left to do? I frown at my brother, but if he sees me, he ignores me, happily eating his food. Nirri and Imani eat their food as if they didn't hear the brief conversation that went on. I look to Mason and he shrugs, digging into the meat on his plate.

Whatever it is, I don't want to know. I have enough to worry about besides their boyish pranks.

With an empty plate and full belly, I lay back on the grass. Mason's head rests on my belly, and we intertwine our fingers. The canopy, despite the darker hour, is still restless with the calls of birds. Stars poke their way through scant patches of the canopy, and I watch as they shimmer in the breeze, the winds of earth playing with the reflections of the heavens. I wonder if Hanola is watching us. Can she see us? Does she know what we are about to do? I wonder if she knows what waits for us after the next few days.

I slam my eyes shut and breathe through the fear that snakes its way around my spine. Sickness rides up my center and I swallow it back down. I do not have the luxury of being afraid. That would only result in poor decisions, haphazard fighting, and lives lost. I decide in this moment to tamp down fear and focus on outcomes. Tactics and strategy.

I study the faces of my family and find mixed emotions etched over each face. I sit up and Mason groans at me, eyes closed. He must have been almost asleep. I trace a finger over his jaw and his eyes open. I bend down and dot kisses over his mouth and nose and along his jaw as it feathers under my lips.

"We should go over plans one last time before we turn in," Harm says, breaking my moment with Mason.

I straighten. "Sure." It seems leaders think alike. Harm will make a brilliant leader for the desert sector, or whatever it ends up being after the dial is changed. I hope for their sake the earth can be redeemed, and that they flourish.

We lazily pull to our feet, one after the other. Slowly, we wander to the center of camp, dropping onto the logs laid out around the large firepit.

"So, I have been mulling over our original plan for days," Harm starts. "It is solid. But I think we really need to stick to the timelines and tactics we have come up with if we want this to play out in our favor."

"Agreed. We strike the day after next. Any longer, and it just gives the Chancellor time to discover where we are and work out our plans," Mason says.

"We need both sides to make the numbers, or we won't be able to take the savages. Before, we had a great chance; now, our chances are less. It could go either way," Callian adds. His words leave my stomach upturned.

"Okay, so, we have three ranks: our larger center army, and one flanking each side. Archers in the trees. Healers just beyond the battle lines. Once the fighting turns in our favor, Imani and I go after Arthur and his personal guard. Harm, you make for the tower. We are close enough to it that if any of the savages go after you, we will see. Change that dial and remove the power source, then get the hell out of there and back to the fight for the finale. Everyone has a job.

"Are we all on board with the order of things?" I finish.

"Solid plan," Imani says.

"Yep, all good here," Mason says.

Harm nods. "Yes. Simple, but effective."

"Ready when you are, sis." Callian smiles.

"I do have one request," Nirri says. Every gaze swings to her.

"What is it?" Mason asks.

I hold my breath, hoping it is not something I can't grant.

"Promise me you will all still be standing when this is over." Nirri studies each of our faces in turn, the silver in her eyes illuminated by the dancing reds and oranges of the fire.

Mason stands and walks to where she sits. "I promise, Nirri." He leans down and wraps her in a brief hug. She forces a wobbly smile. Harm stands and repeats the action. A tear spills over her porcelain cheek. Callian watches her, his face twisted with love and agony.

Imani stands and walks a few paces, halting inches from her. "You have my word, little sis." She kisses her on the forehead and leaves. I stand and track the now-worn grass to Nirri.

"I will bring him home for you, Nirri." I rest my hands over hers.

"All of you, Catori. Every single one of you," she rasps, helplessness piercing her gaze. Not being on the battlefield with us, beside Callian, must be eating her alive.

"I promise. When the last of them fall, all six of us will be standing."

She nods, the movement sending tears down her face. I cup her cheeks with both hands. How did we get so lucky as to have a sister so loving, so selfless, so brave as to remain behind and care for the injured while her heart is on the battlefield, beating where my brother stands. Where each of us fights. I drag in a deep breath, fighting for air over my quickly closing throat. She rests her hand over mine and closes her eyes.

Callian's eyes are trained on her face, his arm wrapped around her waist. He dips his head to hers, her pain written over his face.

"Night, Nirri," I whisper.

She lets me go, her trembling hands finding my brother's. I walk to my tent, pulling the flap back. I pause before entering and look up. Through the gap in the canopy, I count six shimmering stars. One for each of us.

And just like that, my mettle hardens. I push my shoulders back. The savages don't even realize it yet, but their breaths on this earth have just been numbered. The weight in my chest vanishes, and I slam my right fist over my heart.

Time is up, Chancellor.

I toss and turn on the hard bunk Mason and I were issued. He lies beside me, awake, fingers laced under his head, releasing a chuckle. "You are going to send me flying off this bunk any second with your tossing and turning. Do you need another blanket?"

I grunt and roll over to face him. I touch his jaw with my hand, and his smile softens. He pecks a kiss to my forehead.

"Maybe."

Without a word, he rises from the bunk and walks from the tent in search of a blanket. Nirri has them stashed in her bulk storage tent by the healer's tent. I roll onto my back and count each breath. After I count past one hundred, I sit up. Mason should be back by now. Worried he got talked into helping someone, I stand and hold back the tent flap. A few people mill about in the light of the center fire, shifting things, chatting softly. I scan the space between our tent and the healer's.

No Mason.

The swish of trodden damp grass from behind startles me. I go to turn but a sack falls over my head and a hand presses roughly over my mouth. I try to kick the intruder, missing. Two firm hands clasp over my right arm, another two over my left. My breath stops, not returning. The material is thick; I can't see through it. I glance down to see the grass move as they shove me forward.

No one speaks.

Just heavy breaths from the owners of the four hands digging into my arms, the hand around my mouth still too firm for me to scream. So, three people, then?

If this is the Chancellor's idea of an abduction, he needs to learn a few things about the trade. Once this hood comes off and we are clear of my people, I will snap each of their necks with my bare hands.

Is this some kind of tactic? Is he taking leaders before the battle to instill fear into the rebels, giving him yet another advantage? The weight in my chest returns and I struggle to shake off the firm grip tugging me forward.

I am pulled to a stop.

Wait, we only went a matter of feet. The heat of the fire is to my right, its crackles and pops making it to my ears despite the growing whispers around me. Are they going to execute me in my own camp? In front of my family? Fire courses through my insides, sending fury to my cheeks.

Another group of footsteps approaches, stopping an arm's length from where I stand. At least I think they do.

I smell him before I hear his familiar, fast breathing.

Mason.

Dammit. If they lay a hand on him, I will slaughter every last one of them. The hands around my arms lighten before falling away completely. People are walking around us, muttering in low whispers. To my left, I hear sand hissing, something snapping, and an object thudding into a wooden surface. A piney, green smell meets me. Is that leaves?

Some kind of ritual.

I raise my hand, searching for Mason.

My stomach plummets as his jaw feathers against my palm.

CHAPTER 35

MASON

Catori's hands are on my face.

My heart thunders in my chest.

What is happening? I wrap my hands around hers. Every breath is so deep, stars encroach my black vision. We haven't walked far enough to have even breached the camp boundary. Her hands move on my face, and I lean into her palm. Body rigid, waiting for what will happen next, I listen as the hushed movements around us turn to whispers.

Familiar ones.

The bag is tugged from my head. Catori is still covered in hers, her breathing turned shallow. Harm stands to my right, and the smile across his face melts the knots in my gut. Imani stands behind Catori, as if waiting for her.

Callian removes the sack from Catori's head, and she whips her head around, the anger on her face falling as she meets her smiling brother's gaze. His firm grip around her arms falls away and she gasps, looking from Callian to Harm. It is now that I notice a small altar behind him with a glass of sand and a bowl of leaves, Nirri standing behind it. I move, and the crackles of forest leaves and branches ebb from underfoot.

I glance down. Laid out all over the communal area by the central firepit are large green leaves, the same type from when Catori was inaugurated as leader of the forest people. She follows my gaze, taking in the same things I do. We look back at Harm, and he nods to Imani. Catori turns and watches as Imani steps up beside her and hands her a small bundle of flowers from the forest floor's abundant supply.

This is our Blending ceremony.

The smile that wraps around Imani's face is met by the moisture that leaves her silver-lined eyes. My breath leaves and doesn't return. Harm takes my hands. They shake in his and he tilts his head with a smile. Callian takes Catori's, dropping them into my upturned palms. She pulls in a long breath and shuffles closer. Her green eyes, now holding a fine line of silver, meet mine as she laughs through a wobbly breath. Her night tunic, soft and thin, rises and falls rapidly with her chest.

I rub the backs of her hands with my thumbs and try to swallow past the rising lump holding back each breath.

Harm clears his throat.

He looks to Catori before his gaze settles on mine. "You ready?"

"Absolutely."

Catori nods, her chin wobbling.

My chest explodes with the love that pours from her to me. Tears streaking down each of her cheeks, she grips my hands tight.

Harm begins.

"On this very day, two people become one. The sands of the desert meld with the leaves of the forest to be Blended for eternity. A union like none before; may your love, loyalty, and courage never leave your side. May your hearts always find their way back to each other, no matter what this life or the next plants in your path."

He pauses and studies our faces. Catori glances at Harm briefly before returning to me. My heart thunders in my chest, the ground beneath me moving of its own accord. I pull in a breath, shove my shoulders back, and hold her gaze.

She is my strength, and I hers.

Harm glances at Imani, lost in thought for a second before turning back to us. No doubt he is remembering the day Hanola Blended him and Imani. Now, I realize I am sorry I wasn't there for it. Catori squeezes my hands, bringing me back to the present moment.

"May you both be carried by the wind, never separated. You are now and forever entwined, like the sands of the dunes, like the falling leaves on the wind's breath. Blended to each other, forever loyal and holding strong through the storms that weather both sands and forest alike. Now and always." Harm raises his hands above his head.

"Now and always!" the people surrounding the ceremony chant, patting their right hands over their hearts twice, like a heartbeat. Catori's warriors file in, making a circle around Catori and me, Harm, Imani, Nirri, and Callian.

"Okay, brother, you may kiss your wife." Harm winks.

For the first time since the day I met her, I see Catori blush. The smile that explodes over my face stretches my heart. I step into her space, and her eyes darken as they meet mine. Her hands find my face, and she pulls me closer. My mouth finds hers. We lose sight of everything around us. She presses her body to mine. My hand slides to her waist, gripping her hips as we spiral with the heady kiss.

Imani's laugh pulls me back. Catori stills, but her hands run through my hair. "I love you, Mason Rayner. More than you will ever know." Her words are barely a whisper.

The corner of my mouth tugs up. "I love you too, Cat. Always will. This life and the next."

Her fingers tremble as they fall from my hair to my jaw, and then to my chest.

Harm lifts the glass of sand and pours it over the leaves in the bowl. Nirri takes a small dagger and swirls it through the grains of sand and glossy green leaves, blending them together. Blessings from both her and Harm. I lace my fingers through Catori's, and Harm nods behind us toward the crowd of waiting forest people. We turn to face them.

"Now and always!" Harm calls.

The crowd echoes it back twice.

Catori smiles, taking in every beaming face. I dot a kiss onto her forehead and the crowd explodes with cheers. I loose a laugh and walk with her toward her people.

Our people.

The circle of warriors breaks to let us through, and we greet each person in turn, hugging every single person who has not only come to brave the Chancellor, but has welcomed me into their home, their forest, their life. And I will be eternally grateful they gave me the chance. I will be forever grateful Catori saw me for who I was and gave me a chance when I needed her so much, from that very first session at Hanola's. My heart will always be hers.

With the prospect of battle only two nights away, Catori insists that rest is better than celebration tonight, promising our family that our celebration will be twofold after we take the battle. She leads me toward our tent after tight hugs from Harm, Nirri, and Callian. Imani kisses my cheek then releases me to Catori, her eyes still lined with silver. I pull her back into a hug and cradle her head with my hand.

"Hey, it will be okay. We can do this. We will all be standing on the other side. I promise you that, little sister."

She struggles through a whimper, as if our ceremony has just reminded her of how much we all have to lose if things don't go in our favor. She pushes off my chest with splayed palms and sucks in a breath, nodding before turning back and wandering toward Harm.

I watch her go, and Catori's hand slides into mine. "We will be okay," she whispers into my neck.

I close my eyes and let the burn of tears take hold. I open them to a blurry vision of Harm wrapping Imani into his chest. Callian and Nirri stand by, consoling each other, their faces torn by happiness, love, and the agony and fear of losing anything in the following few days.

I turn back and scoop Catori into my arms, acutely aware of the little time we have left before the battle begins. I don't plan on wasting a second.

I reach our tent and spin to walk backward through the flaps. Catori chuckles and grabs my face with both hands, pulling my mouth to hers. I step cautiously backward until my legs hit the bunk. With a half turn, I lower her onto it. She lays down, chest cycling through ragged breaths, green eyes dark but soft, her beautiful face turned up in a cheeky smile.

"No walls here, Cat," I say, low and breathy.

"Anywhere with you is more than enough for me."

I tug at my shirt and pull it over my head, letting it drop to the floor. I pause to look at her. How the hell did I get so lucky? An ache grows, spreading from my chest to my core. Fire flickers in my veins, filling every inch of me with need for her. Catori sits up, her eyes still locked on mine. Her hands make quick work of the fasteners on my pants, and they hit the floor. She studies my body with a slow gaze upward until she meets my heated stare.

"Come here, husband," she whispers.

Damn, that sounds good.

I kneel on the bed before crawling over her on all fours. Amusement fills her face, her eyes darkening again. I nuzzle her neck before nipping at her skin. She wriggles beneath me, sending a surge of heat through my limbs before it settles in my core. "Too many clothes," I rasp out.

"Get them off me, Mas."

I kiss my way down her chest and clamp my teeth over her nipple through the threadbare sleep tunic. Her back arches up to me instantly. I rise on my knees and lift her tunic up. She wriggles as I slide it up over her head and toss it onto the floor. Her hands wrap around my neck, and she smashes her mouth into mine. Heat and want consume me. I break from her kiss, and she studies my face, pupils dilated fully.

"Nothing on this earth will ever compare to you, Catori."

She huffs a wobbly breath through a crooked smile. "Or you, Mason. Do whatever you want with me. I am yours."

I bend down, finding her peaks with my mouth. She whimpers, her body pressing into my hard center. I track my hands down her waist and over her hips, sliding them under her sleep pants. She moves off the bed to allow the clothing to move, and I push it down. I rise, crawling back up to meet her mouth with mine. She slides her hand around my neck and into my hair.

This right here is heaven.

When there is nothing between her and me, I nudge her legs apart with my knees. Her fingers curl in my hair, the barest of whimpers slipping into my mouth from hers as I find her center, driving deep into her warmth. Her body trembles under mine and her eyes glaze. I watch as her face twists with the beautiful agony I elicit from her with every stroke. But laying under me, a passive participant, has never been Catori's style. I pause and she finds my gaze.

Still joined, I wrap her in my arms and sit back on my heels. Her hair falls over her shoulders and frames her face. Her hands find my face, her mouth finding my own. She takes up the cadence between us, and it takes everything I have to hold back. Running a hand over her chest, I trace circles around each nipple, earning a disapproving growl from her. I clench my teeth over one peak, knowing exactly what she wants. Her rhythm quickens and my breath turns to ragged huffs.

I grip her hips and shuffle off the bunk. In a few long strides, we reach the table covered in maps, strategy papers, and months of planning between both sides. I lower her to the table, and her legs trap me where I stand. She leans back, hands splayed over the papers behind her, propping herself up. I move to take up the cadence and she sits up, pressing a hand to my chest.

"Take your time, husband." She trails a hand through the valley of my chest, over my hardened stomach, and toward the place we are joined.

"I intend to, wife." I slide almost all the way out, and her gaze burns into mine. She smiles at me, huffing a sweet laugh. I slam into her, and she releases a sweet cry that sees my heart burst. Out again, then I slam into her. Her legs tremble, hugging my hips tighter. Again and again, backing out to the tip, only to plunge as deep as I can go.

Catori explodes around me, pulling me under with her. I lean over her, gripping her wrists tight with both hands. Heat coils at the base of my spine, and I can't hold it any longer. The release barrels through my body, riding higher with every stroke that follows. Catori's chest heaves under me and I drop my head between her shaking breasts.

Many breaths later, I rise to find her watching me. Her soft green eyes are now lined with silver. If she is feeling anything like what I am, she is terrified to lose what we have found.

Each other.

I release my grip from her wrists and scoop her off the table. She nuzzles into my chest and closes her eyes. I lower her to the bunk. She rolls over to face me, still watching every move I make. I swallow down the agony of knowing this could all disappear in the space of a breath. Laying down beside her, I kiss her neck, then her cheek, then her lips. Her hands find my face and I close my eyes.

"Mas, whatever happens. Please know that I am grateful for any amount of time with you."

I open my eyes, searching her face. Tears track down her face onto the pillow. "Don't say that. We are both going to get through this."

Her finger presses against my lips. "I hope things go the way we want them to. But I have been a warrior for long enough to know that not every battle can be won, and most of them come at a high price."

My heart thunders in my chest, faster with each word she says. "I am not leaving your side in the that battle, Catori," I growl.

"You will do what you are required to do, Mason. And so will I. We both need to focus, or the people we love will be at risk. Promise me you will stick to the plan, *no matter what*. That's what I need you to do."

I suck in a handful of burning breaths. She is right. I know she is. Getting emotional doesn't help us. But just knowing she is going up against those savages terrifies me.

"I will do whatever needs to be done. But you promise me, Catori Rayner, you will be standing there waiting when this is all over."

She chuckles into my chest before pushing her head back on

the pillow to find my gaze. "I promise. And you, Mason Rayner, promise you'll be still standing when I come find you."

"I promise you the rest of my life and every one that follows, Mrs. Rayner."

She huffs another laugh.

I study her face. "What's so funny?"

"We don't have last names here. I guess now I do. I kind of like it." She pecks a kiss to my nose and snuggles in close, trailing circles over my chest like she has many times before. Like her lullaby to me. I close my eyes and let her drag my weary body and worried mind into oblivion beside hers.

A shard of a scream rips through the humid air inside our tent. I sit up, lightning surging through my veins. The sound curdles my blood, allowing fear to pierce my core. Catori stirs beside me. I shake her awake, pulling on my pants as I stand and pluck my shirt from the floor. Catori springs to her feet and is dressed in seconds. I snatch my weapons from the table and shove them into my belt before tossing Cat hers. A ruckus is growing on the north side of the tent. I step through the tent flaps and the sounds abate.

The dawn's early rays split the space between the trees. The sounds stop, as if cut off. Nothing else stirs for a moment.

It's too quiet.

No animals.

No birds.

No sounds at all, save the wind in the trees over us. It's as if everything is hiding, and a hideous snake of fear slithers up my spine. I take a step toward the camp center, scanning the tree line as I go. Catori is close behind me. A muffled sound comes from behind us.

It is then I see an arm wrapped around one of the trees just beyond our camp. No grey; just ragged brown clothing.

Savage.

I freeze and look back at Catori.

She has seen it too. Her face is stone, hands on her weapons. Someone is here. I search the trees for more savages. I make my way to Harm's tent with casual steps, resisting the urge to grip the hilts of my blades. I slip inside his tent and Catori stays outside to watch for movement. Our tasks are predefined. No words are needed—we know our parts well.

I shake Harm hard, rousing both him and Imani. The panic on my face must be vivid, as Harm's expression transitions from happiness to brows pulled down, mouth agape and worry pinching his eyes without a word from me. Imani sits up, flying to her feet the second her gaze meets mine. They don their weapons without a word. We slip outside, and Catori heads in the direction of Callian's tent. Moments later, the six of us are standing beside the dying fire, armed to the teeth, including Nirri. Callian nods to the trees to the east and west. More climbers cling to the branches of the forest timbers.

"What is happening?" Nirri whispers.

"They are here. The same tactic we were going to use. Surprise. Heaven knows how many of them are hiding in the undergrowth," Callian whispers back.

Nirri's eyes widen.

"We are not ready. Without the desert side, we don't stand a chance," Imani says.

Harm pushes his shoulders back and searches my face before settling his gaze on Catori beside me. "We hold them off for as long as we can."

"Agreed. Not like they gave us a choice. Wake up the warriors, starting with the outer tents and working your way to the center. We take up defense position," Callian says.

"The quickest way to lose a fight, brother," Imani growls.

"Running isn't an option, Imani." Catori fixes her gaze to Imani's.

If our only two options are defense or fleeing, things have gotten very bad, very quickly.

"We stand and fight. Let's hope there are enough of us still standing when the desert rebels get here," I say, sliding my hand into Catori's. A moment later, she hovers an inch from my face. "Make sure you keep your promise, husband."

"I would walk through hell for you, Catori. I will be here."

"As will I," she says and winks as she stalks off to the eastern ring of tents. Callian, Harm, Nirri, and Imani do the same, heading in separate directions. I hover by the center of camp for a heartbeat and watch as my family walks away from me, straight into the face of danger. Right now, I wish I could check out, like I did so many times as a Guardian.

Because, deep down, I know this is going to hurt.

So. Damn. Much.

CHAPTER 36
IMANI

With our backs to each other, every last warrior stands in a large circle, weapons drawn. You could hear the heartbeat of an insect right now.

Nothing stirs.

We stand in silence.

And it is deafening.

With every passing minute, I spot another and then another armed savage partially concealed by the forest's generous foliage. With each one I find, my stomach twists tighter and my heart races faster. Harm stands at my right, Father on my left. They are making us wait. The longer we stand here, the longer fear has to set in, rattling us to the core.

I can't see them, but I know Catori and Mason are on the opposite side of the circle, facing the south. Callian and his men are spread throughout the circle we made, strengthening it by spreading their skill amongst the newer warriors.

We wait.

Feeling every heartbeat.

Every breath.

A ring of silence.

Loud booming splits the painfully quiet air. To their credit, the warriors we have trained do not flinch. They stand taller, as if lightning from the forest storms courses through their veins. Their bodies are rigid and alive with anticipation. The rhythm of the sound grows, louder and faster.

Drums.

Harm shoots me a sideways look, his throat working, his face stone. I hold his gaze.

"Where you go, I go," I say.

"Together," he says. The one word almost wrecks his face, but he schools it back.

My heart flings against my ribs, making each breath shallower than the last.

The drums stop.

Silence echoes and we wait, shuffling into a tighter circle. Father catches my gaze and nods. The fire in my core roars to life. This is for every last person we lost.

I close my eyes, sucking in a long, steadying breath. Air fills every inch of my chest.

The roar of men yelling and the crashing of the forest undergrowth flies at us from between the trees. Every warrior tenses, steadying their position, waiting for Callian's order.

And then I see them.

Hundreds of them.

Savages.

Their hideous fur-wrapped hulking bodies, rough faces covered in scars and beards. They seem like giants. Ghastly weapons raised in their hands. Curved blades, jagged swords, and something like round, spiky axes.

A yelp sounds from beside Harm.

Marshall.

Harm spins on him, breaking formation. "Get back to Nirri!"

"I just—I wanted to fight with the warriors." His face has paled.

The savages fly toward us, tens of them, from the trees.

No Guardians.

"Go! Now, back to the shelter!" Harm's words are desperate. Marshall stands shaking on the spot, staring at the armed savages bounding toward us at a disturbing pace.

Harm turns and shakes his shoulders. "Marshall, run. Get out of here!"

Marshall's gaze meets Harm's like slow-moving tree sap.

"I—" The word dies out in his throat.

"Nirri needs you in case they break through our ranks. Now, brother!"

Harm shoves him around and barks the order to run.

Marshall takes off, sprinting toward the shelter. He looks back at us briefly, horror creasing his young face.

Thoroughly rattled, I turn back.

"Imani," Father grinds out.

He is reassuring me, making sure I'm ready.

Harm stares at me, eyes tense, before dotting a kiss to my forehead. He turns back and raises his weapons.

I widen my stance and inhale, long and slow. Both fighting knives in my hands, I fondle the hilts, rolling them in my hands.

Three paces out.

Two paces.

One.

A savage, dressed in dark furs with a ridiculous grin plastered over his face, raises his blade, sending it crashing down toward me.

I meet his force with my crossed knives before spinning out of range. His grin falters slightly and he stalks toward me. Fully aware

I have broken the circle, I skip around him until my back is against Harm's.

"Nowhere to run, little girl." He chuckles.

I step sideways and back into position in the circle, standing sideways as to not expose my back to the oncoming savages. "I'm not running. You're trapped."

He growls and lunges at me, eyes darting around. My blades hit against his. He tries again and gets the same result. Another savage rushes me from outside the circle. I fend him off with one knife, the other busy with the man I have trapped inside the circle. This is not sustainable. Savages have stopped pouring from the tree line, at least.

The man outside the circle lunges again, and I step backward. He stumbles past me and into his comrade. I fill the gap in the circle again. Two trapped.

But I can't fight in both directions.

This was a mistake.

Standing on wide footing, both blades dangling in my hands and chest heaving, I flick my gaze from the two men homing in on me, to the tens moving toward us from in front of the tree line. I search the men's faces, waiting for their next move. Harm fights beside me, his sword against an axe. Father holds a savage with a long, curved blade at bay with his two fighting knives, similar to mine.

Seconds tick past.

The two trapped men move as one toward me, exchanging feral looks.

A savage rushes me from outside the circle. I meet his wielding axe with a knife to the throat. His stunned face crumples as he falls to his knees, hands gripping his neck. Roars explode from the two trapped savages. They raise their weapons and stalk toward me, the hate in their eyes plain as the blood-tinged air around us.

With only two fighting knives against their multiple weapons, I change tactics. Sheathing my knives, I draw the twin swords from my back.

They quicken their pace for the last few steps. Four blades against two. Two men against my smaller frame. As if they have just realized the odds, stupid grins split across their faces simultaneously.

A heartbeat.

Another step closer.

Inches away.

I let my swords swing in my grip as everything slows down. The raging faces of the bearded giants hurtling toward me grow sluggish. For a brief second, and against my better judgment, I close my eyes.

Hanola is there.

Standing in the grassy space we fight on. But it's empty. Only fog drifts around her clean cream-colored robes. Her amulet pulses on her chest. Something like a fever dream.

"You can do this, my child. You are strong enough, Imani. You are quicker than they are. Remember your fire, girl."

I hold out a hand to her. "I don't know if I can, Hanola."

"Go, child. Go, now!"

I snap my eyes open. Four blades are falling just above me. Instead of meeting their steel, I flatten against Harm's side. He grunts in acknowledgment but keeps fighting. The two men spill into the fray of their comrades. They turn back to me, eyes blazing.

Keenly aware they just lost their prey and now face the three of us, their faces harden. Father dispatches the man in front of him and steps by my side. The man in front of Harm falls to the ground, and he scans the area in front of us before stepping beside me.

"Need the big men to fight your battles, little girl?" one spits.

Harm shakes his head.

Father exhales, a growl lining his breath.

I fly at the savage, both blades whirling. He steps back but holds his ground. Harm meets the man beside him. Another rushes to my left, and Father meets his sickening-looking blade with a fluid motion that disarms the overgrown Neanderthal. He runs him through and takes a moment to find the next target.

Metal clashes with metal as I hit the brute force of the man who now stands towering over me. The stupid grin that hasn't left his face now looks so familiar.

He's the one who held Nirri, who tried to get Catori to submit to his bed.

"Ah, now she remembers me," he drawls.

I grit my teeth as fire flies around my body in ebbs and waves.

He is a dead man.

I step back.

He straightens, and the grin curls to a sneer.

I sheathe my swords in exchange for my favorite weapons. Fighting knives. I step back again, and he cocks his head to one side.

"Don't be afraid, little one. I'll make it quick."

He steps forward.

I spin the knives in my hands, waiting for him to still.

"Come at me, then, girly."

I don't move.

"Still waiting for your big men to fight your battles?"

Inhale.

Shoulders back.

Loose grip.

Relax my wrists.

"I think they're too busy to save you, how sad," he coos.

Exhale.

I throw both knives. A risk—he could deflect both.

He flinches and deflects one knife, aimed for his heart.

The other sinks into his neck.

He grabs it and yanks it from his pulsing throat.

Bad idea.

Blood spurts out in a gorge of red.

He growls through his teeth.

I take a step forward.

No weapon in hand.

He draws his blade with his free hand and staggers toward me. I spin around him, ripping my dagger from my hip and lodging it in between his ribs as I go. He turns to face me, inside the circle again. My prey, again. I pluck my fighting knife from the ground and take a side stance in my place in the circle again.

He screams, rough and low, and runs at me, a rusted, filthy curved blade in his hand. I meet his blade this time, and he presses down until he towers over me. *Good, keep going. Lower.*

He grunts spittle landing on my face.

My arms shake with the heavy weight of his downward force.

I rip the last dagger from my left hip and, with one swift upward motion, plunge it into the soft patch between his throat and chin.

His eyes widen. Blood gurgles from his mouth, splattering my face.

I retract the blade and watch as he slumps to his knees.

I lean down, inches from his now-twisted face.

"I prefer to do this part myself." For good measure, I whip my knife across his throat and step back before lodging a foot into his chest. He collapses to the muddy grass, breath rattling to a halt.

I spin back into formation. Harm has bodies at his feet. Some of the savages walk over them, some haul their dead comrades away to allow the better fighters closer proximity to our circle. Our circle of silence has turned to a circle of death—for them. I take a brief look around the circle; only three of our warriors have fallen so far. Better trained and better fed, most likely, we have an advantage. I scan the circle for my family. Catori, Callian, Mason—all still standing. A whimper leaves my throat and I school my face before emotions get the better of me.

Callian calls for tighter formation and the entire circle moves back three paces, tightening our ranks. Protecting the three fallen warriors. They may still be alive.

As if he read my mind, Callian is barking for them to be taken to Nirri. Six forest people appear to cart the three limp bodies off on flat bunks, each easily handled by two people.

And then everything goes still.

Again.

The savages retreat.

Back to the tree line.

We stand our ground and wait as before. Waiting for Callian's order.

A small parcel of relief lodges in my core.

Is it over? At least for now?

Both of my knives hang from my fingertips. I inhale and close my eyes. Nothing gets the tangy smell of copper out of my senses.

Harm turns and inspects me head to toe before sheathing his weapons. He pulls me toward him and grips my face with his hands. I smash my mouth to his, choking through a breath. His hands curl around my neck.

A chuckle from behind splits us apart.

I turn to see my father watching us. But instead of the irritation with Harm that usually lines his eyes, there is only admiration and gratitude.

"I see keeping you two apart was a mistake," he says.

"You think, Father?" I roll my eyes at him, and his laugh echoes through the silent, blood-filled space.

No sooner do we turn back and heed Callian's next instruction, than the trees shake, our archers ascending the bark-covered trunks. Callian nods to someone in the closest trees. Jeselle swings out and signals ready.

We wait. That seems to be the only tactic the savages have for us. It is as simple as it is tedious.

The savages cluster into smaller divisions. Warriors around me check their weapons for damage.

Nothing happens for what feels like an age.

Waiting again in silence. We don't have the numbers to attack in case more savages arrive. If that happens, our odds plummet. Significantly.

Callian raises a hand and closes his fist. Hold. He is moving his head to the side watching between the trees.

Jeselle starts signaling wildly.

The roar is almost deafening. And seconds later, hundreds of savages pour from the forest around us.

We won't last the hour.

The sun is at its apex, and still no desert rebels have come. Metal clashes around me; the tang of blood has turned to thick sap in my senses. My hands tremble around the handles of my fighting knives.

The circle is breaking.

Warriors I have trained with for months, who have been honing their skills every day for this their entire life, are starting to falter. The clean line of our circle is more like the murky edges of a spoiled puddle, misshapen and temporary.

Callian barks for us to hold.

Over and over.

Harm is slowing, his movements less precise, less effective with each savage he takes down. Father is breathing heavily beside me. Every blow he meets with a raw grunt.

I meet the long axe of the savage in front of me with both blades. He bears down and a sickening sneer splits his face. I push back, but he doesn't budge. I try to spin from his hold, and he sidesteps, matching my movements. I can't get out from under his weapon. My arms shake, and I stifle a groan.

Air burns its way in and out of my lungs.

He pulls his axe from my blades and swings it into my side. I stumble sideways. The ragged edge of his weapon slices the skin at my ribs. Blood instantly soaks my tunic, running down my side. But I know better than to drop my weapon and try to staunch the flow of blood. He is waiting for me to do that.

Instead, I step out of range, breaking the circle again.

On wobbly legs, I draw in a long, steadying breath. I reaffirm the blades in my hands, tossing them over and over, willing my trembling body to relax.

The savage rushes me, axe wielded high. I exhale, flinging both blades toward him. No accuracy this time. Just a desperate, wild throw.

With a sickening thwack, both blades lodge in his body—one in his neck, one into his chest at his heart. He tumbles into me. I stagger backward, falling onto the muddy ground. A second later, the huge, bearded man crumples over me, pinning me into the crimson-washed mud and grass.

"Get off me!"

I wriggle and try to dislodge him. His weight crushes my chest.

I scream, all semblance of bravery lost to panic.

I can't breathe.

Pounding my fists into his limp body, I cry out through a guttural scream. Thick, warm blood spills from his neck onto my face. With my last scrap of energy, I push on his chest. My breaths are so shallow now, stars line the sides of my vision.

He jerks on top of me and rolls to the ground.

I close my eyes, pulling the stale, copper-filled air into my lungs. A rough, warm hand lifts me to sit up. I open my eyes to find the worried face of my father.

"Imani, are you hurt?"

"I'm fine."

"Come on, my girl. Up before another one finds you on the back foot." He lowers a hand. I take one last long, luxurious breath before slapping my hand into his. He pulls me up with a swift motion and we spin back to the fight.

A man similar to the one I just put down steps into my father's space, too close for the weapon that is now dangling in his hand to be of any use. I spin back and pluck my knives from the fallen savage's body. A grunt leaves Father's mouth.

I turn to see him drop to his knees. The savage standing over him sheathes his curved blade and pulls a sword from his back. Father is kneeling in the mud, hands pressing into his stomach.

Blood seeps through his fingers.

No. Please, no.

I just got him back.

This. Is. Not. Happening.

CHAPTER 37
IMANI

I throw a knife into the man's chest. It sinks into his skin briefly, wobbles, and then falls to the ground.

"Imani, no," Father chokes.

He is still protecting me.

It will cost him his life, and he is still protecting me.

Fury lights my entire body with a heat that sears my insides. I meet the gaze of the savage in front of him.

"Leave. Him. Be." Each word comes out a hideous growl.

The savage laughs, tossing his head back.

I toss a knife into the exposed thundering vein in his neck.

I pull the sword from my back and stalk to where he stands, grappling with the knife in his throat. His eyes wide, he staggers back a step.

Thunder roars through my head.

He holds up his sword, trying to fend me off with one hand. I swipe his blade sideways, and it drops to the ground. Blood splatters from his mouth with every shallow, quick breath.

I step between the savage and my father.

The hilt of my sword turns in my fingers.

The savage pulls the blade from his throat. It doesn't help.

He rushes me and I run him through.

He stops awkwardly, inches from my face.

"Go to hell," I grind out.

His face twists as he gasps for air and slumps at my feet.

I stand and watch the light leave his eyes.

Sheathing my sword, I turn back to find my father crouched over on the ground. His hands are covered in blood.

I need to get him to Nirri.

Fast.

But I can't leave Harm.

Torn between my father and my husband, I kneel in front of the man who raised me.

"I need you to stand," I say, resting my hands on his face.

He nods.

His breathing is too shallow.

Harm growls behind me. I turn and find him fending off three savages. My heart lodges in my throat.

Dammit.

Always another impossible choice.

My chest tightens under the load of choosing between them. My father, who I only just got back. Or the man I love, who has literally given up the world for me, again and again.

A strangled moan rips through my throat.

Things may get harder before they get better. The words Hanola said to Harm, so many months ago.

This is hard. This is harder. Harm falters backward under dual blades.

"Lay down; don't move. As far as they know, you are dead. Got it?" I say to Pa.

He nods, watching my gaze fling between his face and Harm's back. "Go to Harm, Imani."

He sounds like he is giving up.

Air leaves my chest and tears burn my eyes. His hand lands on mine. "Go, my girl. I'll be here when you're done."

Tears fall from my blurry vision as I shake my head. "No."

"Imani, you cannot lose him. I promise I will be here. Go, please."

I press a kiss to his blood-streaked forehead and stand.

I turn back and set my shoulders. Harm falters again. I draw a breath and fly into the savage to his left. I sink a blade into his neck and lodge another between his ribs. He drops and I waste no time slicing his neck before kicking him to the ground.

Harm runs through the man in front of him, who is too stunned by his fallen comrade to defend himself. As one, we turn on the last man. He growls and lunges at me. I block him with both knives. Harm sheathes his sword and pulls a dagger out, stepping up behind him. A second later, the sharp edge of his knife is cutting into the man's Adam's apple.

"Get away from my wife."

Harm's deep brown eyes meet mine. He winks at me, and I smile. I slam both blades into the man's chest, as Harm runs the dagger into his neck, spilling blood in an instant. We let the man fall to the grass.

"Harm, Father is hurt badly. I need to get him to Nirri."

"We can't break the circle."

"I can't—" I twist to look at the helpless body of my father, laying in the mud. "I can't lose him again, Harm."

"Callian won't be happy about it."

What else can I do? I can't leave him to bleed to death. He can't fight; he can barely stand.

The clang of weapons dulls to the sounds of thunder. Yelling and hollers sound from just beyond the tree line to our right.

What on earth? Someone releases a cheer. Harm and I stand, waiting to see what is happening. He grabs my hand and pulls me into his side.

Then we see it. Hundreds of desert rebels wielding weapons have broken through the eastern side of savages. Two older men cut their way through the now-thinning group of savages.

"Jonah!" I cry.

"Christopher," Harm chuckles.

Thank the heavens.

"Let's get your Pa to Nirri," Harm says.

Thickness swallows my breath. He called him Pa. I nod and follow as he picks him up. I walk in front, fending off any hapless savages who decide to attack. We reach the opposite side of the circle, and Mason finds me.

"What happened, Imani?"

"He was defending me and got stabbed."

Mason's face crumples a little and he pulls me into a hug. He smells of sweat, mud, and blood. His muscular body is alive with exertion. I push out of his hold.

"Make sure you're alive when the last savage falls," I say.

"I'll be here." He ruffles my hair and spins back to the fight beside Catori, still steady and precise. She winks at me, meeting the twin blades of the savage in front of her.

We make it to the healer's shelter with little hassle. Harm lays Father on the closest bunk and Nirri runs over. I stand at his head.

"Daniel!" She gets to work removing his shirt.

"Harm, help me sit him to get this shirt off."

Harm lifts Father from the bunk, and Nirri rips the shirt up the back.

And then I see them.

Scars.

Similar to Harm's, but many, many more.

Lashes.

From the Chancellor?

"What the hell?" I gasp.

"Lashes," Harm mutters.

Nirri gestures for him to be laid back down, and Harm lowers him slowly. Blood trickles from his wound. His face is pale, his breaths short.

"Need some help?" The kind voice of Flick fades in.

I jump and turn to face her.

"Yes, we do. Abdominal wound. He's fading," Nirri says.

Flick ties her hair up and Nirri hands her an apron. The two women get to work on my father. Harm pulls me from the shelter by the hand.

We stop a few paces from the door.

"Imani, there are others who need our help now," he whispers, folding me in his arms.

I breathe him in.

Others.

Mason.

Catori.

Callian.

Jonah.

Luca.

Christopher.

My family.

I dig deep and find the coiled-up part of me that holds my fire. Before I open my eyes, I replay Miya's words to me: *That fire of yours will serve you well, girl.*

I push from Harm's hold and stalk back to the battlefield.

I'm exhausted. I hardly slept last night. Today we travel to the rendezvous point to intercept the Chancellor's army. Nirri, Flick, and a handful of healers are following, putting up a makeshift shelter. My bones are weary; my muscles are tender and sore. The desert rebels' arrival meant we won the last battle. Just.

Callian wants to keep at it while we have the upper hand, saying the odds can change in a second and we need to make use of every advantage we have. He is right.

The Chancellor hasn't put his precious Guardians into battle yet. It's making me nervous. There are hundreds of them. They are more coordinated than the savages. More disciplined. And now, armed with real weapons instead of canes, they pose a threat. I can see what he is doing. Using soldiers he's not afraid to lose to weaken us, before sending in the favorite children to finish off the job. It not only means he will lose less Guardians, but also that they will cement their place as oppressors and the dictators to our lives by literally pounding us into the mud.

We cannot lose this battle. The moment we see a glimpse of those grey uniforms, we have to make every minute, every action count.

I find a place beside Luca. He gives me an encouraging nod before returning his gaze to the trees. Once rallied, we travel as one to the rendezvous point Callian had pinpointed for us originally. Where we have the advantage of proximity to the tower and the Chancellor. Where we have plans to carry out.

Nirri and Flick trail behind with a handful of their healers, ready to set up a few hundred feet from the battlefield. Harm walks beside me, lost in thought, rucksack bulging and heavy strapped to his back.

Mason and Catori walk together in front of us. They have been inseparable the last few days. He doesn't show it, but I know Mason is terrified of losing Catori in the battle. Every spare moment he has, he is watching her, admiration and agony fighting for control of his face.

As we all are watching our significant others.

By midday, we arrive at the site, and Callian orders his warriors to take up posts, the archers to the trees, and the healers to set up as fast as they are capable. Nirri is busy, but the stress of having Callian front and center of this battle sees her snap out short instructions to the healers she is in charge of. The moment this is all over can't come soon enough.

An hour after we have positioned ourselves between the trees, waiting for the Chancellor's next move, the drums start again.

My heart flings in my chest as the events of yesterday replay in my head. The hulking savages, their sickening weapons, the smell of blood that I will never clear from my senses or my memory as long as I shall live.

"You okay?" Harm wraps an arm around me.

I lean into his warmth.

"No," I say on shaky breath.

He pulls me around to face him.

"Nirri will take care of him, Imani. Your father will be fine."

I lift my face to meet his gaze. Deep, gorgeous brown eyes scan my face. The slow reverberating sound of the drums plods along behind the quickening pace of my heartbeat. I grab his face with both hands and press my forehead to his lips.

"I know. It's not my father I am worried about."

Harm's strong, corded arms fold around me, like they have hundreds of times before.

My stomach flips.

Breath lodges in my swollen throat.

"We will all get to go home when this is over," he whispers into my hair.

I hope so.

Dammit, I really hope so.

Callian's order cracks through the forest around us and we file into line. A shoulder bumps mine. Mason. A cheeky smile lights up his face. And I can't help but choke out a wobbly laugh.

"Hey, don't go getting sentimental on us now, Travesci," he says, lowering his head to meet my gaze.

Travesci. He hasn't called *me* that before.

"Not likely, Rayner," I huff back.

He raises a fist, and I pump mine into his. He roughs up my hair before resting his hands on his weapons. I stare at him. So calm, his courage outweighing anything else. I turn and throw my arms around him and squeeze tight.

A strangled laugh rumbles from his chest. "I love you too, little sis."

I peck a kiss to his cheek and roll my eyes at him. His laugh echoes over the drums. I turn to find Harm smiling at us both. He winks at me and leans down, lips brushing my ear.

"You know, I love you too." He nips my ear and I turn my head, planting my mouth over his.

The drums stop.

Silence crackles through the air.

We break apart, scanning between the trees that sway on the indifferent breeze.

Moments later, the underbrush hisses, jerking with the intrusion, and the thunder of hundreds of men rushing toward us steals my breath.

Harm wraps a hand around my neck under my hair, pulling me into his hold.

"Where you go, I go, my love." His voice is raw; his face is stone.

His words are my order to stay alive.

"Where you go, I go," I whisper into his chest.

He releases me, drawing his weapons from his chest.

I pluck both fighting knives from my hips and widen my stance.

I stand, gaze locked with Harm's, the thunder of armed men closing the gap between us, faster by the second.

An hour later, trembling with exhaustion, our lines are scattered through the forest. Blood, dirt, spit, and mud cover every inch of us all. The drums sound and the savages hover before retreating.

What is going on?

Our warriors are on edge, weary from the battle yesterday. Tens have fallen today. Groups of women and men were carried to the healer's shelter. Nirri and Flick will have their hands full.

"Fall back," Callian calls, his voice hoarse.

We stagger back toward the camp. Women from the villages are handing out water and small portions of food. Harm leads the way through the crowd toward the healer's shelter, accepting food and drink for the both of us.

We sink to the ground by the closest tent. I peel off my weapons belt and toss my knives on top, on the ground. They may be light, but at this moment they may as well be made of solid stone. I lay my head back on the tent and close my eyes. A cup is placed in my hands, warm hands curling my fingers around the vessel.

"Drink."

I sigh and open my eyes. Harm is watching me, his face heavy with worry and exhaustion. I sip from the cup. The water cools me from the inside as it slides down. I drain the cup. Harm holds out a chunk of bread and a portion of cheese. I pluck the cheese from his fingers with a smile and almost swallow it whole.

He chuckles at me.

I bite into the bread and watch as he eats his food. Mason and Catori slump to the ground beside us. Callian heads into the healer's tent, bypassing our little group sitting on the ground without a word. I imagine he is desperate to see Nirri.

A whimper followed by a low groan sound from inside the tent. Callian has no doubt wrapped himself around Nirri, and she would be inspecting every inch of him, agonized by what she does and doesn't find.

"Sounds like he found her," Catori says with a smile.

I lean into Harm and breathe him in. My chest feels set to explode. We have been at this for a day and a half, and the savages don't seem to be thinning out or slowing down.

They are more than we can fight, even with the desert rebellion. The thud of boots on wet ground has me pushing from Harm's side. I track up the length of man in front of me. Old, worn boots, ragged beige pants and shirt, and weapons strapped to his large frame.

The wide smile of Jonah meets mine, and I spring from the ground into his embrace.

"How you holding up, my girl?"

"I'm fine." I push from his hold.

"How's your father?"

"He's doing okay, last I heard. I will see him before we go back out."

Jonah nods and smiles at Harm.

"You stay safe, please, Uncle Jonah."

"I will do my best."

His kind face studies mine.

"What?"

"I am so very proud of you, my girl." The last two words wobble their way out.

I smile, breathing past the lump in my throat. I rest a hand on his cheek, and he turns his head in my hold, pressing his lips to my palm. With a rough motion, he tugs me back into a hug before squeezing tight.

He releases me and meets my gaze. "See you in a bit, hey?"

"You have my word."

Before I have a chance to tell him I love him too, always have, he is walking away from me, back to Christopher and a group of desert rebels. I watch as his big form moves through the people.

Harm stands, leaving for a moment to where Christopher sits. He wanders toward our tent, returning with two bulging rucksacks that he drops at the door of the large tent.

I turn back and make my way into the healer's shelter. Nirri is standing over my father, the dressing on his wound peeled back. She looks up as I stop beside her.

"How is he?" I ask.

"It looks worse than it is," my father says, opening his eyes.

"He was lucky; Flick was able to open him up and tie off some small bleeding. The blade missed all the vital parts. I am glad we brought him with us though, he is burning up."

"I will be fine, Nirri."

"Can I sit with you for a moment?" I say to Father.

"You don't need to ask."

I sit on the side of his bunk. He grabs my hand, squeezing it.

"What were the lashes for?"

He stares at me for a heartbeat, then looks away. "Punishment."

"What punishment? You are the Chancellor's commanding officer. I mean, were."

"It doesn't matter, Imani. Everything has changed now."

"Please tell me."

He shakes his head and closes his eyes. I stand and stalk over to Nirri, working with a mortar and pestle.

"What were the lashes for? Were you there?"

Her eyes widen as she realizes what I am talking about, and her hands stop on the tools.

"Tell me, Nirri, what was he punished for?"

"I was there, Imani." She drops the tools and pulls me further from the bunks. "He didn't tell you?"

"Nirri," I grind out.

She wipes her hands on her apron before removing it. "They were handed down to Fletcher for every crime you committed. He took *your* punishment, so you didn't have to."

Her face is stone.

My breath stops.

A weight crushes my heart.

My chin wobbles. "What?"

"He was ordered to give you the punishment. He traded your freedom in exchange for accepting the punishment and one other condition. I am surprised my grandfather agreed to it, but he must have had some reason to. Maybe he didn't want to lose his highest-ranking officer."

"What other condition?"

"You would have to ask him that."

I storm to where my father lays, eyes closed, breathing steady.

"Why didn't you tell me? And if you are capable of such compassion for me, why were you hunting Harm? What was the condition you agreed to with the Chancellor?"

His eyes open slowly, and he struggles to sit up, wincing with the painful movement.

His gaze meets mine, tortured and lined with silver.

"It was you or him, Imani. That was the choice I was given.

Take your punishment and bring in Travesci, or you were to be executed. I chose you."

I try to form words. Instead, I stand shaking in front of my father.

"Imani, I am sorry. I will always choose to protect you, even it meant the worst for Harm." He holds his hand up to me, and I stare at it.

He wore my punishment. He chose me over anything else. He protected me the only way he knew how against the Chancellor. I drop to my knees and grab his hand.

Ringing fills my ears.

All the years we wasted.

Every horrible thing I said to him.

Sobs chug from my throat and his hand rests on my hair.

"I would do it all again, if I had to. You're my baby girl."

"I'm so sorry, Pa."

"Don't ever apologize for doing the right thing, Imani. You have more gumption than the rest of us put together. I did my part so you could keep doing yours."

The drums start and Callian's order snaps out over their hideous sound a second later. I clamber from the floor and press a kiss to my father's tear-streaked cheek before rushing out of the tent.

We hurry to form our lines, Harm on one side of me, Mason the other.

We wait for the thunder of the savages.

For the assault we have been barely holding off for the last forty-eight hours. Anything else, and we are screwed. Anything more advanced than the messy, erratic, and undisciplined fighting style of the savages, and we are in a whole world of trouble.

I stand frozen, straining to see between the green.

And then I see it.

A glimpse of grey.

Guardian after Guardian pops out from behind the forest.

Adorned in weapons, moving as one unit, the Guardians march toward us.

I catch Harm's gaze before he turns back to the force raining down on us. His jaw feathers, his throat working.

We are done for.

CHAPTER 38
MASON

Hell just got handed to us in a neatly woven grey handbasket, trimmed with epaulets and decorated with far too many weapons. Catori throws me a worried look. I lace my fingers through hers. We wait for Callian's order.

Fifty paces.

Forty paces.

Thirty paces.

Twenty.

Ten.

"Weapons ready!" Callian hollers.

Every warrior clad in green and beige steadies themselves. The exhausted faces around me have been tightened by the threat in front of us. Catori releases her fingers from my hand. My gut flips, my racing heart a thunderous noise in my head.

Five paces.

I widen my stance and dig my back foot in. The twin swords in my hands turn over in my inpatient fingers.

"Now!"

I lunge, attacking the man rushing me. Getting him on the defensive as fast as I can.

Clash.

Metal grinds on metal as the man in uniform holds under my downward force. After a moment he buckles and spins out of range. I stalk toward him, blades whirling, trying to remind myself that we are to render them unconscious, to try and save them later.

He stabs at me with the blade in his hand. I swipe his half-hearted attempt away and move into his space.

"Surrender or die," I bark.

He mutters something before laughing at me. I sheathe a sword and knock the weapon from his hand, grabbing him by the collar.

"Surrender or die!"

"It's not us who are going to be dead in a matter of hours," he drawls, spitting in my face.

The warm spittle drips from my chin. I curb the need to run him through and sheathe my sword before ripping a dagger from my chest. He squirms in my hold, and I stab his arm to take the fire out of him.

He screams and I pluck my knife from his arm, returning it to my chest. "Which one is it?" I bark.

"See you in hell, traitor," he snarls.

I throw a fist into his face, and he slumps to the ground.

"Not part of the plan, idiot."

I drag him to the nearest tree and secure him there, making sure his wrists are tied tight behind him. Turning back, I see Harm is taking down two Guardians. I bet he has waited a long time for this moment. Imani fights another by his side.

Catori. My gaze settles on my wife. She has a man with his back against a tree. He is shaking his head wildly, not surrendering. She runs him through. His limp body slides down the trunk of the tree. She spins and meets my gaze through the chaos around us. The sweetest smile lights up her pretty face. A Guardian runs at her. And she meets his strike with her own. I stalk to where they stand and pull a dagger from my chest, resting it around his throat.

"Surrender or die? You get to choose."

"Get off me, filth!"

"I guess that's not a surrender?" Catori plays with the words.

"Doesn't sound like it."

She runs a finger across her throat and makes a choking sound.

"Fine, okay! I surrender!" He gasps beneath my blade.

"Good choice." Catori winks at him.

I pull a sword from my back, gripping below the hilt, and slam it into the back of his head. He drops to my feet, and Catori and I drag him and tie him like the last.

This is taking much longer than we had anticipated. At this rate, we are going to be exhausted before we have even made it halfway.

"Mas, incoming," Catori snaps.

Two groups of Guardians stalk our way, weapons drawn. Five men head toward Catori, five toward me. From behind her I see another eight bound for Callian. They are picking out the leaders. Catori runs at them with twin swords flying as she screams a sound so raw it would scare the bones from a grave. I pull my second sword and launch at them at a run. They falter slightly before standing together. As I slow down to take my aim a few paces away from them, they split, forming a circle around me. Surrounded, I spin around, counting the blades they carry, sizing up the largest of them to fall first.

As a unit, they tighten the circle, stepping in. Any closer and my swords will be redundant. Fighting knives are not my strong suit. I meet the officer's blade in front of me with one blade, and another comes at me from the left. I hold him off with my other sword, but the angle is wrong and the movement messy. Catori would have barked at me about form by now. Right now, I would take her pretty face scorning me over this lot in a heartbeat.

I spin from the man on the left and use my left blade to run the first through. He drops like a stone in stagnant water, slow and unsteady. His comrades pay him no heed, their eyes well and truly glazed over now. Poor buggers. If they survive this, that one's going to hurt on the other side of the mind control treatment.

The hair on the back of my neck prickles and I spin back. Two blades careen toward my chest, and I swipe them away with one blade. Their numbers don't match my skill, but they have me blocked none the less.

"Mason!" Catori yells.

"Yeah?"

Clash. Metal on metal. The vacant man before me bears down hard.

"Callian!"

I track my gaze to her brother.

Elijah.

Hell.

That bloody snake has Callian surrounded and wounded. I grind my teeth together, mulling over how to help from where I am. I stab my blade into the shoulder of the man standing over me.

Callian growls, fighting off four men. Elijah watches as his men are cut down, but not before cutting into the big warrior badly. The Guardians have had some serious training.

Catori is frantically fighting off the men in front of her as more file in, surrounding her.

Clash.

I meet the distracted movements of the next officer. I take my chances and move into his space. Ripping my dagger from my chest, I run it across his throat. At this point, it's them or us. We have run out of time and strategy to be able to save as many as we can.

It's them or us.

I choose us.

I choose Catori.

Harm.

Imani.

Callian and Nirri.

Clash.

Catori's grunts turn to whimpers as she takes down the man in front of her, eyes glued on her brother. Another five move in, surrounding him. He pulls fighting knives from his chest. He must be exhausted if he thinks his hulking size is going to be agile enough to wend around swords to make an impact with those short, close-range weapons. That is Imani's style, with her small size and quick feet.

A heartbeat later, he is on his knees, one blade to his throat and another to his chest, Elijah's fist pulling his head back by the shaggy blond hair that flops in his face.

"Callian!" Catori screams, louder than thunder itself. "Callian! Stop! Please, no! Callian!"

Every soul on the battlefield slows. Catori's tortured scream echoes through the trees. The tang of blood carries on the breeze, carrying her cries toward the south.

Elijah bends down and whispers something in Callian's ear.

The warrior's face hardens, jaw tensing, hands balling to fists.

Elijah adjusts his weapon over our brother's throat.

My stomach plummets.

"Stop! Please, Elijah, stop! Callian!"

Elijah pauses, looking directly at Catori, then to me. His cold stare turns to a sneer.

The men around us slowly come back to life, and a blade rains down toward my chest. I meet it with twin swords and push him back.

Callian.

Catori is fighting wildly, but more keep coming.

"Callian, brother, no," Catori cries between clashes of her sword against the men surrounding her.

Harm and Imani are on the other side of the battlefield, surrounded as we are. They have singled us out.

Callian struggles in the hold of the four men now holding him.

Elijah laughs.

"You lay a finger on her, and I will kill you, pretty boy," Callian growls out.

"You won't be around to stop me, you idiot."

Nirri.

Elijah is talking about Nirri.

As if the thought of her name could conjure her, Nirri bursts from the healer's tent. She scans the field before finding Callian. Tens of men lay between her and him.

She stares at Elijah, his hand at Callian's throat, and her body stills.

She plucks a bow and quiver from the pile by the tent door, slinging it over her shoulder, and takes off running. Men step out to intercept her, and she flings the knives on her chest at them one by one, lodging steel into flesh. Every few meters, she sinks an arrow into another man.

Clash. The blade to my right thunders down on mine. I turn and push him off before running him through. Another one down. Another one files in.

Nirri ducks and weaves through the Guardians and remaining savages, eyes locked on Callian. She stops a handful of steps behind Elijah, chest heaving. I doubt it is from the run. Her face is pure hatred. Wild.

A grunt comes from beside me, and I raise my weapon to meet his before slamming my dagger into his neck. He falls at my feet and another files in. Convenient.

Elijah turns slightly to meet her gaze, his hand still firmly against Callian's working throat.

Guardians file in around Nirri, grabbing her arms. Her bow falls to the ground. Callian growls, deep, throaty, and raw, pulling against the hands of the men holding him.

"Stand down," Elijah says to the men holding Nirri. They release her.

Their mistake.

Catori is still fighting, now six men.

I pray she doesn't lose concentration because of her little brother and get herself hurt.

"Let him go, Elijah," Nirri says, low and shaky.

"You know, I don't think I will."

"Yes, you will. Now!"

An officer points a blade into Nirri's neck and Elijah raises his chin.

Callian strangles a moan.

"And what do I receive in return for that generous act, Miss Nirri?"

"What do you want?"

"You know exactly what I want. My rightful place beside the next Chancellor."

Dammit, he's talking about Nirri.

The blood drains from Callian's face. "No, Nirri." Our brother's words are broken.

Nirri holds Elijah's sickening gaze.

"Fine. You get what you want Elijah."

"Really? You are just going to swap sides and do what I ask to keep this Neanderthal alive?"

Nirri's gaze meets Callian's. Her hands shake by her sides. She swallows and closes her eyes briefly.

"Nirri, don't do this, please," Callian pleads.

Nirri opens her eyes. Her face is pure agony. She turns her gaze to Elijah.

"Yes. If you promise to let Callian live, I will go with you."

Callian's raw scream echoes through the forest, his entire body shaking in the grip of the four men around him.

"Good choice, Miss Nirri," Elijah coos.

Nirri screws her face up. She tracks her gaze to Callian's broken face.

"Let him go. You heard her." Elijah gestures to his men.

He holds his hand out to Nirri.

She stares at it with wide eyes.

The sword of the man in front of me swipes my shoulder, and blood seeps through my sleeve. I send him backward with one thrust and step into his space, running him through with my blade.

Elijah grabs Nirri's hand and drags her toward the tower. Passing his officers holding Callian, he nods slightly. He's going to kill him anyway.

A Guardian steps into Callian's space and rams a dagger into his shoulder.

Callian roars.

Nirri spins back in Elijah's grip, horror etched over her elegant face.

She pulls from his grip and flies to where her bow and quiver lay on the ground. She pulls the string taut, aiming at Elijah. Guardians surround her in an instant.

"Let. Him. Go!" she thunders.

Elijah steps toward her.

He is a dead man.

"What, so you can run back to him whenever you feel fit? I am not as stupid as your grandfather. I do things properly the first time. Your grandmother pined for the traitor, even decades later. At least if he"—he points to Callian—"is dead, you won't be pining, Nirri. You will be where you belong. With me, leading the people. We will rule the next generation of this ring."

Ring?

What the hell?

Elijah draws a dagger from his hip and presses it into Callian's bounding throat. Blood trickles down his neck, spoiling the tunic over his heaving chest.

"No. Elijah. You do *not* decide for me."

"You women always think you get to have a mind of your own. When are you going to learn that's not how it works, you stupid little girl?"

I dispatch the last of the officers surrounding me and weave my way toward Nirri and Elijah.

Catori is still fending off three men. She can handle them. I will not let her lose her little brother.

Using the movements we were taught at regime training, I step up into line beside the officers, and then, when none take note of my appearance, slip past them and behind Elijah.

I pluck a fighting knife from my chest and slam it into his back. He gasps, dropping to his knees.

Wildly, he twists to see who has stabbed him in the back. I smile at him, malice lining every inch of my face. He turns back to Nirri, choking on the air in his lungs.

She steps forward and aims the tip of her arrow at his face.

"Please, Miss Nirri," he pleads, hand raised to her.

She holds his stare, face like stone.

"It's just Nirri."

She lets the arrow go.

It lodges into his eye, bursting through the back of his skull. He falls to the ground like a sack of stale, old flour.

Nirri nocks another arrow.

"Get away from him!" she warns the remaining men. They raise their hands in surrender begrudgingly and step away from Callian. His face is pale, breaths shallow and fast.

"He needs Flick," Nirri chokes out.

I grab Callian under the arm.

Nirri points her arrow at two of the officers. "You two, help him!"

They help me pull Callian to his feet and we weave our way back to the healer's tent with Nirri's arrow aimed at the back of their heads.

Go, little sis.

Moments later, we are in the tent. The two Guardians hover around, watching as Flick and Nirri attend to Callian.

Something like shock is on their faces.

"What, you've never seen a man be treated before?" Flick snaps, annoyance twisting her face.

They exchange a look. I know what it is. Arthur lets his men die, not bothering to waste resources on the injured. Their outcomes in this battle are far less pleasant than ours.

CHAPTER 39
IMANI

I fly into the tent, Harm right behind me. Nirri and Flick are working on Callian, fast hands finding every wound and potential threat. Mason sits beside Callian, holding pressure to a wound. Catori rushes into the tent, slamming into Harm. He guides her round, and she rushes to her brother.

"Callian!" she whimpers, sinking beside him, grabbing his hand. Nirri and Flick exchange a look. We are slowing them down.

"Let them work," Mason says to Catori, extending a hand. She buries her head in the pillow beside her brother's head. He turns and kisses her hair.

"I'll live." His voice is gravel.

She nods into his neck and runs a hand over his messy blond hair. "I will be outside."

She stands and takes Mason's hand. We wander from the tent, stopping outside.

"We need to get to that dial, brother," Harm says to Mason.

He is right.

Mason holds up a fist to Harm. They bump before he pulls Catori to his side and plants his mouth over hers.

Harm kisses my forehead, hands gripping my hips. We part and Harm picks up the rucksacks he dumped at the tent earlier, tossing one to Mason. The boys take off back to the fray at a jog.

"This ends right now," I say.

"Agreed. I'll get Nirri."

Catori disappears for a moment before returning with an armed Nirri.

"Flick has Callian sorted for now. The others will help her. Let's do this," Nirri says.

Catori fights her way through Guardians and savages as we make a line directly to the tower. Time slows and speeds up all at once. The one thing I have been thinking about doing for almost a decade is finally here.

End the Chancellor.

Nirri walks in front of me, quiet, as Catori pulls up just outside the base of the tower. The servants' entrance the forest people have used for decades is wide open. The officers must have filed out of this and into the forest to join the battle. Instantly, the three of us wrap up our hair and faces, hands double-checking we have every weapon.

"His personal guard will no doubt be close, and maybe others," Nirri says softly. Her face is unreadable.

"No one does anything rash; we work our way in like any other mission, dispatch anyone we find and lastly, the Chancellor. Then we get the hell out of this bloody tower before the boys leave?" Catori asks, scanning both our faces for agreement. When Nirri and I both nod, she steps into the darkened corridor of the ground level of the tower.

It's empty.

Quiet.

Silently, we make our way through the corridor and up the winding stairs to the next level. I can only imagine what Nirri is going through right now. Her last living relative is about to be put down. She shows no sign of worry or even upset. If it was my father about to be toppled, I think I would feel something, even if he hadn't defected. Even if I hadn't come to realize all the ways he protected me since the day I left home.

We make it to the bridge before Catori spots a handful of Guardians. Armed with one small dagger and a cane, they fall like leaves in the morning breeze. Catori and I turn back from the bridge to find Nirri staring at their limp bodies.

"You okay?" Catori asks Nirri, resting a hand on her shoulder.

"If you don't want to be here, you don't have to," I offer.

"No." She meets my gaze and pushes her shoulders back. "I want to be here, Imani." Her eyes turn dark, as if she is replaying every horrible memory under Arthur's care. Every despicable thing he ever said to her. The death of Emmie.

"Let's get this over and done with, then." Catori's words snap Nirri from her daze.

On quiet feet, we wind our way to the level of the Chancellor's meeting rooms, with his large wooden chair. Three Guardians stand watch at the door.

Catori and I lunge at them. I cut one down before turning to see Catori run a blade through each of her opponents. Three officers lay lifeless on the floor, and we cross the threshold into the meeting room.

Ten officers stand around the room, guarding the Chancellor. Armed to the teeth. These men were at least given a fighting chance.

Nirri comes to stand at my left, Catori to my right. Catori's twin blades flick over in her hands, hilts gleaming with sweat. She scans the room, sizing up the men between us and our target.

I roll the hilts of my fighting knives over in my hands, realizing in the moment that I inherited that habit from Catori. I smile to myself.

"What are you waiting for? Kill them all!" Arthur screams.

He just ordered his granddaughter's death.

His vile behavior never ceases to amaze me.

All ten Guardians lunge at us.

Fifteen minutes later, half lay at our feet, either dead or almost so.

The remaining five men hover in front of their leader, the smug looks they held before upon seeing three women enter the room having long fallen.

Arthur shifts in his seat, face tight with anger and laced by something I think is fear.

"You will not get away with this! My new commander will see you all hang!" Arthur yells, his gaze burning into Nirri.

We step forward as one. Catori smiles that predatory smile of hers before flying into two Guardians to our right. I rush the middle two, drawing them away from the Chancellor. Nirri stalks around the remaining man, no weapon in her hand yet. The officer huffs a weak laugh and steps toward her. She tilts her head to one side before drawing her bow and nocking an arrow.

Without a word, she lets the arrow go, sending it right through his left eye. Arthur's face turns to pure fear.

I dispatch the two men in front of me and fall in beside Catori, who finished moments ago and now stands watching the scene between grandfather and granddaughter unravel at the seams.

"Whatever you want, you can have it. Please, just don't—" He holds both hands up. "Please don't kill me, child."

Nirri steps over to where he squirms on his seat. He stands. Nirri tucks her bow back into its sheath.

"Give me one good reason why you should live," Nirri hisses.

"I—" He pulls a fighting knife from under his tunic and lunges for her.

Nirri's face crumples in disappointment, as if she was hoping there was something salvageable, but found nothing.

She steps backward out of range. "That's what I thought."

She nods to Catori.

We move around the Chancellor, circling him like prey.

Catori pauses, shoving both blades in one hand, the other going to her wrap.

"For Miya," she says, tugging her wrap off and tossing it to the floor. Her blonde hair tumbles around her shoulders. Her eyes burn into the Chancellor's.

I sheathe a fighting knife and rip the wrap from my head and toss it away. "For Harm's family."

Nirri stills, her eyes never leaving her grandfather's face. She plucks her wrap from her head, and golden curls fall around her face and shoulders. "For every last person you ever hurt. This is for them."

As one, we ready our weapons and start circling the old man again. He holds both hands up and starts laughing.

"Okay, you have had your fun, girlies; you can put the weapons down."

"I don't see any girls here, do you, Imani?" Catori says.

"Nope, just warriors. Nirri?"

"You will find in this room, Grandfather, two warriors and one healer, maybe somebody akin to an archer. But no, there are no girls in this room."

Arthur stares blank-faced at Nirri.

"Please, Nirri, don't do this."

"You did this to yourself, Chancellor," I spit.

Catori nods and we fold the circle in half, pinning him down.

"Nirri, please! I am begging you! What will happen to the

people if I am gone? They won't last. They will wither and snuff out in a few short years without my order."

Nirri pauses her slow footsteps and briefly looks at Catori, then me. "When you are gone, they will be free."

"You don't know what you're playing at, girl," he snaps.

"I know hurting people is not the answer, Grandfather," Nirri says, her voice ice.

"You stupid girl; you were always a disappointment!" His face turns red, hands balling into fists.

"That doesn't work on me anymore, Chancellor," Nirri says.

Catori lunges both blades toward him as I slice lines up his back.

The longer this takes, the better. Nirri stands in front of him as Catori digs the tip of her blade into his ribs.

He roars with agony, and I sink both blades into his back just below his ribs. Catori holds another blade across his throat.

I pull my knives from his body and slam one into each shoulder. He drops to his knees. I lean over, my mouth by his ear. "This is for every last thing you did to my father," I whisper.

I slam both blades into either side of his neck and he chokes through a whimper.

Catori runs the blade across his throat, spilling pearls of crimson onto the gleaming wooden floor. He slumps to the ground, gasping for breath.

Nirri steps over, stopping at his head.

He holds up a trembling hand, the other over his gaping throat.

"Nirri," he chokes, blood spluttering over his face with the word.

She nocks an arrow. "Enjoy hell, Grandfather." The arrow sinks into his heart.

He jerks and stills.

The light dims from his eyes.

I wait for a moment, making sure that his chest stays still and the life really has left his body. Catori waits at the door. I sling an arm around Nirri's shoulders and turn her away from the lifeless body of her grandfather.

We wander back down the stairs, Catori alert, weapons in hand.

On the last flight of stairs, we release a collective wobbly laugh, and Catori pulls us both into her embrace. Nirri holds me tight, as if she will lose it if she lets go.

We did it.

Finally, the man who has destroyed our world for decades is dead.

And by the hands of three women, no less.

CHAPTER 40
HARM

I leap up the stairs, suspiciously vacant of Guardians, with Mason close behind me. The rucksacks on our backs bounce with every step. Winding our way up to the highest level, we round the corner to the dial room. Two Guardians stand, weapons in their hands, gazes vacant. What just happened?

Mason and I draw our blades, flying into the offense. They barely bother to defend themselves. Mason shoots me a concerned look and we step back, blades dangling in our hands.

"What's wrong with you two?" Mason snaps.

Neither responds for a time, and I study their faces. Mason keeps an eye on the stairs behind us.

"Surrender or die," I finally say.

One officer looks to the other, his jaw feathering. "We're dead if we don't. You saw what those women did to the Chancellor." His words are thick, cracking under the strain of his terrified face.

What the women did to the Chancellor?

The girls have been here.

And Arthur is dead.

They did it.

I pray they got out safely.

"Well?" Mason says from by the door.

They drop their weapons and raise their hands above their heads. I sheathe mine, hovering for a moment to test their sincerity. When neither moves, we tie their hands behind their backs and sit them on the top step. Mason stands watch as I open the door to the dial room and set my rucksack down carefully. The four crystals we fought so hard to retrieve and keep fill the bulging bag. As Nirri taught me, I lift the latch on the base of the pedestal, open the curved door, and slide out the bottom wooden tray. It scrapes on the floor, warped with age and the moisture of the forest sector. After wiggling and coaxing it for a moment, I have it all the way out. Six metal bases line the tray, five making a circle and one in the center. I pull a crystal from the rucksack and slip it into the closest one. It eases in, resting on the bottom, but nothing happens. I pull another from the bag and slide it in next to the first. Nothing.

I grab the remaining two and push them into the holders on the opposite side. I push the tray back into the pedestal and click the latch shut. Standing, I run a hand over the face of the dial. Dust floats away from it, the symbols smooth under my fingertips.

Still, nothing happens.

I must have the crystals in the wrong spaces. Grinding out a moan, I drop to the floor and open the door, tugging out the now-heavy tray. The four crystals could make tens of different patterns in the base. It would take me an age to test each one.

"Does one need to go in the center, Harm?" Mason asks.

Possibly.

"Maybe. Let's try that."

I grab the crystal closest to me and push it into the center base. Sliding the door shut, I run my hands over the ancient machination one more time.

Nothing.

"Dammit." I rest my head on my arms. Why can't anything just be easy? We have fought so hard. My breaths shallow and I grip the edge of the dial with both hands, suppressing the urge to shake it from where it stands.

With a low, breathy growl, I straighten before dropping back to the floor and ripping the door open.

I pluck each crystal from its base and lay them on the rucksack. Which pattern would seem to be the most even? I bend down, sticking my head into the empty column of the pedestal. Small gold wires run from the back of the tray, up the back wall of the pedestal to the underside of the dial itself. I snatch up a crystal and place it in the center, then put the remaining three in the spaces closest to the back, to the wires. I shove it in and slam the door shut.

I run a hand over the dial again. Still nothing. "Dammit."

I'll try blood.

Nirri said it is activated by blood. Maybe that means the power part as well. I rip the dagger from my chest and slice my palm. Blood swells from the two-inch cut, and I let it pool while I search the dial for where to spill it. The face is divided into five sections, much like our world has three. Each sector has a symbol that Nirri taught me corresponds to a season or environment. Much like the sections of the fruits they cultivate here in the forest, evenly divided and coming to one central point. One section has all four symbols.

I tilt my hand and let the blood drip into the central point where it divots, sinking into the lines that divide the sections. It wells there for a second before traveling down each line simultaneously, spreading to the far edge of the dial. Still, nothing lights up. I squeeze my hand and lose more blood to the dial. The crimson liquid streaks down the sides of the pedestal in the channels that follow over the edge and to the floor, ending in a small, lipped rim. It snakes its way around the base, meeting at my feet.

The moment the blood completes the circle, the dial hums to

life, its face lighting up with the symbols in each sector. I slam my hand onto the section with four symbols, holding it there. Mason watches, eyes wide, mouth agape. I close my eyes and wait for what comes next.

I am just about to open my eyes when the section under my hand depresses a half inch. The humming dies off and the dial dulls, my blood in the channels turning dark.

I step back and Mason moves to my side. "What happens now?" he asks.

"I don't honestly know."

We watch the dial, waiting for it to do something. I press my cut palm into my hip, stemming off the bleeding. Mason rips his sleeve, the cleaner of the two, and gestures for my hand. He wraps it before tying it off. "Do we just trust that it worked?"

"I can try again. Maybe it—"

The ground trembles, the tower swaying under our feet. We rush to the window, searching the vast space outside. The Guardians' training grounds, the forest, the battle still going on below us. The ground rumbles and groans. The air around us turns hectic, winds lashing everything it can find. We raise hands over our faces and watch as the space over the wall quivers like a piece of transparent material.

Boom!

Some sort of veil above the wall separating the sectors wavers and snaps. The crack is so loud it sets my ears ringing.

Mason grabs my arm. "You did it, Harm!"

The wide smile over his face lights up his eyes. I can barely hear his words.

I stand staring at him. We have lived for this moment for years. Finally here, it feels strange, to say the least. I take in the ecstatic face of my brother. He slaps a hand on my shoulder and shakes his head, grinning.

"We should get this tower sorted out," I say, the smile on my face growing with Mason's infectious laugh.

I realize I have never seen him this excited, ever. Warmth grows in my chest, and I wrap an arm around his shoulders and walk back to the stairs.

"Right, we split up, and plant these with the running fuse. As many as you can on each level; try to make it even. That's what Christopher said." I hand over half of the contents of the rucksack to Mason. He nods and flies down the stairs two at a time.

I turn back to the two Guardians still waiting on the top step. "You two are going to help me."

They exchange a look before one utters, "Fine."

I plant explosives around the top levels, ensuring one rests at the base of the dial, as Mason does the lower sections. When all of mine are set, I release the two Guardians at the servants' entrance with instructions for them to find Catori and Nirri. They nod and leave. Whether or not they turn themselves in doesn't matter much anymore.

I jog to the level of the bridge. "Mason, you done?"

"Yep, just one more."

I race up the stairs and light the first fuse. We have thirty seconds before the spark reaches the first explosive. Christopher told me, in no uncertain terms, we have to be at least two hundred feet away from the closest one, or we will end up injured. Or worse.

I snap the flint against the stone and hold the heat to the fuse. It takes up immediately, winding its way toward its target. I fly back down the stairs.

"Mason, get out now, brother!"

Twenty-five seconds.

No reply.

I run down the stairs, legs wobbly from the speed of my

descent. I hear a muffled reply from Mason as I reach the last set of stairs. Good, he is coming.

I rush through the servants' entrance. Catori is fighting off three Guardians, who have the two men we held behind them, looking bashful. Imani flies out the door I just came from.

Twenty seconds.

"What on earth were you doing in there?"

"I was just helping Nirri grab some things."

I look at her hands, loaded with Nirri's possessions.

Hell.

"Where is Nirri now?"

"She's right behind me."

Nirri bursts over the threshold, arms loaded up with her things. Books, instruments for healing, important items.

No Mason.

Fifteen seconds.

"You need to get away from the tower, back at least two hundred feet! Go, now!"

The two girls take off running.

Come on, Rayner. Get out, brother.

Ten seconds.

Dammit.

If he doesn't come in the next few seconds, he won't clear the explosion.

I won't clear the explosion.

With a raw growl I take off back through the door and up the stairs.

"Mason!"

Nothing.

Shuffling, running footsteps.

Five seconds.

Bloody hell.

"Coming!" He sprints toward me.

I turn and run down the stairs.

Three seconds.

We aren't going to make it.

I fly down the hallway toward the servants' door.

Two seconds.

Sunshine hits my face and I fly across the grass. Mason is a few feet into the hallway, just inside the door.

One second.

Catori stands with Imani and Nirri, her face frozen with terror as she waits for Mason to appear.

Crack!

Boom!

Crack! Crack! Crack! Crack!

Boom!

I fly face down onto the muddy ground, trying to get my legs to propel me away from the explosion. Stone falls like rain, slamming into my body, hitting my back, legs, shoulders.

Thwack.

Pain splits my vision.

Imani's screams barely echo over the thunder behind me.

Darkness.

Softness has my face wrapped in its firm grip. I force my eyes open and ringing floods my ears. Warmth trickles down my face and I press a hand to my head, fingers hunting for the open source of the leak. Imani's face blurs and clears, then blurs again. Her hands are on my face. I slump, and darkness swallows me again.

Shaking grips my shoulders. I crack my eyes open. The dirty, tear-streaked face of my wife hovers inches from my face. Her whimpers, cascading from her chest, are laced with desperate words.

"Harm, wake up. Please, wake up!"

I pull in a ragged lungful of air and press my arms into the ground, pushing up. Dizziness cradles my head and I lose my stomach to the grass beside me. Soft hands turn my head back, wiping away the spit and bile. Her brilliant blue eyes find mine. She sobs through a ragged cry and presses her forehead to mine, hands on either side of my face. I wrap my arms around her waist and pull her as close as she can get.

"I nearly lost you," she chokes out.

"Still here, my love."

Like rain, small bits of paper float down from the sky. A larger piece falls onto my lap. It's a map, with rings dotted all over it.

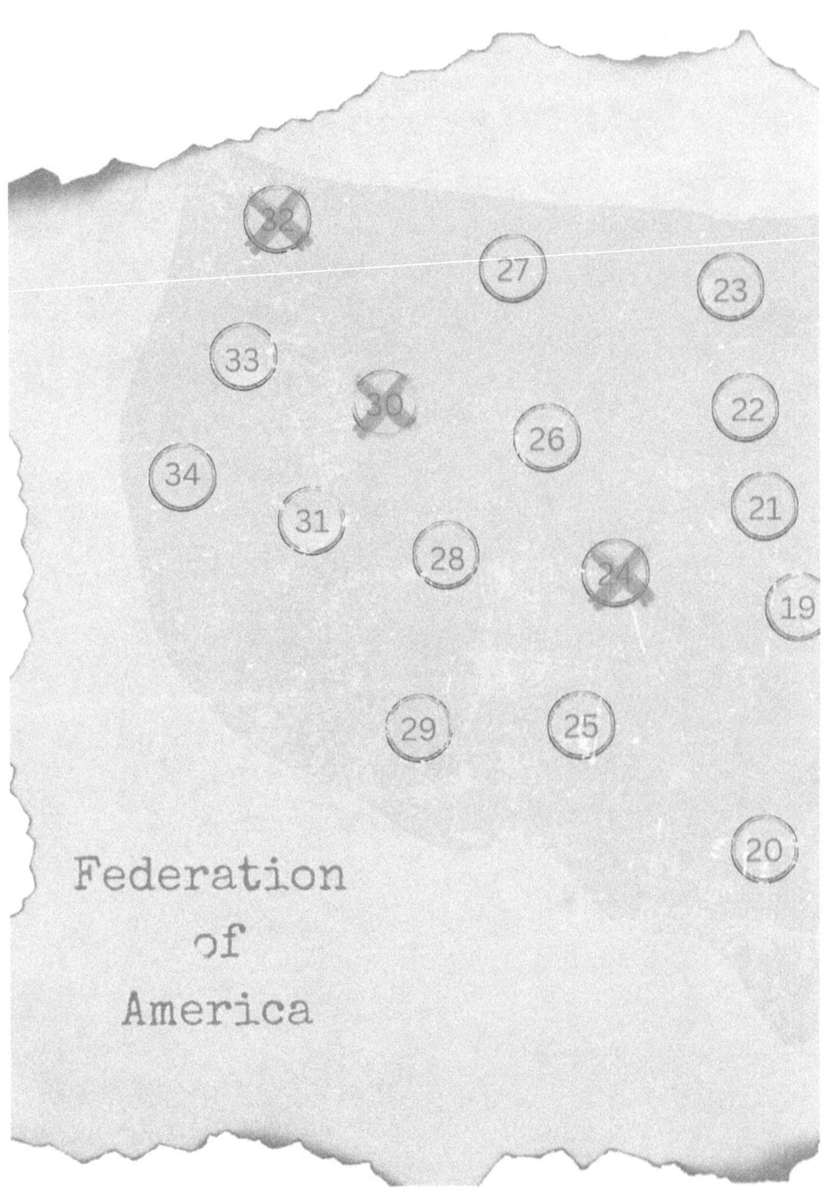

32
27
23
33
30
22
26
34
21
31
28
24
19
29
25
20
Federation
of
America

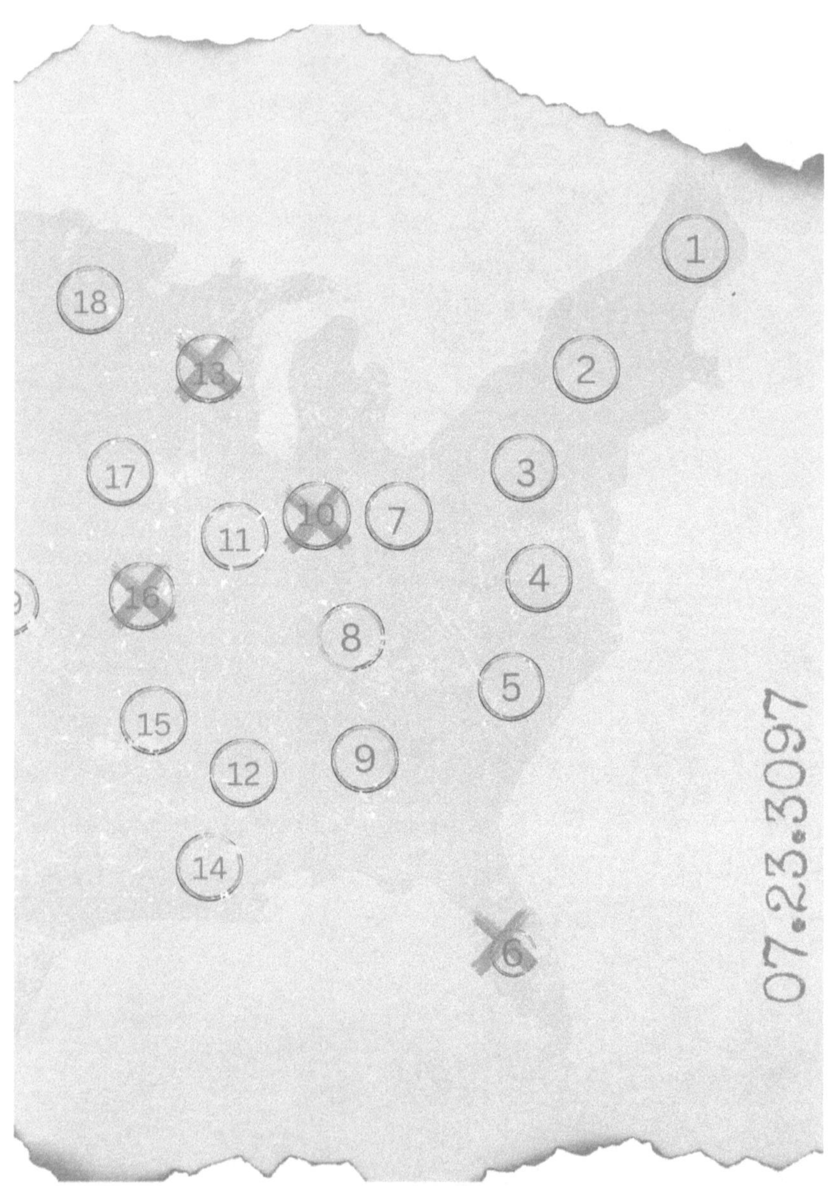

Imani places a hand on the other side of the paper and her shocked gaze finds mine.

Imani catches another, covered in words. She hands it to me, and I scan the paragraphs, my mouth falling open. Two pages are stuck together... I pry them open.

Federation of America

Statement of Legislative Agreement

The apocalyptic fallout has forced many changes to our once democratic society. The remaining leaders of the Americas convened on the 1st day in May, 2935.

The following outcomes were accepted for the greater good of country and for the people of America moving forward.

1. Each state will be allocated resources to build a protective ring. It will allow security for all ring dwellers.
2. The wealthiest families of each state will be selected as the governing family.
3. Each governing family will decide upon the laws and legislations they govern by.
4. There will be no outside interference to the government of individual rings.
5. Ring leadership will decide whether they chose to remain in contact with other rings or isolate themselves. But once the choice is made, it remains.
6. Ring leaders may choose the people that they allow into their rings, under the laws and legislation they develop.
7. Punishments for crimes committed by ring dwellers is the jurisdiction of the ring leaders.
8. Air space above individual rings is off limits to any other ring.
9. Resources may be shared between rings only if the rings in question have open communication policies.
10. Technological advancements of any kind remain the property of the ring it was developed in.
11. There will be no mandated religion or practices forced upon any ring. This is to be decided by individual ring leaders.
12. The council of the Federation of America will reconvene in one hundred, five hundred, and one thousand years from the date of this statement. Failures, successes, and prominent occurrences will be reported at each of the dates.

Residing President: ________________________   05.01.2935

<u>RING 26 – Statement of Policy & Legislation</u>

Policies and legislation – RING 26.

1. ONLY Caucasian descendants of European blood are permitted. After the intial intake of three months, RING 26 will be sealed.
2. RING 26 will remain in communication with the following rings, 27, 12, 3 & 30.
3. No technology or technological advancements are to be shared with RING 26
4. NO RELIGIOUS IDEALS PERMITTED.
5. Interracial persons will not be permitted.
6. The governing family hold the right to deny access to any persons who do not abide by the set regulations, which are policies 7-15.
7. All currency is hereby banned.
8. The barter system will replace any leftover currencies.
9. From the age of 10, all persons inside RING 26 will work.
10. Women are assigned to work inside the home and child-rearing ONLY.
11. Men are to work to build and establish each village, and after establishment take up a trade.
12. Trades shall be organised by village leaders, so there is an appropriate number of each trade persons in every village.
13. Healers will replace commercial medicines, using herbal and natural remedies ONLY.
14. Trading will take place between villages and counties.
15. Lastly, the authoritarian force for RING 26 will be the Guardian Regime. They will ensure order and protect the people.

1st Chancellor RING 26: ....

06.06.2940

I drop my head to her shoulder, breathing her in, foreign words whirling through my mind.

Catori's scream splits the air.

Instantly, I jerk, remembering Mason.

Imani moves from my lap, turning to see Catori frantically plucking up rubble, tossing it aside. Nirri stands for a moment, hands clasped over her mouth, before rushing to Catori's side.

"On no!" Imani sobs, sprinting toward the rubble. I clamber to my feet and limp to where they are moving the chunks of strewn stone.

Oh, brother.

Mason. No.

I tug stone from where his leg extrudes, bent out of shape, the rest of him buried under the remnants of the tower. What feels like an age later, we have him uncovered.

He's not breathing.

His head is bleeding.

Catori drops to his side and rests her head on his chest, with the most painful scream I have ever heard. Tears course down Imani's face, her chest heaving.

"Flick. I'll get Flick," Nirri sobs and takes off toward the battle, unarmed.

I stand over my brother, taking in his lifeless body.

His brilliant smile only moments ago replays in my head.

My heart twists with the weight of a hundred stones. How many times have I had to watch the people I love die right in front of me?

Not today, Rayner.

"I need to help him," I say to Imani. She chugs another breath before trying to pry Catori from his chest.

"Move, sister," I say, softly resting a hand on her shoulder.

Her broken face finds mine. She shakes her head.

"No, Harm, no. I can't lose him."

Imani grips her shoulders. "Give him space to help." Her words are calm but firm, tears dripping from her chin.

I move in over Mason, pressing my ear to his chest. Nothing moves. No sound.

I slam a fist into his chest. His body jerks with the impact, and blood trickles from his mouth.

"Stop. You're hurting him, Harm," Catori whimpers.

I shake my head at her.

I raise both hands and lace my fingers together. I slam down over his heart as hard as I can.

Again.

Again.

Crack.

A rib, or two, gone.

"Oh, please, stop," Catori wails.

Imani holds her in place, barely breathing as she watches her best friend lay limp under each of my sickening blows.

A crack followed by three more echoes through the trees, sending birds aloft. The wall. Christopher has taken out the wall.

I search Mason's slack face.

I roar and slam into his chest harder again.

"Come on, brother!"

Flick rushes to Mason's head, sliding onto the ground.

"Keep going, Harm, I will help him breathe." She holds his head and blows a breath into his mouth.

Catori's eyes widen. Callian, bandaged and wobbly, limps to where his sister stands and folds both girls into his side, wincing with the movement.

I raise both hands again and slam them down, this time pumping my fists into his chest every second. Flick breathes for him every other second.

I pause, hands held high.

Mason jerks and shakes; his chest rises and then falls. Then stills.

"No!" Catori folds in half, dropping to her knees at her brother's feet. Callian's face is twisted with agony, his gaze alternating between his sister and Mason.

Imani curls into Callian.

Nirri steps into his space, resting her head on his chest. His hand automatically runs behind her neck and into her hair as he plants a kiss on her head.

"Come on, Rayner. Not now, brother!"

Flick blows a long, slow breath into his mouth.

I slam down with everything I have.

Crack!

Catori crawls over the debris of stone and mud and ashes, stopping at Mason's side.

She sobs, resting a shaking hand on his face.

"No, no, no, no, no. Mas, please, no."

She rests her head on his chest before rising to kiss his mouth. Her hands steady on his jaw, she leans back on her heels. Looking to the sky, she screams to the heavens.

"You send him back!"

It's as if she's talking to Hanola.

"Now! Send him back to me!"

She withers, face coming to rest on Mason's still chest.

Tears streak down her face, soaking his shirt.

"Mas, please. I don't want this life if it's without you."

We watch, our hearts being shredded to tiny pieces, each of us choking on the smoky air that wafts around us. Flick bends down and blows another breath, giving me a hard look. I move to Mason's other side and rest both hands on his chest, pressing down hard.

"Mason Rayner, you come back to me! Right now!" Catori's strangled cry cracks what's left of my heart.

She plants her mouth over his and blows breath.

She looks to the sky again. "Please! I am begging you, send him back to me." Her shoulders shudder, and she collapses to the ground beside Mason, hands still clutching his face.

Mason's chest jerks.

Flick blows another breath.

A shallow rasp leaves his lips.

I run a hand up and down his chest roughly.

Another raspy, jerky breath.

Catori rises, her face torn between agony and hope.

Flick meets my gaze, her face stone, before she watches his chest for the rise and fall.

Catori shuffles closer, whispering softly against his cheek.

His hand moves.

"Mason. Open your eyes, brother," I say.

He lifts his hand and lets it fall, finding Catori's.

A soft moan rises from his chest.

A tortured whimper leaves Catori as she runs her hands over his face. "It's over. You're okay."

His mouth lifts to a tender smile.

Imani moves to where I sit beside Mason. Dropping into my lap, she buries her head in my chest, her hand finding Mason's other.

Callian holds Nirri as she sobs into his chest.

The smile and pride on the warrior's face sends a stream of tears down my cheeks.

It almost cost us everything.

But we did it.

We are free.

CHAPTER 41

EPILOGUE

HARM

ALMOST TEN YEARS LATER...

The groan of the buggy grows nearer. I finish the last sweep of sanding down the long, grained-swirled timber top. It's ready for finish now. Dusting my hands on my trousers, I chug back a mug of water and push through the door into the backyard. The sinking sun has almost reached the horizon, and the colors of the rainbow flirt around each other in a colorful display. The warm, humid air hangs like an invisible cloud. Rain is coming, maybe in two days' time, maybe less, by the feel of it. Birds dart about, finishing their day's work before the sun sets, their calls piercing the air overhead.

Two little figures scurry about, holding branches loaded with wide, glossy green leaves. The wooden apex I made for them yesterday stands patiently as Amaya and Arlo lean each fresh green branch against the timber frame, making a tepee, Amaya checking every branch Arlo positions.

"Amaya, Arlo. Mama is nearly here, you two."

"Race you!" Amaya squeals. They drop the branches and fly across the grassy expanse of our backyard toward me.

A smile cracks over my face and a chuckle reverberates from my

427

chest. Amaya hits me first, slamming into my side and wrapping herself around my leg. I run a hand through her dark hair, her excited brown eyes lit up over her wide smile. Arlo, smaller and a little slower, having lost the impromptu race against his older sister, hangs his head and trudges over.

I squat down as he reaches me. His brown hair is filthy and tousled from playing.

"Hey, buddy, you will be bigger than her one day. Then she won't stand a chance." He shrugs his four-year-old shoulders, looking sideways with his big blue eyes.

"You want to go and meet Mama?"

"Is she coming in the buggy?" Amaya asks.

"Yep. Let's go and see if they're here yet." I lift Arlo onto my shoulders and stand, lifting Amaya onto my hip. I push through the screen door of the house my father built with my precious, giggling cargo. I take exaggerated strides, pretending to bounce my way to the front door. The buggy comes to a stop in front of our house as giggles echo through the hall. Arlo pushes the front door open for me from above and I step onto the patio.

Two travelers in the buggy unwind their scarves, one grey and one blue, and push back their hoods. Imani's gaze finds mine instantly and her face splits into a grin. She jumps out of the buggy. Landing on the grass, she pulls out her hair from her hood. It falls around her shoulders, framing her face. Her thinned blue scarf rests over her chest as always. Amaya wriggles from my grip and runs for her mother. I bend down, and Arlo climbs from my shoulders but stands by my leg, twisting his body around mine. Imani scoops Amaya up, kissing every inch of her face. She squeals and twists in her hold. Imani laughs, dotting more kisses on our daughter. The sound fills my chest with warmth. Arlo hangs by my side, waiting.

Imani's gaze drifts to Arlo, and she puts Amaya down.

She kneels on the grass and tilts her head, offering him a small smile.

"Hey, my little man, you okay?" she says gently. Arlo flies into her arms and snuggles against her chest. I follow behind him, and Imani stands with Arlo in her arms. He buries his head into her neck.

"Hey, you," she whispers to me.

"Hey, yourself." I kiss her forehead. She grabs my shirt and pulls me into the hug with her and Arlo.

"Uncle Mason!" Amaya squeals, running up to him as he rounds the buggy. He lifts her high in the air, throwing his head back to talk to her above him as his hood falls back.

"Hey kiddo! Being good for your father, hey?" He shakes her in the air playfully.

She nods furiously, and he sits her on his hip. She plays with his shirt, flipping his driving goggles around their laces.

Mason lets out a chuckle and looks at me. "Hey, Harm."

"Mason." My smile widens as my gaze reaches my brother.

"So? Can you teach me to drive this thing now?" Amaya insists.

"When your father tells me it's okay, then I can teach you, alright?"

"Please Dada, can I have a lesson now?" Her grubby hands clap together in a plea.

"Maybe another time, May May. Uncle Mason is probably tired. It's a long way to his village, remember?"

Mason sets her down, and she climbs up into the buggy and grips the steering wheel. She makes buggy sounds and twists the wheel side to side.

Arlo climbs in the passenger's side and copies his big sister. The mad driving noises escalate, and the three of us chuckle.

Imani huddles into my side for a moment, watching them play.

"Catori says hi," Mason says.

"How is she?" I ask.

"Big. Any day now. Hopefully, this one is quicker than the first." He runs a hand through his hair.

"The second one is always faster. Plus, you have Felicity coming, don't you?" Imani asks.

"Yep. She arrives the day after tomorrow, thankfully. Catori is the strongest person I know, but I still worry about her."

"You should see little Miya, Harm. She is almost crawling now. Gosh, she's so adorable." Imani sighs. I tug her closer to my side and lean into her ear.

"You want to make another one?" I ask.

She leans her head against mine and blows out a laugh.

"Maybe, or maybe just practice." She tilts her head and winks at me, and I kiss her neck.

"Uncle Mason, what happens if I turn the keys?" Amaya asks.

"Your father will skin me alive, kiddo."

"Oh, come on Dada," Amaya pleads. I shake my head, and she pouts over the steering wheel.

"You just missed Callian and Nirri. They were here yesterday for lunch. One of Nirri's ex-Guardian patients had a house call. Nirri is running herself ragged still, helping those men. Callian was trying to tell her to slow down. But she's Nirri and gives more than she has, every time. He will never stop fussing over her. They headed home yesterday. Callian's buggy-driving skills are nearly as good as yours now, Mason."

Mason throws his head back and laughs before turning to watch the children.

I turn to face Imani and brush her hair out of her face. She slides her arms around my neck. My forehead rests on hers, and she smiles. I lean in, brushing my lips against hers, and she claims my mouth. I slide my arms around her waist and pull her against me, removing any space between us.

"That never gets old for you two, does it?" Mason chuckles over his shoulder.

"Nope," I utter between kisses.

Mason walks over to the buggy and starts explaining the parts of the dash to Amaya.

"I missed you," Imani whispers, leaning back to study my face.

"I missed you too, the whole seven days you were gone."

She grips my collar and pulls me back into her kiss. A handful of heartbeats later, she breaks away and stares at me, her eyes lit up. "Oh, I have been dying to tell you something."

"What is it? Something from the meeting?"

"Yes. The Guardian men who Nirri worked with, they have begun building a solar compound. They found old blueprints and more parts in the tower basement. So, it is possible that some buildings may have sun power in a few months. Jonah and Christopher have been building small units and testing them. Catori has plans to expand it to every village eventually, including our territory. Life is about to get a whole lot easier."

I pull back a little and stare at her.

"That's brilliant. Can it be used for other things?"

"They are not sure at this stage. Cat has people working through the rest of the documents and parts in the basement, and they are finding remnants from the world centuries ago that are very promising. But..." She looks past me and hesitates.

"But what?" I ask.

"There was a development," Mason intercepts, stepping toward us.

"What kind of development?" I ask. Imani studies my face, as if deciding to tell me.

"They found someone on the border of the mountain wilds, near the wall," Imani says.

"The external wall," Mason says, folding his arms over his chest. "They were not from our territories."

"Not from any of our territories, Harm. They came from another ring," Imani says, her brows lowering.

My mouth falls open, and I grab Imani's hand. She squeezes it and I pull her close. My heart flogs against my chest. Another ring still exists, even centuries later.

"What do we know about this person?" I ask.

Mason draws his brows down. "Not much; they were dehydrated and almost dead from exhaustion. She was wearing something around her wrist that was constantly making a screeching noise. She hasn't said much yet, mumbling constantly about her sister. But her name is Clara. She's from another ring, Harm." He repeats, and his frown slips, giving way to excitement.

Another ring.

Damn.

Acknowledgments

We did it!!

Stuck by Harm, Imani and Mason through thick and thin! Oh gosh was there some hard moments... But the ending was so damn worth it.

This series was made possible by every person who has read, edited, designed and waited on it. ARC readers, beta readers, editors, proofreaders and cover design make this series what it is.

So, thank you, to every person who has been involved in the series and Harm, Imani and Mason's journey to freedom.

Onto the next!!

Thank you to every reader who has found themselves on this page (and perhaps in these pages), you are truly rockstars!!

About the Author

Perched on a thin limb in a tree that had stood for decades, was a skinny, little farm girl. Her focus was solely on the scrappy notebook and pencil in her hands. Oblivious to the swaying branches around her and the voice of her mother calling her down, she scratched out a story. For the first time her imagination made it to paper, and she was obsessed.

Rose-Marie is a mother to four vivacious daughters, wife to a grazier, sister, daughter, etc. Stories and her little bunch of humans keep her alive and give her purpose every day, and the reason she spends a disturbing amount of time with imaginary people, in imaginary worlds, most days.

www.ingramcontent.com/pod-product-compliance
Lightning Source LLC
Chambersburg PA
CBHW050106120726
47904CB00004B/1233